MW00329313

MAKING WHOOPIE

HOT CAKES BOOK THREE

ERIN NICHOLAS

Copyright © 2020 by Erin Nicholas

All rights reserved.

No part of this book may be reproduced in any form or by any electronic or mechanical means, including information storage and retrieval systems, without written permission from the author, except for the use of brief quotations in a book review.

ISBN: 978-1-952280-05-4

Editor: Lindsey Faber

Cover design: Angela Waters

Cover Photography: Lindee Robinson

Models: Cristy Mazaris and Michael Pack

MAKING WHOOPIE

This marriage of convenience is about to get sticky.

Getting hitched for the health insurance is not Jocelyn Asher's idea of romance.

But the hospital quote has really frosted her cookies, and suddenly, "I'm rich. We should just get married," sounds a whole lot more swoony.

Especially when the man proposing is this gorgeous. And takes her to parties featuring champagne and petit fours. She's a sucker for anything with bubbles or icing. And just like that she finds herself married to a near stranger.

Grant Lorre is usually allergic to spontaneity.

So why did he ask the beautiful small-town baker he had a one-night stand with to marry him? Somehow watching her lick batter off a whisk--not a euphemism--made a wedding and a little fraud seem like a sweet idea.

They'll just play house and make some whoopie--pies, of course--for a few months and then move on with their separate lives. Until then, bring on the cream filling. And that is a euphemism.

But as things heat up even outside of the kitchen, they quickly realize there's no recipe to follow when it comes to love.

1

No one fell in love over cheesy potatoes.

That was ridiculous. There was nothing sexy about cheesy potatoes. Or potatoes without cheese, for that matter.

But lust? Well, that was a possibility. Apparently.

Because watching Grant Lorre eat cheesy potatoes across her best friend's mother's dining room table was making Jocelyn Asher hot.

Of course, Maggie McCaffery's cheesy potatoes were award-winning. Seriously. She'd taken home the purple ribbon four times from the Dubuque County Fair and twice from the Iowa State Fair. And Grant seemed to agree that they were delicious. He'd made a sexy groaning sound when he'd first taken a bite, and Josie had been mesmerized as his lips closed around the tines of his fork. Never mind how her heart rate had picked up when he'd turned the fork and *licked* it.

She was a mess. Purple ribbon or not, Josie was pretty sure that getting worked up over watching a man eat potatoes meant she was hard up.

She took a long drink of iced tea and tried to remember the last time she'd had sex. If she wasn't forgetting anyone—and how sad would *that* be—the last time had been with Ben Davis. After Kara Davis's, now Tibbin's, wedding.

Last week Kara had been into Buttered Up, the bakery where Josie worked with her best friend Zoe, to order a miniature version of her wedding cake to celebrate their first anniversary.

Josie sighed. That had to explain the sexy potato thing going on across the table. It had to.

But then Grant laughed at something Aiden, his best friend and Zoe's fiancé—yes, it was one big happy group at this table —said, and Josie felt her neglected lady parts clench. Yeah, it wasn't the potatoes.

Thankfully.

Kind of.

As weird as getting turned on by potatoes might be, it *might* have been preferable to being turned on by the man who had been coming into the bakery nearly every morning for the past two weeks, but hadn't so much as asked her to have a cup of coffee with him.

He'd asked her if the blueberries in the muffins were locally sourced. He'd asked her if they had any gluten-free cinnamon scones. He'd asked her for a lemon slice for his cup of hot water. But that was pretty much the extent of the things he'd asked her over the course of the time they'd known each other.

Oh, and he'd caught her when she'd fallen. Twice.

The first time she'd been up on the stool reaching for a bag of flour. Her shoulder pain, which was becoming more and more of an issue, had jabbed her hard, and she'd dropped the flour and slipped off the stool.

But Grant had been there. He'd caught her. In his arms. Very gallantly.

The second time, she'd been up on a ladder, dusting the bakery's shelves, and he'd startled her. She'd twisted, and her foot had slipped off the rung—or something. She wasn't totally clear on what had happened because she'd been all about Grant then too—and he'd, again, swept her up before she'd hit the floor. Like a freaking knight in shining armor.

But both times he'd simply set her on her feet and gone on with his day.

She, on the other hand, was now getting hot and bothered by side dishes.

Honestly, he'd probably even make green bean casserole sexy and that should truly be impossible.

Then he'd started coming into the bakery every day. He placed his order with Zoe some of the time. When he did order from Josie that was *all* he did. It wasn't like they'd even been flirting. But every freaking time he came through that door, she felt herself get a little happier.

It was like when five-year-old Sammie had come in that afternoon and seen the unicorn cupcakes Josie had made. The little girl had *lit up*. Everything about her had gotten brighter.

Josie felt for Grant the way Sammie felt for unicorn cupcakes. For sure.

"Are you all right, honey?"

Josie pulled her gaze away from Grant's fork—which was lying innocuously next to his plate—to look up at Maggie. "Oh yes. I'm fine." She gave the other woman a mostly sincere smile. Maggie was lovely and Josie, and Jane, Zoe's other closest friend, had dinner with the McCafferys almost once a week.

At least, it used to be that way. Before Aiden had moved back to Appleby and he and Zoe had fallen in love and he'd become a regular at the table. And before Jane had fallen in love with Aiden's friend Dax, and he'd taken up the third seat on Maggie's right.

Not that Josie didn't love Aiden and Dax too. But things around this table had changed, and she'd been feeling like a fifth wheel for the last couple of weeks. Henry, Zoe's little brother, had told her she could be his date. He was cute, smart, and funny. But he was also only eleven so she was still, for all intents and purposes, the single girl at the table.

"You've barely touched your food," Maggie said with a worried little frown. "Are you sure?"

It was very unusual for anyone to leave food at Maggie McCaffery's table, it was true. And it wasn't because Josie didn't love Maggie's pork chops, and yes, cheesy potatoes. She'd just been distracted throughout the meal. Which was entirely Grant's fault. Which made no sense.

He was a suit-wearing, rich city boy who worked in an office, loved spreadsheets, drank hot water with lemon and worried about gluten, and who was, apparently, not attracted to her.

She didn't need him. There were dozens of guys in Appleby —okay, *a dozen*, plus or minus—who were interested in her. Guys who happily ate gluten—a good thing for a guy dating a *baker*. Guys who wore good old blue jeans and worked with their hands and appreciated every dollar they earned and freaking drank *coffee*, the hot beverage God intended to be paired with baked goods. Gluten-free or not.

"I'm... feeling a little off," Josie said, deciding to be as honest as she could. She wasn't sick. She was annoyed. But that was "off" for her. She was bubbly and happy and optimistic, and much to her chagrin, sometimes, romantic.

A guy who caught her from falling off a ladder, who literally had swept her up and saved her, was supposed to at least want to take her on a date.

Especially if he was her age, handsome, and looked amazing in a suit.

She'd always thought she was a blue-jeans-and-flannels girl. Grant Lorre was making her think she'd been wrong about that. Very, very wrong.

Even tonight he was wearing a button-down shirt. He didn't have a tie or jacket on, but he'd paired the shirt with jeans, and she would very likely always find flannel shirts lacking now. Which was going to be a problem. Small-town Iowa guys liked their flannel.

"Oh, honey." Maggie put her hand on Josie's forehead in a very maternal way, and Josie had to fight a smile. "Do you need some ibuprofen? Or how about lemon cake?"

That made the smile even harder to hide. The McCaffery family absolutely felt that lemon cake—or really any cake—was as medicinal as *actual* medicine. And Josie had really never had reason to doubt that belief, as a matter of fact.

"No, I think maybe I just need to head to bed early tonight."

That wouldn't *hurt,* and just getting away from Grant's sudden presence in her social circle and his cheesy-potato sexiness was probably all the remedy she really needed. She hadn't been expecting him to be here tonight. That was probably what was throwing her off.

She didn't know the guy. She saw him for, like, three minutes each morning. Sure, she'd felt his rock-hard chest and his big biceps and had slid along his long, firm body as he'd caught, held, and then lowered her to the floor. Twice. But she was probably making it all better in her memories than it really was. Like how people remembered movies as being better than they really were. Or high school.

She just needed to get her mind around the fact that he was, evidently, sticking around Appleby. So she'd be seeing more of him. Even though he was from Chicago. And lived in Chicago. And worked in Chicago. And had come to her tiny hometown only because his best friends had decided they were all going to buy a snack cake factory, and Grant, from what she'd overheard from Aiden and Dax, was the money guy and kept everyone else in line when it came to business and investments.

So he was here babysitting his friends. Helping them get

things going with their new venture. Making sure no one blew through several million dollars without any supervision.

Josie internally rolled her eyes. It was weird to her that Aiden and Cam—Zoe's older brother—were millionaires. They'd met Dax and Ollie and Grant in college and had accidentally invented the fastest-growing online gaming phenomenon of the decade. So they were *accidental* millionaires. She supposed it was good they had someone like Grant around. Twentysomething guys fresh out of college with unlimited disposable incomes and no accountability could definitely get into some trouble.

Not that she knew anything about disposable income. She'd never had it and doubted she ever would.

Anyway, Grant was still here. Possibly because Aiden and Dax and the others still needed overseeing. But how long was that going to go on? Aiden and Cam were almost thirty. Dax and Ollie were twenty-eight or -nine. Did they really need Grant looking over their shoulders indefinitely?

And if so, did he have to do it with Buttered Up muffins and scones in hand? Couldn't he just go straight to the office in the morning? Oliver seemed to manage. He was the only one of the five partners who she'd only met a couple of times. Ollie didn't make regular stops at Buttered Up. He survived.

Then again, his assistant, Piper, did come in regularly and took treats back for Ollie, so there was that. But surely Piper could get Grant's scones too.

Now, though, Grant was showing up at Maggie's for dinner too. That was way worse than the few minutes in the bakery. He'd been charming and sophisticated and polite and intelligent tonight. She assumed. She'd kind of tuned out a lot of the particulars of the conversation, but he'd smiled and laughed and made others smile and complimented Maggie, and in general, seemed like a really nice guy.

Great.

Hot and nice.

She really needed him to have a flaw. Or four.

No, just one. She could cling to one.

Like the hot-water-with-lemon thing. What was that? That wasn't a real drink. At least not in the morning before starting the workday.

Yeah, that was a flaw. She could work with that.

That was good because she didn't want to start avoiding Maggie's dinners altogether, and she was not going to keep leaving early and missing dessert. Buttered Up bakery had been in the McCaffery family for three generations. These people knew how to bake. Plus, she really did love the camaraderie and fun of the dinners at the McCaffery house. Even with the lovey-dovey new couples who made her own romantic heart yearn for what they had.

Yes, she yearned. For love. She was the romantic of their group. Zoe had always been too picky to really fall in love, and Jane had been too busy to even entertain the idea of letting a guy into her life full time. Josie, on the other hand, had been wanting it to happen for... ever.

And now she'd had not one, but two, incredibly romantic moments with a guy who only wanted lemon slices—for hot water, for heaven's sake—from her.

"Well, okay, honey," Maggie said, still looking worried. "I could get you some hot water with lemon and honey."

"No!" Okay, that was a definite overreaction. Hot water with lemon was not the problem here. Josie smiled. "No, I'm okay. I'm just going to head out."

"All right. But text me tomorrow and tell me how you are."

Maggie leaned over and kissed the top of Josie's head. Josie did feel cared for with the gesture. Maggie had been like a second mom to her all her life. She and Zoe had been best friends since first grade. Josie's own mom and dad lived about fourteen blocks from here, but she loved Maggie and Steve dearly.

"Okay," she promised Maggie. Her smile was much less forced this time.

As Maggie moved away, Josie's gaze drifted to her best friend, sitting a few seats down.

Zoe was looking at her with an eyebrow up. Yeah, Zoe wasn't falling for it. They worked together long hours every single day. Zoe had known Josie most of her life. They'd shared all their secrets. Zoe knew that Josie was fine. At least physically. And she was going to want to know what was going on.

So far, it had gone mostly unnoticed that Josie wasn't talking much or paying attention to the conversation. That was one positive about having Dax Marshall around. He could talk to anyone about anything and made it a personal mission to have everyone laughing and enjoying themselves no matter the occasion. She swore that he could make a root canal fun. But she should have been doing a better job eating. A too-full plate would not go unnoticed at Maggie's table.

"You're sick?" Jane asked, pulling Josie's attention to her other best friend as Maggie and Steve carried dishes out of the dining room. "I saw you eat the last piece of carrot cake in three bites and chug a cup of coffee just before we came over here."

Josie scowled at her. "Shh." She did *not* want Maggie to overhear that.

"What's going on?" Jane asked. Though she did lower her voice.

"Nothing. I'm just... full."

That would make sense. She had just eaten cake and coffee before coming over, and that should definitely mean she was full. Of course, her body didn't work that way. She had a crazy-fast metabolism, which sounded like a blessing, and most of her girlfriends assured her that it was, but was actually a pain in the ass. She was hungry all the time.

Still, it did help since her career was making cakes—and pies and cookies and everything in between—and she really liked sweets. Being around sugar all day made it difficult to resist, and the stuff she and Zoe did with sugar was amazing, if she did say so herself.

"You're just full," Zoe said in a very yeah-right tone. "What's really going on?"

"I'm just in a weird mood." Josie flipped her hand as if to wave it all away as no big deal.

She really needed them to drop it. At least as long as Grant was around. She had no qualms telling her girlfriends that she was all mixed up about Grant. She was pretty sure they suspected it anyway. But no way was she admitting it to him. Or his friends.

She had been stoically avoiding looking at him since she realized she was fantasizing about him and root vegetables, but now she sneaked a glance.

Surprise and heat arrowed through her when she found his eyes on her.

He was watching her as if he knew exactly what was going on. Which was crazy. How could he know? They hadn't even talked about the weather. How would he know that she was borderline obsessed with him?

She frowned. Maybe this happened a lot. Maybe women became obsessed with him all the time. The dark good looks, the air of indifference, the money, the suits, the smooth sophistication. Sure, those could do it. Some women might even overlook the hot-water-and-lemon thing.

Dark good looks made some things easier to overlook for sure.

"So I'm just going to go," Josie said, scooting her chair back and standing.

It seemed imperative, suddenly, that she get out of here.

"You really think you're just going to get away with acting weird and leaving?" Zoe asked. "Really?"

Josie gripped the back of her chair and pressed her lips together. She looked from Zoe to Jane. Then to Grant. She lingered there. Then looked at Zoe again. Josie shook her head. "No, I know you're not going to let it go, but for now, it would be great if you'd just... give me some space."

Zoe's eyebrows went up again, but her look didn't say you're-full-of-shit. She looked concerned. "Just tell me you really are okay. Like mostly, generally, for the most part, okay."

"I am," Josie promised. "It's just... weird. You're going to think it's super weird when I tell you, I promise."

"You're going to tell me too," Jane interjected. "For sure."

Josie nodded. "Absolutely."

"Will we need wine?" Jane asked.

"Spiked lemonade," Josie said. "Lots of spiked lemonade."

"Got it," Jane said.

For the three of them "spiked lemonade" generally meant there was a family issue or a guy issue they needed to talk about. Otherwise they stuck with the mellow, happy effects of wine. Spiked lemonade was for the serious stuff that needed numbing or the tearing down of inhibitions or both.

"'Night, everyone," Josie said, looking around the table. She saved Grant for last.

She didn't know him. He wasn't a friend or a member of her friends-that-were-family family. He was a friend of a friend—two of them actually—so that meant that he had potential to be a part of that family though. Eventually.

And she was really going to have to figure out how to not have dirty thoughts about him when they were doing the simple family stuff with the rest of these nice people. Especially if, God forbid, he ever brought a date.

She shuddered. Then rolled her eyes at herself. She was

jealous of a possible future date of the guy who wasn't her type and who didn't even like her cupcakes?

Everyone liked her cupcakes.

She couldn't date a guy who didn't like her cupcakes.

That would be like a... painter who dated a guy who didn't love art. Or woman running a dog rescue who dated a guy who hated dogs.

No, actually, no one should date someone who hated dogs. That was just wrong on every level.

Still, *she* couldn't date a guy who didn't swoon over her cupcakes. Period.

Grant Lorre only bought muffins and scones. Those were Zoe's specialties. Everything in the bakery was made from Zoe's family's recipes, of course. But Zoe wasn't as... culinarily gifted... as Josie was. It wasn't an insult to her friend. It was just a fact. Like saying Zoe had more freckles or Josie had bigger boobs. Josie was just better in the kitchen. So Zoe stuck to the basics. Muffins, cookies, scones. Zoe could decorate the basic cookies and cupcakes, of course. She'd been doing it since she was old enough to hold a whisk. But if anyone needed something special—a cake that looked like a dinosaur or cupcakes that looked like cats—that was Josie's expertise.

She always did a few cute little things for the bakery case to go alongside the basic vanilla, chocolate, and strawberry with the swirled icing. And she wouldn't lie, she loved the fact that her stuff usually sold out first.

But not to Grant Lorre.

Grant stuck with the basics.

He had no idea how moist and sweet her cupcakes really were.

And yeah, she meant that to sound a little dirty. Even if it was only in her head.

She was losing it.

"'Night, Jose," everyone echoed in multiple variations as she started for the front door. She couldn't face Maggie again. Maggie would either get even more worried... or she'd figure out Josie was lying about not feeling well.

She was feeling fine. Horny. But fine.

She really didn't want to explain that to the group at dinner.

"I'm going to head out too."

Josie froze in the doorway between the dining room and foyer as Grant spoke. She slowly turned back.

Grant was getting to his feet. He laid his napkin by his plate and smoothed a hand over the front of his shirt as he stepped around his chair.

"No dessert?" Dax asked. Dax Marshall never skipped dessert.

"Nah. I have some stuff I need to do yet tonight," Grant said.

"Something more important than lemon cake?" Dax said, clearly not believing it.

"Definitely," Grant answered.

Then he glanced at Josie.

2

Her heart stopped.

Just for a second. Maybe two. But it actually happened. And she realized that, for some reason, Grant Lorre was following her out of the house on purpose.

"So, I'll see you tomorrow at the office," Grant said to Aiden. "And you... sometime, I assume?" he asked Dax.

Dax grinned. "I'll stop by. I know you miss me when I'm not there."

"Yep. That's exactly what I was thinking."

Dax had been a partner at Hot Cakes, the snack cake company that Aiden and Grant, along with their other partners, had taken over. But Dax had given up his shares so that he could date Jane. Since she worked for the company, she'd refused to go out with him while he was her boss.

Dax giving up the potential for millions of dollars of profit to be with Jane was the most romantic thing that Josie had ever heard, and she sighed a little every time she thought of it.

He now owned the nursing home where Jane's dad lived and was working to remodel it and introduce several new, innovative eldercare programs. Honestly, that was also all because he'd fallen in love with Jane, and Josie knew that any guy who came along for *her* now was going to be measured by the Dax Marshall standard.

She was so screwed. Who was going to be able to compete with all of that?

And it wasn't even the money. Dax definitely had enough of that to throw at any and all of Jane's problems. Whether or not she would *let* him do that was another issue, but still, money was no object. But Josie wasn't expecting to meet a guy whose wallet could measure up to Dax's. It was his heart that she admired. His willingness to do whatever it took to make sure Jane—and the people she loved—were safe and happy.

But while money made that easier, it wasn't the primary factor. Her father and grandfather were two of the most romantic, caring, generous men she knew. And neither of them had ever had more than a couple thousand bucks in the bank at one time. They'd both lived paycheck to paycheck—her dad still did—but they still provided a safe, happy, loving home and treated their wives like queens.

Just queens without jewels or gold or servants.

That was what Josie wanted. Just to be loved with someone's whole heart. Even if all they had to give in the romance department was a Netflix subscription and microwave popcorn every weekend. That would matter as much as someone else giving her diamonds and trips to Paris.

"You already made it through that month's supply of gummy bears I sent you and you need some more?" Dax asked Grant with a grin.

Grant lifted a brow.

"He donated them to the Candy Apple," Aiden said, referring to the candy and ice cream shop in town. "They're making some special sundae with gummy bears on top. What's it called again?" He directed the question at Grant. Aiden wore a grin that said he knew the answer, and he was enjoying this immensely.

Dax turned interested eyes on the more serious of his two friends. "Yes, what's it called, Grant?"

Grant shook his head. "I don't remember."

"The Gooey Gummy Grant," Henry piped up.

Everyone looked at him. The little boy had been so quiet Josie had almost forgotten he was there. Okay, she'd probably almost forgotten because she'd been too distracted by Grant tonight to remember much of anything. Like to keep her heart beating steadily, for instance.

"No they're not!" Dax crowed, clearly delighted.

"Seriously," Henry said. "It's strawberry ice cream and marshmallow fluff with gummy bears and whipped cream and sprinkles. They sell it for twenty-five percent off the price of the other sundaes because the gummy bears are free because of Grant."

Dax's mouth was hanging open in obvious glee when he looked back to Grant. "I. Love. Everything. About. That."

"That was *not* what was supposed to happen," Grant said. "I went back in and asked them to not call it that but they insisted."

"You mean Betty insisted," Aiden said. "No one says no to Betty."

It was true. Betty Andrews was the owner of the Candy Apple and was sweetest woman on the planet. She had a way of making the people around her feel like they had brought such joy and sunshine into her life just by *being* there, and no one ever had the heart to say or do anything that might disappoint her.

Josie found herself fighting a smile as she watched Grant. He was clearly uncomfortable with being associated with something *gooey* and *gummy*.

And now she wanted to cover him in marshmallow fluff.

Which was a vast improvement over cheesy potatoes, so there was that.

"You gave Grant a month's supply of gummy bears?" Zoe asked, going back to the previous point. "Question one, how many is that? And question two, *why*?"

"Well, assuming that a guy would need about four to five ounces of gummy bears a day," Dax said seriously. "Rounding up, of course, to be safe, that comes out to about nine and a half pounds of gummy bears for a month."

Zoe's eyes widened. "Nine and a half *pounds*?"

"Roughly," Dax said with a nod.

Aiden was laughing out loud now.

"And to answer your second question," Dax said, glancing at Grant, "because Grant needs a little sweetness in his life, and if I'm not there for him every day, that is going to be sorely lacking."

Zoe laughed and Grant rolled his eyes. But his expression was one of resigned affection.

That did something funny to Josie's stomach.

It was one thing to see him every morning just looking good —confident and sophisticated and powerful in his suit and tie. It was something else to see him charming and friendly with Zoe's parents and then goofing around with his friends. Not that Grant was goofing around. There was definitely something about him that made Josie certain Grant Lorre didn't goof. But the way he rolled with the punches from Dax and Aiden—and yes, the way it was clear he cared about his friends, even if he and Dax were night and day in personality—made her like him.

Dammit. First romanticizing the way he'd caught her in his arms, then lusting after him, and now liking him *too*? Great. That wasn't the way to get over a crush.

"I don't know," Zoe said, looking from Dax to Grant to Josie. "Grant's been coming into the bakery really regularly.

Maybe he's found another way of getting a little *sweetness* in his day."

"Has he now?" Dax asked, arching a brow at Grant.

"I need to get going," Grant said. He started for the front door.

Which meant he started in Josie's direction. For a minute there she'd become a simple observer of the scene playing out in front of her. But she was still standing here, and he was now coming toward her, and pretty soon he was going to be right in front of her and...

She suddenly straightened, her heart pounding as he drew near.

"I'll walk you out."

Her eyes widened at his words. It wasn't really a question. Or even an offer. It sounded a lot like a command.

"I'm... fine."

He was only a few inches away—the doorway was only so wide after all—and he smelled really good, and he was really tall next to her, and yeah, she remembered that chest and those arms really well and...

"We're going in the same direction," he pointed out.

Right. They were both walking out to their cars, which were parked in front of the McCafferys' house. It didn't really matter if she was fine. Or not. Him walking out with her was more of a just-the-way-it-was-going-to-happen than him taking care of her.

That was a very weird thought to go flitting through her mind just then.

He didn't really come across as the warm-and-fuzzy-nurturer type. She also didn't need anyone taking care of her, thank you very much.

Still...

"Are you sure?" he asked.

Sure of the marshmallow-fluff-all-over-his-body thing? Or

the curl-up-in-his-lap thing? Or the big-hands-rubbing-her-feet thing? Because yes. To all of that.

"About?" she asked.

"Being fine?"

She was kind of staring at him. And not moving. And not turning and walking toward the front door of the house the way she should be.

"Oh yes. Mostly," she said.

He didn't seem convinced. But he didn't press. He just gestured toward the door.

She gave the dining room—which was surprisingly quiet at the moment—a little wave, carefully not making eye contact with anyone. Zoe and Jane were no doubt watching her with what-the-hell expressions. Then she pivoted and made her feet carry her toward Maggie's front door.

Grant reached around her to open the door for her, emphasizing that he smelled good and that he was a gentleman, in spite of barely speaking to her after catching her in midair —twice.

She stepped out onto the porch and sucked in a deep breath, hoping that would help. But Grant stepped out behind her and shut the door. Which meant they were now alone. In the almost-dark of the early summer night. And that didn't really help with her lust-and-like-and-why-isn't-he-attracted-to-me daze at all.

The disappointment of that last part was the sharpest. That surprised her. It wasn't as if every man she met fell at her feet. It wasn't as if every man *she* was attracted to was automatically attracted to her. It just didn't work that way. But she was far more disheartened by Grant Lorre's lack of interest than she had been in a long time. Okay, ever.

Mostly, Josie believed that when the time was right, the right guy would come along, and she'd get her happily ever after. That had been validated even further by her two best friends finding true love when they'd been least expecting it. Falling in love wasn't something you could put in your planner.

So when things didn't work out with a guy she liked or even one she'd gone out with a few times, she didn't get overly upset about it.

But Grant Lorre was upsetting her.

It was crazy.

She stopped at her car, debating what to say to him. Just a simple good night seemed most appropriate. She turned to speak and was startled to find him right behind her. Very close. Closer than two casual acquaintances should probably stand in the dark.

Close enough it should have seemed creepy.

It didn't. At all.

She wanted to take the little step that would bring her right up against him and press her nose to his chest and take a big, deep breathe. She would bet the combination of his cologne and laundry detergent would make her stomach flip a lot like it had when he'd reacted to the Gooey Gummy Grant.

"It's not really my business, I realize," he said.

Was it the dim evening light making his voice sound huskier?

"But I don't really think you are okay. Is there anything I can do?"

Josie peered up at him. He was tall. Well, she was short. So he was definitely tall next to her, but he was just tall too. He had to be about six-three or so.

"I'm..." She really did almost say fine. But at the last minute she said, "Stupid."

Clearly that wasn't the answer he'd been expecting. "Stupid?"

She blew out a breath. "Yeah. But it's not really anything for you to worry about. It's not fatal or anything."

"Is it chronic?" he asked.

And the corner of his mouth curled.

And she was never getting over this crush now.

She nodded. "I think so. At least, very long lasting."

"How long?"

"How long are you going to be in town?"

Oops. That she had *definitely* not meant to say.

He frowned. "That's a good question. But I'm not sure how it relates to your stupidity problem."

She sighed. "I bet if you think about it you could come up with a guess."

He did think about it. Seemingly. Then he took a small step forward. "I have something to do with your stupidity?"

Oh what the hell? He was a friend of a friend, but he didn't live here. He didn't know her. Her friends were going to find out soon enough—from her—that she had a thing for this guy. They were hopefully going to help her drink it away. So what would it matter if she confessed?

"You have everything to do with it."

His eyebrows rose. "How?"

"Well, it seems that I have a little thing for you, and it was fine when you had only saved my neck. But then you started coming to the bakery and I saw you every day. But you didn't even really want to talk to me. You definitely didn't want to flirt. Which I didn't love, but I could get over after you walked out with your scones and hot water."

Why did she mention the hot water? She wasn't sure. Maybe just because it was definitely a sign her fascination with him was crazy.

"But now you're coming to dinner here. At this place I love with these people I love. And you're being charming and… long suffering, which I find funny and endearing… and it just makes it harder to not be disappointed that my crush on you isn't reciprocal."

She took a deep breath.

"But," she added, before he had a chance to respond, "it's fine. I'm a grown-up, and while getting worked up over cheesy potatoes is annoying, I can deal with it."

He seemed to hesitate for a moment. Then asked, "Cheesy potatoes?"

She nodded. He had to already think she was a little cuckoo, so what could it hurt to go all in here? "I found it sexy how you ate the cheesy potatoes."

Yeah, that was definitely a look of surprise on his face.

"So anyway," she concluded, "I'm not exactly *fine*, but I'm going to survive. Especially if you could just, you know, go back to Chicago. But until then, it will all be okay."

There, that hadn't been so bad. She turned and started to open her door.

"Jocelyn."

But his deep voice—and her full name—stopped her.

He knew her full name?

She turned back. And swallowed hard. There was no way she could have labeled the look on his face, but it was... not uninterested.

"Yes?"

"You have a crush on me?"

She felt her cheeks heat a little, but she rolled her eyes. Come on. He had to hear her say it twice? Really? "Yes."

"And you think that it's not reciprocal."

"Right."

"And that's why you've been acting strange tonight? Because you've been uncomfortable around me because you think you have unrequited feelings?"

She blew out a breath. "Is this the serious-businessman thing? Like how much you love spreadsheets and stuff? You have to go over every single point and make everything really black and white?"

His lips curled again. "Probably. Though it might also be that I want to be very sure about your feelings right now."

"Why is that?"

"Just tell me all of that is true."

She threw her arms wide. "Okay, fine, yes, Grant. You got it all right. That's all true."

"Very good to know." Then he reached up, cupped the back of her head, stepped her back until she was against her car, and kissed her.

Oooo-kay.

So maybe indifferent wasn't quite the right word to use.

Grant did *not* kiss her as if he was indifferent to her. He kissed her as if he'd been thinking about it as long as she had. And had been thinking about covering her in cheesy potatoes.

Then he gave a little groan, tipped his head, pressed even closer, deepened the kiss, and all she could think was *no, marshmallow fluff. For sure.*

Josie felt every stroke of his tongue in her lower belly and between her legs. She was immediately up on tiptoe and gripping his shoulders, arching closer.

They kissed for long minutes before Grant finally lifted his head. They were both breathing hard and just stared at each other for several seconds.

Josie licked her lips. He let her go, and she lowered back flat on her feet.

"Very reciprocal," he finally said.

"The first day you just walked out of the bakery," she said. That was the part that had been bugging her the most.

He nodded. "I was afraid you were going to make me want to stay in town."

Oh. That was definitely not what she'd expected him to say. And she was equally surprised by how much she liked that answer. "But you *are* still in town."

"I guess I didn't get out of the bakery fast enough."

Her eyes widened. "You're still in town because of me?"

"Yes."

He didn't even hesitate. He didn't blunt the answer. He didn't even blink.

He was a very straightforward guy. She was used to the charming, flirtatious guys she'd grown up with.

"So why haven't you asked me out?"

"You don't seem like the casual dating type of girl."

She thought about that. Was it casual dating when you literally fell into the guy's arms and you locked eyes and you both became immediately smitten? But he was right. She nodded. "I'm not really."

"Exactly."

She should let it go. If he just wanted to casually date and she wasn't the type for that, then she should let this go.

And she might have, if he hadn't kissed her.

"Did you really have something else to do that made you leave before dessert?" she asked.

"Yes. I needed to walk you out and make sure you were okay."

That clinched it. "Well, I need to go home and bake."

He seemed confused.

"I bake on the side. For people who have last-minute work potlucks or kids' school parties they don't have time to bake for themselves. It's purely to help people out. Stuff the bakery doesn't do," she added quickly. "You can't tell Zoe." She felt a flicker of guilt. That was familiar, however. She always felt a little guilty when she baked behind her best friend—and boss's —back. Well, when she did it for money, anyway.

"My lips are sealed."

His lips. Yeah, she really liked his lips.

"So I was thinking... if you just stopped by my house tonight and sampled a few things for me then that's not really a date, right?"

Hey, she couldn't be held responsible if he took "sampled a few things" as innuendo.

His eyes flickered first with understanding, then heat. "No, I wouldn't call that a date."

"Four Fifteen Elm Street," she said. "The kitchen door will be unlocked."

"I just have one more question," he said.

"Okay."

"Can you be late for work tomorrow morning?"

Heat flashed through her. His meaning was clear. Her reaction to it was as well.

"Yes," she told him simply.

Hell, she could play up the I'm-not-really-feeling-well thing in the morning too if necessary.

And after that kiss, it was going to be necessary.

"Great. I'm definitely in the mood for something sweet."

She had never had a one-night stand. She'd never slept with someone she hadn't known for at least a year. Actually, if she thought about it, she probably hadn't slept with anyone she hadn't known for three years or more.

But Grant was Aiden and Dax's friend and partner. Aiden Anderson, her best friend's fiancé, had known and worked with and trusted this man for nine years.

"I'll see you there," she told him. Then she got into her car and headed for home, her heart pounding, her breathing uneven, and her panties much warmer than even the early summer night should account for.

She had nothing to worry about with inviting Grant over to her house for... whatever.

Except that she was ninety percent sure she didn't have any marshmallow fluff at home.

That was really unfortunate.

3

This was really one of the worst ideas he'd had in a long time.

Grant acknowledged that even as he followed Jocelyn Asher home.

He didn't have bad ideas very often. In fact, it was pretty typical that he was saving others from *their* bad ideas.

But even the taillights on Jocelyn's bright blue Ford Fiesta were tempting him. He wanted to follow her home. He wanted to back her up against the wall of her—no doubt—bright, cute, sweet kitchen. And kiss the hell out of her.

He had an inkling of what the draw was here.

There was no question Jocelyn was gorgeous. She had long, wavy blond hair that fell nearly to the curve of her lower back. She had big blue eyes. She had a tiny body with sweet curves and a bright, quick smile. She had a tinkling laugh.

Yes, tinkling. Like bells or wind chimes or something. Something bright and cheery and impossible to hear without it making you feel happier.

She was clearly a bubbly, sweet, happy, sunny person.

Not his type at all.

Yet he hadn't been able to stop thinking about her since she'd fallen—literally—into his arms the first time he'd set foot in the bakery where she worked.

It was very likely that fall—and the one that had happened the second time he'd ever seen her, also at Buttered Up—was messing with his subconscious.

He had a hero complex. He saved damsels in distress. Not in the old-fashioned, slaying-dragons way. Not in the I'll-physically-protect-you way. Not in the putting-himself-in-danger or sacrificing-for-them way. In fact, damsels kind of annoyed him.

That sounded cold even to his own ears. But he was determined to make sure that the women in his life were strong and confident and knowledgeable and never dependent on anyone else for survival or happiness.

He didn't teach self-defense classes or anything, though he was a big supporter and advocate of those. He wasn't a psychologist or a counselor. Though, again, he was a big fan of those. He was a financial coach, who worked almost exclusively with single moms and widows. He taught women how to make, invest, and spend their money so that they were financially independent.

He didn't feel worried or protective of his clients. He felt motivated. Energized by the opportunity to help. And often frustrated. With the women who thought they were "dumb about money" or "not good at math" and couldn't handle their finances. And the men who liked having women depend on them. He also got exasperated with the women who attended his seminars and then hit on him. It was like they weren't listening at all. He wanted them to leave his seminars understanding that they didn't need a man.

He'd also recently been very uncomfortable with one of his attendees. His most recent seminar had been Michelle's third time participating, and she'd made it very clear afterward that she was only there because of him.

Finding a woman naked in his bed in his hotel room had been a shock. That was the kind of thing that happened to Dax and... No, really only Dax. Grant had quickly dissuaded her of any idea that he was interested and had told her he thought it was best she didn't come to any more seminars. He'd been able to get her out of his room without getting hotel security involved—which, according to Dax when he'd heard the story, meant the woman wasn't *really* a fan—but Grant had decided that he needed to start wearing a wedding ring and talking about his "wife" at these seminars. Or at least bringing an assistant along. He thought, for the right price, Piper would accompany him, but he wasn't sure he could afford her.

Jocelyn Asher, however, was neither a mom nor a widow. And she was most definitely making him feel protective. And he'd love to find her naked in his bed.

He didn't like that. He didn't want to nurture or take care of someone.

But he couldn't stop thinking of her.

Following her out to her car tonight had truly, initially, been out of concern. She'd seemed quieter than he'd expected her to be at a meal with her friends. Then when those friends had commented that she'd been acting strange, and Maggie, clearly the mother figure to all of her daughter's friends, had seemed legitimately concerned, *he'd* gotten concerned.

But then Jocelyn had told him it was because she was attracted to him, and he couldn't keep his lips off her any longer.

Once he'd tasted her, resisting her was futile.

He was going to have to figure out why she was making him feel so protective. But first, he was going to get her naked.

Again, maybe not the wisest decision, but fuck it. He had no idea how to fight it. Nor did he want to.

Dax and Ollie got to make dumb decisions all the time, and they always landed on their feet. This was Grant's turn.

ERIN NICHOLAS

They pulled between two stone columns with lamps set on top and drove up a curving driveway.

Grant knew his eyes were wide as Jocelyn stopped her car in front of a three-car, carriage-house-style detached garage. The garage was set back from the main house. An enormous 1800s Victorian mansion, to be exact. The house sat back from the road several yards and was surrounded by trees, grass, and flowers.

The fading light of the evening didn't give him a perfect look at everything, but his first impression was that of a gorgeous, peaceful, old, and majestic property, and he knew his mouth was hanging open as he got out of the car and met Jocelyn at the front bumper.

She was wearing a pale pink sundress with a subtle flowered pattern. The skirt hit her just below the curve of her calf and her dainty feet were in nude-colored sandals that showed off pale pink toenails. The bodice of the dress, however, was strapless, leaving her shoulders and arms bare, showing off lots of smooth, pale, creamy skin. The top of the dress cupped her breasts and fit to her narrow waist before flaring slightly at her hips. It was a very feminine, sweet dress. With her long blond hair falling in soft waves to her lower back and her general gorgeous-girl-next-door looks and easy smiles, she was so unlike the polished city women at the top of their corporate game in law, real estate, marketing, and sales of all kinds, that he could only shake his head in wonder. He'd bet Jocelyn didn't have a single pantsuit in her closet.

Why was he drawn to this woman? This woman he knew next to nothing about and who he had nothing in common with?

Then again... he glanced at her house. Maybe there were layers upon layers of things he didn't know about her that he'd find fascinating and familiar. He was definitely used to spending time with women who were from old money. He didn't visit them at home, but he could imagine some of his clients having stately old mansions that sat at the back of humongous lawns and had gardens overflowing with flowers behind them. Along with stone cherubs dotting the property and wrought ironwork that was older than his grandfather.

Jocelyn took in his expression as he looked up at the house.

She smiled. "I inherited it from my grandparents. My great-great-grandparents lived here, then my great-grandparents, then my grandparents. Now they live in a small, much easier to care for townhouse about ten blocks away."

"This is..."

"Surprising?" she asked.

"Yes."

She laughed, and he thought of the comparison to wind chimes again. The sound was light and happy and soothing. He focused fully on her, forgetting about the house.

"The house has been paid off forever, so I only have to come up with the money for the utilities. And the repairs. I was the only one who wanted to take on the upkeep. It's gigantic and... old. There's lots of issues with pipes and electric and creaky floorboards and leaky roofs. But our family has a ton of great memories in this house, and there was no way I could let it go."

Grant felt himself frowning. "How do you take care of all of that?"

She shrugged. "Myself, when I can. Favors, when I can't. Pinching pennies when that doesn't work."

"You have people who can do some of that stuff for you?"

She nodded. "I've lived in this town all my life. I know everyone. And I'm an amazing baker. You'd be surprised what people will do in exchange for free cookies." She peered up at him, a tiny crease between her eyebrows. "Actually, you probably would be surprised."

He was aware of how short she was when she stood looking up at him like that. When he'd kissed her just before, it had been obvious. He'd had to bend, and she'd had to stretch. But tasting her, touching her, absorbing her little gasp and then moan had been at the forefront of his mind then.

"Why would I be surprised by that?"

"You don't really like cookies."

He lifted a brow. "I don't?"

"You never get cookies from the bakery. Or cupcakes." Her frown deepened.

"I come to the bakery at seven thirty in the morning," he pointed out.

"You could get them and eat them later."

She seemed offended that he'd never bought cookies or cupcakes. And she'd been paying attention to what he bought. Maybe she knew everyone's order. That wouldn't surprise him actually. Appleby was a very small town, and the bakery seemed to have a lot of regulars. As she'd said, she'd lived here all her life. Still, he liked that she'd paid attention to his order.

"Remember what I said about if I got to know you I'd want to stay around?" he asked.

She nodded.

"I was pretty sure if I ate your cupcakes, I'd never want to stop."

Did *ate your cupcakes* sound as dirty to her as it did to him? He hoped so. Because it was true. In the sex sense *and* the cake sense. There was something about this woman that made all kinds of warning signs flash for him.

Yet here he was.

Jocelyn smiled at him then. And the warning sign flashed even brighter.

But did he turn around and get back in his car?

No, he did not.

"So you were avoiding the good stuff at the bakery because you were afraid of it?" she asked.

That was so true. On so many levels. He nodded. "Definitely."

"You might not want to come into my kitchen, then," she said. "I'm trying something new tonight, and I think it's going to be amazing."

He was trying something new tonight too. Sleeping with a sweet, small-town baker, who wore pink, flowery dresses and didn't date casually. She was also friends with the fiancées of two of his best friends. Which meant if he hurt her, he'd be fucking a lot up.

"I'm absolutely coming into your kitchen tonight, Jocelyn."

Yep, that definitely sounded dirty.

He was, apparently, also making bad decisions he knew were bad going in. Which was also new.

Heat flickered in her eyes and she took a quick breath. Then she nodded. "Okay, then."

She led the way across the loose white rocks that covered the drive toward the steps that took them up to the back porch. She turned the knob and pushed the door open.

"You don't lock your doors?"

"In Appleby?" She laughed. "No. Besides, I don't have anything worth stealing."

He frowned. "Someone could just want *you*. They wouldn't necessarily want to steal anything."

She just laughed and stepped inside.

Grant didn't think it was funny. He stepped through the door, but nearly plowed her over when she stopped and bent to slip her shoes off.

His hands landed on her hips, her ass pressed against his groin. The position was provocative but clearly unintentional. Still, his body responded.

Well, nothing like getting up close and personal in minute one.

Jocelyn straightening quickly, jerking her head around to look at him, her hair whipping against his face. "Sorry!"

Grant didn't remove his hands. "I'm not."

She ran her tongue over her bottom lip. He was certain she had no idea she'd even done it. "I... go barefoot a lot."

That fit, somehow. "Want me to take my shoes off too?" He, on the other hand, never went barefoot.

"You don't have to. The whole house is marble or hardwood floors."

"Your feet don't get cold?" He had no idea why that was the thought that occurred to him.

She seemed equally surprised. And amused. "They do sometimes," she admitted. "I have a huge collection of socks."

"But you just don't like shoes?"

She shrugged. "I don't know. It's just here that I go without them. It feels less homey to wear shoes in my own house. I've crawled on these floors, slept on these floors, danced and fallen and bled and puked on these floors. Feels weird to be formal on them. And shoes seem formal."

He just stared at her. He'd never known anyone who was attached to floors. Who had even given that much thought to floors. Then again, he'd probably never known anyone who'd lived in a place where they had history like that. Except Aiden and Cam.

His two friends who were also from Appleby. There was definitely something about this little town that seemed to make it hard for people to leave. Permanently, at least.

Aiden had been gone from home for nine years, but he was definitely back to stay now. Cam seemed determined to avoid his hometown except for the random weekend where he'd come back and donate a boatload of money and accept a boatload of praise and thanks for it. Like when he'd paid to build the youth athletic complex or when he'd saved a historic bridge that ran across a small river outside of town. He did love being the hometown hero even though he seemed a bit allergic to actually being in the town. Still, he'd been fully on board with the idea of their company saving Hot Cakes, the local snack cake factory that employed a huge percentage of the town.

"I think I want to take my shoes off on your floors," Grant said. His voice was strangely gruff.

Jocelyn rewarded him with a smile. "Okay."

He let go of her finally and bent to remove his shoes. He was stupidly aware of his footwear for the first time in maybe ever. The shoes were leather, lace up, casual men's shoes. They weren't tuxedo shoes. They weren't the most expensive shoes he owned by a long shot. But they weren't tennis shoes or work boots, that was for certain, and he was suddenly aware Jocelyn probably saw a lot of both of those. He shouldn't assume that, of course. She was, after all, attracted to *him*. And she was single. Gorgeous, sweet, a hometown girl, *gorgeous*. It was almost ridiculous that she was single. Unless small-town, blue-collar country boys didn't do it for her.

Maybe Grant was exactly her type.

But she went barefoot at home because she felt attached to the floors. In the one-hundred-plus-year-old house that her family had owned for generations. In the town she'd lived in her whole life. Where she worked in a bakery with her best friend and went to dinner once a week at her friend's mom's house. Where they served things like cheesy potatoes and lettuce salad with ranch dressing and breaded, baked pork chops.

He wasn't her type.

She didn't know many guys like him. If any.

He'd bet a million dollars on it. Literally.

After he'd kicked his shoes to the side, she took him through the three-season room and into the kitchen.

She set her purse and car keys on the little table just inside the doorway and then headed to the sink. She washed her hands and then grabbed an apron—one of four—from the little hooks on the wall.

"What are we making?" he asked. He wanted to watch her bake. It was as strange as wanting to go barefoot, but hey, he was willing to roll with things at this point.

He'd been friends—and a pseudo babysitter—to Dax Marshall and Oliver Caprinelli for nine years. He was the voice of reason, the guy who talked them out of the dumbest ideas and the one who paid the bail for the ideas he couldn't talk them out of. Generally, he was the guy who kept them out of the *worst*-case scenarios.

And he'd learned the best memories and stories were never the ones where people were toeing the line.

Dax and Ollie had more fun than Grant did.

Sometimes he was a little jealous of that.

Like right now when his head was telling him he should turn around, leave Jocelyn's house, leave Appleby, leave Iowa. But his heart was saying *this is going to be so, so good. Crazy, but good.*

She smiled. "You want to help?"

"I want to watch."

"You want to watch me bake?"

"I do."

"Is that a fetish I'm not aware of?"

"For me, as of tonight, yes," he told her truthfully.

Her eyebrows rose as if surprised, but her smile was sly and pleased. "Well, okay, then."

She crossed the room to the stove and grabbed the tea pot. "Hot water?"

He frowned. "For?"

"To drink?"

"Uh, no. Do you have coffee?"

She turned to face him. "Of course. But you drink hot water with lemon, right? Not coffee?"

Ah, his order from the bakery every morning. "That's for Piper."

Jocelyn tipped her head. "So you drink coffee."

"I do. Strong. Black."

"Oh." She seemed relieved. "But you don't like our coffee?"

"I get up early and usually have already had a cup or two by the time I come in," he said. "And there's more at the office if I need it." He peered closer. "Does that offend you? I'll gladly drink your coffee, Jocelyn. If that would make you happy."

That sounded a little like innuendo as well. He meant it that way too.

She gave him a little smile. "Actually, Zoe makes the coffee, so no. But I *do* want you to eat my sweets tonight."

That was definitely innuendo. Though it was also literal. She was going to bake. And he was going to strip her naked and take her right here on one of her countertops.

"I can't remember the last time I had a craving like this," he admitted.

She pressed her lips together but then gave a little nod. She turned to the Keurig coffee machine. "Regular or decaf?"

"Regular."

She fixed his coffee and set the mug on the center island. He grabbed it, then propped a shoulder against the doorway that led into the dining room. He figured he'd mostly be out of the way here but could see everything she was doing.

Jocelyn bustled around the kitchen, retrieving ingredients and bowls, spoons, whisks, and spatulas from the fridge, cupboards, and drawers. She had flour, eggs, cocoa, buttermilk, and various other small bottles and cans laid out before she stepped back to survey the assortment.

Grant cradled his cup between his hands, mostly forgetting about his coffee. He was intent on the woman who was muttering to herself as she moved around. He was quite sure she was unaware of the way she talked to herself and he found it endearing.

"Buttermilk, soda, salt, eggs... *butter*. Dammit." She turned back to the fridge and retrieved the butter.

"Buttermilk," she started again, to herself. "Soda, eggs, butter, cocoa, salt... brown sugar. Fuck."

She headed for one of the cupboards and Grant grinned. For some reason, he hadn't pegged her as someone who said "fuck." It didn't offend him in the least, of course. It was one of his favorite, most used, words. But Jocelyn gave off a sweet and sunny air that didn't quite line up with someone who muttered curse words to herself in the kitchen where she created things like the cupcakes he'd seen just that morning.

They'd been freaking caterpillars. Of course, you had to buy three cupcakes to get the full caterpillar—head, middle, and tail. Which was brilliant marketing, in his opinion. They had been done in bright colors and each head cupcake had sported a huge smile. Now he wondered how many *fucks* Jocelyn had dropped while making those brightly smiling cupcake bugs.

She set the canister of brown sugar down on the worktop with a *thunk* and a frown. "Buttermilk," she muttered again, sounding irritated. "Eggs, butter, cocoa, soda, salt, sugar and... *flour*! Fucking *flour*!"

He chuckled at that, but when she looked up with a frown, he quickly lifted his cup to hide his mouth. She narrowed her eyes but turned to stomp into the pantry, retrieve the flour, and return to the work area.

Grant didn't know what was going on, but she surely didn't usually have this much trouble baking every time she tried. She might be Zoe's best friend, but Zoe couldn't afford to pay someone who took this long just to gather ingredients.

Jocelyn started measuring and mixing, but she stopped after adding three ingredients and swore.

"Son of a *bitch*."

Grant couldn't hide his laugh this time.

She looked up and scowled at him. "You're very distracting."

"I'm the problem here?"

"Do you really think *this* is how it usually goes when I bake?" she asked.

"What just happened?"

"I just added the buttermilk to the flour and soda."

"The recipe needs buttermilk, right?" he asked.

"It does. But not *now*."

"Oh." He didn't understand.

"The texture of the cakes depends on how you mix the ingredients together. I can't just add the wet ingredients in with some of the dry now and then more later." She sighed. "Ugh!" She grabbed the bowl and turned to the sink, dumping the contents and washing them down.

"Can I help?" Grant asked.

"Can you be less hot and stop watching me, like you're imagining me doing this naked?" she asked.

"Um... no," he finally said. "At least not the last part. For sure."

She shook her head. "Maybe we should have sex first. Then I can come back down and bake later. I'll be a lot less flustered and distracted then."

Grant pushed away from the doorframe and crossed to where she stood. He set his coffee cup down and crowded close to her. "Well, one, we're not going *up* anywhere. I'm taking you right here, in this kitchen."

Her lips parted and her breathing sped up. "Oh."

He nodded. "From the first second I met you, you've had flour on your cheek or sugar in your hair. You smelled like cake the first time you fell into my arms—and the second, for that matter—and I've had some very specific and erotic images of you, sugar and flour, and lots of bare skin since then."

She wet her lips and stared up at him, her eyes wide. "Like... what?"

"Like my flour handprint on your sweet ass," he told her bluntly and honestly. "Like your nipples coated in sugar. Like icing and batter streaked over your tits and stomach and ass and clit."

Her pupils dilated, and he wondered if he'd gone too far. He barely knew this woman. Just a minute ago he'd been shocked to hear her say the word *fuck*. Maybe she wasn't the type he should be saying *tits* and *clit* to.

"Holy hell, *yes*," she said breathlessly.

Or maybe she totally was. His body went hot and hard and he leaned in. But he didn't kiss her. "Mix up some batter, Jocelyn," he practically growled.

She wet her lips and nodded. "Yeah."

"But I think maybe you need a plan B for whoever it is you're baking for tonight. Because that batter isn't going to make it to the oven. And you're not going to have much time between now and tomorrow morning."

"I was thinking about trying something new for her. But I have cookies in the freezer I can give her."

Wow, he loved that needy, husky tone in her voice.

"Excellent," he told her.

Jocelyn stood, just staring up at him. Well, at his mouth.

"Jocelyn?"

"You should call me Josie."

"Why?"

"That's what my friends call me. People who know me well. And... you're going to know me well." She gave him a sexy-but-shy smile.

"I am," he agreed. "Very well. But Jocelyn fits you."

"Josie doesn't?"

"Josie is cute and sweet," he said with a nod. "It fits. But Jocelyn is gorgeous and sexy and makes your eyes darken."

"It does?" Her brows rose.

"It does."

"I think that's actually because of how you say it." She wet her lips. "You make it sound sexy and a little bossy."

The corner of his mouth curled. "I tend to be bossy."

"I like it."

"Do you? Is that one of your turn-ons?" God, he could boss her around all fucking night long.

"I don't know. There isn't a single guy in this town—in this *county*—who would be bossy with me."

"No? Why's that?" His palm itched to reach up and tuck her hair behind her ear.

"Because they've known me forever," she said, lifting her shoulder. "Because they know my family and it would feel disrespectful maybe? Or because they know my friends and are afraid they'd kick their asses?"

"Or because they think they know you, and you've always been sweet and friendly, and you probably helped them with their homework or worked on a school play or at a fair stand with them or went to Sunday school with them, and they can't imagine saying something like, put your hands on the counter, bend over, and let me lick your pussy," Grant said.

Her eyes flared with surprise and heat. She bit her bottom lip and nodded. "Yeah, maybe that."

"Then it's a good thing I came along. Because I have no qualms about saying that to you."

4

"Wow." Jocelyn practically breathed the word. "First it was catching me from falling and then it was the potatoes. I didn't even know that there was all of *this* to look forward to."

"This?" he asked.

"The dirtiness. The confidence. The bossiness."

He nodded. "There's a lot of all of that."

"That's so good." She said it with just a touch of wonder.

"What about the potatoes?" he asked with a frown.

"You're sexy when you eat potatoes."

"Am I?" That wasn't something he'd ever heard before.

She shrugged. "To me."

He leaned in. He towered over her and found he loved the size difference between them. He loved how little she was and the images of lifting her up and putting her on the counter or against the wall. Or throwing her over his shoulder and heading for her bedroom. But no, he really did want to lick chocolate cake batter from her tits first.

He ignored the niggle that said *she makes you feel possessive and protective.* It was just the alpha-manly-testosterone thing that was rushing through him with all the sex talk and knowing she liked being bossed. Or would like it. Or thought she'd like it.

He loved the idea that other men hadn't been like that with her. These small-town farmer guys had probably been nice and gentlemanly toward her. Which was great. In fact, they better fucking have been. She deserved that. But if she wanted a little dominating, he was happy to oblige. It didn't mean he *felt* anything soft or serious for her. In fact it was the opposite, right? Bossing her around? Being dirty with her? Those were the opposite of soft. He liked being in charge. So he could give her a little of that while he was in town. Then she could go back to the nice guys, and one of them could get her a white picket fence and a puppy.

"Jocelyn," he said, making sure his voice sounded gruff and a little firm.

"Yes?"

"Make us some chocolate cake batter to play with."

Play. And sex. While talking about dominating her. It didn't seem like all of that should go together. Play and sex didn't really go together for him usually. He just didn't… play. In general. Much.

Dax made sure he did some. But women never did. He dated sophisticated women who liked sophisticated things. Being covered in chocolate cake batter didn't seem very sophisticated. But he'd been absolutely honest when he'd told Jocelyn that he'd been having very specific fantasies about her and baked goods.

And she was the type to play. To giggle and tease with chocolate and Lord knew what other fun, sweet, sticky stuff.

As evidenced by the, "Yes, sir," she gave him and the smile she flashed as she turned toward the worktable and started pulling ingredients toward her and mixing them up.

He braced a hand on the table and leaned his hip into the

edge, settling in to watch her. "You don't seem to be having trouble remembering how to put this all together now," he commented, watching her confident moves.

"I guess I'm very focused now," she said, grabbing the whisk and beating the buttermilk and vanilla together.

"But I'm still here."

She nodded, reaching for the hand mixer and turning to plug it into the outlet behind her. "And I'm very motivated to get this done."

He smiled. "What's this supposed to be?"

She gave him a sly grin that made his cock harden. "Whoopie pies."

He lifted a brow. "Seriously?"

"Seriously. You know what they are right? Chocolate cake sandwiches with cream in the middle."

"I've maybe seen them, but I've never had one."

"Oh, well, just wait."

"I will. But only because you're sexy as hell when you're baking. And in that apron."

She gave him a sexy smile, then got to work.

She beat the butter and sugar together, then added the egg. She slowly added the dry mixture and the buttermilk mixture into the bowl in small alternating batches, scraping the sides of the bowl down periodically. Finally, the batter was well combined and smooth.

She shut the mixer off and then blew out a breath and looked up at him.

He leaned in. "Now we have to taste test it, right?"

Jocelyn dipped her whisk into the bowl, then lifted it to her mouth and took a little lick.

Watching her tongue run over the curved metal of the whisk made Grant's body tighten. And his smile grow. He liked Jocelyn flirting and teasing.

"Oh no, I need to feel your tongue on *me*." He dipped the tip of his index finger into the batter and then lifted it to her mouth.

She obediently moved the whisk out of the way and opened her mouth. He set his finger on her bottom lip and she closed around it, sucking lightly, then flicking her tongue over the tip.

His nerve endings lit up. Just that one little graze of her tongue and he wanted it all over his body. Some places more than others, of course.

He pulled his finger from her mouth, cupped the back of her head, and brought her in for a kiss. He didn't go slow. He opened his mouth on hers, running his tongue over her bottom lip where his finger had been a moment ago, then sliding in deep along hers, tasting the chocolate and the sweetness that was all Jocelyn herself.

She arched close, her hand going to his cheeks and holding his face as she met him stroke for stroke.

He reached to bump the bowl of batter to the side and then lifted her to the island, stepping between her knees, all without breaking contact with her mouth.

She seemed perfectly fine with the change in position. Both of her arms went around his neck, and she welcomed him into the V between her legs, tightening her knees on either side of him.

He reached for the bow at the back of the apron, pulling it loose, and then separating from her only enough to whip the apron off over her head. But he took her mouth again immediately after the pink frilly thing was gone.

He ran his hands over her body. He wanted to know every curve. He wanted to know which spots made her gasp, which made her moan, which made her arch closer, which made her beg.

Especially the ones that made her beg.

She was already arching closer and moaning. Her hands were also roaming, and Grant felt them run up and down his back, over his ribs and then to the front, where she slipped them under the bottom edge of his shirt and onto bare skin.

He sucked in a breath as her palms glided over his abs and to his chest. Her hands on him were heaven and hell. She seemed to want to explore thoroughly, and his skin felt like it was burning.

He wanted some of that action too. He found the zipper on the side of her dress, grasping the tiny tab and pulling on the delicate fastener. The bodice gaped, and he tucked his finger in the front and tugged it down, freeing her breasts.

He tore his mouth from hers, needing a good look at her. She was panting, her mouth shiny and pink from his. Her pupils were dilated as she blinked up at him. The bra she wore was also strapless and pale pink, nearly matching her skin. It wasn't completely sheer but her nipples were darker and he could see the stiff points against the thin fabric. He ran a thumb over one and she gasped.

"Need this off too," he said gruffly.

"Need this off, then," she said, tugging on the bottom of his shirt.

His fingers went to his buttons, his gaze locked on hers. She reached behind her for the hooks on her bra.

She got done first.

The pale pink silk dropped away from her body, revealing the most perfect breasts he'd ever seen. He wasn't picky about breasts. Any size, any color, they all made him happy. But these... these were his favorite. Ever.

"Fuck, you're gorgeous," he told her.

"Keep going," she said, her voice husky.

He realized that he'd stopped unbuttoning and quickly went back to it, debating about just ripping the damned thing off.

But then she started to wiggle, and he was fine with taking his time on those buttons, so that he could watch her.

She was shimmying her dress down her hips and legs. The movement made her breasts bounce slightly, and obviously revealed even more of her gorgeous body. By the time she kicked the dress to the floor and hooked her thumbs in the tops of her panties—also pale pink and also tiny—and wiggled them down and off, Grant's shirt was hanging open, his mouth was dry, his heart was thundering, and his cock was harder than it had ever been.

"Damn," was all he could manage.

Jocelyn met his eyes. Her expression was sexy and almost devious as if she knew exactly what she was doing to him and had him right where she wanted him.

Well, if this was where this goddess wanted him, he was all in. He didn't care about tomorrow or next week or, hell, five minutes from now. He just wanted *this*. Her.

She reached out and dipped her finger in the cake batter, then painted a swirl of chocolate on her stomach. She trailed the finger up toward her breast, but the chocolate ran out by the time she got to the glorious mound. She reached for more batter, then made Grant the happiest man on earth. She leaned back onto her other elbow, hooked one heel on the edge of the counter, and drew the chocolaty finger around her nipple.

"Take your clothes off, Grant," she said softly, playing with her nipple, coating it in chocolate and making it pucker even tighter.

He couldn't speak. He could barely breathe. He shrugged out of his shirt, toed off his shoes as he tore at his fly, and pushed his jeans and boxers to the floor. He stepped out of them, kicking them to the side.

Her gaze roamed over him, taking in every detail. "Oh my God, you are so hot," she told him. Her eyes lifted to his. "So big."

He grinned and stepped forward and ran a *big* hand up the outside of her thigh. "Ditto on the hot part. Very much ditto."

"I'm serious," she said, looking very sober suddenly. "You're huge."

"I'm a big guy," he said soothingly. "But this will work. No worries."

She laughed. "Well, yes, I'm sure it will."

He lifted an eyebrow. Okay, so she wasn't *worried* about his size exactly. She was a tiny woman, and he was a big man, if they were talking averages anyway. But hey, maybe the guys of Appleby, Iowa were well endowed.

"But you're going to have to do a little extra work first." She quirked an eyebrow. Then handed him the bowl of cake batter.

Oh, he liked this girl a lot.

He took the bowl with a little growl. "Lie back, Jocelyn."

She took a quick, deep breath, and shook her head. "Yes, sir." She eased herself onto her back.

Her blond hair spread over the work surface. He was sure there was going to be flour and sugar in it when she got up. But she was going to be a lot messier and stickier than that before he was done with her.

He let his gaze take in every inch. He ran a hand over her stomach, causing her muscles to clench and her to suck in a breath. He spread the chocolate swirl she'd drawn into a messy smear of sticky brown. Then he lowered his head and took a long lick.

It was delicious. But that had everything to do with the silky, hot skin underneath. And the moan that it elicited.

"Grant."

His name was breathless on her lips and he fucking loved it. He followed the chocolate trail up her stomach, over her ribs, and to the lower curve of her breast.

She was already wiggling and her fingers slid into his hair.

"So, the way I understand what you need, is that I have to

make sure you're nice and hot and wet and slick so that I can ease into you without any trouble," he said against her breast, before swirling his tongue around her nipple.

"Grant... yes..." Her head moved back and forth on the tabletop.

He really liked how easy it was to get his name out of her. He drew her nipple into his mouth, sucking all the chocolate from it, then sucking harder, then even harder.

Her hips lifted from the table and he grinned. Okay, sensitive nipples. Very nice.

He trailed his hand up her thigh, circling his thumb over her hip bone, then sliding along the crease that led to her mound. "And is there anything specific that really does it for you, or can I just go according to the gasps and *yes, Grants*?"

"You can..." She gave one of those gasps as he brushed over her clit. "You're doing fine."

He chuckled. Fucking chuckled. During sex.

That was strange enough for him. But now he was about to smear cake batter all over a woman. No one would believe it.

As he looked down at the naked, wriggling woman spread out like a dessert buffet for him, he knew he wasn't telling anyone a damned thing about this though.

He reached for the cake batter, and rather than dipping just one finger, he scooped up a handful. He let it dribble onto her stomach. She sucked in a breath. He drizzled it up and over her breasts, down the valley between them, swirled it around her belly button, and down to her mound. He moved his hand back and forth, painting swirls there, then dripped it down her thigh.

He followed it from top to bottom with his tongue and lips, making sure to get every drop and to spend extra time on each spot. By the time he moved his thumbs to part the sweet folds between her legs and flick his tongue over the slick, swollen bud there, she was whimpering and begging, and she came almost instantly.

"Oh my God! Grant!" Her toes actually curled and her back arched. Her body shuddered, and she gripped his forearm tightly.

Grant lifted his head to look at her. Her entire body seemed flushed, but her face was a darker pink and she was breathing hard, her chest rising and falling.

One lick? He'd made her come that easily?

Damn, that was good for a guy's ego.

Several long moments passed as he just stroked the outside of her thigh into the curve of her ass and waited. She wasn't begging him to *keep going, please don't stop, oh, that's so good,* so yeah, he assumed she needed a second to regroup.

Finally, she put a hand over her eyes and gave a sobbing laugh. "Oh wow."

He squeezed her hip. "Why, thank you very much."

She laughed again. "I can't believe that happened so fast. And easy!" She moved her hand to look at him. "You hardly even did anything down there!"

Grant gave a choked laugh. "Hey, I was willing. I was just getting started!"

She grinned. "I know! That's... wow. You have a magic tongue. I mean, it definitely got a workout everywhere else." Her smile was a combination of amused and shy. "You're good with it, I'll give you that. Maybe it would have been too much if it had been... applied directly."

He laughed again. He wasn't sure what to expect to come out of her mouth. "Jocelyn," he said, his tone serious even though he was grinning like a damned idiot. "You *will* find out what it's like when applied directly."

She blushed deeper but also grinned. "Good."

"But now—" He shifted so he was straighter and reached to

take her ass in both hands. "I think we've completed the prep work."

She blew out a breath. "Boy, have we. I've never been... prepared... quite like that."

Damn right she hadn't.

It was the kind of thought that should have him worried. He never cared about the men that came before him—or after, for that matter—with the women he dated. They simply didn't matter. The relationship was about Grant and the woman he was with for however long it lasted. He didn't think much—and certainly didn't *worry*—about the woman's history before him or what happened after.

That might make him an asshole, but he cared about a lot of women outside of the bedroom. Women who needed someone on their side. Who had a lack of allies in their life and needed a coach and a cheerleader and a teacher.

He never dated women like that. Women who *needed* things.

But Jocelyn needed something. Him. And another orgasm. Right now.

He'd worry about the other things she was making him feel later.

Because he needed something right now too—her. And he *never* needed anything.

Focusing on the naked, post-orgasmic-glowing woman before him, he ran the hand not covered in chocolate up her thigh and eased a finger into her pussy. Definitely slick and hot. And tight. Still really damned tight.

She said his name in that breathy, begging way again, and he added a second finger, gliding in and out, loving the feel of her already.

"How do you want me, Jocelyn?" he asked, circling his thumb over her clit.

She bit her bottom lip. Oh, she had a request. He could tell. She wanted him to be bossy but she had an idea.

"Tell me," he said firmly, curling his fingers into her G-spot.

She gasped and let her head drop back. "You..." She took a breath. "You mentioned flour handprints on my ass."

Oh. Fuck. Yes.

He removed his fingers, pulled her off the island and turned her to face it in one swift, smooth move. He leaned in, his front to her back, his whole body against hers, his cock pressing into her ass. "You like being spanked?"

"I have no idea," she said softly.

Even better. He ran his hands down her arms to her wrists, then lifted her hands to the table. "Don't move them," he said, pressing them into the wooden top.

She nodded.

He reached around her, running his palms through the flour that had spilled and was now spread over the work surface by her body. He leaned back, seeing that white powder already dusted her back and her ass. He put one hand over her right butt cheek, pressing and squeezing slightly, making a perfect handprint.

"Oh yeah, that's pretty," he said.

She arched her back, almost instinctively, as if offering her ass up to him. He gave her a little swat as a reward. She gasped, more from surprise than pain. He leaned in, his mouth against her ear. "How was that?"

"Hot," she said, her voice husky.

He bit her earlobe and she moaned. He dragged his mouth down her neck, making sure the scruff on his jaw abraded the sensitive skin. Goose bumps broke out and her nipples tightened. She groaned. He bit the curve of her neck where her shoulder began, and the groan turned to a whimper.

"Fuck, you are so good," he told her. "I am going to love fucking you."

She shivered at his graphic language. He leaned back and gave her another swat, this one a little harder.

"Yesss," she hissed softly.

They barely knew one another but she clearly trusted him. That fired his blood and made his cock rock hard. He would take such good care of her. Did she sense that somehow? Did she sense the way he was feeling? This protective, possessive thing that he didn't want, but couldn't deny?

He rubbed her ass then swatted the other side, rubbing away the sting immediately as she pressed into his hand. Covering her in flour from his hands was strangely erotic and satisfying. As if he was marking her.

He was in so much trouble.

"Grant, I need you," she said, her voice pleading.

He ran his hand over her sweet curves again. "I know, sweetheart, I know." He leaned over and snagged his pants, pulling out his wallet, and then a condom. He'd had no idea he'd need this tonight, but he was always prepared. At least where condoms were concerned.

He wasn't sure he was truly prepared for Jocelyn Asher at all.

"Please." She pressed back when he'd straightened again, her ass against his cock. "Please."

"Please what?" He ripped the condom packet open, then rolled the thing on one handed. "Tell me what you want."

He wanted to push her. Just like her letting him swat her ass, he wanted to know what all she'd let him do, how far she'd let him go. How much would she trust him?

"Please. I want you inside me."

He put his mouth on her ear again as a *need* to push—and more, a need to see how far she'd trust him—rose inside him. "I want you to ask me to fuck you," he said, his voice rough. He reached up and took a nipple between his thumb and forefinger. He plucked, then pinched.

She moaned, her head falling back against his shoulder.

"Say it, Jocelyn. Tell me you want me to fuck you. That you'll just stand here, hold on, and take it."

"Yes." Her voice was wobbly. "Yes, I'll take whatever you want to give me."

A surge of emotion went through him, and he took her hips in both hands. He wasn't going to try to define that emotion. Or analyze it. At least not beyond the realization he was in way too deep with this woman already. That he recognized without giving it a single bit of focus. That was a subconscious resignation.

As he positioned himself at her entrance, he vowed to go slow. Yes, he wanted to push, and he'd never been this worked up and she was, after all, begging. But he didn't want to hurt her.

Of course, she surprised him again. She leaned over, pressing her breasts and cheek to the table, completely at his mercy.

"Damn," he muttered. It was part *oh-damn-I'm-so-screwed-here* and part good old-fashioned awe.

He slid into her in one long, slow thrust.

They both groaned. Jocelyn gripped one edge of the table. She couldn't reach both sides at the same time, but she held on to the one and tucked her other hand underneath her chest. There was something about the sweet pink nail polish on the fingers curling over the edge of the table, hanging on as she was fucked from behind, that was insanely hot.

Grant withdrew and thrust again. She took him easily enough. It was a tight fit, but in a glorious, hand-in-glove way that pulled at his balls, and his restraint. He wanted to pound into her, make the table rock, and make her scream.

Every time he pulled out, her body clenched and clung, not wanting him to go. Every time he sunk deep, she made sounds that made his balls, gut, and even his chest draw tighter.

He ran a hand up and down her back as he thrust, loving

the silky feel of her hair over the back of his hand and wrist. He loved the curve of her back and her hips. He loved the color of her skin. He loved the way she went up on tiptoe to take him and the way his name fell easily from her lips.

But he couldn't hold on for long. Her body was heaven, and her pussy milked him relentlessly.

"Jocelyn, I want you to come again for me," Grant said through gritted teeth.

"This is so good," she said.

"It is. Jesus, honey, it is. I can't last too long." He thrust deep. "I want you to come on my cock. I want to feel the way you come apart."

She gave a little groan. "Oh yes. I'm so close."

He gripped her hips and changed the angle just a bit, hitting more toward the front. Her pussy responded with a tighter clenching, and she said his name breathlessly.

"I need you wider, Jocelyn," he said. "I need your pussy wide open and taking me."

"Oh God," she whimpered.

He grasped her knee and brought it up. The table was too high to rest it on the edge, so he just held it, surging deeper into her body.

"Step stool," she gasped.

"What?"

"Under the table. Stool."

He paused. Somehow. Unbelievably. He felt underneath the edge of the table with his foot and located the leg of what must have been a stool. He pulled it out by hooking his foot around it. Sure enough. It was a little wooden stool that would boost her up about three inches. It looked more decorative than functional. But he wasn't picky at the moment.

Jocelyn reached back, grabbing his ass. "Don't leave me," she said. Then pressing into him, she stepped up onto the stool.

She put her own knee on the edge of the table.

"Oh wow," she gasped.

She was spread wide and Grant nearly lost it. She really was going to do whatever he told her. And she was going to trust him for all of this.

"You're... amazing," he told her.

"Keep going, Grant," she told him, gripping the edge of the table again.

"My fucking pleasure." He gripped her hips and drove deep.

She moaned and pressed back against him. He did it again.

"Yes!" she called out.

"Come for me," he demanded.

She reached for her clit, circling it as he continued to thrust, and a minute later he felt her pussy clamp down, and her cry was an even louder, "*Yes!*"

He picked up the pace, thrusting into her hard and deep until he let go, his release rushing through him.

Gasping, Jocelyn slumped onto the table and Grant pulled out, still gripping her hips. He tipped his head back and worked on sucking in oxygen.

His thoughts stopped spinning a minute later and he focused. He ran his hand over her flour-covered ass. "Yep, that is really pretty."

She giggled. "I am going to get so horny every time I bake in here now."

"Good." He didn't know why he said that. Why was that his first reaction?

He wanted her thinking of him whenever she came into her kitchen? Why? This was a one-night fling. Maybe a couple-weeks-long fling. She was a small-town baker. A *sweet* small-town baker who wore pink sundresses and was attached to an old house in her hometown that was very far from Chicago. She was not his type. It was cruel of him to want her thinking of him all the time after he left.

But even as he moved to the sink to deal with the condom

and clean up, he couldn't deny that seeing his handprints on her, knowing that she trusted him, thinking that chocolate cake might always make her think of him, definitely made a surge of something go through him.

Something that was probably best labeled *I was right to not eat her cupcakes.*

5

Somehow Josie managed to push herself up from the table. She didn't want to move. She'd never felt this good in her entire life. She never wanted these blissful waves of thank-God-bodies-could-do-that-to-each-other to fade. She never wanted to use this tabletop for anything *but* what she and Grant had just done.

And that was saying a lot because she loved all the things she did with flour, sugar, and butter.

But now that she'd had sex with Grant Lorre, she was never going to love anything more.

And that had been *sex*. Hot, dirty, take-over-every-sense *sex*. The kind she'd always hoped was possible. It hadn't been, so far, in her love-slash-sex life. But she'd held out hope. She was, after all, an eternal optimist. That didn't have to just apply to the state of world politics and her ability to save even the worst cake fails.

She hadn't officially named her side business where she baked for overworked moms who'd forgotten they had to provide dessert for the next day's office potluck or kid's class party. Or those who didn't have time to bake four-dozen anything. Or those who were just not good at baking, period. She was unofficially known in the circles she helped as Bakery 9-1-1. She loved that.

She'd met women in the gazebo at the park to give them their goodies.

On Tuesday, she'd met Travis, a divorced dad, on the seventh hole on the golf course—the one with the most trees— with three-dozen caramel-stuffed Rice Krispie treats. She'd helped him take them from the box and put them into his own plastic containers and even brought extra caramel to put on his shirt so that *he* could be his son's hero at the birthday party at his ex's house.

She'd met Nancy, a fifty-something corporate executive, behind the nursing home last Saturday. Josie had handed off a strawberry shortcake made with Nancy's mother's recipe for her mother's eightieth birthday. Nancy had *needed* that cake to be perfect. She just hadn't had the time to make it.

Josie was happy to help.

All of those people had the best intentions of doing it them-selves. They wanted to take the time and put the effort into making something special for people they cared about. But time worked against them. Or their lack of experience. Or their lack of the right equipment—like a big enough mixer to handle the job or the right ruffle decorating tip. Or their realization at midnight that they didn't have enough eggs.

So Josie's personal cell number had gotten passed around. She liked being able to help those people have the special goodies they needed without the stress and hassle that some-times came with making it themselves. She didn't mind if they passed her treats off as their own.

Besides, word was getting around. She'd actually had to hold back on those Iron Man cupcakes to make it at least *a little* believable that Travis had made them. That had been difficult for her. She'd had some really cute ideas for them. But a simple vanilla cupcake spread with red icing and a yellow mask—that she'd had to redraw twice to make it *worse*—in the middle had had to suffice.

As she forced herself upright and smoothed her hair back, she heard the water running in the sink behind her. Grant was cleaning up, and she should do the same, she supposed.

She looked down. And giggled.

Her front was covered with chocolate and flour and sugar. She knew her back was similarly messy. Her body tingled as she thought about how all of that had gotten on all of those places.

She'd suspected things would be hot between her and Grant the second he'd kissed her. Hell, she'd been the one thinking about his naked body and cheesy potatoes and marshmallow fluff—not together—so combining food with sex had seemed inevitable. But this cleanup was going to require a shower.

She grabbed for her apron, rather than her clothes, and slipped it over her head, tying it at her back.

Grant turned from the sink and stooped to grab his boxers, but he froze as his gaze landed on her.

His mouth turned up in a slow, sexy smile. "Fuck, that's hot."

She loved his smile. She also really loved his gruff voice and the way he was looking at her.

"I'm thinking that if we did something like this at Buttered Up, we could increase sales," she said, doing a little turn.

"Don't even think about it."

His voice was firm, and he was frowning when she faced him again.

Her brows went up. "No?"

"No." Again firm. And serious. He jerked his boxers up.

He didn't seem to be kidding around. "I was just joking,"

she said. She thought that was really an unnecessary clarification to make.

"I know." He was still scowling.

"Are you okay?"

"The idea of you... showing anyone any of... you," he said, seemingly at a loss for words as he tried to explain. "Makes me... irritable."

That wasn't funny, exactly. Still, she laughed. He frowned harder.

"Grant, there's no way I'd go to the bakery like this."

He grabbed his pants and yanked them on. He drove a hand through his hair, let out a breath, then focused on her again. Shirtless, his hair disheveled, his pants unzipped and loose, he looked so sexy she sighed.

"No," he agreed about the apron-only idea at Buttered Up. "But you might wear that here for someone."

She studied his face. What was going on? "I guess. Maybe."

"And that makes me... irritable." He paused before that last word again. As if that wasn't quite the word he was looking for. Or as if he was avoiding that word, possibly.

Josie didn't know what word he *was* thinking, but she liked that he didn't *like* the idea of her here with someone else. She stepped close and put a hand on his chest, rubbing in a little circle. "Is there anything I can do to make you feel better?"

"Never have sex with anyone else."

That wasn't what she'd been expecting. "Um. Ever?"

"Ever."

"I thought you didn't want to stay in Appleby."

"I don't."

"So that would mean no more sex at all for me?"

He nodded. "Except for the times when I visited."

She gave him a little smile. "You're good, Grant. You're very good. But unless you're visiting here several times a week, I don't think you're good enough to keep me satisfied indefinitely."

He gave a little growl at that, and her inner muscles tightened in response. Yeah, she was going to need a lot more of everything he had to offer. And not long distance or over the phone.

"But I'm very happy to give *you* full access to my... kitchen... for as long as you're here," she said with a grin and what she thought sounded like a pretty saucy tone.

He nodded. "And no one else."

She widened her eyes. "Of course not." Okay, she'd been pretty bold tonight, at times, but she was a one-man-at-a-time kind of girl. In fact, a one-man-at-a-time-with-lots-of-time-in-between-men kind of girl, actually.

"Good."

Wow. That sounded... possessive.

She liked it.

Also wow.

"I think I need to go," he said after studying her for a long moment.

"Enough kitchen time for one night?" She sensed there was something else going on. He wasn't leaving because he was done with her. He was leaving, maybe, because he *wasn't*.

"I basically want to throw you over my shoulder, take you to bed, and stay there for a month or two," he said.

"So you're leaving instead," she clarified.

"Right."

"This is like the reason you didn't ask me out."

"Right."

She got to him. Somehow, for some reason, she—little Josie Asher of Appleby, Iowa—got to this guy. She was making him act out of character. Apparently. And feel things he wasn't used to feeling.

Her mouth curved into a wide smile.

He lifted a brow.

"Okay," she said. "You can go."

He narrowed his eyes. "You look very smug suddenly."

She nodded. "I'm feeling smug."

"About?"

"Scaring you."

He frowned. "You don't..." But he didn't finish the sentence. He took a deep breath. "I'll see you tomorrow."

"Will you?" She wasn't sure how far and for how long a guy like Grant might run from something he was afraid of.

She felt herself smiling again. Yeah, she liked that she shook him up. It was all just a feeling she had about a feeling she thought he maybe had—so, obviously, nothing tangible or even confessed-out-loud—but the fact that Grant was acting possessive while also claiming that he hadn't wanted to ask her out because it would have made him want to stay, all made happy bubbles of emotion fizz through her body.

That was damned romantic.

He might be fighting the feelings, but he was having them.

She liked that a lot.

He nodded. "You'll see me tomorrow."

She grinned. "I thought you kind of thought you should stay away."

He sighed. "Yeah."

"So..." She trailed off on purpose, really wanting him to fill in that blank.

He hesitated for just a second, then he backed her up against the island where they'd just been *very* friendly, braced a hand on the counter next to her, and leaned in. "So..." he said, his voice low and husky. "Now that I've had a taste of your cupcakes, I have no chance of staying away."

That was exactly what she'd wanted him to say. Or a very nice variation of it anyway. She looped her arms around his neck and went up on tiptoe, pressing her lips to his. He didn't move his hands or lean in any closer, but he kissed her back thoroughly.

When she pulled back she said, "I like your cupcakes a lot too, Grant."

He gave a short huff of laughter. "My cupcakes? That's not very manly."

She arched into him, pressing against his cock that was already hardening again. "Your Yule log?" she asked, then giggled.

He growled and kissed her again, deeply and hungrily. When he lifted his head, she was breathing hard. "I'm going to go," he said firmly. "But I'll be thinking about your cream filling all night."

Her eyes widened for just a moment. That was surprisingly dirty. And funny. And hot. "I hope so," she told him honestly.

Lord knew *she* was going to be lying in bed thinking about him. She loved the idea that it would be mutual.

Grant grabbed his shirt, donned his shoes, and headed for the back door with a final, "'Night, Jocelyn" as he paused at the threshold. Then he was gone.

Josie gave what could only be described as a swoony sigh as the screen door slapped shut behind him.

She surveyed her kitchen. It was a disaster. And it made her smile.

Then, still wearing only an apron, she pulled the frozen cookies out to thaw for Karen for the next day and she went to work baking cupcakes for Grant. Very special cupcakes. Just for him.

———

"Is this a pussy cupcake?"

Dax was standing in front of the bakery box Grant had set on the table in Aiden's office. Dax had just lifted the lid to check out the goodies.

Grant crossed the room quickly. He looked down into the box.

Of pornographic cupcakes.

His mouth twitched.

Jocelyn had baked him cupcakes. Especially for him, or so she'd said when she'd grinned at him as if she'd never been happier to see anyone in her life and handed over the bright yellow Buttered Up bakery box.

He'd been downright dazzled by that smile. He'd had a hell of a time falling asleep after leaving her, and he swore, even after a shower, that his skin still smelled like chocolate cake. And Jocelyn.

Then he'd walked into the bakery, and her face had fucking *lit up* when she'd seen him. He couldn't remember the last time someone looked at him like that. He did get a lot of admiration and general gratitude from the women who attended his financial seminars. But this had been different. He hadn't helped Jocelyn pay off her credit cards or refinance her house. He'd just laughed and fucked and had fun with her.

And she'd looked at him like seeing him had made her entire day.

Damn. That had jabbed him right in the chest.

He'd still been thinking about it when he'd taken the box of cupcakes and headed for the office. He'd still been thinking about *her*. And how eager he'd been to see her too and how much he wanted to carry her into the kitchen and take a nice deep taste of her. Her mouth. Her breasts. Her pussy.

Yeah, her *actual* pussy had definitely been on his mind. Which was why he hadn't looked inside the bakery box—

where she'd given him another sweet, sticky, delicious pussy to start his day—before bringing them in to share with the guys.

He'd figured he wasn't going to be able to eat six cupcakes anyway, and he'd looked forward to the guys wondering why Jocelyn had made *him* special cupcakes.

That was pretty obvious now. But how could he have expected the woman who made caterpillar cupcakes to make him sexual cupcakes?

There were six. Two were breasts, complete with hard nipples. One was a mouth. One was a butt—with a flour hand-print on it. He really liked that. One was an erect penis. She'd made that cupcake extra big, which definitely made Grant chuckle. And the sixth was clearly a pussy. He would bet a million dollars it was cream filled too.

He quickly reached out and snagged that one. He actually wanted to keep them all to himself now, but he was certain Dax wasn't going to let that happen.

"Tell me it's cream filled," Dax said, clearly thinking along the same lines.

Grant bit into it, then turned the cupcake to face Dax. "Of course."

"That"—Dax informed him, pointing at the cupcake—"is awesomely naughty. I love it. Whatever you did to that girl—and I have a general idea and don't need details because I need to face her at the bakery later, and I don't want to be blushing and stammering—was well done."

Grant shook his head. He'd just barely kept from groaning out loud over that first taste of Josie's cupcake. Much like the night before. "When have you *ever* blushed and stammered?"

Dax shrugged. "Picturing Jocelyn Asher, sweet, smiley, always upbeat baker extraordinaire, letting you do things to her that led to pussy cupcakes in the morning? That might do it."

"Pussy cupcakes?" Oliver walked in just then. "You'd better mean cupcakes that are shaped like cats. Piper will never let us introduce a porn line of baked goods. Though that would be awesome. We could sell online only." Ollie's brain had clearly started spinning already. That was common. A single sentence, a simple mention of something, and his imagination would take off. "It would be kind of a secret, off-menu thing that only our special clients know about and people only find out about by word of mouth."

"No." Piper, their executive assistant—who was five years younger than the youngest of the partners and five times as bright, or so it seemed—breezed through the doorway a second later. "Absolutely not."

"It could be huge," Ollie said.

"No," Piper said again, handing Grant the files he'd asked for when he'd passed her desk earlier. "No pussy cupcakes."

Ollie sighed and looked at the guys. "Told you."

"I'm totally giving that idea to Zoe," Piper said with a smile. "*She* can have a special off-menu, word-of-mouth-only line for bachelorette parties and gag gifts and such."

She turned and sashayed out of the office. Piper almost always sashayed. It was part attitude and part the way she dressed. The pinup girl skirts and dresses, the heels, the bows and scarves, the glasses, the lipstick... it just all seemed to call for sashaying.

"Dammit," Oliver said. "My great idea, stolen right out from under me by female empowerment. Typical."

"Don't feel bad," Grant said dryly. He was certain Ollie did not, in fact, feel bad. No one was more dedicated to their company and its growth and well-being than Piper. If Piper had thought that was a good idea for them, she would have looked past any misgivings she might have had about the actual product and encouraged it. "Jocelyn made these cupcakes. If Zoe wants a line like that, she's already got the idea and the best baker in town."

"Best baker in town, huh?" Ollie asked, dropping into one of the armchairs. "You've sampled a lot of *baked goods* in this town, then?"

They all knew that was not the case. Whether they were talking about actual or figurative baked goods. Grant had no intention of dating anyone—or sampling anything from anyone—in Appleby. Of course, that had been blown to hell the minute Jocelyn fell into his arms.

"No," he answered. He put the rest of the pussy cupcake into his mouth. Damn, it was delicious. And he wanted Jocelyn again. Right now. As badly has he had before.

"So you're just assuming that Jocelyn is the best?" Ollie asked.

"You don't have to try *all* the cupcakes to know when you've found the best ones," Grant said.

He heard a snort to his left, and he glanced over to find Dax grinning.

"What?" Grant asked.

"You're almost kidding around," Dax said. "And it's not even ten a.m. I feel like we *all* need to start the day with Josie's pussy cupcakes."

"No." Grant said it firmly. More firmly than needed.

Dax lifted a brow and looked at Ollie. "What if I called her up right now and said, 'Hey, Josie, I'd love some more of your pussies?'" Dax asked.

Grant knew Dax was messing with him. He knew the other man was just poking at him, trying to get a reaction. He knew Dax was expecting a certain reaction, in fact. Grant knew he should not give Dax that reaction. He didn't care. "I'd kick your ass," he said simply.

Dax nodded as if Grant had given him exactly the right answer. "Even if I was referring to the actual cupcakes?"

"You won't ever say the word *pussy* or *pussies* to Jocelyn," Grant said. "And those cupcakes are *mine*." He reached out, took the box, closed the lid, and tucked it under his arm.

Dax shook his head as he moved toward one of the other chairs and sank into it. "Wow, that was fast. Like *really* fast. Maybe faster than me and Jane."

"What's fast?" Grant asked.

"You becoming smitten," Dax told him. "But you're totally the type to see something you want and to just *take* it, so it doesn't really surprise me, I guess."

Grant frowned at him. "I'm not smitten."

"Oh, you're totally smitten," Ollie said, nodding.

"Fuck off," Grant said. But he was afraid they were right.

Dammit. This is what he'd been trying to avoid. Jocelyn Asher was exactly the type of woman that men became smitten with. They didn't just lust after her. She was too sweet for that. They didn't obsess. That seemed too crazy. They just fell head over fucking heels for her.

He did not want to be in love. Or smitten. Or obsessed, for that matter.

Lust he could handle. He could cope with liking her for sure.

But anything more than that would mean that he'd feel responsible—for her happiness and her safety. He didn't want that. Women needed to be responsible for their *own* happiness and safety. Men fucked that up way too often. They couldn't be trusted.

He'd seen that personally. With his grandmother and his sister. Men couldn't actually be trusted to take care of women in the way they needed. To care for them and love them without smothering them or making them feel helpless.

What the hell did he know about taking care of someone? Not physically, of course. But emotionally. Men just weren't equipped to take care of women emotionally.

Aiden and Dax might be the exceptions. But Grant had to say, and he thought his friends would agree, that Zoe and Jane were strong women who had been taking care of themselves very well before the guys showed up and were willing and able to call the guys out on their shit if they started thinking they were somehow in charge of things.

Aiden was an amazing supporter of Zoe's, encouraging her to grow her business and try new things. Dax was the perfect guy for the strong but sad-around-the-edges Jane who took on the weight of the world. He made her laugh and made sure she had fun.

So yeah, his friends were exceptions to the rule of men sucking when it came to women. There were a few of those. Grant ran into them once in a while.

But mostly men sucked.

It was why women were paid less, held fewer CEO positions, held fewer seats in Congress... he could go on and on.

He wanted to help women see that they didn't need men. The way he'd done for his sister. The way he'd done for his grandmother. He'd done it for dozens of women in the seminars he taught.

He wasn't about to start taking care of a woman now. He didn't want to feel protective and possessive and like her happiness and safety was his one and only priority in life. Jocelyn didn't need that. And he sure as hell didn't.

"Piper said I needed to check out the cupcakes," Aiden said, coming into his office and rounding the desk. "Something about a new product line for Zoe?"

Grant recalled Jocelyn confiding in him about her side business and saying that Zoe didn't know about her baking special projects outside of Buttered Up. He couldn't let on to Zoe's fiancé that Jocelyn was doing side projects.

He liked the idea of Jocelyn having a side business. It gave her more security. He knew from a few conversations with Aiden since he'd been back and gotten involved with Zoe romantically, that the bakery didn't offer a lot in terms of benefits for its owner and single employee. That bugged Grant. More than it should.

He would frown on any business not offering its employees as much security as possible, of course, and he would have been tempted to go to Zoe, as a female business owner, and offer his financial consulting services if she didn't have Aiden. But the fact that Jocelyn was her one employee made him even more irritated by the idea that the two young women were just flying by the seat of their pants.

"These cupcakes were made exclusively for me," Grant told him. "It's not going to turn into anything regular at the bakery."

As much as he liked the idea of Jocelyn having a side hustle, he did *not* like the idea of her making pussy cupcakes, or breasts or butts for that matter, for anyone else.

That was as stupid as his sudden desire to start her a 401K. She wouldn't even have to know about it. He could just contribute to it monthly. He'd have to have Cam look into the legalities of paying that out to her when she retired, but he was sure it could be done. Almost anything could be done with the right lawyer drawing things up. And Cam was one of the best.

Grant shook his head. He could not start Jocelyn Asher a secret 401K.

"Okay, well, good," Aiden said, looking confused. "I guess." He took his seat behind his desk and shuffled some papers to the side.

The guys had gotten into the habit of convening a short meeting every morning. Or they'd revived the habit, actually. They'd worked together in the same space for the past nine years. Their company, Fluke Inc., had taken up the entire thirty-ninth floor of their building in downtown Chicago. They'd each had an office, and there were two big conference rooms as well as various other rooms and offices for their product development team. But every morning they'd come together, just the five of them, in the smaller of the conference rooms to touch base and start the day together.

It had almost started by accident. They'd never made it a formal meeting. But it seemed that they needed to physically see and talk to one another before going their separate ways for the day.

They grounded each other. Even though when the five of them got together the ideas and brainstorming and crazy plans flew, they also kept each other anchored. The morning meeting was their way of just being *them*. Giving each other shit, catching up on things outside of work—women, parents, hobbies, and such—and just remembering where they'd started before they went out and met with their young, energetic, wildly creative development team, or made marketing calls, or fought a copyright infringement, or the many other tasks they each handled to keep the company safe and growing.

They'd all found each other in college. The online game, *Warriors of Easton,* had become a huge phenomenon almost overnight, launching five young guys to millionaire status and pseudo fame—at least in certain circles—so quickly that it had taken them a long time to really come to grips with their new reality.

They'd been busy and in demand and very wealthy, and it had all happened by accident. None of them had known that the game would take off the way it did. They'd simply been drawn together, like pieces to a puzzle, each fitting in their space just right to make the big picture come together. They'd sensed a chemistry between them, and that had turned into friendship, and that had turned into "Hey, what the hell, let's see what the world thinks of this" and... nine years later, they were millionaires, with a huge fan following and a solid friendship that would last the rest of their lives.

Then they'd bought Hot Cakes.

The factory in Aiden and Cam's hometown had gone up for sale and the town, and the three hundred or so people who worked for the company had feared that it would be bought out and changed by a much bigger company, or that it would close. Aiden had wanted to step in to save it, and as always, the other four had his back.

So they now owned a snack cake factory in a tiny town in Iowa, and frankly, they were all realizing they weren't nearly the master businessmen and managers they'd all thought they were.

But they were trying. And learning. And so far, anyway, they hadn't fucked anything up.

"I thought Cam was coming in today," Dax said, tossing a handful of gummy bears into his mouth one by one.

Grant had no idea how the guy could eat candy this early in the morning. But his grip tightened on the bakery box as he realized that the cupcake he'd greedily shoved in his mouth had more sugar than those gummy bears did. And he didn't regret a thing.

"I am. I had to flirt with Piper," Cam said, coming through the door. "I haven't seen her in weeks."

"You talk to her every day," Ollie said.

"It's not the same." Cam grinned. "She's awesome all the time, but so much better in person."

"Thank you!" Piper called from her desk outside the office.

Grant had to admit that Piper was a force of nature even via text, but there really was something about seeing the woman in person. She could put you in your place and make you laugh about it at the same time. And she was a knockout.

"But I definitely think I deserve a pussy cupcake for driving all this way," Cam said, dropping onto the couch near the window and stretching his legs out.

"You drove in last night," Aiden said. "It's not like you got up at the crack of dawn."

Cam had been the only one of the five partners to stay in Chicago. He'd come to Appleby briefly when Aiden had needed to break the news to Cam's family—Aiden's adoptive family—about their purchase of the company that was the McCafferys' archrival. But Cam had hightailed it back to Chicago shortly after their town hall meeting announcing the purchase and introducing themselves to the town. The town knew Cam after all, and he'd moved on to bigger and better things. Or so he claimed.

His four closest friends knew that his reason for keeping a healthy distance between him and his hometown was the woman who'd broken his heart over a decade ago. Whitney Lancaster. The granddaughter of the Hot Cakes founders.

Aiden had been very happy with Cam's choice to stay away. Cam was a troublemaker. Always had been. Not a happy, have-an-adventure-take-a-stupid-risk type like Dax and Ollie but a cause-a-bar-fight-take-people-down-in-court type.

And he had a chip on his shoulder about Whitney. And Hot Cakes. And Appleby, Iowa to some extent.

According to the story Aiden had told Grant, Dax, and Ollie —because Cam didn't talk about it—Cam and Whitney had fallen in love in high school, but because their families had been feuding for two generations, they'd kept their romance a secret. As graduation approached, Cam had asked Whitney to run away with him. She'd said no. He'd told her he'd stay in Appleby rather than go off to college on the full-ride football scholarship he'd been offered. She'd broken up with him.

She'd gone to work for the family company. He'd gone to the University of Chicago, and he'd long believed that she'd chosen her family business over him.

"That pussy cupcake?" Ollie asked. "It's from your sister's bakery."

Cam made a horrible face. "Ew. What the hell, man?"

Dax laughed. "Josie made it, not Zoe."

"Jesus, that's an important distinction." Cam scowled at Ollie. "You're a dick."

Ollie nodded. "Sometimes."

"Anyway," Dax said. "Grant's not sharing the cupcakes. Josie's cupcakes are all his."

Cam looked over at Grant. "Is that right?"

"Not all of her cupcakes," Grant said mildly. Not her literal ones anyway. "I want no part of the caterpillars."

"Guessing you're not into the ladybugs or the rainbows or the high heels and hair bows either," Aiden said dryly.

Ollie laughed. "Nope. Just her pussies."

"Well, he's not sharing her butt, mouth, or tits either," Dax said.

He absolutely fucking wasn't. Thankfully, he didn't say that out loud.

Grant wondered why he didn't have better friends. He *chose* to stick around these guys. He could have made just as much money in a number of other businesses.

"What about the cock?" Ollie asked. "I specifically saw a cock." He looked at Grant.

"All of the above are between Jocelyn and me," Grant said, refusing to rise to their bait and give them any kind of reaction. Well, any *further* reaction. "You all knock yourselves out with the high heels and hair bows."

Cam shrugged. "Once it's in my mouth, I don't really care what it looks like."

Dax snorted. "That attitude can lead to a lot of bad, contagious things."

"Your *sister's* bakery," Ollie reminded Cam.

Cam shook his head. "Now I know we're talking about Josie. That's different."

Grant felt his grip on the bakery box tighten again.

"Is it?" Dax asked, casting a sly glance at Grant.

"Josie's the best," Cam said with a nod. He crossed his arms over his chest, his huge biceps bulging, the tattoos that decorated one arm from shoulder to wrist and the other arm from shoulder to elbow, jumping as the muscles flexed. "And she's always been cute, but she's definitely turned out hot."

Grant gritted his teeth. He needed to *not* react.

Cam had known Jocelyn for years. She'd been his little sister's best friend since they were kids. They were probably more like brother and sister than anything else.

He glanced at Aiden. Then again, Aiden had been Cam's best friend for just as long and Cam's sister, Zoe, should have been like a sibling to Aiden too. She wasn't. At all.

"I'll never forget that first summer Josie had boobs," Cam said thoughtfully, as if reminiscing about days gone by. "She was probably about fourteen. She came over to sunbathe with Zoe, and she walked through our kitchen in a bikini, and I dropped an open two-liter bottle of soda, and it sprayed all over everything."

Grant ground his teeth.

Dax laughed. "How'd you explain that?"

Cam shook his head. "Josie was sweet and innocent. She had no idea that had anything to do with how she looked in that swimsuit."

"So, of course, the question is," Ollie said, glancing at Aiden, "if Josie had come to you at some point and asked you to be her first, what would you have said?"

Aiden rolled his eyes. "Fuck off."

Zoe had done exactly that to Aiden just last Christmas. She'd been a twenty-five-year-old virgin, and she'd been ready to get her first time "over with"—her words to Aiden. She'd tried to seduce Aiden. And he'd turned her down.

Needless to say, when he'd come back to Appleby to tell her he was in love with her, he'd had a lot of work to do to win her over.

"Oh, I would have *absolutely* helped her out with that," Cam said, completely seriously. "Once she was old enough, of course."

Grant breathed in and out steadily. His friends were just fucking with him. He knew that.

"I still would help her out with that," Cam went on. "I mean, I taught her to roller skate and how to play poker. And I gotta say, she's really good at both now."

"Enough."

Grant's response quieted the room, and his four best friends looked at him. But not with surprise. With *aha* expressions.

Grant rolled his eyes. Cam had been back with them for ten minutes, and he'd already joined right in with the bullshit without missing a beat.

Grant had resisted. He really had. But he wanted to punch someone in the face right now.

"But you really do need to let her sell these cupcakes," Ollie said. "It's a good idea. Maybe she could do, like, a liqueur filling. Make them very adult themed."

"It's not up to me to *let* her do anything," Grant said. Which was true. He was feeling possessive of her—and the dirty, flirtatious cupcakes she'd made just for him—but he wasn't about to tell *her* she couldn't sell them. Hell, he should encourage it.

"Did you see them?" Dax asked Ollie. "The nipples on the boob cupcakes were hard candies. So you could suck on them." He grinned. Then he looked at Grant. "Hey, was the clit a candy you could suck and lick too?"

"Shut the hell up, Dax," Grant said.

"I'm being serious," Dax said, sitting up straighter. "That's creative and perfectly, hilariously dirty."

Grant sighed. It was. "It was a hard candy," he conceded. Then added, "Cherry flavored."

Dax shook his head, looking a little awed. "Perfect. That sweet little lady has a naughty side. That's amazing."

It was. It was sexy as hell. And Grant was thinking about taking the rest of the day off and camping out at Buttered Up just so he could watch her bake again. Everything about her turned him on, and he couldn't wait to see her again.

"The liqueur center of the pussy cupcake should definitely be cherry flavored," Ollie said, nodding.

"But the pussy cupcake is *cream* filled," Dax said. "Come on. We can't mess with that."

There was a beat, then Ollie and Dax said together, "Cherry-flavored cream."

Grant groaned. This was how it so often went. Ollie could not shut his imagination off. He would let things just fall out of his mouth, Dax would pick them up and run with them, and Grant would blink, and everything would snowball.

Cam had swung his legs around and was leaning onto his thighs now. "Zoe and Josie are going to do this at the bakery?"

"It would have to be a side thing," Aiden protested. "They couldn't put those in the bakery cases."

"Of course not," Ollie said. "But they could easily let people know they were available and take orders without displaying them."

Cam was nodding. "That would be hilarious."

Aiden seemed unsure. "The nice little family-owned small-town bakery?"

"People who really knew my grandma knew she wasn't always nice," Cam said.

"I'm just saying, I'm not sure that's on brand," Aiden told him.

Grant nodded. "Agreed. They should *not* do this."

Mostly because it had been Jocelyn's idea, and if *she* wanted to sell these cupcakes, then she should do it herself. She didn't have to give this idea to Zoe.

Though Grant needed to check with Cam on that. Did Jocelyn have a contract with Zoe that would prevent her from baking for profit outside of the bakery? If Zoe didn't have a contract like that, she maybe should. But he wouldn't be the one suggesting that now because he was absolutely Team Jocelyn.

Which meant he probably shouldn't bring it up with Zoe's brother, who might mention the idea to her.

Dammit. This little town and this group of people was so intertwined, everything got complicated very easily.

"Oh, they should absolutely do this," Ollie said. "And if you think I wouldn't send each of you cherry-cream-filled pussy cupcakes on your birthdays, you are crazy."

"Pussy cakes for everyone," Dax agreed.

"Um..."

They all swung toward the feminine voice.

Whitney Lancaster, their VP of Marketing and Sales, the granddaughter of the Hot Cakes founders, and Camden McCaffery's ex, was standing in the doorway.

6

"I can come back later," Whitney said, looking very much like she would love to turn around and leave, in fact.

Aiden sighed. "No. You're right on time. Come on in."

"You could have warned us, Piper!" Ollie called out. "Or her!"

"No way! This is way more fun!" Piper called back from her desk.

"Sorry," Aiden said to Whitney, rising, and rounding the desk.

Whitney cast a glance toward Cam but then gave Aiden a smile. "Guess I'm not used to the changes around here yet. My dad doesn't have much of a sense of humor."

Cam snorted at that and Grant looked over at him. His eyes fixed on Whitney.

"Hey, Whitney," Dax greeted as he popped up from his chair, offering it to her while he propped himself on the corner of Aiden's desk.

"Hi, Dax." She gave him a smile as she accepted the seat. "Hi, Ollie."

"'Mornin', Boss," Ollie greeted.

She actually laughed lightly at that. "I told you before that nickname wasn't going to stick."

Ollie grinned. "Trust me. After you tell them all your new idea, it will. You should definitely be the one in charge around here."

Grant agreed. Whitney had grown up in the company and had been officially the VP of Marketing and Sales for the past ten years but functioned very much like a CEO. Her grandparents had started the company. The idea and recipes and original baking had all been her grandmother's, but her grandfather, Dean, had been the one to truly grow it into the national brand that it was today. Whitney's father, Eric, had taken over after Dean retired, but Eric had never been enthusiastic about Hot Cakes and had focused his attention and time on growing another food brand based out of Dallas. Whitney had stepped up and taken the reins at Hot Cakes even though her father had never given her a change in title.

Grant and the guys were fortunate that she'd been willing to stay on when they'd taken over. What they lacked in knowledge about, well, everything having to do with running a commercial snack cake factory and business line, Whitney had been able to help with.

If it hadn't been for her past with Cam, they would have likely already offered her a partnership. As it was, they were happy to have her in charge of marketing and sales for them as well, with a hefty salary, and wait for the dust to settle a little before they made any huge changes.

Of course, that meant that Cam was Whitney's boss now.

One of them anyway.

"What new idea?"

On cue, Cam spoke up. He stretched to his feet and approached Aiden's desk and the chairs in front of it. He stayed off to one side, near the potted tree by the bookcase, but he was intent on the meeting suddenly. He had his arms crossed and seemed unable to stop looking at Whitney.

Whitney, on the other hand, seemed determined to *not* look in his direction.

It wasn't as if they hadn't seen each other. Every time Cam was in town it seemed they ran into each other. Always unintentionally. Though sometimes literally. Like when he'd almost hit her in the crosswalk at Christmastime, causing her to drop her box of cookies and bag of panties all over Main Street. And then had to help her gather those panties up off the icy pavement.

Grant was sure that interaction had stayed with them both.

"New product," Ollie said. "Whitney thinks we need something new to invigorate things and that it's the perfect time with the change in ownership and everything. We can bring our own flavor—so to speak—to Hot Cakes."

Aiden had run this all past Grant and Ollie a few days ago, and Grant was completely on board. Not only would a new product bring in additional revenue, which would help cover the costs for improving their employee benefits, but this was a great thing to get Ollie focused on. His visionary friend needed projects or he got bored and came up with his own. Which were usually wild and expensive and sometimes completely unrelated to anything else. This would give him some creative outlet while also benefiting the company.

Grant also liked this chance to pull Whitney in more and get her involved with the team. She was sharp and experienced, but he got the impression she hadn't been encouraged to share ideas or head up projects when her dad and grandfather had been in charge. Grant would love to see her shine, and this seemed a great place to start.

"More cake? Bring it on," Dax said. "I'm feeling lemon."

Dax was no longer a partner in Hot Cakes so was here this morning as a consultant only. Well, he was here because they always had a morning meeting, and he would have wanted to know if anything happened between Grant and Jocelyn after they left the McCafferys' together last night. But he was also here to weigh in on the new idea. There was rarely an idea that Dax couldn't embellish.

For better or worse.

"You're 'feeling lemon'?" Cam asked.

"Yeah," Dax said. "We don't have anything lemon." He looked around. "Do we?"

"No," Cam said. "But if we're doing something new, it better be coconut."

"Come on," Dax said. "No way is coconut better than lemon."

"It most definitely is," Cam said. "And then there's caramel. That would be the second thing we do. Way before lemon."

Cam was here, though, because he was a partner, and he had to have a say in big initiatives. A new product would mean work for all departments from actual production in the factory to legal paperwork for trademarking and so on. They all had to be involved.

But that meant he had to work—at least partially—with Whitney.

Aiden had been concerned about that, and after he'd shared more of Cam and Whitney's history with Grant and Ollie, they'd agreed. But Grant would love to see them working together and getting past some of their heartbreak and history.

And if Cam was a nice, guy-next-door type, Grant would think that was a possibility, and they'd have nothing to worry about.

But Cam was Cam. He loved to argue, which had drawn him to law school, and he could hold a grudge like no other. To think that he might have a little revenge on his mind was not a stretch.

"We'll have to vote," Dax said. "That's the only fair way to do it."

"You're not a partner anymore," Cam reminded him. "So your vote wouldn't count anyway."

"But you all really value my input," Dax said.

Cam snorted. "I could arm wrestle you for it," Cam said, seemingly nonchalantly flexing his arm.

Dax shook his head. "Ping-Pong tournament."

"No fucking way," Cam said. Cam sucked at Ping-Pong.

"We have a better plan than any of that," Ollie broke in. "We're going to have a contest."

Cam cocked an eyebrow. "A contest?"

Ollie nodded with a grin. "Tell them, Boss," he said to Whitney.

She swallowed and glanced at Cam, then quickly looked at Dax instead. "I was thinking that if we had a baking contest, then a few things could happen. One, we don't have to develop a brand-new product from scratch without knowing if anyone will like it. Our customers can bring products they'd like to see to us. We can pick and choose from the entries. That gets us the basic recipe to adapt. Two, it gets the community involved. It would have to be open nationwide, I would guess." Again she looked at Cam. These were the kinds of things they needed legal counsel for—"but even so, it would get our customers involved. They could compete to be the ones to submit the final recipe to us."

Dax was already nodding. Clearly, he liked the idea. Of course, he liked any kind of game or contest and was a pro at interacting with fans. Customers of Hot Cakes weren't exactly the same as the fans that played *Warriors of Easton* and showed up at Comic-Con, but they were still the people purchasing from them repeatedly. Interacting with them was a good idea.

"We can have rounds," Dax said. "We have taste testing to narrow down the entries. We can get the town involved in that part. That shows them that we really want to be a part of the community, and it gets them invested in the company and the new things we're doing."

Whitney was smiling more genuinely now. "So we have all of the entries put to a taste test by the people of Appleby." She nodded. "I like that. We can have people send entries in from wherever they are, but we have community judges narrow things down."

"Then the top ten get flown in then," Ollie said, picking up the thread. "We bring them to Appleby, put them up at the B and B, make it a whole event."

"And," Whitney said, "we have special judges for the final rounds."

"Like the mayor or something? Maybe your grandmother?" Aiden suggested. "That would show she was happy with the transition and was giving it her blessing."

Whitney nodded slowly. "That's not a bad idea. Maybe she can be the very final judge. Like when we get down to the last two or three?" She grimaced slightly. "She has some dementia. I don't know how much she'll really understand about it all. But if we give her two desserts and ask which she likes the best, she'll be able to pick. Just having her involved in *all* of the final few rounds might be a lot."

Aiden nodded, a sympathetic look on his face. "I'm sorry."

She smiled. "She's still healthy and has some really good days." She looked at Dax. "She's really excited about her new apartment at Sunny Orchard."

Dax grinned. "Having her there will be huge for us."

"She's moving into your nursing home?" Grant asked.

"Yep. She's going to have one of the first deluxe suites when they're finished."

Grant actually felt a surge of pride when he saw the work his friend was doing and how excited Dax was about it. Dax had found a fabulous way to apply his love for fun and willingness to go over the top and try new things. If anyone was going to try new programs for enriching the lives of people living in nursing homes, it would be Dax.

"That's really great," Grant said sincerely. "Good for both of you."

Dax and Whitney shared a smile.

"Until then," Whitney said, "Grandma and I are living together in her house." She laughed lightly again. "She doesn't need twenty-four-hour care but shouldn't be totally alone either. So it's working out, but it can be... interesting. But yes, I'm sure she'd think it was fun to be involved."

"If you think she should be the final judge, how should we handle the prior rounds?" Ollie asked. "We could put together a community panel. Or maybe a group of employees."

"Well..." Whitney bit her bottom lip.

Aiden lifted a brow. "What are you thinking?"

"You might hate this idea," she said hesitantly.

"Lay it on us," Ollie encouraged. He loved brainstorming.

"Well... we could play up the Hot Cakes name by having hot guys be the judges," she said, her cheeks getting pink. "I know that's gimmicky, but it would draw an audience, I promise you. We could show everything online too, and I'm sure we'd have people watching. We find, I don't know, a handful, of young, good-looking, charming guys. We make sure everyone knows who they are." She looked around. "With the right guys, it could be a big hit."

Ollie was sitting forward in his chair now. "What if we make the contest three days? We bring those ten finalists in. We have a big event space, a stage, the whole bit."

"Oh, the hot-guy judges could each *make* one of the finalist's dessert submissions," Whitney said. "We could set it up so it's like a little cooking show. Women love men who can cook."

Dax was nodding. "We could do a bachelor auction. The women bid on the guys, and the date includes the dessert that guys makes and maybe wine or coffee at some location around town."

Grant caught Aiden's eye. Wow. Whitney was sitting between Ollie and Dax. All three of them were leaning in, talking excitedly, the ideas bouncing around and growing as they went.

The last thing they needed was a *third* person who dreamed big and was willing to go over the top.

Still, he couldn't help but grin. The tension in Whitney had completely relaxed, and she was clearly in her element. He had to wonder how much creativity she'd been able to show with her grandparents and father. From what he could tell, Hot Cakes had been very much the same for most of the fifty years it had been in existence. The logo had been freshened up about ten years ago—likely Whitney's doing—but the product line hadn't changed at all.

Now, watching Whitney brainstorm with Ollie and Dax, Grant could tell that she'd been stifled and was thrilled to have a chance to think outside the box.

And to have two partners in crime.

Oh boy.

"Okay, maybe before we put up a circus tent and start selling off bachelors, we should hammer out some details?" Grant said, interjecting the voice of reason as he so often did.

"Well, I want in," Ollie said. "I want to be one of the bachelors."

Grant looked at him in surprise. "Really?"

"Sure. I'll taste test new products. And I can bake."

"You can?" Aiden asked as surprised as Grant.

"Well... probably," Ollie said with a shrug. "I know the basic principles."

"I don't know—" Grant started.

But Whitney was nodding. "That's perfect. It would be hilarious to have a guy up there who doesn't really know what he's doing but who can be funny and charming about it."

"Uh." That came from Dax. He looked at Ollie. "I love you like a brother, but funny and charming aren't really your forte."

Ollie frowned. "I can be funny and charming."

"He'll be great," Whitney rushed to assure them. "Girls love hot nerds."

"What?" Ollie asked. "I'm a nerd?" He didn't question the hot part.

Whitney laughed. "You didn't know that?"

"Well, I..." Then he nodded. "Yeah, okay."

"But it will be great. If you're a little awkward up there, the women will eat it up."

"I want to do this too," Dax said.

Whitney grinned at him. "I don't know how Jane would feel about you going on a date with someone else."

Dax sighed. "True." He looked over at Aiden. "Guess that means Aiden's out too."

Aiden laughed. "Thank God."

"Oh, you wouldn't have wanted to be up on stage, acting all cocky while you frost some cookies, having girls ooh-ing and ahh-ing over you?" Dax asked.

"I would kick all of your asses," Aiden said with a nod. "I've been... frosting cookies... at Buttered Up for most of my life."

Whitney lifted a brow at the way he paused before "frosting cookies." "Yeah, that innuendo stuff will definitely work." She glanced at the others. You have to do that."

Aiden laughed. "Yeah?"

"Women are going to love this," she said confidently.

"You only want women interested in this?" Grant asked.

"I want everyone interested," Whitney said. "But if the women get interested, the men will be too. They'll want to see what the girls are into. Maybe they'll want to try a recipe to impress their girls." Whitney grinned.

"Oh, we should *encourage* that," Dax said. "Have them send in stories and videos of it."

"Yes," Whitney agreed enthusiastically.

"Okay, so Ollie's in. Aiden and I are out," Dax said. He gave Grant a look.

"What?"

"You should do this," Dax said.

"No way."

Whitney turned in her seat to face Grant fully. "You should."

"Not my kind of thing." And he was kind of seeing someone. Except that he wasn't. He was... obsessing about someone. That was not the same thing.

"But we've got the hot nerd," Whitney said, gesturing at Ollie. "We could definitely use a bossy CEO type."

Grant crossed his arms. "Aiden's the CEO."

"Aiden's off the market," Whitney lobbed back. "Ollie can do the smart, hot, adorably awkward thing."

"Hey," Ollie protested.

"And you can do the broody, sexy suit-and-tie thing," Whitney went on.

Grant lifted a brow. "Broody?"

"You're totally broody!" Piper called from her desk.

Grant rolled his eyes. "These guys all wear suits and ties."

Whitney nodded. "For this, we'll have you each play up your type. Ollie will wear his glasses and a button-down with jeans. You'll wear the tie."

"What will I wear?"

Whitney pivoted at Cam's question. Her eyes were side, and the tension that had melted out of her was instantly back. "What?"

"What will I wear for my type?" Cam asked.

"Leather jacket and jeans!" Piper called.

"Just get in here so you don't have to keep yelling!" Ollie yelled.

Piper appeared in the doorway a moment later. "Cam's the hot bad boy."

Grant looked at Whitney. Her eyes were on Cam. She swallowed hard. "You're going to do this too?"

"Damn right," he said.

"The adorable nerd, the broody suit, and the hot bad boy," Piper said with a nod. "The perfect trio."

"You think I'm adorable?" Ollie asked her.

"I think other women will think you're adorable," Piper told him. "Since none of them have to work for you."

"And Cam's a fantastic baker," Aiden said.

"Really?" Grant asked. He did not know that about his friend.

Cam shrugged. "Yeah." He said it as if it was no big deal at all.

"He's been baking all his life with his mom and grandma," Aiden added. "I can see it now. Ollie will just throw things together and probably forget at least two ingredients. Grant will measure every damned thing to the exact line on the measuring cup. And Cam will be over there whipping things up without even using a recipe."

Whitney actually laughed, seeming a little more relaxed. "This could be really fun."

"So leather jacket and jeans, huh?" Cam directed the question to Whitney rather than to Piper. He seemed to be wanting something from his ex.

Attention? Acknowledgment that he'd look hot in leather? Grant rolled his eyes.

Whitney's smile faded a little, and she took a deep breath. "Can you bake in leather?"

"I can do anything—"

"Tight t-shirt," Piper interjected before Cam finished his

answer. "One that will show off your muscles and tattoos. You can arrive on stage with your jacket but then take it off." She nodded. "Yeah, for sure."

Whitney just wet her lips.

"I'm not wearing a suit to bake in," Grant said.

Whitney was the one to look him over. "Jeans are fine but with a button-down shirt and tie. That you take off before you start baking."

"Oh yes on the taking-off-the-tie thing," Piper said to Whitney, her eyes on Grant. "And he unbuttons the cuffs and rolls up the sleeves." She nodded. "Yes, definitely."

Whitney nodded her agreement.

Grant felt like a piece of meat. Or one of Jocelyn's cupcakes being perused by a customer. A hungry customer.

He wondered briefly what Jocelyn would think of him being in a bachelor auction that included baked goods. Specifically Hot Cakes snack cakes. Hers were far superior to the mass-produced and prepackaged snack cakes.

"And I suppose I'm going to wear a sweater vest or some fucking thing?" Ollie asked, frowning at Piper.

But for just a second, Grant thought maybe he was frowning over Piper's attention to, and appreciation for, the attributes of other the men.

"No. You need to wear one of your nerd t-shirts," Piper said. "And your glasses."

"My nerd t-shirts?" Ollie glanced at Cam. "He'll already be in a t-shirt. That's not overkill?"

Piper chuckled. "Cam isn't going to wear his t-shirt quite the way you will."

"What's that mean?" Ollie planted his hands on his hips.

"Cam's t-shirt will be tight and plain. Probably black," Piper said thoughtfully.

"And mine?"

"I think you should wear the one that says *I Paused My Game to Be Here.*"

Ollie frowned. But then said, "I love that shirt."

"It's a great shirt," Piper agreed. "It's very you."

He gave her a look that said he really didn't know how to take that, but Aiden jumped in before Ollie could respond.

"Okay, so we can deal with the details later. But we've got three judges, a general plan, I think we can go ahead."

Everyone nodded.

"And I think we need to pull Piper in," Aiden said.

"Obviously," Whitney said.

"I suppose I could squeeze it into my schedule," Piper said.

They wrapped the meeting up in the next few minutes, and Grant kept an eye on Cam and Whitney as the brunette rose from her chair and smoothed her pencil skirt. But Cam did nothing more than watch her leave the office.

Grant waited to see if his friend would say anything about his ex, but Cam just blew out a breath as Whitney disappeared through the door.

It seemed maybe Cam was as tense about Whitney as she was about him.

"This is going to be great," Dax said, rising and clapping his hands together.

"The bachelor-cake auction?" Aiden asked. He shook his head. "It might be over the top."

"It's definitely over the top," Dax agreed. "That's what makes it great."

Of course Dax would think so.

"You think people will really care about three guys making cake and blind dates?" Grant asked.

"I do," Dax said. "It's fun." He shrugged. "You guys underestimate the power of doing things just because they make people smile. It will call attention to Hot Cakes and our new product.

That's the main goal. This will definitely accomplish that, but it will also give the whole thing a fun air. There is nothing wrong with the new Hot Cakes management being associated with fun and laughs and good times." He pinned Grant, Ollie, and Cam with a serious look. That alone was unusual for Dax, but then he said, "You guys better pull this off."

A warning about stepping up from the goofball of the group? Really? Grant lifted a brow. "You think we won't?"

"I think you need to not take it too seriously," Dax said to Grant. Then he looked at Cam. "And you'd better not make this all about making Whitney jealous. This is about Hot Cakes, not some little vendetta you've got tripping through your head now."

Cam narrowed his eyes. "You think she'll be jealous?"

Dax sighed but didn't respond. He looked at Ollie. "And you have to stay focused. Like you have to actually show up."

"I'll show up," Ollie said. "Jesus, you guys—and girls"—he frowned toward the office doorway—"make it sound like I'm a fucking flake."

Dax shrugged. "You're a damned genius. But you also don't have a lot of time or patience for things that you aren't a hundred percent into. You have to at least fake it for this."

"I'm one hundred percent into the launch of a new product," Ollie said. "I'm just not thrilled about playing the part of nerdy, hot guy."

Grant snorted at that. "Well, I don't know how much playing you'll be doing."

"And it's creepy to hear you call yourself hot," Cam said. "So knock it off."

"You didn't protest when Piper called *you* hot," Ollie said with a frown.

Cam lifted a shoulder. "Because *Piper* called me hot." He gave Ollie a little grin. "I didn't say it myself."

"Bad boy," Ollie muttered. "Whatever. Just because you have tattoos."

"You wanna go get a tattoo?" Cam asked him, flexing the arm that had the full sleeve, on purpose. "I'll take you and even hold your hand."

"I don't need a tattoo to feel confident," Ollie said.

Cam grinned and nodded. "Okay."

"Once you're up on stage making cookies you won't seem so badass," Ollie told him.

"I'm not worried," Cam said.

"Women love a man who knows what to do with a tube of frosting," Dax said. He looked at Aiden. "Right?"

"Well..."

"No," Cam said, holding up a hand. "No. I'm cool with you being with my sister, but frosting talk is my hardline. We're not going there."

"Want to hear about strawberry pie filling?" Dax asked.

"Fuck, no," Cam told him.

Dax just laughed.

Grant shifted, his body remembering every single thing about chocolate cake batter from the night before. He was grateful, not for the first time, that he was the quiet one of the group. When Dax was around, no one else really needed to talk, and when Dax, Ollie, and Cam got going, no one would notice that Grant wasn't contributing much to the conversation. Or was lost in thought. Or more specifically, distracted.

Which meant they wouldn't ask what he was distracted by.

Or who.

Grant ran a hand through his hair.

Following her home last night had absolutely been the worst idea he'd had in a long time.

He should probably regret it.

But he didn't. Not a bit.

7

"Hey, Jos?"

Josie looked over from where she was pulling a pan of cupcakes from the huge oven in the bakery's kitchen. "Yeah?" she asked Zoe.

Her friend, and boss, had been out front, as usual, tending to the counter and frosting cookies in between customers, while Josie worked in the kitchen, baking and doing the bigger decorating jobs.

"I was just wondering... are we going to make any cupcakes today that aren't chocolate?" Zoe held up a cupcake. "This is our last vanilla, and I noticed everything you're bringing out today is chocolate."

Josie looked down at the pan of cupcakes in her hand at the moment. They were also chocolate. "Oh."

Zoe grinned. "What's going on?"

"I'm just... craving chocolate today, I guess," Josie answered, her cheeks feeling hot. But she couldn't help her smile.

She definitely had chocolate on the brain. Well, she had Grant on the brain. And last night. Which also meant chocolate. Lots and lots of chocolate.

"Are you?" Zoe gave her a quizzical look. "You seem to be feeling a lot better than you were when you left Mom's last night."

Josie set the pan of cupcakes down on the worktable in the middle of the kitchen and pulled off the oven mitts. She was surprised Zoe had waited until now to ask about that. She'd texted both Zoe and Jane that she was fine, feeling a lot better, and heading to bed last night after Grant had left. Well, after she'd made him his special cupcakes.

All of which was true. She'd been feeling *a lot* better after Grant left, and she had been heading to bed when she'd texted them.

But Zoe, Jane, and Josie told each other everything. She'd expected to be questioned first thing this morning. She and Zoe opened the bakery at 6 a.m., and Jane was always first through the door, needing her sugar fix for the day.

They'd been busy this morning, though, and Jane had been running a little late—something that had been happening more regularly since she'd gotten together with Dax. Josie and Zoe suspected it had to do with Jane being more reluctant to leave her bed now that there was a hot, funny millionaire in it.

Josie had known she wouldn't get off completely free of sharing what had been going on with her last night though.

"I'm *much* better," Josie told her friend.

"And to what do we owe this miraculous recovery?" Zoe asked, seemingly innocently. But there was a twinkle in her eye that told Josie Zoe knew something.

Josie put a hand on her hip. "What do you mean?"

Zoe laughed. "Aiden texted me that you gave Grant pussy cupcakes this morning."

Josie felt her face flush, but she grinned too. Those cupcakes had been inspired, dammit. Dirty, but inspired. She was surprised Grant had showed them to the guys though. "Only one was a pussy," she said, her grin growing.

Zoe laughed harder. "Jocelyn Elaine Asher! You made him a pussy cupcake?"

"And boobs and a butt and a cock," she said. She knew she probably looked proud. Because she was.

"Wow. You and Grant." Zoe looked thoughtful.

"Yeah." Josie smiled. "You're surprised?"

"I am. He doesn't seem like... your type."

"Hot? Romantic?"

"He's romantic?" Zoe did seem surprised by that.

"He's..." Josie thought about that. He'd seemed romantic, yes. The night had. Their connection had. Something had.

"I think of your dad and your grandpa as being romantics," Zoe said.

"Or Dax," Josie added.

Zoe added. "Definitely. Grant seems too gruff for that or something. But if you're happy, I'm happy. He's a good guy. Just not someone I would have put you with."

"He's..." Josie frowned. "He's been trying to stay away from me actually."

Zoe's eyebrows went up. "What?"

Josie nodded. "He felt drawn to me but was trying to fight it. He followed me out last night because he was worried. But he doesn't really want to be worried." She hadn't thought much beyond the sex and the cake batter, but now that she was talking it out, Grant really didn't seem like her type. Again. She'd thought it before. His mouth and hands and other body parts had distracted her from it. But it was true.

"But he felt drawn to you," Zoe pointed out.

"But he was trying to fight it," Josie repeated. She frowned again. "I don't want a guy who fights his feelings for me."

"Well..." Zoe said slowly. "What if he's not winning that fight? That's kind of romantic—or something—right?"

"What do you mean?"

"Aiden said he would not share his cupcakes once he saw what they were," Zoe said.

Josie had to admit she liked that.

"And he's out front now. So he's not doing a very good job of staying away from you."

Josie's eyes flew to the swinging door that led to the front of the bakery. "He's here now?"

"Yep. He's talking with George and Phil."

George and Phil were bakery regulars. They were two older men, seemingly complete opposites, who came in every day after the morning rush and sat and read the newspaper and had coffee and muffins. Not together. They sat at separate tables and barely spoke to one another. But they came in at the same time every day, did the same thing, and stayed the same amount of time. It had been their routine since their wives had passed away.

"What's he talking to them about?"

"Something about them going into business together?" Zoe asked with a shrug. "I'm not sure. But he definitely glanced around as if looking for someone else when he first came in."

Josie's heart kicked against her ribs at that. Wow. She needed to get over this crush, if this crush was so intent on getting over her.

Then again, he was here.

Maybe to talk to George and Phil.

But maybe not.

"Did he look around as if trying to be sure I wasn't around? So he could avoid me?" she asked. "Or did it seem as if he was hoping to see me?"

Zoe smiled. "Well, Josie, he was *very* adamant about not sharing your pussy cupcake. I'm guessing he was hoping to see you."

Josie couldn't help her smile. "I guess that does make sense."

But nothing else about her and Grant really made sense. It was all kind of crazy really. How attracted she was. How hot they'd been together. How she'd made and decorated X-rated cupcakes for him without even hesitating to wonder if she should. How happy she'd been to see him this morning. How much she wanted to see him now.

As she stepped out from the kitchen, Grant looked up from where he was sitting at one of the little round bakery tables with George and Phil. They were at the same table for a change. They had their heads bent over some papers. That alone was strange. But seeing Grant there with them was even more so. Josie hadn't been aware that Grant even knew the two older men. He was sitting back, one ankle propped on his opposite knee, a cup of coffee cradled in his hand, almost as if he was observing the meeting between the other men, but he was clearly welcomed there.

His gaze met hers across the bakery counter, and she stopped and took a deep breath.

It was really too bad that he was from Chicago and not into dating a small-town baker, who wanted to get married and have a dog and a couple of kids. Because her heart had never thumped like it did when she looked at him. Even now. No need for nakedness and cake batter. Just him sitting there doing normal things in a normal way looking very normal made her stupid stomach flip, like she'd gone over the top of a roller coaster.

She gave him a smile and made her feet approach the counter. "Hi, Grant."

"Jocelyn," he greeted.

She actually sighed at the sound of his voice.

She never should have had sex with him. How was she supposed to get over him now? He'd been so *good*. Sex like that was not run-of-the-mill sex. That had been ruin-her-for-other-men sex.

"Did you come to talk to George and Phil?"

George and Phil both looked over.

"Phil's going to start renting out his rig," George said. "I'm helping him get that going. I know about loans and capital. We figured maybe Grant knew something about contracts like this."

Phil had been an over-the-road trucker for years, while George had been a banker in Appleby for as long as Josie could remember. The two men had very different backgrounds and lifestyles. George was a burly man who wore slacks and a button-down shirt every day, was clean shaven, and wore his hair neatly trimmed. Phil was lanky, pulled his long gray hair in a ponytail, often had scruff on his face, and wore jeans and t-shirts. It was interesting to see them working together on a project.

Josie looked at Grant. "Do you know something about all of that?"

"Yes."

Of course he did. He was the epitome of a polished businessman who knew everything about mergers and expansions and every other business term.

"But Cam's the one they really should talk to."

Josie nodded. "So *you're* here because..."

"Of you."

She felt her shoulders relax as he filled in the blank the way she'd wanted him to. She smiled and crooked her finger at him. He lifted a brow but got up and approached the counter. She leaned in when he was close.

"I'm sorry about the cupcakes," she said softly.

Grant frowned. "You're sorry?"

"Yes. I realize now that those were inappropriate."

Grant tucked his hands into the pockets of his pants. He'd been wearing the full suit when he'd come into the bakery that morning as usual. Her heart had stuttered when she'd seen him. She'd been stupidly attracted to him for a long time, but that morning, after last night in her kitchen—now that she knew how his mouth felt against hers, and against other parts of her, how his hands felt on her skin, how dirty he could be, how *good* he could be—she hadn't been able to do anything but stare at him for a full ten seconds when she'd first seen him.

Now he was wearing everything but the jacket. He even still had the tie on, though it was loose at the throat.

Josie had to curl her hands into fists to keep from reaching for the knot and pulling it loose. She wanted to see the tie hanging loose around his neck, those top buttons open, exposing the skin at the base of his throat. Even if she went on tiptoe she'd barely be able to press a kiss there.

"Why do you think the cupcakes were inappropriate?"

Her eyes widened. "There was a—" She cast a glance at George and Phil. She leaned in closer and lowered her voice. "A c-o-c-k cupcake."

The corner of Grant's mouth curled. It reminded her so much of her kitchen the night before and how much more open and relaxed he'd seemed that she pressed her lips together. *Don't say anything stupid. And don't kiss him. That would definitely be inappropriate.*

"I think George and Phil can spell."

She gave a little huff of laughter. "Right."

Grant just looked at her for a long moment. He seemed to be trying to figure out what to say. Or maybe how to say it. "Jocelyn," he finally said. "The only thing I didn't like about the cupcakes was the idea of you making those for any other man. Ever."

That sent a shaft of heat through her. He said the most preposterous and possessive things. They really did barely know each other. So why did he feel that? And why the *hell* did she like it?

"I've never made those before."

"But you could make them again," he said. "They'd be a great line to offer as part of your side business. Bachelorette parties, gag gifts, that kind of thing."

Josie felt her eyes widen again. "You think so?"

"Well, yes." He seemed reluctant to admit that. "But like I said, I don't like the idea of you making them for anyone else."

She couldn't help but smile at that. "They're just cupcakes."

"They were just cupcakes for me?" he asked. His voice had dropped to a husky, lower tone. "Because they felt like a dirty, private joke just between us designed to have me thinking about your sweet pussy and tits and ass all day and making me eager to get my mouth on them all over again as soon as possible."

Josie sucked in a sharp breath as all of those parts, and well, every nerve ending in her body, it seemed, responded to that.

He leaned in a little more. "Tell me they weren't that, Jocelyn."

She swallowed hard. "They were," she said softly. Huskily.

"And you thought that would be inappropriate?"

She nodded.

"After I had my mouth all over your body last night?" His voice was quiet too, but George and Phil were completely silent and leaning in to hear better.

She wet her lips. But nodded again. "I wasn't sure you'd actually want to again. The cupcakes could have been kind of pushy."

He did that half-smile thing again and her belly flipped. "Push me, Jocelyn. Please."

Now *she* smiled even as her entire body got hotter. "Yeah?"

"Yeah."

She couldn't hide her grin or her blush.

"Good. I still want to try my hand at those whoopie pies. I was thinking about seeing how the cream filling turns out tonight."

Her inner muscles clenched at the look on his face now. He looked... hungry.

Damn. Okay. So he'd changed his mind. He knew she wasn't the casual type, and he'd just said that the cupcakes were fine. In fact, he wanted more.

She giggled.

"What?" he asked, a smile still tilting his mouth.

"Everything about the bakery suddenly sounds dirty in my head," she said.

His eyes darkened slightly. "What time do you get off work?"

"Five."

"I'll meet you at your house at five oh five."

"Okay."

"And I'm going to have quite the appetite."

A hot shiver went through her. "Noted."

Finally, he lifted his hand and tucked a strand of hair behind her ear. And she melted a little.

He was sweet. He was gruff and dirty and even a little reluctant to get involved at all, but he was also sweet and possessive, and... he'd fallen under her spell. Even though he hadn't wanted to. She had to admit that made her feel powerful. Romantically powerful.

This was how romance worked. It was a force you couldn't fight and you couldn't deny.

Not even Grant Lorre.

And it was *her* making him feel that way.

Okay, so the rom coms didn't have pussy cupcakes in them or naughty kitchen sex. But that honestly just made all of this so much better.

"I should get back to work," she finally said after staring at him for several long seconds and just basking in how all of this was really worth all the frogs she'd kissed so far.

"Yeah. Okay." He seemed reluctant to let her go. "I'm just going to watch."

She laughed. "Right. Your newly discovered fetish."

He nodded. "Yeah."

She was now going to have to find a reason to stay at the front of the bakery today. Grant was a baking voyeur, and she was very happy to help him with that.

8

Josie helped a couple of customers and then pitched in on the last-minute order for four-dozen cake pops Zoe had taken while she and Grant had been talking.

"I think we're going to need more sugar," Zoe said, eyeing the cake-pop embellishments they had laid out. "We have plenty of sprinkles, but there's not as much blue sugar. It will look weird if we do like three-dozen sprinkles and only one with sugar."

Josie nodded. "Well, let's do four different ones, then. One dozen with sugar, one dozen with sprinkles, one dozen with crushed nuts, and one dozen with... crushed cookies?"

Zoe grinned. "Brilliant. Yes. Do we have chocolate cookies?"

"Definitely."

Josie grabbed the short ladder and pulled it over in front of the tall set of shelves set into the wall behind the bakery cases. They stored their canisters of various ingredients on the shelves, making it decorative and functional at the same time. The canister of cookies was on one of the higher shelves, and Josie had to stretch for it.

She felt a twinge in her shoulder blade as she reached but

ignored it. It happened from time to time. It was an overuse injury from stirring and whisking a lot during the day. Probably tendonitis according to Alicia, the nurse practitioner, Josie supplied with seven-layer bars on the side for family functions and potlucks. She'd never formally seen Alicia, or anyone else about the pain that came and went, but she'd mentioned it once, and Alicia had agreed that it was likely a hazard of Josie's job.

It had started about a month ago and had been getting more frequent, but Josie was ignoring it for the most part. She didn't have time to go to the doctor. Moreover, she didn't have time to rest her arm. Her job required her to use it, a lot, every single day. And her job didn't really have built-in sick time. It was just her and Zoe running the bakery. If one of them wasn't here, Maggie could and did fill in, but it wasn't the same, and Josie knew, without any ego, that she was the true talent. People came to Buttered Up for decorated cakes in part because Josie was extremely good at her job. The bakery was a town staple and was famous in this area of the state. Their recipes were tried and true. People bought their pies and cookies and cakes because they would be delicious every single time.

But since Josie had started at the bakery, right out of high school, they'd seen a definite increase in demand for specialty cakes for birthdays and other occasions. She could create anything out of cake. And word had spread.

So she had to be here. Zoe and the business depended on her.

Besides, she didn't have insurance to pay for a doctor's visit or treatment anyway. As a very small business, Zoe didn't offer insurance. Prior to Zoe owning Buttered Up, it hadn't been an issue. Zoe's grandma and then her mom had run the bakery, and they'd been covered on their husband's plans. Zoe was covered on her dad's plan, and once she and Aiden were married, he'd cover her. Josie had been on her dad's insurance up until about two months ago when he'd been reduced to part time. It was good for him. His job at the egg factory was hard on him physically and cutting back helped immensely. But financially it was going to be tough until her mom could find something.

And that left Josie without insurance coverage.

She hadn't told Zoe. It would make her friend feel bad and maybe even cause her to panic buy something to cover Josie that would cost far more than it needed to.

Aiden was a millionaire and could just buy a policy probably, but neither he nor Zoe wanted that. Buttered Up was *her* business, her legacy, and she wanted to do this herself. Aiden respected that and didn't expect to become a partner. And a guy couldn't go around just writing million-dollar checks to his girlfriend's business without some legal considerations.

So he was helping Zoe get policies and things caught up at Buttered Up. The fact that they didn't have things like employee benefits bothered him a lot. But it was taking a little time, and they both had a lot going on. So Josie just wanted to give them a chance to get it all straightened out. She could deal with her tendonitis until it all got figured out.

But as she pulled the heavy ceramic canister from its spot on the shelf, the pain grabbed and she gasped.

It was either the surprise of it or the actual nerve suddenly refusing to fire, but her grip loosened and the canister slipped. The ceramic jar hit the hard linoleum with a loud crash.

Everyone in the bakery jumped and swung to face her.

"Oh my God! Josie, are you all right?" Zoe came forward quickly. She was frowning, clearly concerned.

Josie realized she was holding her shoulder. And probably grimacing. Because she felt like someone had a hot poker and was stabbing it under her shoulder blade. She was having a hard time taking a deep breath. She nodded but was grateful for Zoe's hand on her other arm as she stepped down. She didn't trust her painful arm to help.

Suddenly Grant was there, big and glowering, practically pushing Zoe out of the way.

"What the hell happened?" he demanded, seeming almost angry.

But the huge hands on her waist, that plucked her off the step and turned to set her on the counter were gentle.

"I just... my shoulder hurts," she said.

"Can you move it?" He was still scowling at her.

She frowned back and lifted her arm. She had full range of motion, and it didn't hurt to move it. Well, it didn't hurt *more* to move it. It still hurt. Especially when she took a deep breath. What the hell? She was able to reach overhead and circle it.

"What did you do?" Grant asked. His voice had calmed a little, but he was still standing very close, nearly hovering.

"I didn't do anything. I grabbed that canister, and it made my shoulder tendonitis twinge, and—oh no!" Her eyes flew to the smashed pieces of ceramic on the floor behind Grant. "Oh, Zoe!" She found her friend standing to the side, watching Grant fuss over her with an amused look on her face. "I'm so sorry!"

Zoe shook her head. "Don't be silly. You didn't mean to drop it."

"No, but I feel terrible. It was your grandma's."

Zoe waved toward the shelves. "I have lots. No worries. I'm a little concerned about your shoulder though." She gave Grant a look. "Are you going to be okay?"

Josie waited until Zoe's gaze swung back to her. "Oh, me?"

Zoe chuckled. "Well, both of you. There's a lot of... something going on around here."

Grant didn't look amused. "I'm just concerned."

"Me too," Zoe agreed. "So it's tendonitis? Should you see someone? A physical therapist or someone?"

She probably should, yes. But that would cost money. Josie gave her friend a smile. "I talked to Alicia about it. She said ice, rest, ibuprofen, all of that. She said massage might help."

Zoe nodded, but Grant asked, "Who's Alicia?"

His voice was gruff and he was still frowning.

He seemed legitimately worried and that made Josie feel warm. Warmer than how Zoe's reaction made her feel. Zoe made Josie feel cared for and loved, but she didn't make her feel *protected* the way Grant did.

Lord, she really needed to like that a lot less. She didn't need Grant taking care of her.

But then he put his hand on her shoulder and started rubbing.

Okay, she didn't *need* him to take care of her. But damn if she was going to fight it. She was independent. She lived alone, helped Zoe run their business, took care of her friends and family when they needed her. If a big, hot guy who could melt her like butter on a muffin wanted to rub her shoulder—or anything else of hers—she was not going to say no. Independence didn't have to mean using a self-massager... on any part of her body... did it?

His thumb found a knot in her shoulder, and she made a soft moaning sound without meaning to.

"Jocelyn." His voice was softer now. Less angry. Maybe even a little amused.

She forced her eyelids open, not having realized they'd slipped shut, and sat up straighter as she found she was leaning into his touch. "Um..."

His expression was definitely more relaxed now. "Who's Alicia?"

"My doctor. Nurse practitioner actually."

His frown was back. "She's not even a doctor?"

"She's great," Josie protested.

"Yeah, I wouldn't pull the you're-not-even-a-real-doctor thing on her," Zoe said. "She's brilliant and beloved."

"But she's not an orthopedic specialist," Grant said.

Josie's eyes widened. "I don't need an orthopedic specialist." Lord, she could have sworn she heard her wallet whimper in the other room just from the word *specialist*. Her shoulder throbbed a little more too.

"You might. What if this is a rotator cuff tear and not just tendonitis?" he asked.

"Well..." Shit. This really could *not* be a rotator cuff tear. She didn't have the money for that, but she also didn't have time for that. *Zoe* didn't have time for that. Buttered Up was a two-woman job.

"Maybe I just need more massages." She literally batted her eyes at him. She liked him protective, but she didn't like him pointing out truths that she didn't want to think about. "Last night my shoulder felt great," she added.

Grant froze at that, clearly surprised. His gaze locked on hers, hot and dark. "Well, I'm no expert, but I'm aware that endorphins can be powerful things."

She nodded, darting her tongue out to wet her lips. His eyes dropped to her mouth, and she felt heat tingle through her belly and between her legs. Yeah, see, all she needed was more Grant.

"So maybe I just need another dose of those," she said. She definitely did. Regardless of what the hell was going on with her shoulder.

"Endorphins only cover things up," he said, dragging his eyes back to hers. "If you have an actual serious medical issue, you need to get it looked at."

"Maybe you're just overreacting," she told him. But there was a niggle in the back of her mind. Not the one that said having him worry about her was kind of nice. The other one. The one that reminded her that Alicia had also mentioned something else that could cause stabbing pain in the shoulder blade area that came and went. And there was the *other* niggle that reminded her that she'd had pain two days ago in her stomach.

"Maybe I am," Grant said, agreeing with her overreaction comment. "But I'd rather assume it was something worse and be wrong than risk underestimating it."

She tilted her head. "Why is this bothering you so much? I didn't drop *your* canister."

He opened his mouth. Then shut it. Then looked at a spot over her head. Then met her eyes again and said, "I think you know. It's the same reason I'm still in Appleby after deciding I was going to leave two weeks ago."

Her heart did a happy little flip. See? *That* was romantic. He was smitten. It wasn't love—that would be ridiculous—but he felt drawn to her. She sighed. She'd always wanted someone to be smitten with her.

"You don't look sorry," he commented wryly.

She widened her eyes. "About?"

"Keeping me here. Making me worry about you."

"Well, good," she said. "I'm not sorry about that one bit."

He laughed lightly and her inner muscles tightened.

"I appreciate your honesty."

"And I appreciate your... endorphins," she said with a grin.

"Zoe?" Grant asked, without looking away from Josie.

"Yeah?"

"I don't suppose... in light of the shoulder injury and all... that Josie could get off early tonight?"

Zoe laughed. "Do you actually think that's subtle? At all?"

"No." He gave Josie a small grin.

"So what you're really asking is can you take my best friend home and kiss it all better?"

Grant's grin got bigger. Josie smiled in return. She loved Zoe.

"Yeah, that's what I'm asking."

"Then yes," Zoe said. "You can. *If*," she added, "you make her take ibuprofen, and you put some ice on her shoulder at some point, and you talk her into making an actual appointment with Alicia, not just a casual chat when they're at the post office."

Josie felt a flicker of guilt. She hadn't run into Alicia at the post office. She'd asked the nurse practitioner about her shoulder when she'd been dropping bars off at Alicia's house. Bars that had not been made at Buttered Up. Of course, they didn't have those bars on the menu. Buttered Up's menu had been the same, for the most part, since Zoe's grandmother had first opened the doors over fifty years ago and seven-layer bars hadn't been a part of her plan.

But still, Josie could never fully shake the guilt of baking for money on the side.

"You think I can convince her?" Grant asked.

"I think you have some... leverage," Zoe said with a nod. "You know... withhold a few *endorphins* until she agrees. Something like that."

Grant blinked but then slowly grinned. "Interesting idea."

Josie's eyes went wide. "Hey! No fair!" She leaned around him to glare at her best friend. "Whose side are you on?" Whoa, that leaning thing made a pain jab her in the side. What was that? Josie worked to not wince or gasp.

"Well, Grant's, obviously," Zoe said with a shrug. "As long as his side includes you being safe and healthy."

Josie swallowed and sat back—carefully—and looked up at Grant, batting her eyes again. "Oh, you wouldn't do that, would you? I mean, withholding *my* 'endorphins' would mean fewer 'endorphins' for you too."

"Would it?" he asked, his eyes hot. "I'm not so sure about that."

Something in his tone and their teasing made her whole body heat and she leaned closer. "Oh?"

He shifted, bracing a hand beside her hip on the counter and put his mouth near her ear so no one else could hear. "I think teasing you until you're begging and need me more than anything, keeping you right there, knowing that I have total control over everything you're feeling, would give me plenty of endorphins." He slid his hand to her hip and squeezed. "And there are lots of ways for me to have all kinds of fun while you're frustrated and on edge."

He would just use her for his own pleasure? What would *that* be like?

"You don't seem like the selfish type," she told him softly, nearly panting. In fact, he seemed the exact opposite of the selfish type. He seemed very concerned with her and how she was feeling and her being happy as a matter of fact.

"But you don't know me very well," he said gruffly.

Then he nipped her earlobe.

Lust shot through her and she gasped.

"Okay, okay, okay," Zoe said.

She hadn't needed to have heard all of that to get a pretty clear idea of what they'd been talking about with the way Grant was leaning in. And the way Josie was nearly melting into a puddle.

"No endorphins on my bakery countertop," Zoe said.

Josie knew her cheeks were pink but not because she was embarrassed. She was just plain *hot*. She leaned around Grant to grin at her friend again. "Oh, like you and Aiden have never gotten *endorphins* on these counters."

"Not these," Zoe said, shaking her head. "Too many windows." Then she winked. "Get out of here and 'nurse your shoulder.'" She added air quotes when she said those last three words.

"Gladly," Grant said gruffly as he helped Josie off the counter.

She had a feeling he meant them literally, though, as well as metaphorically. She might get some "endorphins" from him, but she was also going to get a big, hot, protective nursemaid.

Which didn't sound at all like a hardship.

"Are you okay to drive?" he asked as she collected her stuff from the kitchen and pulled her keys from her purse.

"Yes." She smiled up at him. "I'll take any excuse to get you over to my house again. But I'm fine to get there, I promise."

"You don't need an excuse," he said. "You just have to ask."

"Really?"

"Really."

"But you're not thrilled about the... effect I have on you?"

"I'm getting more thrilled with it," he said.

"Oh?"

"Yeah." He did that thing where he tucked a strand of hair behind her ear again. "You have a way about you."

She smiled, happiness bubbling up in her chest. "Thank you. I'm pretty thrilled that you're getting more thrilled."

He gave her a slow smile. "I really want to take care of your shoulder tonight. For real."

She nodded. "I know. And I want you to."

"Yeah? You like being bossed around?"

"Definitely not."

"Then why do I get an invite to play doctor tonight?"

"Because I like your hands on me."

His eyes flickered with heat. "Well, then we're going to get along just fine because I'd very much like to have my hands all over you."

"Meet you there."

J osie had already let herself into her house through the back kitchen door by the time Grant pulled in behind her car. He'd just been here last night, and yet he felt like he'd been waiting to have her again for weeks. Maybe months.

This woman was getting to him. He should truly want to be anywhere *but* here. She was distracting him. And not just with thoughts of last night flashing through his mind at inopportune times during the day or with her flirtatious, dirty cupcakes. But now he was feeling protective and worried.

He fucking hated worrying. He wanted everyone in his life to just make good choices, make the right decisions based on data and knowledge and calm, rational thought. He didn't expect them to be perfect and to always have all the answers, but he did expect them to listen to him. When he gave advice, he knew what he was talking about. If he didn't, he found out before he gave advice.

But now the woman who had rocked his world with cake batter—both by its use during sex as well as when she actually baked it into cupcakes—was making him worry. And she wasn't listening to him.

She had an injury. He had no idea how serious or mild. But she wasn't taking care of it. She was shrugging it off. She wasn't even making an actual appointment at a medical clinic to discuss it with a professional. Okay, maybe she didn't need an orthopedic surgeon at this point, but she'd only talked about it in casual conversation with her nurse practitioner. Probably while they'd been discussing the weather or some new cookie recipe.

People who didn't make good choices made him crazy.

People who didn't listen to him when he gave them instructions and advice made him angry.

Ollie and Dax made stupid decisions sometimes. They were usually driven by a desire to entertain their fans... or to entertain Grant. They weren't just total fuckups. He'd learned that pretty early on. They were creative and natural risk-takers, and sometimes that manifested itself in doing things like hang gliding off the top of a building on the Vegas strip or losing their shoes to a street magician in Paris. Those sounded bizarre, he completely agreed, but the hang gliding had been a part of a fundraiser, and the street magician had been research for a new addition to their video game. Or something. At the time they'd explained it, Grant had understood. At least enough to say, "Fine. Whatever. I've booked you on a flight home, and there will be shoes waiting in the car that's coming to get you."

But Ollie and Dax listened to him. After they gave him shit, of course. But they still did what he told them. When he said, "Get your ass back to Chicago. The flight leaves in three hours," they showed up at the airport. When he said, "You should get that casted in Vegas, or your flight home will be miserable," they went to the hospital and got a cast put on Ollie's wrist before coming home.

Jocelyn wasn't listening to him. Yet.

He also hadn't fully turned on his bossiness.

He wasn't above using whatever leverage was needed to get his way. That was just who *he* was. Ollie and Dax were the creative risk-takers. Cam was the I-don't-give-a-shit-what-you-think guy. Aiden was the charming leader. And Grant was the I-always-know-best guy.

Grant climbed the back steps and let himself into Josie's kitchen. She was expecting him after all.

"I was thinking that—"

Whatever he'd been about to say was cut off by the sight of her doubled over, gripping the edge of the counter.

He crossed to her swiftly. "Jocelyn."

She looked up at him and gave him a weak smile.

"What's going on?"

"Um, pain," she said.

"In your shoulder?"

"Kind of. Yes. But not just there." She took a deep breath.

Grant worked on breathing too. He was shocked by how hard his heart was suddenly pounding. This woman had him in knots. He didn't even know what was wrong, but seeing her beautiful face scrunched up in pain was making adrenaline surge through him.

"Tell me what's wrong." His voice was far sharper than he'd intended, but he couldn't help it. He needed to fix whatever this was, right now.

"I just am having more pain suddenly," she said. "Which is strange, right? Because I'm not really using my shoulder."

"How about we let a doctor decide what's strange?" he asked. "Is there an urgent care here?"

She shook her head. "I don't need urgent care." She straightened, though the move seemed to take longer than it should have. She gave him a smile. "It's not urgent."

He frowned at her. "How about we be sure?"

"How about you distract me from this little muscle strain by stretching some of my *other* muscles?" She winced. "Did that sound dirty or weird?"

He gave a short laugh. "A little weird."

"Yeah, that's what I thought."

He noticed that while it looked like she had her hand on her hip, she was actually pressing her fingers into her side.

With a frustrated grunt, Grant pulled his phone out and searched for urgent cares in the area. There wasn't even one in this town? The closest was about eight miles away. Fuck. Where the hell were they?

He took a deep breath. Okay, eight miles. Hell, the closest one to his apartment in Chicago was possibly farther than that. Just the idea of this one being in another town made it feel farther away.

He eyed the blond who was making him worry and fret and

cuss. If he kept going here, he was going to be in over his head. He should call Zoe. Or Jane. Or even Aiden or Dax. They would definitely jump in here and take care of her. Zoe and Jane might be even more effective in getting her to the doctor. They knew her better. Had known her longer.

But even as those thoughts occurred to him, Grant knew he was the one who was going to be taking her to urgent care.

"How long has this pain been going on?" He especially eyed her hand pressing into her side.

"My shoulder started bugging me a few weeks ago, I guess," she said. "But this... is different." She grimaced slightly.

"How?"

"Well, the pain has been coming and going ever since it started, but this time it's not going away as quickly and it's not just my shoulder."

"You know that means we need to get it checked."

Her eyebrows rose. "We?"

Yeah. Fuck. *We.* He nodded. He could just pick her up and carry her out to his car, but it would be nice if she'd *agree* to let him take her to see someone.

He *really* liked it when people listened to him and did what he told them.

"I'd really like to be sure you're all right."

She gave him a little smile. "That's really nice."

"Well, if your appendix ruptures, it will be a while until I can... stretch you."

She gave a short, surprised laugh. "See, now when you say it, it kind of sounds dirty."

He grinned.

Then she frowned. "Oh my God, you think it's my appendix?"

"I have no idea. That's why we should talk to a doctor," he said, trying to be patient.

She bit her bottom lip. "Maybe I can just call Alicia. I don't think she would mind."

"Jocelyn," Grant said, firmly and with a touch of warning.

"I um..." She was studying the buttons on the front of his shirt instead of meeting his eyes. "I can't... it's cheaper if I just talk to her."

Grant realized that he and his friends often didn't consider the financial implications of the things they did and suggested. He was better about it than Ollie, Dax, and Cam because he worked with people on their financial plans all the time, but he did sometimes forget how easy it was for him to do or obtain things he wanted without thought to the cost. Still...

"Yes, I would certainly think that removing your appendix on her kitchen table with a couple of shots of tequila to numb the pain would be cheaper than the hospital," he said dryly.

Jocelyn frowned. "I'm just saying that she could help me know if that was necessary."

He looked at her side again. "It's getting worse."

"It's easing up a little now," she said.

"In *general*," he said through gritted teeth. She was so sweet, and she'd certainly taken direction last night when he'd been saying things like *bend over* and *spread your legs*. Now he was seeing a stubborn side that was annoying the fuck out of him.

But then she nodded. "Yeah, it is."

"Let me take you to urgent care," he said. "Please."

Her eyes flew to his. It seemed she realized that *please* was not a regular word in his vocabulary.

"I don't have insurance," she blurted out.

He frowned. "What?"

"I don't have health insurance."

"Zoe doesn't provide benefits?" He was surprised Aiden was okay with that.

"I was covered on a family plan with my mom and dad until recently," Jocelyn said. "Zoe was on her dad's too. The bakery has always been small, and there hasn't been a need for comprehensive benefits. If someone is sick or needs vacation time, we just... make it work."

"Do you get paid for sick time?" Grant asked, feeling his frown deepen.

"Well, no, not exactly. But she gives me bonuses when she can and..."

"That's not okay," he broke in. "That's not fair to you."

"It's fine," Jocelyn insisted. "I knew what it was when I went into it. It's really more like it's my business too."

"But you don't have insurance," he pointed out flatly.

"I did have. But my dad got cut to part time recently."

"And Zoe didn't offer to help out?"

"I haven't told her," Jocelyn admitted. "I knew she would feel terrible and that it would be a big financial burden on the business. She's been looking into plans and things with Aiden's help. We're just not there yet."

"But now you need it."

"That's not her fault."

Grant sighed. "I'll pay for it."

Jocelyn's eyes went wide. "No." She said it quickly and firmly. "Definitely not."

"You don't have a choice."

"I do! I'll make payments to the hospital or whatever. I'm not taking money from you for this." She wrinkled her nose. "That would be... really icky."

"Icky?" He felt his frown relax slightly. "How so?"

"Well, we're not related, and we're not really friends. I mean, why would you give me money? For sex? I can't take money for that!"

"I would be giving you money for your *health care*," he said. "Not for sex."

"But the only thing I'm giving *you* is sex."

"It's not related. The sex was before this," Grant argued.

Why was he arguing this? Why couldn't she see that this was a great option? He had plenty of money. And he had an intense desire to be sure she didn't have an internal organ that was about to explode.

"But there will be more sex after!" Then she narrowed her eyes. "Won't there? I realize this isn't very sexy. And if I do have to have my appendix out..." She paled slightly and took a shaky breath. "That's going to put a damper on things."

He stepped closer to her. "There *will* be more sex." That was maybe the only thing he knew for certain at this moment. "But the two things aren't related. I'm paying for peace of mind here." He decided to use a new tactic. "We *are* friends. I care about this. Let me help make sure things are all right. Or if they're not, let me help make them right." Because they weren't all right. Something was going on with her and he needed it fixed. It was a strange drive, but the idea that Jocelyn was sick and in pain was making him nuts.

Jocelyn stood, blinking up at him, studying his face.

He saw when another stab of pain hit. She winced and held her breath for a second.

That was enough. He bent, scooped her into his arms, and started for the door.

"Grant—"

"We're going to the doctor. We'll figure the rest out later," he said.

"But I—"

"Jocelyn," he said firmly. "You're going to have to learn that I don't really like to be argued with when I'm right about something. And I'm almost always right."

"But—"

"Jocelyn, enough."

She stopped arguing then.

But only because she threw up on him.

9

Well, she might have ruined Grant wanting to take care of her no matter what.

In the process she'd probably taken care of him wanting to stick around Appleby indefinitely as well.

She'd definitely taken care of the ever-getting-naked-together again.

But honestly, at the moment, she couldn't care.

She felt horrible. She was huddled against the door of Grant's car trying with everything in her to not throw up again. She'd heard him talking brusquely to someone, asking them to meet him in Bridley, the town eight miles away that had the closest urgent care clinic. She assumed it was one of the guys and they were bringing him a change of clothes. She also assumed that whichever guy it was, soon Jane and Zoe would know about what was going on.

This could *not* be her appendix. She could not have her appendix out. Besides, not being able to take time off from work for that and not being able to afford it was terrifying. Taking internal organs out of her body? Yikes. Yeah, she knew that millions of people walked around without that particular organ. It was pretty routine surgery. The appendix was, arguably, not all that useful. Still, the whole thing made her feel even queasier than she already was.

They pulled up in front of the clinic minutes later, and when she reached for the door handle she got a firm, "Stop."

Grant got out, rounded the car, and again scooped her up into his arms. Even after she'd thrown up on him. That was pretty nice.

She actually thought she could walk at this point. She was still not feeling *good,* but she didn't feel like she couldn't walk. Then again, if Grant wanted to snuggle her against his hard, warm chest, who was she to argue. After the puke-down-his-left-arm-and-shoe thing, this might be the last time she got to be this close to his chest. So she rested her head on it and closed her eyes.

She heard him talking to whomever he needed to tell what was going on.

She thought she heard the term *girlfriend,* but she couldn't be sure. She *was* sure she heard *cash.* She really should argue with him about paying for this. But she didn't have the energy. Not because she wasn't feeling well but because, dammit, Grant was bossy and stubborn and always thought he was right. He'd said so.

She'd deal with how to pay him back later. And no, it wouldn't be in sexual favors. That was tempting, for sure. But also gross. Kind of. Somehow. Immoral anyway. Kind of.

Yeah, she'd think about all of that later.

Grant settled into a chair in the waiting room, with her on his lap.

Reluctantly, Josie lifted her head and started to get up to get into a chair of her own. Grant's arms tightened around her. "Just stay," he said gruffly.

"But—"

"Stay," he said again, pulling her up against him.

And really, why argue with a guy who was saying things that you liked and wanted to agree with?

She relaxed back into his hold.

"Are you okay?" he asked against her hair.

"Um..." She thought about his question. "I don't feel like I'm going to throw up. The pain has lessened. But I feel... weird. And still achy in my shoulder blade."

"Okay."

She didn't know if it was okay exactly, but they were here now. She had to admit that she felt relieved to know that she was with medical professionals, and before they left here she'd have an answer about what was going on. Fixing it was something else. Could she afford it? What would it entail? *Could she afford it?*

But first she needed to know what she was dealing with.

"Hey, here you go."

She looked up to see that Cam had joined them. He held out a duffle bag to Grant.

"Thanks." Grant looked down at her. "Can you sit with her while I change?"

"Of course."

"Grant, I don't need a babysitter," she protested.

"Humor me," he said.

There was something in his eyes. It was almost as if *he* needed Cam there more than she did.

"Okay."

He rose and crossed the waiting room to the door marked as a restroom.

Cam leaned back in his chair, studying her. "You okay?" he asked.

"I'm in urgent care after barfing on the guy I would much rather be naked with right now," she said. "What do you think?"

Cam grinned. "Fair enough. How are you feeling? Physically?"

She sighed. She'd known Cam all her life. She wasn't sure what it meant that Grant had called Cam. Maybe because he wasn't currently dating one of her best friends. But maybe also because Grant knew she knew Cam well and would be comfortable with him.

Cam had always been a little rough around the edges. He'd loved to poke at people and had gotten into more than his share of fights at school and had never missed a chance to tease Zoe, or Josie by extension, but he was a very loyal friend and son and brother.

Josie was completely comfortable with him here. "I'm... fine. Ish. I guess? I'm worried about what is going on," she confessed. "But at this very moment, I'm not in horrible pain or anything."

Cam frowned. "You think it's something bad?"

She shrugged. "Grant mentioned my appendix."

Cam nodded. "Yeah. Guess that would make sense. But that's almost nothing. I got mine out in high school."

She remembered that now that he said it. "Yeah. You're right. It will be fine." She was comfortable with Cam, but no way was she going to tell him that she was worried about the money. Her insurance situation would get back to Zoe for sure. If not directly, then to Aiden. She was sure Cam wouldn't approve of Buttered Up not having solid employee benefits either.

She'd been surprised that the bad boy Cam had gone into law. He'd seemed more the type to become a professional MMA fighter or to go into construction. Something where he got his hands dirty and could swing hammers—or his fists—and knock things—or people—down on a regular basis. She had a hard time picturing him in suits and ties and in courtrooms. But when she'd found out from Zoe that, while he did represent the guys' company, Fluke Inc. when it came to trademarks and contracts and such, he also did a lot of pro bono work for small companies and nonprofits. He loved to go in as an underdog and fight larger corporations that were trying to screw over the smaller ones.

That actually fit. Josie, of course, knew Cam's whole history with Hot Cakes and the Lancaster family and Whitney. She knew he felt that Whitney had chosen her family and their business and money over being with him.

That chip on his shoulder had manifested into him becoming a champion for smaller people fighting against bigger companies and Josie loved that.

Cam was a fighter, and if he could do some good for those who couldn't fight for themselves, then it was a perfect outcome.

"So you've really got Grant all twisted up," Cam said. He had an ankle propped on his other knee, one big hand resting on his leg, his arm muscles bunching. He said it casually, but he was watching her carefully.

She gave him a look. "Do I?"

"You don't realize it?"

"He told me that he didn't intend to stay in Appleby this long, but that he's basically here because of me," she said.

Cam nodded. "That's really unusual for him. Grant never does anything he doesn't want to do."

Okay, it looked like she was going to get some insight into Grant from one of his best friends. She was completely here for this. She leaned in. "How about when he has to go chasing after Ollie and Dax?"

"He only goes if he wants to. Otherwise he'll send someone."

"So sometimes he *wants* to go after them?"

Cam nodded. "Sometimes. Not that he'd ever admit it to them, but sometimes he finds what they're doing is interesting, and he wants to see it up close. Often those things turn into new projects."

"If he thinks what they're doing is silly and waste of time, that's when he sends someone else to bail them out?"

"Right."

"And his instincts are pretty good about which times he should go see it in person and which times it's a waste?"

"Spot on. Every time," Cam said with a nod.

Josie sat back in her chair. "I'm guessing he's been in urgent cares or ERs with them before?"

"More than once," Cam confirmed.

She sighed. "Maybe I'm a project, then? That's what you're saying?"

Cam thought about that for a second. "It's really not apples to apples," he said.

"No?"

"Definitely not."

"Why not?"

"Because he's never wanted to see either of them naked, and I'm certain he's never..." Cam paused. Then grinned. "Eaten either of their cupcakes."

She blushed hot even as she laughed at his innuendo. "Well, that might muddy the picture a little."

"It's just interesting," Cam said.

Interesting. She liked the word *romantic* better, but Cam McCaffery was definitely not the type to use the R word. Actually either R word—romantic or relationship. He'd sworn those off when he'd left Appleby and Whitney behind.

Josie really didn't want to be a project of Grant's. She really didn't. She didn't want to be a problem he had to solve or a charity case he had to take care of. But here she was, in urgent care, and had already promised to pay cash for the visit.

And she didn't know how to change that. She could, *would*, pay him back, of course, but she would have to do it over time.

That wouldn't be humiliating at all.

Her side twinged just then as if to remind her that this wasn't really something she could change her mind about, however.

The bathroom door opened, and Grant emerged, dressed in a pair of jeans and a long-sleeved Henley. He now had more casual shoes on as well. He looked different. Not as buttoned up and perfect. But he still made her heart thump. Maybe even more so dressed like this. More laid back. More like he might if he was just hanging around the house on a Saturday with her. Like if they were in a relationship and he was her boyfriend and—

"Jocelyn Asher?" the nurse called just then.

Josie sat up straight, jerked from her daydream. She opened her mouth to respond, but Grant beat her to it.

"Yes. She's right here." He crossed to her swiftly.

Cam rose and took the bag back from Grant. "You guys good? Want me to stay?"

"Nah, I appreciate you coming though," Grant said, taking Josie's hand and pulling her to her feet.

As if she couldn't figure out how to stand up by herself? She wasn't *that* bad off. Annoyed by the prospect of being a project to him, and annoyed that she wasn't enjoying being taken care of as much now, she pulled her hand away.

Grant gave her a little frown. She gave him one back.

"Right this way, Ms. Asher," the nurse said.

Josie headed in that direction, aware of Grant right on her heels. *Right* on her heels. He literally stepped on the back of her shoe, pulling it off her heel.

"Grant!" she snapped.

"Sorry," he muttered.

Josie wiggled her foot back into the shoe and gave the nurse a smile. "He's a little on edge."

"She's been having a lot of pain. It's been getting worse. She started vomiting tonight," Grant said.

Josie rolled her eyes.

The nurse nodded. "So I read." She looked at Josie. "Do you want your... friend... in the room with you?"

Josie glanced up at Grant. "Quit acting like a weirdo."

He gave her a bemused look. "I'm acting like a weirdo?"

"Yes. Just... relax."

"Not going to happen."

Yeah, Grant wasn't really the relaxed type. He was intense and serious and a little broody and definitely bossy. "Can you just let them do their jobs at least?" Josie asked.

"Are you going to listen to *them*?" he asked.

"I really do need to get you back into a room," the nurse interjected.

Josie sighed and nodded. "We're fine."

She, of course, wasn't sure that was true at all. Physically or emotionally, for that matter. But it also looked like all of this was now out of her control. And not in the fun way that being out of control with Grant had been the night before.

———

Three hours later, Grant followed Jocelyn into her kitchen again.

He got the impression that she wanted him to leave her alone.

Well, that wasn't going to happen.

She hadn't *said* that. She hadn't said much at all since the doctor had told her that she needed to have her gall bladder removed.

Grant had asked more questions than she had.

There had been the routine questions and taking of her vital signs. They'd done an exam which had led to a trip to the hospital in Dubuque for an ultrasound which had confirmed the doctor's suspicion about her inflamed gall bladder.

Apparently an angry gall bladder accounted for all of her symptoms, including the shoulder pain and the fact that the pain had come and gone for the past few weeks. He said he wasn't surprised that she'd assumed she'd injured her shoulder at first. She was young and healthy and not in the typical demographic for gall bladder issues. But there were always exceptions, and the ultrasound had confirmed gallstones.

He said it wasn't something that had to be taken care of immediately—as in that night or the next day—but that her symptoms would definitely continue to worsen. She could control them to some extent with what she ate, but that his recommendation was to have the gall bladder removed. He assured her it was a simple surgery with a relatively easy recovery, especially for someone of her age and health.

Jocelyn had gone very quiet after all of that.

Now, back in her kitchen where it had all started, Grant was starting to get antsy with that.

"Are you going to call the surgeon tomorrow?" he asked point-blank. That was really what he wanted to know. He could offer to make her a cup of tea or to rub her feet or to run out for some antacids or something, but she didn't really need any of that. She needed to have her gall bladder taken out. And *he* really needed to know when she was going to get this taken care of.

"I don't know." She rounded the middle island and went to the refrigerator, taking out a bottle of water. She twisted off the cap and leaned back against the counter, taking a long drink. She seemed lost in thought.

Grant ground his teeth. This was not really any of this business, he reminded himself, but it not being his business didn't seem to keep him from being concerned about it. Or prying.

"You know what the problem is and you know how to solve it. Why wouldn't you just make that phone call?" he asked.

"Because I'm not ready to solve it," she told him, finally meeting his eyes.

She hadn't even looked at him in over two hours.

That had also been grating on his nerves. Not because he needed her to placate him, but because he got the definite impression she was not okay.

"You're not ready to solve it?" he repeated, moving forward to lean his hands onto the kitchen island. "What does that mean?"

"It means, I need some time," she said with a frown.

Lord save him from stubborn women. He had certainly dealt with his share of them. His sister, his grandmother, just to name two. He definitely ran into some in his seminars, but they were in the minority. When women signed up for his seminars, clearly they knew what they were coming for and *chose* to come to get his advice. They came to him. Because of his expertise. Because they wanted to hear what he had to say. Because they acknowledged that he was someone who knew what he was talking about. He could admit that was a part of the job that he really loved.

"Some time for what?" he asked, trying to not let on that he was gritting his teeth. His fingers gripped the edge of the counter.

"Time to think it through and plan," she said with a frown. "It's not something I can just do."

His eyebrows went up. "It's something you *need* to do."

"I have a job, Grant," she said, her tone snippy.

Jocelyn didn't seem the snappish type.

Was that one of the reasons he'd been drawn to her? She'd seemed so sweet and docile and submissive? She'd seemed like the type of woman to listen to him and defer to his judgment?

Fuck.

Yes.

He knew that a woman who was *too* submissive would not be someone he could be with long term, of course. He loved strong, independent women. Hell, he helped women *become* strong and independent. But for a short-term fling, did he like the idea of a woman who would think he had all the answers and would sweetly say yes to him over and over again?

Yep.

That was not Jocelyn Asher after all.

And now, here he was, up to his eyeballs in caring about her and worrying about her enough to seriously consider throwing her over his shoulder and kidnapping her to the hospital to have her gall bladder taken out.

He shoved a hand through his hair.

"Your boss is your best friend. I'm certain if she knew what was going on she'd insist you get it taken care of as well," Grant said, trying to keep his voice even.

Jocelyn narrowed her eyes. "You'd better not even think about telling her. *I* will tell her about what the doctor said."

"You mean you'll tell her a *version* of what the doctor said."

She didn't confirm it. But she also didn't deny it.

"Dammit, Jocelyn." Grant smacked his hand down on the counter. "Be reasonable."

"I'm *being* reasonable!" She frowned at him. "I have a lot to consider here! I told you, I don't have insurance. I need to figure out to make this work. When I *can't* work for a little bit. And when I'll have big bills to pay! Just leave me alone for a freaking minute!"

Grant blew out a breath. This was not his problem. She was not his concern. She was not his responsibility.

That didn't seem to matter.

"I'll give you the money."

She closed her eyes and sucked in a deep breath. As if counting to ten to gather patience.

Oh, *she* needed to gather patience to deal with *him*?

"That's very nice of you," she finally said calmly. "But we're talking tens of thousands of dollars. I couldn't take that kind of money from you."

He had it. It would be no problem at all. But he appreciated someone not wanting to take a handout. Pride was important too. "You can pay me back." There was no way he'd have her pay him back the full amount, but he'd figure something out when the time came.

"I can also pay the hospital back. They'll have some kind of payment plan, I'm sure."

Damn stubborn woman. "Mine would be interest free."

"I wouldn't be comfortable owing you that much money for the length of time this would take," she said, lifting her chin.

Grant ground his teeth. "Borrow it from Aiden, then. He's a friend. Someone you've known forever."

"No fucking way."

He ground his teeth harder even as he made a note that she evidently swore as she got more determined.

"You're being ridiculous," he told her.

"Maybe you should just leave," she responded.

Yeah, maybe he should. Because he was tempted to call a friend of his who was a computer hacker to get into Jocelyn's bank account and make a deposit. Or maybe he could just call the hospital and arrange to cover her expenses anonymously. That he could do, surely. He'd ask Cam about legalities and such. Hell, he'd have Cam just handle it, so the hospital wouldn't even know who it was coming from directly so that Jocelyn couldn't find out.

She would surely guess, but as stubborn as she could be, *he* could be so much more so. She had no idea.

"Fine." He turned on his heel. "I'll leave. But this isn't over." He stalked to the back door.

"I appreciate everything you did to help me tonight, Grant," she said softly behind him.

He stopped and pulled in a deep breath. See? She *was* sweet. She was stubborn and feistier than he'd given her credit for, maybe, but she was also sweet and sexy and had a smile that did things to his heart that had never been done to it before.

"You're very welcome." He looked back over his shoulder. "Call me if you need anything. Please. I mean it."

She didn't reply right away.

"I promise not to yell or nag," he added.

She snorted softly.

"I'll *try* not to," he corrected with a small smile.

"Okay. Thanks."

She wouldn't call him. There was a jab in his chest as he realized it. Dammit. Hopefully she'd call Zoe or Jane. But it wasn't his place to tell them anything about this. Fuck.

He turned back and grabbed the doorknob, but then heard himself say, "Marry me."

10

H e gripped the doorknob, holding his breath, just waiting.

He wasn't panicking. He wasn't hoping she hadn't heard him. He wasn't hoping she'd laugh it off.

He really fucking wanted her to say yes.

Finally she did answer.

"*What?*"

He turned. She was staring at him as if he'd just announced that he was going to take her gall bladder out right here and now with nothing but a butter knife and a bottle of hydrogen peroxide.

"Marry me," he said again. Firmer. "It's the perfect solution."

"To what exactly?"

"All of this." It really was. He hadn't even realized just how perfect until now. As the idea kept going through his mind, it became more and more clear. He nodded. "I want to help. This allows me to do that. You need help. This provides that. You don't have insurance. This would give you insurance. We'll add you to my policy. That won't cost me anything more. I already pay the premiums, and we have an exceptional plan with excellent coverage and a very low deductible."

Those were all true statements. He and Cam had found the best plan for their company. While the five partners were all healthy, single guys and didn't need a lot of coverage, they needed to cover their employees as well, and they'd all agreed that a comprehensive plan that didn't cost the employees much was going to be a perk of working at Fluke Inc. Cam had also agreed with Grant that they needed good coverage, not because any of the partners had chronic illnesses but because two of them had the chronic tendency to do things like travel in foreign countries on whims and skydive with only a couple of lessons.

"But we would have to actually *be* married," Jocelyn said.

"Yes."

"That's... fraud."

"It's not fraud if we're legally married," he said. "They don't need to know *why* we're married. All that matters is that we have a legal marriage license."

"But..." She frowned. "We would have to actually *be* married," she repeated.

"Yes," he said again.

"Why would you do that?"

"For all of the reasons I just listed." He crossed the room, coming to stand right in front of her. "And because I can think of a lot of things far worse than living and sleeping with you every night."

Her eyes widened. "You were just complaining about the fact that I was 'making' you stay here in Appleby longer than you'd intended," she said, lifting her finger to put quotes around *making*. "Now you want to commit yourself to even more?"

Grant lifted a hand and tucked her hair behind her ear. She really was beautiful. She was sassy at times. She had more spunk than he'd anticipated. But she was sweet, and he knew she thought his inability to forget about her was romantic.

"Look, I'm going to be totally honest with you," he said, his voice getting gruff without him even trying. He could convince her of this. He could sweep her off her feet. Not because he was so smooth and romantic but because *she* liked the idea of them having instant chemistry and a connection he couldn't deny.

He didn't want to use that against her. At least, not entirely. He wanted her to know the score.

Her bottom lip was trapped between her teeth as she studied his eyes.

"If it weren't for your gall bladder I wouldn't have proposed already," he said. He gave her a little half grin and was gratified to see her smile in return. "But I wouldn't have been leaving town any time soon either. I would have wanted to keep seeing you. I would have wanted to keep getting you naked. So this is going a little farther than all of that, I'll admit, but it's for a good cause."

She just stared at him, but she took a deep breath.

"And I *really* need to know that you're okay now that I've gotten to know you," he said. "That's who I am. I can't stand leaving people more vulnerable than I found them." He smiled. "You can ask my sister and my grandmother about how stubborn I can be when I decide I need to take care of someone."

Jocelyn blinked. "You take care of your sister and grandmother?"

He nodded. "My sister and grandma needed someone to look out for them and I was that guy. I've helped them become a lot more self-sufficient and independent and I love that. But when they really needed help? Yes, I was there and *insisted* on it."

She pressed her lips together as she searched his eyes. "Why do you think *I* am your responsibility?" she asked softly.

He sucked in a breath and then let it out. He wasn't going to lie to her about this being damned weird and out of character for him. But it was a very real feeling, and he wasn't going to be able to shake it. She needed to know that too.

"I'm not really sure," he admitted. "You clearly have a ton of friends who love you. I know your family is here and I'm guessing would do whatever they could to take care of you. I'm not the type to get deeply involved so quickly with women—or probably anyone outside my family and circle of friends. I'm not spontaneous. I'm not a gambler. But... there's something about you. And the last time I felt this way—caring about someone so quickly—it was when I met Dax and Ollie and Cam and Aiden." He shrugged. "And that's turned out pretty well."

She smiled, the worry lines on her forehead easing.

"And so I'm also not the type to argue against a good idea once I realize it's good," he said. He braced a hand on the counter beside them and leaned in. "And as long as we're going to be seeing each other exclusively anyway and sleeping together, I don't see why we shouldn't have a piece of paper that says you can use my health insurance while we're doing that."

She swallowed. "When you put it that way, it almost sounds practical."

He had her. He grinned. "And," he said, because he felt compelled to lay it all out, "we can get an annulment or a divorce or whatever when you are fully recovered and the bills are all paid."

That made her brows draw together. "Oh. Right." She nodded. "True."

He knew that took some of the air out of her romantic bubble. But they had to acknowledge there was a way out too. They barely knew one another. His life was in Chicago and hers was, clearly, very rooted here. There were lots—lots and lots and lots—of reasons that this wouldn't work out long term. But as a short-term solution to this problem it was nearly perfect.

"How much is the deductible?" she asked.

This was definitely not the way he'd imagined a proposal ever going. Not that he'd ever imagined proposing.

"Two thousand dollars. Maybe three," he said. "I'll check."

"I'll pay you back for that much at least. And any percent of the bills that aren't covered."

He bit back the "No, you fucking won't" that threatened to come out of his mouth. He nodded. "Or you could earn it."

She lifted both brows nearly to her hairline. "Oh?"

He chuckled. "Not like that."

Her brows pulled down. "Then what?"

"You can go with me to my seminars as my assistant. You can help with paperwork and AV and things like that." This was perfect. He could let everyone there know she was his wife, and he could avoid any awkward moments like unexpectedly finding naked women in his bed.

Well, except for Jocelyn, of course.

She was clearly confused. "Seminars? AV? What are you talking about?"

"I'll fill you in," I said. "But I need an assistant on weekends once or twice a month. I have a seminar this weekend, in fact. You can come along and work off the cost of the deductible."

Of course, he didn't give a shit about the deductible, but he knew she did, so if this would make her happy, then fine. She needed time to get used to this, and she was clearly not going to be scheduled for surgery before Monday anyway. So he'd take her to Chicago with him. Maybe they'd pop into the courthouse and get married while they were there. Then everything would be ready to go by the time they got back to Appleby and got her surgery scheduled.

"I don't know anything about AV," she finally said. "But I like the idea of doing something for the help you're giving me."

"I'll teach you."

He reached out, slid a hand around her waist to her lower back, and drew her forward.

"Say yes," he said softly and firmly.

She wet her lips and swallowed. "Yes."

He was shocked by the emotions that rocked through him. Relief was there, for sure. He was going to be able to fix this after all. But there was also a healthy surge of happiness. He was happy about this. Was it unconventional? Absolutely. Was it spontaneous? Definitely. Was it completely out of character? Yes. Yes it was.

Would his friends want *him* to go directly to the doctor for a checkup?

Very likely.

But just as he was starting to feel a little hint of *what the hell did I just do,* Jocelyn leaned in, wrapped her arms around him, and hugged him. And that surge of happiness washed the rest away.

———

G etting married for the health insurance wasn't exactly romantic. Or the way she'd ever thought she'd be saying *I do,* but it was maybe the most practical thing she'd ever done.

And honestly, Grant Lorre was very hard to say no to.

At least for her. She also had a suspicion that he was starting to figure that out. That might be a problem down the road.

Oh, who was she kidding? It was a problem right now. He was talking her into getting *married.* Because her gall bladder was about to bite the dust.

Ugh. This was absolutely *not* the swoony-tell-all-her-girl-friends-about-it situation she'd always imagined.

But her gall bladder stabbed against her side—she was imagining it with a little frowny face and a giant knife that it stuck into her from time to time insisting on being let out—and she realized that she didn't really have a choice here.

She had to get her gall bladder out. No matter what she'd been telling herself and Grant, it *was* getting worse. And now that she knew what it was, she was freaking out a little bit. It made sense that her symptoms had been coming and going. It depended on what she'd eaten that day. She hadn't put those things together, of course, thinking it was her shoulder, but now it made sense.

She did want to get it out. Thinking about having an infected internal organ swelling up inside her and making her sick, not to mention the associated pain, had definitely pushed this to the *must do* column in her head.

And the estimate the hospital had given her had made her feel even sicker.

But Grant was here. Offering a practical solution. That would work. And would keep him around longer, and yes, in her bed. In her kitchen for that matter. In her... life.

Josie knew that her romantic tendencies could be a problem. She knew that real life wasn't like the movies. But... she wanted to date him. She wanted to get to know him better. She wanted to spend time with him. She absolutely wanted to have more sex with him.

Being married was one way for all of that to happen.

It wouldn't be a hardship to let Grant move in here. He was bossy, and yet at the same time, had a way of being protective and caring. It was a potent combination.

She'd watched that combination with her father and grandfather toward her mom and grandma all her life. The men respected their wives and certainly encouraged their independence, but her dad, Chris, and her grandpa, Larry, also took care of them. They went above and beyond to make sure they were safe and healthy and happy.

The happy part had always been what she'd focused on.

The little treats her dad would bring home even though money was always tight. The way he'd whisper in her mom's ear and make her laugh. The way he'd go with her to school events—her mom was a fourth-grade teacher—and would haul boxes and set up huge science-fair displays and would dress up as Aristotle or Sir Isaac Newton without batting an eye. Because it made her mom happy.

He'd always wanted to take her to Italy, but unable to afford that, every year on their anniversary they went to a fancy Italian restaurant, and they'd watch *Roman Holiday* and *Only You*, her mom's two favorite romantic movies, while snuggled up on the couch and would go over the fantasy trip itinerary that they'd started while on their honeymoon to Branson, Missouri instead of Rome.

It was sad that her father couldn't take her mom on their dream trip. But the effort he made to keep that dream alive was incredibly romantic, and Josie swore that her mom was happier with their imagined trip than an actual one at this point. The real thing might not have a chance of measuring up.

But now... looking up at Grant and thinking about something as mundane as health insurance... she had to admit that the "in sickness and in health" part of the whole getting-married thing could be romantic too.

Him wanting her when she was healthy and happy and fully able to be put on the kitchen island and coated with cake batter was one thing. But *insisting* on being with her after she'd puked on him—and likely would again—and would be costing him paperwork headaches, if not actual money, and would probably not be up for kitchen-island canoodling for a little bit was another thing entirely.

She lifted onto her toes and tipped her head, wanting to kiss him. But he was enough taller than her that he had to meet her partway.

Which he did. They kissed, but it was sweet.

That was nice. It really was.

But she wanted more. Josie arched closer, gripping the front of his shirt, and opened her mouth.

Of course, just then her bastard gall bladder decided to remind her that he wanted *out* and the sooner the better. She felt the stab under her ribs and gasped.

Grant seemed to realize it wasn't a gasp of pleasure—or maybe it was the way she stiffened in his arms suddenly—but he lifted his head frowning down at her.

"Are you okay?"

Josie pressed her hand into her side even though she knew that wouldn't help. She gave him a smile. Or she tried to. The way his frown deepened, she was pretty sure her smile had come off as more of a grimace. "Sorry," she said.

"Jesus, don't be sorry."

He bent and lifted her into his arms, tipping her so quickly her head spun a little. He kept doing that—picking her up as if it were nothing.

She liked it.

"Let's get you to bed," he said, starting in the direction of the main part of the house. It was really the only direction to go from the kitchen other than out the back door again.

"This isn't really how I imagined you saying that to me," she said, pointing toward the staircase.

He started to climb. "Not how I imagined saying it either."

"Ugh!"

He chuckled. "One thing at a time, tiger. I'll be taking you to bed every night for a long time."

Her heart stuttered at those words. That sounded amazing. She wouldn't even mind if he *carried* her to bed. She would never admit that to her strong, feisty, best friends, but yeah, she liked this. A lot.

But would he be doing it for a long time? Maybe to Grant a long time was three months. To her a long time, at least in terms of marriage, was fifty to sixty years. She sighed. *This* marriage was practical. It would be fun and sexy too, which was great. But it was not a till-death-do-us-part kind of marriage. In fact, she'd kind of like to leave that out of the service, come to think of it. She did not want to promise that in front of her friends and family and God and all, knowing that it was until her stomach healed and her debt was paid off.

She was going to have to look up how long it took people to recover from gall bladder surgery. She was guessing that, even if she milked it a little, it wasn't going to get her to her silver wedding anniversary.

"Which one?" Grant asked at the top of the stairs.

"Second on the right."

He stepped through the doorway to her bedroom, and Josie was struck by three things at once. How damned big he was, how feminine her bedroom was, and how much she wanted him to stay.

This wasn't the master bedroom of the house, but it was the one that Josie had stayed in when she'd been a little girl visiting her grandparents. Even though she'd lived in Appleby too, spending the night at Grandma and Grandpa's house had been a treat, and she'd slept over often. She had incredibly good, warm, happy memories here, and when she'd moved into the house, it had felt wrong to sleep in any other room.

Grant set her down on the edge of her bed. The duvet was a light green that went with the pale green walls and white wood trim around the doorway and windows and the baseboards. She had only sheer curtains over the windows because she loved the sunlight, and this room got amazing morning sun.

All of her white, wooden bedroom furniture had been handed down to her with the house, including the rocking chair in the corner with the pile of books next to it and the green, blue, and white blanket that her grandmother had knitted for her draped over the arm. She'd slept in this bed, though she'd replaced the mattress a few years ago, when she'd been a little girl. Her mother had rocked her in that rocking chair. She'd played dress-up with dresses and hats and shoes dug out of the large trunk that sat at the foot of the bed and had played with makeup in the enormous round mirror over the dressing table that sat across the room. It had been her mother's. Kate Asher had done her makeup and hair at that dressing table for her dates with Josie's dad.

The trunk now held blankets and photo albums and the dressing table drawers were full of the actual makeup Josie used now, but everything in this room had memories attached to it. Lifelong memories.

And she was about to marry a guy with the intention of it being short term.

Looking at the trunk where she hadn't even realized she'd planned to store her wedding dress and veil after her wedding, she decided that they couldn't have an actual wedding. No gorgeous dress with a long train. No veil. No flowers. No photographs. Hell, they shouldn't even have a ceremony.

"Do you think we could elope?"

Grant's attention came back to her immediately. He thought about her question. "Absolutely," he said after only a few seconds.

Wow, that hadn't been difficult for him to decide. But Josie refused to let that bother her. She nodded. "Great. I think we should go away for the weekend, let everyone know that—well, maybe not my grandma," she said with a frown. "But our friends, I mean. We'll go away for the weekend saying that we're having such a good time that we decided I should go to your seminar to help out. Then we'll find a justice of the peace? A judge? Whatever. And when we come back we'll tell them that we... got drunk and a little crazy, but that we're going to see what happens."

He nodded. "Okay. On all of it except the drunk part."

"No?"

"I don't get drunk."

That didn't surprise her. "Okay. Then we'll just get caught up in the moment. The romance. The sex. Whatever."

"I don't really do that either."

She nodded. "You're going to have to sell it. I mean, what other story are we going to use?"

"Well, fortunately you sent me those cupcakes," he said, the corner of his mouth curling slightly.

"Oh?"

"I acted... uncharacteristically happy and possessive about those," he said.

"Did you?" She liked how that sounded. At least this wasn't completely platonic. It wasn't a business deal. It was... it was kind of a business deal. She could admit that. But they were... friends. Kind of. He was a friend helping her out with something. There was *some* emotion here. A lot of it was lust, maybe, but it went a little beyond that. Fuck buddies didn't sit in urgent care. Or offer to commit insurance fraud.

"I did," he said. "And I think that made the guys think that something was going on that was more than... anything else before."

She lifted her brows.

He blew out a breath, tucking his hands into his pockets. He looked a little uncomfortable or... vulnerable. That's what it was. He looked vulnerable.

Josie sat up a little straighter.

"I like you," he finally said. He was looking at her knees. "I like you, and I feel very strangely protective of you, and I'm... addicted to something here. Something that makes me want to stay and have more. More of... whatever it is." His eyes lifted to hers. "And yes, the men who have been my friends and partners for nine years can tell all of that."

Okay, *that* was all pretty great. It wasn't madly in love and wanting to spend the rest of his life with her, but it wasn't *I basi-cally see you as a charity and need to make a big donation so I can sleep at night.*

"So they might believe this?"

"They might." He shrugged. "I'll make them believe it."

She smiled. She believed *that*. Grant definitely had a way of presenting his arguments. She figured he didn't lose very often.

"Will your friends believe it of you?"

"That I ran off for a romantic weekend with the guy who has *literally* swept me off my feet and ended up married to him?" She gave a soft chuckle. "I should actually probably be worried by how easily they're going to believe that."

He gave her a little grin. "So we can pull it off?"

"I think so."

"We can fly to Chicago tomorrow," he said. "I can make some calls and get something arranged with a judge. The seminar is on Saturday. We can stay Sunday and... see the city. And we can be home Sunday night in time for you to call and schedule your surgery Monday."

See the city? She didn't want to see Chicago. She wanted to spend the day in bed with her hot, would-be-by-then husband.

Then again... she kind of wanted to see the city. Her parents and grandparents both always wanted to travel and had never been able to. She was excited about the idea of the plane and everything that this would entail.

"That sounds good." Then she tipped her head. "Will it look suspicious if we get married, and three days later I'm sched-uling surgery?"

He shook his head. "Zoe saw your attack today at the bakery. We'll just say that it happened again and the surgery was emergency."

"But Cam knows we went to urgent care," she pointed out.

"Cam won't say anything," Grant said easily.

"You're sure?"

"I totally trust him."

"Oh, I do too. But will he know he shouldn't say something?" Josie wanted to know.

"I'll fill him in."

"So, Cam will know our secret. That we're married for the insurance."

"Yes. But he'll have to help with the paperwork and everything anyway," Grant said. "I'm hoping he can pull strings with one of the judges."

She nodded. "Okay."

Grant moved to stand in front of her and tipped her chin up with his finger. "What's wrong?"

She shrugged, feeling silly. "I just... I know it's not going to be real, but I thought if we were the only ones that knew that then maybe it would... feel a little real."

"It's going to be real, Jocelyn," Grant said. "The marriage will be real."

"But it's not..." She took a breath. She was *not* going to whine to him about how they weren't in love. He knew that. And he did not want to be stuck, even temporarily, with a crazy, love-at-first-sight believer. "It's not like we *want* to get married," she finally said.

He crouched in front of her, taking her chin between his finger and thumb. "I do want to marry you. Maybe the reasons aren't entirely conventional, but the desire to be your husband is real."

She so appreciated him not saying *maybe I don't love you but...* She smiled and leaned in, putting her lips against his. "Okay."

He kissed her, then pulled back. "By the way, I'm staying tonight."

"Good."

"But no sex."

She pouted. She knew that made sense. Her side was achy,

and she was still freaked out, and things between them were a little weird. Mostly good weird, but still weird. Still... Grant in her bed all night without any of *that*?

"You need to rest tonight," he said, smiling at her disappointed expression. "You've had a lot of pain, and it's been emotional, and you need your sleep."

He was even taking care of her now.

"And I'm going to text Aiden and have him tell Zoe that I'm whisking you off to Chicago tomorrow and that you won't be in."

"No!" She gripped his wrist. "No. Seriously, Grant. I have to work in the morning. It's our busiest time, and it's too late for her to get her mom to help fill in."

"She knows you weren't feeling well."

"I would have told her by now if I couldn't be there," Josie insisted.

Zoe depended on her. Yes, it made taking time off and sick days complicated, but Buttered Up was Josie's too. Not officially. It had been in the McCaffery family for three generations and the family was... traditional. Okay, that was a nice word for set in their ways. Stubborn. Stuck.

Still, Josie loved Buttered Up and working with Zoe, and she truly felt as invested in the bakery as if it *was* partly hers.

"I'll be okay. I'll rest, and I'll eat carefully in the morning. We can head to Chicago in the afternoon."

He didn't look happy but he nodded. "Fine. But we'll leave right after the morning rush. Not afternoon. Maggie can get there by then."

It was a compromise. And Grant coming in and whisking her off for a surprise getaway would be an easier sell than Josie planning a trip. That just wasn't something she would normally do. She'd never been on an airplane. Never been to a city bigger than Des Moines. Never gone out of town with a boyfriend.

It would also play into *something is different about Grant and Josie* that would help when they came back married.

"Fine, but you have to come in as if it's a last-minute-surprise romantic trip," she said. "You have to basically kidnap me."

He gave her that half smile. "Hmm. Should I bring handcuffs and a blindfold? That could be fun later in the weekend."

She felt a hot shiver go through her. "I wouldn't say no."

Something flickered in his eyes as his smile grew. "Yeah. That's something I really like about you."

She smiled. "Okay, so if there's no sex tonight and I'm going into work in the morning before we leave, you don't *have* to stay."

"Yes, I do. In case you get sick in the night or need something."

He said it firmly, and she felt her head nodding. "Okay."

It wasn't needy of her to want him to stay. She just... wanted him to stay. She liked him, and she was kind of hoping this might turn into more than just a favor—and a little insurance fraud—between friends. She wasn't going to lie about wanting it to be more. If it didn't turn into more, fine. They were going in eyes-wide-open. She wasn't going to trick him or manipulate him. But could she show him what a real relationship with her would be like and hope that he liked it? Why not?

They were going to be married. Might as well give it a fair shot. She couldn't, in good conscience, stand up in front of her family and friends in a church and take wedding vows that she knew might not stick, but once she was bound to Grant legally, even if he saw it as temporary, she could definitely try to make the marriage real and enjoyable for the time they had. She knew a lot about happy marriages. Maybe not from her own experience, but she'd been around two, observing them daily, up close, her whole life.

Of course, she needed to get past the puking and stabbing

pain and then the bloody bandages and possible post-op puking part of all of this first. She really needed to look some things up about gall bladder surgery. Still, it was probably the least sexy thing she'd ever done with a member of the opposite sex.

"Okay," Grant repeated. "Great." He seemed relieved she wasn't arguing.

He stretched to his feet and toed off his shoes as he started to undo his jeans.

She blew out a breath. She'd really love to stay and watch him undress. "You're going to strip right in front of me and then tell me we can't have sex?" she asked, watching his long, thick fingers undo the buttons and zipper.

He paused. "I... yeah, I guess that's what I was doing."

"You could sleep in the guest bedroom," she suggested.

"I'm not doing that."

She looked up at him, just then aware that her gaze had still been on the fly of his jeans. "Why not?"

"You're going to be my wife. I'm sleeping in your bed."

Dammit. It wasn't *really* real but when he said "my wife" her heart flipped over. "Even when I'm sick?"

"Maybe especially when you're sick."

See? *That* was romantic. She didn't care what anyone said.

She took a deep breath. "And the sex thing tonight? Definitely off the table?"

"As much as I'd love to," he said. "I think it's best. It would really bother me for you to have pain in the middle of it."

She believed him. If nothing else, she already knew that Grant was very bothered by her pain. That was also romantic. "Okay. Then I'm going to go brush my teeth while you undress. You be under the covers when I get back." She pointed at the bed.

He grinned. "Yes, ma'am."

She smiled and stepped around him.

"Hey, Jocelyn?"

"Yeah?" She looked back. She was stunned by how much she liked seeing him undressing next to her bed. It was a physical reaction from her attraction to him, for sure, but there was something softer too. A comfort in having him there and just a feeling of rightness.

"Could you put your pajamas on while you're in there? I see what you mean about the stripping in front of each other."

She grinned. "Well, I should maybe torture you a little since this is your rule."

She loved the idea that she even *could* torture him. That his attraction to her was strong enough that watching her undress would have been tempting too.

"But," she went on, "yes, I can do that."

He blew out a breath. "Thank you."

She put a hand on her hip. "You really thought I'd make you watch me undress?"

"You're... sassier than I expected," he told her. "The torture things seems like something you might do."

Josie lifted an eyebrow. "I'm sassy?"

"You have some definite sass in you," he said with a nod. And a tiny frown.

She liked that. She was nothing compared to Jane and Zoe. *Nothing.* Those two were fighters and the epitome of sassy. But it was inevitable that they would rub off on her a little, she supposed. "Well, thank you."

His tiny frown grew bigger. "I'm not sure it's a compliment. I don't love it."

"You mean, you don't love it when I'm using the sassiness on you."

"Exactly."

She laughed. "You like when people listen to you."

"Love it."

"Yeah, I've already figured that out, and we haven't even known each other that long."

Why people *wouldn't* listen to Grant she couldn't really say. He wasn't just bossy. He exuded confidence and assuredness that was downright comforting. He was clearly intelligent and successful. Why wouldn't someone assume he knew what he was talking about?

But she hadn't just gone along with his ideas, had she? She'd fought him on going to urgent care. She'd fought him on letting him pay her bills. She'd been worried—for the right reasons—and wanting to take care of herself. She'd made him compromise and come up with a plan that she could live with. That wasn't perfect but... was kind of perfect in many ways. And when he had finally presented the compromise, where she got something she wanted and needed and so did he, she'd agreed.

She hadn't just fallen at his feet, but she hadn't stubbornly insisted she was right to the detriment of everything.

She'd like to think that was all very reasonable.

"And I can already tell that you're going to be difficult some-times," he said.

Josie nodded. "That's probably true."

"I'll be sure to have the judge add the 'honor and obey' line to our wedding service," he said, the corner of his mouth curling up.

She rolled her eyes. "Well, that will make me *really* compliant with my medical orders so that I heal and recover as quickly as possible."

So that they could annul the marriage or whatever they were going to do as soon as possible.

She didn't add that part, but they both knew that's what she was referring to.

She didn't like that part. She'd admit it. She'd never imagined being someone who would marry for anything less than true love and forever.

But interestingly, Grant didn't laugh or smile or even nod agreement with her statement.

"I hope you're compliant and get better quickly because I hate seeing you not feeling well," he said. Sincerely.

That. Was. Romantic. Dammit.

She sighed. She wasn't in love with him. She couldn't be. She wasn't even falling in love with him. Yet. But she wanted to fall in love with him.

"I'm going to brush my teeth. And change into my pajamas."

"I'll be right here when you get back."

It was going to be a long night lying next to her romantic-even-though-he-didn't-mean-to-be, saving-her-ass, mostly-naked, sort-of fiancé.

11

It had been a long night.

He had not only spent it in a queen-sized bed—Grant couldn't remember the last time he'd slept in something smaller than a king—but he'd spent it next to the woman he wanted more than he'd ever wanted a woman. Who wanted to have sex with him. Who he was, basically, for all intents and purposes, engaged to.

She smelled good. She looked good. She felt good.

She'd snuggled right up next to him in the night as if they'd been sleeping next to one another for years. Her sweet ass pressed right into his crotch, her head tucked right underneath his chin, her feet sandwiched right between his. As if that was *her* spot and she'd never been more comfortable in her life.

He didn't know if she'd done it to torture him—since she'd kindly skipped the striptease—or if she was just a cuddly-touchy-feely type even when she was unconscious but... it was the most heavenly hellish way to spend the last three hours of his night.

He guessed it was the cuddly-touchy-feeling-type thing, honestly. She was bold and stubborn at times, but Jocelyn

Asher was not vindictive. He didn't know how he knew that with such certainty, but he did.

When her alarm went off at the ungodly hour of 5 a.m., she stretched like a cat, rubbing that ass—and the rest of her—against him, probably without even realizing it.

Until she felt his erection pressing into her.

And became aware of his body snuggled tightly up against hers. His arm draped over her waist, his chin resting on the top of her head.

She froze. Then slowly turned. Her eyes widened, and she quickly whipped her head back to face away from him. Then she scooted out from under his arm and to the edge of the bed, nearly jumping off the mattress.

He blinked. "Um, good morning."

She ran a hand through her hair and gave him a little smile. "Hi." Then she spun on her heel and practically ran from the room.

Okay. So she hadn't snuggled up against him on purpose. She'd seemed shocked to see him in her bed as a matter of fact.

Grant stretched and yawned and also got out of bed. Though less as if his ass was on fire and more like a normal person. He was dressed, but shoeless when Jocelyn came back into the room wrapped in a bathrobe, her hair in a ponytail.

He watched her for a sign about how to proceed here.

"So... hi," she said again, this time with a smile.

"Everything okay?" he asked, moving around the edge of the bed. Maybe she'd felt sick and had run to vomit.

She nodded. "I'm not used to waking up with men... well, people of any gender... in my bed."

He came to stand in front of her. "Can't say I'm not happy to hear that," he told her honestly.

She gave him a small smile. "I panicked about the morning breath."

He nodded. "Understandable."

Her eyes went wide, and her hand flew up to cover her mouth. "Was it bad?"

He caught her wrist and chuckled. "No."

He started to lean in, but her hand went to his chest.

"I brushed my teeth," she said.

"Okay."

"You haven't."

Right. He grinned and straightened. "On my way." He stepped around her but paused in the doorway. "Just for the record though, there's *lots* of places I could kiss you in the morning where you won't notice—or care about—morning breath." Then he continued on to the bathroom.

It must have taken her a second to recover from that because as he was closing the bathroom door he heard her call, "There's a new toothbrush in the second drawer!"

Grant chuckled. In fact, he found himself smiling through the entire teeth-brushing process and a quick shower.

By the time he made it to the kitchen, Jocelyn was dressed, had another apron on, and was making what appeared to be French toast.

Any man who claimed that the adage about getting to his heart through his stomach wasn't true was a damned liar. At least in part. There was nothing bad about sleeping with a woman who could cook. Except maybe the extra couple of miles he'd need to add on to his daily run.

"You probably shouldn't eat that," he said, leaning onto the kitchen island, loving everything about watching her in the kitchen.

She looked over her shoulder. "I'm not. This is for you."

"You're making it just for me?" he asked, surprised and stupidly touched. She was just being a good hostess.

"I am." She turned from the stove with a spatula holding two pieces of French toast and slid them onto a plate. They were perfectly golden brown. She turned to take a small saucepan from the stove and proceeded to spoon syrupy, cinnamon-smelling apple slices over the bread. Then she reached into a bowl and took a pinch of powdered sugar, dusting it over the French toast before pushing it in front of Grant.

Then she went for the coffeepot.

Grant just stared at the plate in front of him. This wasn't just plain old French toast. Of course it wasn't. This was Jocelyn Asher. Nothing was *just plain old* with her.

"Wow," he finally said as she set a cup of black coffee in front of him. "This looks amazing."

She nodded. "I know you go for scones and the simpler muffins at the bakery, but I'm determined to win you over to the decadent side of life."

He nodded. "Done."

"You haven't even tasted it yet."

"I licked cake batter off your naked body. It doesn't get much more decadent than that." He picked up his fork as her mouth fell open.

He cut into the French toast and took a big bite.

Yep. Decadent. That was a pretty damned good word for it. He groaned.

Jocelyn gave a happy sigh.

He met her eyes as he chewed and swallowed. "You look happy."

"I *love* making people make that sound because of my food."

He almost made a quip about making him make that sound with other things, but he didn't. He just nodded. Cooking and baking, creating things that made people happy, was her life. She clearly did love it, and she was very, very good at it. "You keep doing this for me and this marriage is going to work out just fine," he told her with a grin, cutting into his breakfast again.

Her smile faded just a tad. If he hadn't been watching her, he wouldn't have even noticed.

"We can probably make it through my whole breakfast and brunch rotation once before it's over. But I have a lot of great recipes," she said.

"Well, I wouldn't want to divorce you before I've tasted them all," Grant teased, trying to keep the moment light. "But I wouldn't mind extending it to include *this* at least one more time."

Her smile was definitely smaller, but she nodded. "I can slip it in again, I'm sure."

She turned back to the stove and made him three more pieces, which, of course, he had to eat regardless of calories or fat content. Not that he minded.

She started doing the dishes as he ate.

"What are you eating?" he asked.

"I already had some toast and some berries," she said. She glanced over her shoulder at him. "I'm fine. I'm feeling good today."

"Okay. Good. I don't want you skipping meals because you're afraid it's going to flare up though."

She nodded, reaching for the dish towel. "I'll admit it's in the back of my mind, but I'll be good. I can be careful for a few days."

Grant studied her. She was so trim. Not a bit overweight. Yet she clearly loved food. "Working around sweets all day doesn't make you crave them less? You don't get sick of them?" he asked.

She laughed at that. "No way. I love everything about baking and cooking and decorating. I don't think I'd be as good at it if I didn't like eating it all too. How could I make the raspberry filling perfect or put the right amount of butterscotch chunks in something if I didn't appreciate how delicious it all was and could be with just a few more chunks or just a little bit more vanilla or just a dash more of cinnamon?"

Grant lifted a brow. "Aiden said that Zoe is a stickler for following her grandmother's recipes at the bakery. In fact, he's been a little frustrated by how adamant she is about not changing things down there. That's why you guys doing cake pops and pies in a jar are such a big deal, right? Because it's a change."

Jocelyn nodded, her eyes on the pan she was drying.

"Are you telling me that you sometimes *change* the recipes, Jocelyn?" Grant asked, teasing, but curious about this woman.

Her cheeks were pink, but she still didn't meet his gaze. "I don't *change* them. I might *tweak* them a bit."

"But Zoe doesn't know."

Jocelyn looked up. "Zoe isn't as... particular about her baking as I am."

He couldn't help it. He grinned. "What does that mean?"

"She follows the recipes to a T. And they're awesome. So there's nothing wrong with that," Jocelyn said. "But she doesn't sample everything, and she doesn't pay *that* much attention. So she... doesn't know when I tweak things."

"And your tweaks make them better?"

She nodded. "They do."

"Better than tried-and-true recipes that have been used and become famous in this area for half a century?" He wanted her to say yes. With confidence. He loved seeing her sure of herself and her talents and willing to defend them.

Jocelyn thought for a moment. Then she said, "Yes." She hesitated. "But you can't tell Zoe."

"I've already promised to keep your secrets," he told her. "I'm one hundred percent Team Jocelyn. I like that you know when to tweak something, when to lean on your talent and knowledge."

She took a deep breath. Then gave him a small smile. "I've

never told anyone that. No one knows that the butterscotch bars and the raspberry thumbprint cookies are so damned good because I actually changed the recipe slightly."

"They give the credit to Zoe?"

"Well, to the family. Her grandmother, I guess, technically. Everyone knows that we use Letty's recipes faithfully." She shrugged. "Semi-faithfully."

"Does it bother you that they don't know it's you behind the deliciousness?" he asked.

"Not really," she said after a moment. "I consider Buttered Up my business too. Its success—or failure—impacts me directly. So I want it to do well. If people love the butterscotch bars, for whatever reason, it's a good thing for all of us."

He nodded. What she said had merit, of course. He just wasn't used to people not wanting to be acknowledged and applauded.

"Is that also partly why you liked having the business on the side?" he asked. "Because then you can make whatever you want however you want to?"

She nodded. "Yeah. It really didn't start that way. It really started as a way to help the people out who needed that stuff last minute or needed things that we don't make at the bakery. We don't make French-toast casseroles for brunches," she said, pointing at Grant's empty plate. "But a woman wanted to take one to her aunt's house for Easter brunch. She's a terrible cook but wanted to bring something homemade and asked if I could make it for her. She supplied the recipe and said she'd pay anything." Jocelyn grinned. "I love trying new recipes, so it was a win win."

"And you made it even better than the recipe, right?" Grant asked, knowing the answer. "You added something extra to it?"

She smiled. "I did. And when the woman called to tell me how everyone *raved* about it, it made me feel so good. I love when I can help people out, but also, of course, love hearing how much people love what I create. It's just..." She shrugged as if having a hard time finding the words. "It's very fulfilling."

Grant couldn't help but smile back. She was so fucking beautiful and sweet. Yes, a little sassy too. But he was finding he liked that. A lot. That sauciness made her add extra butterscotch chunks to the butterscotch bars at the bakery. Behind her best friend's back, maybe, but it wasn't hurting anything. If anything, it was Zoe's fault for being so damned stubborn. Grant had heard Aiden rant—affectionately but exasperatedly—about his fiancée's obstinacy, so it wasn't just Jocelyn that dealt with it.

But Jocelyn's sweet side was very addictive. Even more so than her French toast.

"So, anyway, I don't think I could ever be sick of the stuff I make." She tilted her head and studied him. "But I couldn't imagine spending every day doing something I didn't really love and believe in. Isn't that how you feel about your work?"

Grant didn't have to think about that for long. "It is. I know it sounds superficial since I'm the money guy with Fluke, but I believe in the guys and the company, and they need me to be as successful as they are. So I'm doing my part. But that's why I do the seminars too," he added. "That's really fulfilling for me. I know how you feel about doing something that makes other people happier and better."

She gave him a soft smile. "I can't wait to hear more about those," she said. "I think. Are they about money and stuff?"

He chuckled. "They are."

"I will *try* to be interested," she said. "I promise."

"Not your thing?" A lot of the women who came to his seminars didn't think money and numbers were their things either. He wasn't worried.

"Not even a little," she said. "That is one reason I'm glad I'm not Zoe's partner. She has to worry about all of that stuff."

"Would you like to be Zoe's partner?"

She shrugged. "I sometimes think so. But I think I am in all the ways that really matter. We work together to make the bakery the best it can be. Everyone knows I'm a part of it."

"They don't know how much you're a part of it," he couldn't resist pointing out.

"They know I decorate all the cakes," she said. "Zoe is great about that. She praises me all the time. Makes a huge deal out of it. She'd be lost without me. She could never do the cakes that I do."

"But you don't make the money that a partner would make. You don't make decisions, like healthcare plans, that a partner would make." Grant told himself he shouldn't push like this. It wasn't his business. Not really. He was solving her immediate problem. What happened long term was not his concern.

"Well, I wouldn't be a very good partner," Jocelyn said, pushing away from the counter. "I don't like the money and business part, and if I had to review healthcare plans I'd fall asleep by page two, I'm sure."

Grant bit his tongue. He couldn't make her want to be Zoe's business partner.

"Anyway, I need to get ready for work." She started out of the kitchen.

"Right. As if you're not being swept off on a surprise romantic weekend trip by your new boyfriend."

She stopped and turned to look at him. "Are we officially calling you my boyfriend?" she asked.

"What else would I be?"

She shrugged. "I guess fuck buddies don't go out of town together?"

She asked it as a question indicating that maybe she'd never had a fuck buddy before. Grant liked that.

"I suppose they could," he said. "I mean, that's a lot of what weekend getaways are comprised of, right?"

"Right."

"But…" Fuck buddy didn't seem right as a label for Jocelyn.

Sure, that's what they'd done. Sure, that's what he hoped they'd do again. And again and again and again. But there was more here. He couldn't explain it. *He* wasn't the in-love-with-love one of the two of them. But he felt something more, something softer and deeper, for her than just a desire to get naked.

"I like boyfriend better," he finally said simply.

She seemed surprised but she nodded. "Okay. If I need to call you anything other than Grant, that's what I'll say." She turned and started for the doorway again.

"I mean, at least until you're back on Monday. Then you'll be able to call me your husband." He wasn't sure why he'd felt compelled to add that.

She stopped again and turned back. "Right." She looked at him for a long moment, then added, "But maybe just sticking with Grant as much as possible would be good all around."

She didn't want to call him her husband?

It was *ridiculous* for that to bother him. This was a short-term fix to a money problem. That was it. It probably took even really-in-love couples time to get used to calling each other *husband* and *wife*. By the time he and Jocelyn adjusted, her gall bladder would be healed, and she would have been his assistant for the three seminars or whatever she would agree would make them even financially.

But as he watched her leave the kitchen and listened to her climb the steps and move around on the second floor while he drank his second cup of coffee and then washed his plate and cup in the sink, he didn't miss how domestic it all seemed.

And how nice it was.

Plus, that French toast? Definitely worth loving and cherishing her, if not until death, at least for a while.

———

"Hey, Josie, do you—"

Josie jumped and dropped two eggs on the hard tile floor of Buttered Up's kitchen.

Make that two *more* eggs. Because she'd dropped three earlier when Zoe had barged through the swinging doors with an order for three-dozen pumpkin-spiced muffins that Mrs. Andersen needed tomorrow.

"*What* is going on with you today?" Zoe asked, eyeing the eggs.

"What do you mean?" Josie knelt to wipe up the mess.

"You're so jumpy."

"You're the one who keeps coming in here and startling me," Josie protested.

But that was a really weak comeback. And Zoe's hand on her hip and raised eyebrow told Josie that her friend thought so too. Zoe came in and out through those swinging doors all the time, all day long, every day. There was no reason that it should be startling Josie. And honestly, Zoe hadn't barged. Not this time or last.

Josie was anticipating Grant's arrival to whisk her off on the "surprise" weekend trip to Chicago, and Josie knew that her chances of convincing Zoe that she'd known nothing about it were a million to one.

"I'm *startling* you?" Zoe asked. "Maybe if you had your mind here at work and not on the hot millionaire who's been rocking your world, you wouldn't be surprised when your partner walks into the kitchen of the bakery that you run together."

Josie realized in that moment that Zoe often referred to them as partners. She often called Buttered Up *theirs*. And Josie had never noticed that it was strange. Or really thought about it being untrue.

But it was.

Grant had made her recognize that this morning.

Of course she knew that she didn't own a part of the bakery or have a financial stake in it. But it really had always felt like *theirs*—hers and Zoe's. Together.

Now, though, it felt weird to hear Zoe say it.

Josie frowned.

"You *are* thinking about Grant and sex!" Zoe said with a huge grin. "I knew it!"

"I'm... yes, I'm thinking about Grant," Josie admitted. That much was true. "I'm sorry."

"Don't be sorry. You getting laid so well that you can't concentrate on baking things you've made so many times you could do it in your sleep is so worth a few eggs!"

Josie blinked. "I'm... wait, what do you mean I can't concentrate? I dropped a couple of eggs but... oh my God, did I make something wrong?"

Zoe laughed. "The blueberry muffins had no blueberries in them, and you left the sugar out of the chocolate ones."

"*What?*"

"It's okay," Zoe assured her.

"It is not!" Josie couldn't believe it. She'd *never* messed up baking like that.

"It's fine. I just told everyone we were already sold out. Which was kind of true. We were sold out of the good ones." Zoe gave her a wink, clearly enjoying this a lot.

Josie groaned. "This is such a mess." Zoe didn't even know all the ways that this was a mess.

A hot, gorgeous, bossy, protective, sweet mess.

Grant Lorre was like a molten lava cake covered in ganache. A little hard on the outside, but softer once you got past that outer layer, and downright hot and even gooey inside.

Okay, gooey might be pushing it. But the hot was exactly right.

Not to mention addictive.

And maybe bad for her in vast quantities...

"Hi!"

Zoe and Josie both swung toward the back kitchen door as Zoe's mom and little brother came through.

"Hi, guys!" Zoe greeted.

She didn't seem surprised to see them. Of course, Maggie and Henry came and went freely from the family bakery but it was early. The morning rush would have just died down, and this was the time Zoe and Josie spent cleaning up, restocking, and then diving into the orders that had been placed. It wasn't as busy as the six-to-nine time frame, but they stayed pretty busy from six to noon every day. It wasn't the best time for visits.

"Where do you want us to start?" Maggie asked, moving to the sink to wash her hands.

"You're helping too?" Zoe asked her little brother.

Henry shrugged. "Mom said I can do cookies."

Zoe nodded. "Great. But they can't all be trolls."

Josie laughed at that. The last cookies Henry had decorated in the bakery—a skill that Maggie insisted all three of her children learn—had been green blobs with eyes. He'd claimed they were trolls, but everyone knew they were Henry-didn't-want-to-decorate-cookies cookies.

"Fine. I'll do some ogres too," Henry said with a grin. "But I'm going to need gray frosting." He looked at Josie. "Do you have gray?"

Josie shook her head. "Sorry. All out. I made a bunch of ogres earlier this week." Of course they *could* have gray frosting. They could mix any color. But Henry needed no encouragement.

He grinned. "Sure you did."

"How about butterflies?" Josie teased. "Or teacups? Mrs. Landers loves to have teacup-shaped sugar cookies with her tea."

Henry wrinkled his nose. "I have no idea how to decorate those."

Maggie nudged him toward the sink. "Of course you could," she said. "But I think Henry can do chocolate chip and peanut butter and the others that don't need to be decorated. That might just be best for everyone."

Zoe laughed. "I don't know. I have to admit that we sold a bunch of those troll cookies."

"All to Henry's friends," Josie reminded her.

"Still." Zoe shrugged. "They had real money."

They all laughed, but then Josie had to ask, "But why are you guys here helping—"

The back door opened again and a head poked through. "Hello?"

"Hey, Kelsey!" Zoe motioned for Jane's little sister to come in.

"Jane said to come to the back, but I wasn't sure if I should just walk in or what," the slender brunette said, coming through the door. There was a pretty blond with her. "You guys know Aspen, my stepsister, right?" Kelsey asked.

"Sure. Hi, Aspen," Zoe said. "This is so great. Welcome." She crossed to give Kelsey a hug, then pulled Aspen in for a quick one as well. "I'm so happy that you're doing this. It will be fun!"

She took Kelsey and Aspen over to the sink and showed them where to wash up and then grabbed them each an apron. Maggie and Henry had already moved to the other side of the kitchen. Maggie greeted the girls too, but she was busy pulling out ingredients and utensils for cookie making.

Josie just watched it all, stunned, and confused.

For one, what were they all doing here? For another, Aspen was here too? With Kelsey? The two girls, only a year apart in high school, fought all the time. Okay, lately they'd been doing better according to Jane. Dax had a lot to do with that apparently. But Josie had never expected to see them out together, just the two of them, on purpose.

Clearly, Jane had recruited them for... whatever this was.

Zoe came back to the middle island. Apparently she was going to teach Kelsey and Aspen cake pop making.

"What is going—"

But the back door opened *again*. This time Josie's mouth actually dropped open.

"Hi, everybody!"

It was Paige.

Her sister.

"Paige! What are you doing here?" Josie rounded the island to go to her sister.

Paige was four years younger than Josie. Their other sister, Amanda, was four years older than Josie. She was married with two kids and was a teacher. She had her shit altogether. She was the epitome of put together and living the small-town dream. Josie was... where she was. Doing okay. Figuring it out. Paige, on the other hand, was a... free spirit. That was how their grandmother referred to her anyway. She wasn't figuring anything out. Nor was she trying.

She owned the yoga studio in town, Cores and Catnip. It was actually a yoga studio and cat café. It was *actually* a yoga studio only because Paige had to have a place to keep her cat collection, and to afford them. And yes, the "collection" was a collection of real cats.

She was a twenty-one-year-old, crazy cat lady.

And completely unapologetic about it.

When people teased her that she'd never find a man who would tolerate that many cats, she always said, "Good." And then got another cat.

In fairness, she worked to adopt the cats out to new homes. But if they didn't get adopted, she certainly wasn't upset.

The craziest thing about Paige being here now, however,

was that she didn't eat white flour or sugar and never baked with either of them.

She was a vegetarian and baked only with things like almond and coconut flours. She never ate from Buttered Up.

"I'm here to help," Paige said with a bright smile. That seemed genuine.

Josie hugged her gorgeous, young sister. "Help bake?"

"Well…" Paige looked over at Zoe. "Or maybe clean up or wait on customers or whatever."

Zoe grinned at her. "I would let you bake if you want to."

"I'm willing to try."

"But you can't sneak in any artificial sweeteners," Zoe said.

"Stevia comes from a plant," Paige told her. "Just like sugar comes from sugarcane."

"You still can't use it."

Paige sighed. "Fine."

Josie shook her head. This seemed like a very bad idea.

"I don't understand what's going on at all."

"Grant set this up," Zoe said, her eyes twinkling. "But that's all I should say."

Grant had set this up? Because he knew that Josie was uncomfortable leaving Zoe shorthanded. That made her heart flip slightly.

"We can tell her now."

The deep voice rumbled from the doorway leading from the front of the bakery.

Josie pivoted to face Grant.

He had her so mixed up that she was leaving the blueberries out of the blueberry muffins, but just looking at him made her heart thump hard. She gave him what was surely a goofy smile. "Hi."

"Hi. I have a surprise for you," he said. He was also smiling.

It was one of those smiles that a few weeks ago had been

impossible to imagine on his face. But damn, he looked so good wearing it.

"Oh?" She played along.

"I'm taking you to Chicago for the weekend," he said, coming into the kitchen.

Josie was very aware that everyone had stopped what they were doing and were watching her and Grant closely. She widened her eyes, focusing on him, determined to make this look convincing. "Really? Chicago? What for?"

"A romantic weekend away," he said, coming to stand so that she had to turn slightly, putting her back mostly to the room.

She relaxed then. Without them all able to see her face it was easier to pull this off. She appreciated that he'd realized that. She smiled up at him. "That sounds amazing."

He nodded. "I have a seminar on Saturday. I was hoping you'd come with me, and we could spend some time together just the two of us before and after the seminar. I'll show you the city. We can go to some of my favorite places. There's a fabulous restaurant that overlooks the city that I think you'll love. Their desserts are to die for."

Josie tipped her head. That all did sound amazing. "I love dessert."

"I know."

His voice was a little gruffer with that reply, and she wondered if he'd done that on purpose. It caused heat to skitter down her spine anyway.

"So when are we leaving?" she asked. She glanced over her shoulder. "Looks like things are covered here."

Everyone was watching them. All of the women in the room were watching with wide eyes and big smiles. If she wasn't mistaken, even Paige was looking a little swoony at all of this. Henry was less impressed. But he was an eleven-year-old boy. She knew that Grant could win him over too if he started talking about the video game he and the guys had developed. It was Henry's favorite thing in the whole world.

Grant had officially won over the entire room.

"Right now," Grant said. "I have a bag packed for you in the car."

She looked back up at him. "Wow, really?" She'd packed the bag that morning before leaving the house.

"Yep. Everything is taken care of. All you have to do is say yes." He held out his hand.

Saying yes to this man wasn't difficult. And she was afraid that was going to be a problem. But she didn't even hesitate a second before taking his hand and saying, "Yes."

There was a collective happy sigh in the room, and Josie rolled her eyes at Grant even though she was smiling.

"I'll bring her back safe and sound," Grant said to the room at large.

"When?" Zoe asked, her tone teasing.

Grant looked down at Josie. "I think I'll keep her as long as she'll let me."

Ugh. See? That was romantic.

It was fake, of course. For the sake of their audience—who gave another collective sigh—but it still sounded good. And he was also referring to their trip. Not to their marriage—that no one else in the room even knew was on the horizon. Not even to their relationship. Just this trip.

Still, even Josie fell for it. For a second.

She kind of wished Jane was here. Zoe had never been a huge romantic before Aiden, but she was getting soft. Jane was still more practical, even with the love of her life, Dax around. She was softer around the edges too, but she wasn't the swoony-sigh type.

"Well, let's see what you've got, Mr. Lorre," she said, trying to sound flirtatious and not like she was torn between melting into a puddle of goo and crying because this wasn't even real.

"Oh, I've got a lot." He started tugging her toward the front of the bakery, not even realizing how what he'd just said sounded.

Josie giggled and looked over her shoulder. "Uh, see you?"

"Have fun!" Zoe waved at her, actually *beaming*.

Her friend and partner was so happy for her. It actually made Josie's heart twinge a little knowing that this was all made up because she needed her stupid gall bladder taken out.

The most *un*-romantic thing ever.

12

"I can't believe they all showed up," she said, tripping after Grant as he strode through the bakery toward the front door.

He lifted a hand to George and Phil as he looked down at her. "They all love you."

She nodded. "Yes. But... Zoe has to love me *a lot* to put up with Paige in the kitchen and Kelsey and Aspen together. The chances of them making it a couple of hours in a confined space without fighting are very slim."

Grant chuckled. "You'll have to tell me more about Paige."

"Okay." She smiled. She'd love to know more about his family too.

It looked like they were about to have a lot of together time. She supposed they could spend some of it talking. They were going to be *married* after all.

"Hey, Josie!" George called.

She looked back as Grant held the front door open for her. "Yes?"

"Maybe take your apron off."

She looked down. Sure enough she was still wearing her frilly yellow Buttered Up apron. She grinned and looked up at Grant. "Grant likes me in aprons though."

He gave a little growl. "Well, when you're in *only* an apron." He said it low enough for her ears only.

Though the looks George and Phil were giving her when she looked back at the older men told her they had an inkling about what Grant had said. Well, they'd both been married for a very long time before losing their wives within a few months of one another.

She giggled. "Maybe I'll just... bring it along." She reached behind her back and untied it.

"Good idea," Grant said.

"Very good," George agreed with a nod.

She blushed and giggled again. Maybe this wouldn't be all bad. It was already kind of fun.

She, of course, couldn't get used to being whisked off, well, anywhere. The kind of guy she was likely to end up with long term would be like her dad and grandpa. A salt of the earth, blue-collar guy who worked hard and was sweet and romantic but could only get her as close to Paris as a movie screen. But that would be enough. Because love was the most important thing, and knowing that he would be giving her as much as he possibly could would mean more than a guy like Grant dropping a few thousand dollars on a weekend getaway. Those few thousand dollars were like pocket change, and weekend getaways were as common for him as going to the movies was for her parents.

She had to remember that.

But when he escorted her onto the private plane waiting for them on the runway in Dubuque and offered her a glass of champagne, and then after landing, tucked her into the back seat of an actual limousine, and then walked with her hand in hand through the Four Seasons Hotel in downtown Chicago, and then opened the door to the penthouse suite, she knew she was going to have a very hard time remembering.

Especially when his answer to her question about why they were staying in a hotel when he lived here was, "Because I figure you've never stayed in a penthouse suite in a Four Seasons Hotel in the downtown of a big city," as he took to her to the window and pulled the curtains back to show her the view of the city and Lake Michigan.

Because that was freaking romantic.

He was making this trip into something special for her. Even if it was fake, or at least temporary, and the reason for them getting married was *not* romantic, he was making the process of doing it romantic.

She wasn't going to have the huge ceremony and the gorgeous dress and the bridesmaids and flowers, but the penthouse suite in the Four Seasons was not bad. At all.

Josie looked up at him. "Wow."

He grinned. "Yeah?"

"Yeah. This is pretty amazing." She looked around. The cream upholstery, the gold accents, the marble countertops. "Though flying on a private plane and the penthouse suite, for my very first time, is probably going to ruin me forever."

Grant paused and gave her a little frown. "Your first time?"

She nodded. "My first time flying. Or staying in a hotel."

"That was your first time flying? Ever?" he asked. "And you've *never* stayed in a hotel?"

Josie shrugged. "That was my first time. This is my first time." She swept her hand to encompass the suite. "I've stayed in two *motels* in my life. One was a family road trip to Six Flags. The other was a school trip in high school with our dance team." She grinned. "We made it to State."

"What's the biggest city you've ever been in until now?" he asked.

"Des Moines," she said.

Grant's eyes widened. Then slowly his mouth lifted into a sexy smile. "This is going to be fun."

"What is?"

"Spoiling you."

She felt her stomach flip.

Yeah, see? That was also romantic.

Dammit.

———

G rant couldn't believe how fun it was to spoil Jocelyn.

He'd bought things for women before. Of course. Occasionally. All right, usually it was just dinner. Tickets to shows once in a while. Sometimes flowers. Jewelry a couple of times.

Nothing compared to watching Jocelyn first step into the massive bedroom in the suite—it was one of two, but there was no way she was sleeping anywhere but in that master suite with him—and see the dress he'd had delivered for her.

Zoe, through Aiden, had helped him with the size, and he'd had Piper call and order something appropriate for a night out wining and dining—and getting married. Yeah, he'd had to confess to Piper that he and Jocelyn were eloping.

The thing about Piper was that nothing any of the guys did fazed her. Sure, it wasn't usually Grant doing crazy, spontaneous things. He was sure she'd blinked a couple of times when he'd first made his request, trying to figure out if he was serious. But Grant was always serious. And as crazy as eloping with a woman he'd known for about a month was, it really wasn't that nuts compared to some of the stuff Ollie and Dax had pulled. So Piper, being unflappable and amazing, had helped him with multiple last-minute details. A dress, a ring, flowers.

It was also the reason for his reaction when Whitney had

texted him, *This contest to find the new snack cake is out of hand. Already. We can't do it.* First he'd asked why, and she'd replied, *Ollie is... a lot.* Grant had simply laughed—because it was true—and replied, *Get Piper to help you with Ollie.* Hell, that's what he would have done if he was there and was finding the project getting big and crazy. Whitney hadn't been around Ollie long enough to understand that projects *always* got big and crazy when he was involved. She needed to learn now how to use all of the resources at her disposal. And Piper was definitely the best way to handle Ollie.

Piper could do anything. Even pull off a wedding with a few hours' notice.

This wasn't the wedding of Josie's dreams. It wasn't the forever wedding. But he wanted to make it nice for her. Something to make her smile. Something to make her even think back on it in the future as something a little more than a business arrangement to get her gall bladder fixed.

He didn't spend time analyzing *why* he wanted this day to be a fond memory. He just did. So he was making it happen. With help.

Piper had been able to do everything but one major detail. That, he'd needed Cam for—getting Judge Warren Perkins to marry them after hours.

Thankfully, Cam wasn't *always* an asshole. Or at least, he was an asshole to the right people, and Judge Perkins generally agreed that those people were assholes, so he and Cam were friends. Ish.

Jocelyn gasped and then spun to face him from the foot of the bed. Her hands were over her mouth, her eyes wide.

The dress was hanging from the outside of the armoire. It was white with shimmery threads of silver through it. The hem was uneven and would "swirl around her ankles," according to Piper. It was a sheath dress so would fit to her body and fall straight to the ground. The bodice was a halter style that hooked behind her neck and left her shoulders and arms bare. There was also a light silvery shawl to go with it to keep her shoulders warm when they were outside or if there was a draft in the restaurant.

Grant knew next to nothing about dresses, but Piper had rattled all of that off to him as he'd looked at the photo she'd sent to his phone.

All he'd cared about was the look on Jocelyn's face when she saw it. His instructions to Piper were, "something that will make her feel like a princess."

"Oh my God, Grant!" Jocelyn's hands finally fell to her sides, and she crossed to the dress. "This is completely gorgeous."

"Good." He crossed to the dresser and lifted the royal blue velvet box. He turned with it, opening the top when she looked over.

It was a diamond tiara. It was on loan from the jewelry store where he'd dropped more money than he should have on a ring. The jeweler had been happy to let him borrow the tiara for the evening.

Jocelyn gasped again.

"We have to give this back," Grant said with a tiny smile. "But the dress is yours."

She looked from the tiara to the dress then back again.

"I don't know what to say."

"Say yes that you'll marry me. Tonight." He set the tiara back on the dresser and reached into his pocket and withdrew the ring, holding it up.

She was going to get to keep the ring too. He was hoping she'd sell it, or maybe keep it in a safe deposit box as an insurance policy in case she ever needed it. He knew she wouldn't take a stack of cash or a check from him, but he wanted to be sure she was taken care of even after her gall bladder was out and those bills were paid.

"Tonight?" She stared at the ring.

"I have a judge waiting in his chambers for us," Grant said, stepping forward and taking her hand. "We can be Mr. and Mrs. Lorre by the time we go to the best dinner you've ever eaten, overlooking this gorgeous city." He tugged her forward and slipped the ring halfway down her finger. "And then I'll bring you back here to this suite, strip that dress off of you, and make you come on eight-hundred-thread-count satin sheets for the first time."

She looked from the ring up to his eyes. Her lips tipped into a smile, and he was certain she had no idea how fucking sexy that smile was.

"Yes," she said as she pushed her finger the rest of the way through the ring.

His heart thumped against his ribs, and he had to admit that no business deal had ever done that to him before.

"Get dressed," he told her. "We have a date with a judge."

"You're wearing a tux, right?" she asked.

"I am, actually." He'd wondered if it was overkill, but Piper had insisted he *had* to wear it, so he'd had his housekeeper deliver it from his apartment.

"Oh good," Jocelyn said, her smile bright.

He lifted a brow. "Yeah?"

"Definitely. I can't wait to see how hot you look in a tux."

"You've thought about that?"

"Of course. And of getting you *out* of a tux." Her smile was flirty and sexy.

He watched her move toward the dress and draw a finger down the front of it.

"I hope you're okay with us taking dessert to go tonight," he said, his voice husky.

She looked over her shoulder at him. "Why is that?"

"I'd really love to cover you in chocolate again. On those eight-hundred-thread count sheets."

But she shook her head. "Oh no, Mr. Lorre."

"No?" He frowned.

"For one, I intend to roll *all over* those sheets and I don't want them all messy. And two, that look on your face says there's a chance this dress might get messy too, and there's *no way* I'm letting that happen." She turned back to the dress, stroking it again.

"I can make you not care about the sheets, and I can buy you another dress," he practically growled.

"Nope. I want this one," she said, not even looking back at him that time.

Feeling challenged, Grant crossed to where she was standing, in three long strides. He put his hands on her hips and pulled her back against him. "Or I could just keep you here now, tie you to that bed, order chocolate cake from room service, and make you come over and over again while looking at this dress from across the room."

She pressed her ass against his cock. He was already getting hard just thinking about having her again. He'd truly been concerned last night, wanting her to rest, but she seemed fine today, and he wasn't sure he was going to be able to wait until after her surgery. Unless she was actually in pain, of course.

"You would deny me the pleasure of this dress? And stripping me out of it?" she asked, wiggling her butt against him.

He moved his hand to cup her through her clothes, rubbing the heel of his hand against her clit. She gasped and he said against her ear, "There's so much pleasure to come that I'm not worried."

She leaned back into him, her hand covering his.

It was her left hand. The hand with the diamond ring now on it.

Something about that grabbed him in the gut and twisted. This felt so damned good.

Maybe it wasn't till death—and they were going to have to leave that out of the vows because he didn't make promises he couldn't keep—but for however long it was going to be, he wanted it to be good.

He moved his hands. One slid up to cup her breast, teasing her nipple through the fabric of her dress. The other started bunching the skirt of the dress. He really loved that she wore dresses. It fit her. It was sweet and feminine. Jocelyn was smart and could be feisty, but she just wasn't the power-suit type. And he liked that. If he wanted a woman who could wear the hell out of heels and pantsuits, he could pick from about forty contacts in his phone right now.

Jocelyn was softer but no less strong. She knew what she wanted, where her loyalties lay, what was worth fighting for. They were just very different things than he was used to.

"Hold it up," he told her gruffly as her skirt bunched above her panties.

She did, gripping the fabric and letting her head fall back against his chest.

He slid his hand into her panties, finding her slick and hot.

Her moan as he grazed her clit shot straight to his cock. He pressed his middle finger against her clit and then slid into her tight heat. Her pussy gripped him and he pulled out, dragging his finger against her G-spot, then thrusting in again deep. He looked at her. Her eyes had drifted shut.

"Open your eyes and look at your wedding dress," he told her.

He liked calling it that more than he should.

She did, focusing on the white sheath.

"Now tell me, if I wanted to fuck you while you were still wearing that, would you tell me no?" he asked, his thumb rubbing her clit as he added a second finger.

"*Grant*," she gasped.

"Tell me, Jocelyn," he growled. "If I wanted this sweet pussy while you were wearing the dress you're going to become my wife in, would you deny me?"

Damn, he sounded like a freaking caveman. He felt like it too. She was going to become his wife legally, yes, but only legally. And only temporarily.

Why did it feel like all of this—the words *wedding* and *wife* and *married*—mattered so much?

He continued to stroke her, tugging on her nipple, his fingers thrusting deep. He put his mouth against her neck and kissed her.

"I wouldn't be able to," she finally said breathlessly. "I wouldn't be able to say no."

"Exactly," he told her, feeling satisfaction rip through him. "Because you want me more than a damned dress."

"Yes," she gasped, gripping his wrist where he was thrusting into her. "Yes."

"Good. Don't forget that." He pulled his hand away from her body.

She wobbled a little as he let her go. Once he knew she was upright to stay, he turned toward the bathroom, with a little smirk.

Three.

Two.

One.

"*Grant!*"

He looked back but continued toward the bathroom. "Yes?"

"You... that was... you stopped!"

"Yes. But I didn't stop until I made my point."

"Your *point*?" Her voice rose on the last word. "That's what that was?"

"Of course."

"Of *course*?"

He wouldn't have been surprised if she stamped her foot. He hid his grin by ducking into the bathroom. He washed his hands—though really he wanted to lick every drop of sweetness from his fingers and then put his face between her legs and lick her until she came hard and loud.

Then he walked back into the bedroom, drying his hands with the hand towel.

Her cheeks were pink—partially from lust and probably partially from anger—and her eyes were bright.

"That was mean." She crossed her arms.

"It wasn't as mean as telling me that you were more concerned about keeping the dress clean than you were about fucking me on our wedding night," he told her.

He tossed the towel back in on the counter next to the sink and then crossed his arms as well.

"I never said I wouldn't do that," she said, her chin lifting.

"You said you wouldn't let me cover you in chocolate," he pointed out.

"But that's..." She shook her head and then laughed softly. "That's a deal breaker, huh?"

He narrowed his eyes. "Maybe."

"Or is it that you're just so used to getting your way that you'll dig in on even the smallest thing?" she asked, walking toward him.

"I do really like getting my way."

"So maybe I need to show you that letting me have *my* way sometimes is good too."

"Not if it means—"

But she reached behind her and unzipped her dress then, and Grant forgot what he was about to say. The dress dropped to a little puddle of pale-blue-with-yellow-flowers fabric at her feet. She stepped out of it and reached to unhook her bra. That also fell to the floor.

Grant's mouth went dry. He had to adjust his fly as his cock realized that maybe it didn't have to wait until after dinner.

That had absolutely been the plan. It had been a good one too. Sweet. Romantic. Wait until they were married, wine and dine her, carry her over the threshold, all of that.

But while Jocelyn Asher was definitely sweet and romantic, she wasn't *only* that, and he should probably remember that.

"I'm just trying to show you that letting me get completely naked before you fuck me would be fine too," she said.

"I—" Grant had no idea what he'd thought he was going to say.

She smiled as if she knew she was short-circuiting his brain and went to the foot of the bed. She reached for the duvet, sweeping it to the side. Then she ran her hand over the top sheet. "Eight-hundred count, huh?" she asked, looking back at him.

He'd been studying the way that position made her breasts swing and the curve of her ass. He met her gaze. "Yeah." He didn't give a fuck about the sheets.

"I bet these feel amazing on bare skin." She stood and hooked her fingers in the tops of her panties, pushing them over her hips and down her legs.

As she bent to unhook them from her foot, Grant caught a gorgeous glimpse of the pink between her legs.

Yeah, this woman was going to get anything and everything she ever wanted from him. And she knew it. And he didn't care.

"You could stay just like that," he said, pulling the belt from his pants.

She looked back. And shook her head. "I want to feel these amazing sheets. All over me."

He stalked toward her, but she'd already sat down and then lay back. She stretched, rubbing her body—her completely naked, mouth-wateringly gorgeous body—over the sheets like a cat.

"Oh, Grant, you're right. These are amazing."

He threw his belt to the side, toed off his shoes, tossed a condom onto the mattress next to her hip, shrugged out of his shirt, and unzipped his pants. Then he grabbed one of her ankles and tugged her twisting body to the end of the bed. "Come here."

"Okay." She gave him a sweet smile.

Sweet, his ass. She knew she had him wrapped around her finger, and she was loving every second of it.

Well, so was he.

He shoved his pants to the floor and gave his cock a firm stroke. He watched her watching his hand on his cock. Maybe he needed to regain a little of the upper hand here.

"Come here," he said in a low, firm voice.

"I'm pretty much here," she said, moving one of her thighs to the side, giving him a heart-stopping view. She even ran a finger over her clit.

Oh, he could watch that all day.

He reached for her hand, pressing it more firmly against her pussy. "More."

She rubbed again, then dipped lower. Her breathing hitched, and her other hand found her breast, tugging on the nipple.

"God, yes. Fucking gorgeous," he told her.

She moved her legs restlessly. "I want you, Grant."

"You can have me," he told her, running her finger down and pressing it into her pussy.

"Now. Please."

"Give me your mouth," he told her, meeting her eyes.

Her pupils dilated and she nodded. She rolled to her stomach and moved to the end of the mattress as he took his cock in hand again. He guided the head to her mouth and she dutifully opened.

"Fuck, Jocelyn. Yesss," he hissed as his head slid between her lips.

Her smaller hand wrapped around his base as she licked his crown, then sucked slightly on the tip.

"Harder, honey," he urged, placing his hand around hers and his other hand on the back of her head.

She sucked harder and then opened her mouth wider, letting him slide deeper.

He felt the heat and pleasure to the soles of his feet. Grant gritted his teeth, holding back from thrusting hard into her throat.

He cupped her head and kept hold of his cock giving her only a few inches. But her greedy mouth, the way she licked and sucked and moaned around him, made it the best blow job he'd ever had. She was enthusiastic, if not overly skilled, and just being here with her, the way she'd turned the tables on him, the way she flirted and teased and seemed to relish being able to make him growl and get graphic, made this all so different, and so much more than it had ever been before.

"Need you." He pulled his cock from her mouth and flipped her backward.

"Yes," she agreed, spreading her legs and reaching for him.

But he wanted to see every inch of her. "Like this." He cupped her ass and brought her to the very edge of the mattress so that he was standing and she was laid out on her back on the bed. Taking in every glistening, sweet, pink inch of her, he donned the condom, and then sank into her slowly.

"Oh, Grant, oh, yes, oh, please." She panted in between each word, her body gripping his tightly.

Again, he found himself gritting his teeth to keep from just slamming into her and barreling ahead.

This position was heaven. He could see everything. Every bounce of her breasts, the flush that started on her chest and climbed her throat, her hands gripping the sheets, the way her mouth fell open to make the incredible sounds she made, her gorgeous blue eyes locked on his. He held her thighs in his hands, keeping her wide. She had little leverage, he was completely in control, and yeah, he felt like she had full command of everything—his body, his mind, his heart.

This was dangerous.

And nothing could have stopped him.

"Yes, Grant, oh yes!" Suddenly she was going over the edge, crying out, her body clamping down on his.

Grant thrust hard and fast, feeling the answering ripples of his own orgasm starting.

"Oh *yes!*" she shouted, coming hard, her neck arching, her upper body lifting off the bed. One hand still gripped the sheet, but the other reached for him, grabbing his arm as if needing to touch him.

"Josie!" Grant felt his body erupt, pleasure blasting through him, as her body gripped him, milking him hard.

He braced a hand on the mattress next to her, letting her leg dangle over the end of the bed.

He dragged in gulps of air, watching her work to catch her breath. Her hair was wild, her skin pink, her limbs loose, lying on the bed as if spent.

He realized he hadn't even kissed her. He remedied that. Leaning over, he met her lips with his. He felt her smile against his mouth, then return the lazy, deep kiss. Their tongues stroked, and her arms lifted to wrap around his neck, pulling him down on top of her.

As their bodies cooled, they kissed and ran their hands over each other's bodies languidly.

Finally, Grant lifted his head. "Huh, sex with you is good even without chocolate."

She laughed. "Told you."

He squeezed her ass. "I still want to fuck you in your wedding dress."

She looked puzzled. "Why?"

"I don't know." He couldn't explain it. He ran a hand over her hip. "There's something about it being your wedding dress that makes me feel like I need to *claim* you. Something about the ring. The whole thing."

She didn't laugh. Or look concerned. She just studied him. Then she nodded. "Yeah. You know what? I want to ride you in the back of the limo with you in your tux too."

His eyebrows shot up. "You do?" That sounded fucking amazing.

"Yes. While we drive around this city," she said, nodding.

"Why is that?"

"So that when you wear it in the future, or are in a limo again, or drive around downtown, you think of me," she said.

And that was it. He wanted to make memories. He wanted that dress to be *all* about everything he *could* give her. She'd never traveled before. Not *really*. She hadn't been pampered and spoiled. She hadn't been naughty in a penthouse suite. She hadn't been risqué in the back seat of a limo. She hadn't been married before.

He didn't know if she'd have any of those things again. But he wanted her to remember these firsts, and him, either way.

"I want you to ride me in the back of the limo with me in my tux too," he said.

"Yeah?" She looked excited and mischievous.

He loved that look on her. "Very much so."

"Then let's go get married so we can do that!" she said.

He laughed. "Well, that's one reason to get married."

Jocelyn scrambled off the bed. And gave him a hell of a view in the process.

Grant groaned. "Maybe we should shower separately. So Judge Perkins doesn't have to wait all night for us."

She paused in the bathroom doorway and gave him a sexy look. "Okay. But *next time* I shower, I want you in here with me."

"Done." He wasn't sure he had the willpower to stay out next time, frankly.

He wasn't going to think about the willpower he may, or may not have, when it came time to stay away from her for good. After all of this was over. After she was healthy and stable. After he was back in Chicago again. Alone.

13

There were worse ways to get married.

No one had lost a bet. There were no shotguns involved. No one was drunk.

And damn, her groom looked *good* in a tux. So good. Grant looked good all the time, but when she'd stepped out of the suite's bedroom in her shimmery white dress, she'd actually stopped in her tracks at the sight of him.

It was the tux in part. The man filled it out and wore it with the ease that the men she knew wore t-shirts and denim. But he'd also been wearing a smile that had caused her heart to skip a beat. A smile that had been quickly replaced by a look that was a combination of awe and heat.

"You look gorgeous, Jocelyn," he'd said in a gruff, low voice that had made her stomach flip.

She *loved* this dress. She never wanted to take it off. It glided over her skin like butter. It clung to her in all the right places but she didn't feel like she had to suck anything in or prop anything up with spandex or special bras. She was wearing a halter bra that she'd found in the top drawer along with a tiny silk thong. That was it. Two skimpy pieces of lingerie, the dress, and a pair of heels that she was going to beg to keep after the annulment or divorce or whatever. They were the prettiest shoes she'd ever worn. She wasn't a high-heels kind of girl, but these shoes could change her mind. They were princess shoes. The whole thing was a princess ensemble. Including the freaking tiara.

That she had to give back. She knew that. But that wasn't stopping her from loving every second it was on top of her head.

She felt sexy and beautiful and confident. And when Grant looked at her the way he'd looked at her in the living room of the suite, she knew that tonight was going to be magical.

She'd pushed the thoughts of gall bladders and hospital bills to the back of her mind. She'd crossed the room—she'd freaking *glided* across that room—she'd tipped her head to look up at the downright dashing man standing there, and she'd said, "I love all of this. Thank you."

It wasn't I love *you*, but it was honest, and it was appropriate, and it was better than *thank you for keeping me out of debt.*

"You are very, very welcome."

And that had seemed very honest as well. He'd offered his arm very gallantly and escorted her to the elevator.

"If I hadn't already been determined to take you out on the town," he'd added as they waited for the elevator, "this would have done it. I'm definitely going to be showing you off."

She'd smiled at that. She wasn't sure she'd ever been shown off before.

He'd leaned in just as the elevator car arrived. "And if I hadn't already been determined to fuck you in that dress, this would have done it."

Then the doors swished open, and he nudged her inside, with her heart pounding and her body warm and her new thong damp. But before she could come up with a response, the car stopped on the next floor and opened to let two more couples on.

She had to bite her tongue and Grant chuckled beside her. As if he knew. Well, she would get him back. Making the serious, always-in-charge Grant Lorre lose that control and have some fun had already been very enjoyable. She knew that he hadn't planned on having sex when they were up in the room earlier.

The rush of power that gave her was crazy. But she loved it.

The ceremony in front of the judge was simple. It was nothing like any wedding ceremony she'd ever imagined, but that was good. None of her friends were there. Her parents and grandparents and sisters weren't there. There was no beautiful meaningful music, and the vows were straightforward and basic.

The whole thing took about ten minutes.

And it was good.

Because she never could have gotten through it if all of those people had been there, if someone had sung "A Thousand Years" by Christina Perri, if Grant had said, "Love, honor, and cherish" to her.

She wanted all of that. But this, with Grant, wasn't it. So this ceremony was perfect.

The dress and tiara and ring were all part of this fantasy weekend getaway. Grant was part of that. The hotel suite, the limo, the hot sex. All of that was new, different, probably once in a lifetime.

She was going to remember this as a vacation, a hot fling, a dream. The ceremony was just a ten-minute reality check, and then she could dive back into the dream.

They said, "I do." They exchanged rings—Grant had one for her to slip on his finger as well. The judge pronounced them man and wife. Grant smiled at her. And it was a great smile.

Of course, it wasn't *love* on Grant's face. But damn, he was doing a great job faking it. And she thought she could safely call it affection. Grant liked her. He wasn't *upset* about being here. Starting a marriage with affection and *major* chemistry wasn't terrible. It wasn't even a terrible way to spend the entire marriage. At least when the marriage was going to be about a month long.

And then they kissed.

The kiss felt pretty real, she had to admit.

The way Grant cupped her face with both big hands and leaned in, taking her mouth in a slow, sweet kiss that didn't even involve tongues but promised at more—so much more—later... yeah, that all felt very real.

Then they were back in the limo.

She gave him a grin as the driver pulled away from the curb.

"Dinner first," Grant said.

"What do you mean?"

"I know what that look on your face means," he said. "You just keep your sweet ass on that seat for right now. We're only a few blocks away from the restaurant."

In spite of the wedding in a judge's office, she was feeling good and playful and not disappointed as she'd thought she might. "I don't know what you're talking about," she told him, running her fingertips over the back of his hand where it rested on her knee.

See, if he didn't want to do anything risqué in the back seat of this limo, he shouldn't put his big, hot hands on her. But Grant hadn't stopped touching her since she'd walked out of the bedroom in The Dress.

The Dress was how she was going to refer to it forever.

He'd held her hand, or had his hand on her lower back, or at her waist, or like now, on her leg, ever since she'd taken his arm to walk out of the suite.

"You're thinking about climbing into my lap, unzipping me,

moving that thong to the side, and taking me deep," he said, his voice rumbling, his hand tightening on her leg.

She was thinking about *exactly* that. But hearing him say it made her suck in a quick breath. "Would that be so bad?" she asked.

His gaze dropped to her mouth, then went back to her eyes. "You think you can come in three minutes?" he asked, his hand moving up and down her thigh, rubbing the silky fabric along her skin. "Because that's how far from the restaurant we are. And you *will* come before I let you off my cock."

Her whole body flushed. The sex was so good. That was going to be hard enough to let go of when this was over. But the dirty talk was going to be the biggest loss, honestly. She loved that.

"I think it's very possible that three minutes is enough," she told him, her gaze on *his* lips now.

He smiled, a wicked smile that made her not want dinner at all.

"Challenge accepted."

Oh, *yes*. She slid across the few inches of leather and hiked her skirt up, straddling his thighs.

He smiled up at her. Something in his expression made her pause. He looked far too satisfied. As if this was going exactly according to plan. Huh. That seemed less like she was teasing him to the point of abandoning all of his plans and more like he was in complete control.

He reached behind her neck and unhooked the tiny hook holding her bodice up. It dropped away and he curled a finger into the top of the cup of one side of her bra, pulling it down. He immediately lower his head and took her nipple in his mouth, licking and then sucking hard.

She gasped, arching closer, her hand going to the back of his head.

He ran a hand up her thigh to her hip and slipped a finger

under the lacy edge of her thong. But he simply pulled, rubbing the thong against her clit as he sucked on her nipple.

The car came to a stop, and he removed his hand, pulled her bra up, refastened her dress, and slid her off his lap.

"Let's go to dinner," he said, straightening his tie and then opening his door.

He slid out and then leaned back in, offering his hand. "You coming, Jocelyn?"

Well, she'd been *about to*. She glared at him. "That was mean."

He grinned. "I told you we were close."

"You also said you accepted the three-minute challenge."

"I did," he agreed, snagging her wrist and tugging slightly.

She slid across the seat and let him help her out of the car. Once she was standing, he put his hand on her ass and his mouth against her ear. "I didn't say when the three minutes would start though."

"They didn't start when the nipple made its appearance?" she asked, sounding huffy.

She was just wound up and completely *not* hungry now. Well, not hungry for food.

"That was what we call getting a competitive advantage," he said.

"Listen here, Grant Lorre," she said, sticking a finger in his face. "I *am* going to have sex in the back seat of a limo at least once in my life, and this might be my only chance. So we can go and have dinner and whatever, but you better not think that all you're going to do in that car is tease me."

He squeezed her ass, bringing her up against him more fully. "I have very *big* plans for you and that car, Jocelyn *Lorre*."

Her heart turned over, and her panties got even wetter and it had nothing to do with the *big* promise—that she knew he could deliver on—and all about him using her new last name.

She took a deep breath. "That's better." She wet her lips, smoothed the front of her dress, and stepped back.

He gave her a wicked, knowing smile.

Then they went to dinner.

It was a gorgeous restaurant. Exactly the type of place she'd always wanted to dine. Five courses, white linen tablecloths, multiple forks, the whole thing. The food was delicious, the wine perfect, and Grant was sweet about helping her pick things she'd like from the menu.

Josie had completely intended to tease *him* throughout the meal. Licking her fork and moaning and all of that. A lot like he'd done over those cheesy potatoes at Maggie's. But she couldn't tear her eyes away from the view out the window. Grant sat just to her right, but he'd given her the chair that looked directly out over the city and the lake. It was breathtaking. She'd never seen so many lights all at once in her life. She'd never been up this high. That all sounded so stupid in her head. Very small-town hick, to be honest. But she *was* a small-town girl, who hadn't traveled far beyond her own backyard.

Grant was giving her the trip of a lifetime. She turned to look at him as the waiter cleared their plates.

"Amazing," she said. "This is all amazing."

Grant was sitting, leaned back in his chair, his bow tie loosened, twisting the stem of his wineglass between his thumb and finger, and watching her. She didn't know if he'd looked out the window more than a couple of times.

"I'm really glad you're enjoying it," he told her.

She propped her chin on her hand and looked back at him. "Is it boring by now? You've seen it all so many times that it's nothing special?"

He frowned slightly. "No. It's familiar, yes." He glanced at the window then back to her. "I love this city. It's home. But I love watching you look at it more."

She gave him a slow smile. "That's sweet." It was romantic was what it was.

"You're gorgeous. All the time, but especially when you're excited about something."

The warmth that flooded through her was different than the heat he so easily caused to wash over her. "Thank you. It's may be a little silly to be so excited about all of this. But I've never worn a dress like this or seen a city like this."

He shook his head slowly. "I love seeing you with all of that too, but you're just as gorgeous when you're excited about simpler things. Like the day you handed me the box with the pussy cupcake in it."

She would never not blush when he said *pussy,* she decided. Not because it embarrassed her but because he made the word sound so dirty and delicious at the same time. She shifted on her chair. "I was feeling playful," she admitted.

"I like that look on you," he said. "You also looked beautiful the day Mrs. Milford came in to pick up a cake. You made a point of showing it to her before she paid for it."

Josie felt her eyes widen. "You noticed that?"

"I did. The morning she came in to pick it up, I was still there getting my scones."

Josie smiled about the scones. Those stupid, boring scones. "And you noticed how I looked?"

"Whenever you're anywhere in sight, I watch you."

She took a quick breath. "That should sound creepy."

"Does it?"

"No." It was hot. And kind of sweet. And the R-word.

"You always look very happy to be serving your customers, actually," he said. "And always beautiful. But I can tell which cupcakes you've decorated."

"You can?"

"You light up a little more when someone chooses one of them."

She shook her head. "It's crazy that you notice that."

He shrugged. "Maybe a little creepy too."

She laughed. "Maybe it's crazy that I like you being creepy."

"It probably is," he agreed with a small smile. "So what was it about that cake?" he asked. "You were especially... glowing when you gave it to her."

"Was I?" Josie remembered being not nervous, exactly, but eager to see Mrs. Milford's reaction. When the older woman had teared up, Josie had known she'd gotten it right.

"You were. I wanted to sweep you up and kiss you right there."

Her stomach flipped. "I would have liked that."

He gave a soft chuckle. "I'm glad to know that." He paused. "So what was it about that cake?"

"It was for her husband's college graduation."

Grant frowned slightly. "She looked like she was in her sixties or so. How old is he?"

"Sixty-six," Josie said with a smile. "He went back to college and got his accounting degree. Isn't that amazing? He didn't go to college after high school. He went to work with his dad for the railroad. But he always wanted to have a degree and to do accounting. He was diagnosed with cancer when he was sixty, and after he beat it, he decided that he was going to do the things he'd always wanted to."

Grant was watching her with an expression that was hard to decipher. "That makes sense," he finally said. "That cake was a part of a celebration that meant a lot to them, so you wanted it to be just right."

She nodded. "It's an honor to be a part of people's monumental days. I know it's just cake and it's going to be eaten and disappear. I know as soon as they cut into it, all the decorating and everything gets ruined anyway but... it still matters. To me."

"The cake can still make the day memorable," he said. "It's a part of the whole thing."

She nodded. "I'm glad you don't think that's silly."

"How can you caring so much about someone else's important days be silly?"

And Josie felt herself fall a little in love.

Oops. Crap.

The waiter came over to ask if they wanted more wine. Grant had him fill both of their glasses again, and then with his eyes on Josie, said, "And a piece of the triple chocolate fudge mousse cake."

Josie felt her eyes widen. That sounded sinful. And amazing.

The waiter moved off and Grant said, "It's not the same as someone making a cake specifically for us for today, but I think it's only right we have some cake to commemorate the day."

She nodded. "I agree."

"So what do you like so much about the city?" he asked, tipping his head toward the window.

She thought about his question. "It's pretty," she finally said. "The lights and everything. There's an energy here that's so different from what I know. There are so many things here—things to do and see, opportunities. Museums, shows, libraries. I'm sure there a hundred classes to take. I could learn to cook Indian food or make real Italian pasta from scratch. I could have someone teach me to make authentic baklava." She nodded. "It's all the different cultures and things to learn and experience."

He nodded. "But you could always come here and spend a few days and do those things and then go home."

"Yes. I guess that's true."

"You'd never want to actually live here," he said. He didn't phrase it as a question.

Josie didn't have to think about that very hard. "No." She

shook her head. "I think, for me, that's the intrigue of travel. Seeing things, experiencing things that are different from what I know. But then taking it back with me and making it a part of my 'normal.'"

"Tell me more about that," Grant said.

His posture still suggested that he was relaxed and casual, but he was watching her intently. He seemed completely focused on her.

Grant Lorre's full attention and focus was an intense thing.

Josie swallowed and sat back in her chair too. But she couldn't help playing with the napkin in her lap. "I would love to see the mountains, for instance," she started. "But I think when I got home, the mountains would make me notice the plains in Iowa more closely. I would love to eat authentic Mediterranean food prepared in Greece. But I think when I got home, I would pay more attention to how great the bacon cheeseburgers were. I think seeing the country, even the *world*, would be amazing and would make me appreciate other places, but I think it would also make me appreciate the things I have right at home more too."

He nodded but didn't say anything.

"What do you like about traveling?" she asked. "You do a lot of it, right?"

"I do. But it's more of a necessity. Not that I don't enjoy it," he added. "I've seen amazing places, eaten amazing food. But I don't have that contrast that you do. The places I go are very much like where I live."

"Greece and Rome and Paris and Honolulu and San Francisco are not like Chicago," Josie protested. "Or like one another."

"They're cities where I stay in a hotel that's a lot like the apartment I live in and eat food prepared by professional chefs and ride in car driven by other people," he said. "It's not like Appleby."

For some reason, that made Josie hold her breath.

"Appleby is the kind of place that makes you appreciate all of that," he went on thoughtfully. "Professionally prepared gourmet meals with things like truffle sauce and lobster tail seem fancier because you also know the comfort and goodness of homemade pork chops and cheesy potatoes."

Those cheesy potatoes were going to haunt her forever, Josie decided. But she liked what he was saying.

"The lights of the city seem brighter and more sparkly next to the old-fashioned streetlights and relative dark of the little town," he said. "The museums seem more majestic because you can compare them to the little house at the end of Main Street Appleby where they have photographs and items collected from when the town was founded."

"The museums *are* much more majestic than that house," Josie said with a laugh.

"But they're doing the same thing," Grant said. "They're telling stories about the past, preserving things that are important for the place they're in."

She shook her head. "Wow, you sound almost nostalgic about Appleby all of a sudden."

"Let's just say, I understand the charm," he said.

"I'm glad." She meant that. She didn't know if it meant he'd come back and visit more often. And that maybe she'd get to see him when he did. Maybe they'd try to keep dating. After their marriage was over. She almost rolled her eyes at how ridiculous that sounded. But even if it didn't mean Grant would spend more time in her hometown, she liked knowing that he'd think of it fondly. She could admit that it made her sad to think about a time when she wouldn't see Grant every day though.

Already.

How had this guy gotten to her so quickly?

"What is being here in Chicago making you appreciate about home now?" he asked.

"The darkness," she said with a smile, pushing the melancholy thoughts away. She was here in the big city, amid the bright lights, in a fabulous dress, with the most amazing man she'd ever dated. The man who was her husband. At least for now. She didn't want to waste any of this on being sad. "The quiet, of course. The fact that I can walk to my house from wherever I just had dinner and not have to sit in traffic."

He was her *husband*. Something about that suddenly hit her directly in the chest. He was hers. At least right now he was. They were on their first date, but this was also their *wedding* night.

That filled her with heat and anticipation and an amount of happiness that should have concerned her, probably, and a surge of *hell, yeah*.

She reached out and ran her index finger over his wrist. Just that. A simple, not particularly sexual touch. But she had every right to touch him, didn't she? To tease and tempt him. To seduce him.

She was never going to have a night like this again. She was going to take full advantage of it.

Grant didn't move a muscle, but his gaze heated. "I'm going to make you very happy to have to sit in traffic on the way back to the hotel."

She gave him a slow smile. "You'd better."

The waiter set the plate of cake down just then.

It looked absolutely as decadent as it had sounded.

"Oh wow."

"I want this cake to be memorable," Grant said. "Even if someone didn't bake it especially for us the way you do at Buttered Up."

She smiled, running her finger back and forth over his wrist. "Everything about tonight will be memorable."

His hand tightened around the stem of his wineglass, and she felt a little thrill at the obvious reaction to her. He definitely affected her and knew it. She wanted to make an impression too.

They had two bedrooms in the suite. They could get one of the beds all sticky and messy with cake and then sleep in the other.

"So maybe we could—"

"Go to the ladies' room."

Her eyes widened at the tone in his voice. Firm, commanding. Hot.

"What?"

He shifted, leaning forward, sliding his wineglass to the side and capturing her hand that had been tracing back and forth over his wrist. His finger ran over her palm, the touch igniting her nerve endings from her hand to her toes. Her nipples hardened just from him running the tip of his finger over her heart line.

"Go to the ladies' room, take your panties off, and take this —" He ran his other index finger through the thick chocolate frosting on the cake and held it up. "I want this on your nipples."

Her eyes widened and her breathing caught. "And then what?"

"And then come back out here."

"But—" She glanced around then leaned in so no one would overhear. "Pull my dress back up? With the frosting... there?"

"Yes." He lifted a brow. "I'll get the dress dry-cleaned."

She chewed on her bottom lip, studying him. He was so gorgeous. And hot. And dirty. And fun. And this was a once-in-a-lifetime night. He'd just turned the tables on her—of course. This wasn't going to be her seducing him after all. But how could she say no to this? She wanted him to think about this night as often as she would.

Josie wet her lips and pulled her hand from his. She stood,

set her napkin next to her plate, smoothed her dress, then reached out and scooped a dollop of frosting off the cake. Then she headed for the ladies' room without a look back.

But she could feel his eyes on her as she crossed the elegant dining room. Her stomach flipped and she felt herself smiling. This was more adventurous than she'd ever been. Yet it was still cake frosting. Something she knew very well.

That was funny and sweet and naughty and odd and perfect all at the same time.

She was alone in the restroom, fortunately. Typically, she would have taken a moment to appreciate the gleaming marble countertops and the ornately etched glass of the mirrors and the gorgeous gold fixtures. But all she could think about was the chocolate icing and how it was going to get all over her dress. And how she didn't mind as much as she should have.

She slipped into one of the stalls and reached up for the hook at the back of her neck—the one Grant had undone in the car when he'd been teasing her with the three-minute challenge. Her bodice dipped, and she reached into her bra with her sticky, frosting-coated fingers. She painted the frosting on her nipples, shivering with desire as she did it. This was beyond crazy and weird and sexy. She realized it was only in part about playing with frosting. It was also Grant testing her to see how much she would do for him, how far she'd let him push her.

The answer—very far.

He was her greatest adventure. He was the escapade she was going to remember when she was eighty and thinking back on her life. She hoped a lot of wonderful things filled in the time between now and her eightieth birthday, but she knew that she'd always think of Grant and smile.

With the frosting on her nipples, feeling naughty and slightly uncomfortable, she pulled the dress back up with one hand. She couldn't hook it that way, though, so holding the bodice up with one arm across her chest, she let herself back out of the stall and went to wash her hand. It was awkward, but she got cleaned up enough to redo the hook behind her neck before a woman came through the door.

They smiled at each other in the mirror, and Josie pretended to fix her hair as the woman went into one of the stalls. Once the door shut behind her, Josie quickly reached up under her skirt and pulled her panties off.

She hadn't brought her purse with her so she had nowhere to put them. She looked around for an idea, but finally just balled them in her fist. She looked at herself in the mirror once more.

Her cheeks were flushed, her eyes bright. She was panty-less, with frosting on her nipples, about to go back out and join her new husband for dessert. She grinned.

Best night ever.

14

Grant sucked in a deep breath as Jocelyn rejoined him at the table. She slid into her chair like a queen. Then she gave him a smile and reached over to put something in his hand.

Her thong.

He gripped it tightly and raised his other hand, signaling the waiter. "We'll take the check now," he told the man who appeared almost instantly, handing over his credit card. He didn't need to see the bill.

Jocelyn giggled and his gut tightened. God, he wanted her. He'd never wanted a woman like this. It was actually making him crazy.

He didn't know if he'd ever been with a woman who fascinated him the way she did. The simplest things made her happy. She appreciated everything from the fabric of the duvet on the bed to the fact that the butter pats on the table were in the shape of roses.

She was sweet and genuine and charming. She made him want to continually delight her. She was so in love with her hometown. She was so loyal to her friends and to her job. She did her work with her heart and barely worried about the money. And yet she'd gone into the ladies' room at one of the best restaurants in Chicago and painted chocolate cake frosting on her nipples and taken her thong off. For him.

He loved these two sides to this woman.

He tucked her thong into his pocket, signed the credit card slip, and shoved his chair back. He held out a hand to her.

She smiled up at him as she took his hand and let him tug her to her feet.

He couldn't resist leaning in and kissing her. It was too short, too superficial a touch, but he couldn't not do it. Then he turned her and escorted her to the door.

They waited at the curb for the limo without talking. The driver had been parked only two blocks away so arrived quickly.

Grant helped Jocelyn into the back of the car, then leaned into the passenger side window. "Hey, Tyler."

"Yes, Mr. Lorre?"

He liked Tyler. Tyler was his regular driver. He didn't always work nights, but since Grant had been out of town, Tyler had been happy to drive Grant and Jocelyn to their wedding and then dinner.

"I need you to take the long way back to the hotel."

"Yes, sir."

"The *really* long way," Grant added. "I want to show her the city. Take us by some cool stuff."

"Got it." Tyler was a Chicago boy, born and raised, so he could easily drive them past several sites.

If Jocelyn happened to be looking out the window while he got her naked in the back seat.

Grant climbed in with Jocelyn and shut the door. The partition was up, and they had the whole night.

"I told Tyler—"

But his wife climbed into his lap before he even finished the sentence.

His *wife*. The thought took the air out of his lungs.

Jocelyn cupped his face and kissed him. His hands settled on her hips, squeezing, pressing her against his already hard cock. She ground against him with a little moan.

Okay, so maybe Jocelyn didn't care about the scenery. He'd bring her back to Chicago and show her around any time she wanted. For right now, all he wanted to show her was how quickly he could make her come.

Kissing her deeply, he reached for the hook on her dress, pulling the bodice down, and unhooking her bra. He leaned back to look at her covered in smears of chocolate.

He thumbed her nipple. "See, your bra kept the dress clean anyway," he said, meeting her gaze as he rolled the hard, sticky tip between his thumb and finger.

She nodded. "But I'd better not leave this car with one drop of chocolate on me, *Mr. Lorre.*"

"Absolutely not a problem, Mrs. Lorre." He lowered his head, taking the chocolatey nipple in his mouth, licking and sucking until she was clean—and wriggling on his lap, pressing against his cock.

He moved to the other side and did the same, relishing the feel of her fingers sinking into his hair to hold him close.

"Grant," she said, panting. "I need you."

"There are so many more sweet inches of you to lick and suck though," he said, kissing his way from her breast to her mouth.

He kissed her, letting her taste the chocolate from his tongue. When he let her up for air, she gave him a dreamy, dazed look.

"And if you're going to lick and suck all of me, you'll have to lay me down," she said, her voice husky. "But I want to watch the city lights out the back window of this limo while you're buried deep inside me."

Heat and lust seized him and he squeezed her hips. Okay, so maybe she did care a little about the scenery.

Or maybe she just enjoyed making him crazy.

Either way, he pushed her back just far enough that he could unbutton and unzip his pants and push his boxers out of the way.

Her hand was there, wrapping around his length before he got the condom out of his pocket.

His breath hissed out as she squeezed and stroked and he let his head fall back against the seat. "Damn, Jocelyn."

"Oh, I really like the way you sound right now," she told him.

How this woman, the one stroking him like it was her job, saying things like she wanted him buried inside her while they looked at the city lights, was the same one who made cater-pillar cupcakes and got teary eyed when someone loved a grad-uation cake she'd decorated was beyond him. But she was one and the same.

And he was afraid he was falling in love with her.

He nudged her hand out of the way, rolled the condom on, and said, "Get that skirt out of my way."

She hiked it up, lifting her butt off his thighs to get it out from underneath her. With the skirt bunched at her waist, he brought her forward. He held her just above his cock.

"You ready for me, *wife*?" he asked, the word coming out naturally and making a surge of possessiveness rip through him.

"I am," she said, her voice soft. "So ready."

He brought her down, sinking down. They both groaned. Her hands gripped his shoulders as she took him. It was a tight fit—a holy-shit-nothing-has-ever-felt-this-good tight fit—and he paused, just breathing for a moment.

Then Jocelyn started moving.

He let her set the pace, watching her move up and down on him, her knees on the leather seat, her hands gripping his tux jacket, her eyes on the lights and traffic and buildings outside the car.

Pleasure and other emotions—affection, happiness, more that he wasn't quite willing to name—built as she moved, her pace picking up naturally.

Finally he couldn't hold back. He moved a hand between them, finding her clit with his thumb, rubbing and circling. She gasped and then moaned. "Yes, there."

"I've got you, love," he said, his voice gruff. "Whatever you need."

"Faster." She took a breath and tipped her head back, her hair spilling down her back. "Harder."

He circled her clit faster and leaned in, taking a nipple in his mouth, as he surged up into her. Faster and harder he could definitely do.

It only took a few more strokes to send her flying, and he was right behind her, thrusting into her, chasing that completion that had never been as good as it was with her.

"Fuck! Yes, Josie! Yes!"

Her body gripped him, and he emptied himself, a groan erupting that seemed to come from his bones.

She slumped against him, her arms around his neck. She rested her chin on her arm on top of his shoulder as she caught her breath, and Grant realized she was looking at the lights as she recovered.

He chuckled and ran a hand up and down her back. "And that's limo sex."

She sighed. "Wow, I really liked it."

"Me too."

She pulled back and looked down at him. "Thanks."

He lifted a brow. "Thanks? Seriously? This is the best limo ride I've ever had."

Something flickered in her eyes.

"What?" he asked when she didn't reply.

"I was trying not to say that I hope it's the best limo ride you ever have. Ever."

And this was where things got complicated. Because it was very likely this was the best limo ride he'd ever had, and it was almost over, and he didn't want it to end. Or he at least wanted to know he could do this all again with her—not just the sex either, but the lights and the laughter and the teasing and getting to know her.

For a guy who didn't want to get involved and have a woman too dependent on him—emotionally or otherwise—that all sounded, well, pretty involved.

"It honestly makes me dread riding in a limo with any of the guys at any point in the near future," he said, trying to lighten the tone.

"Why?" But she was almost smiling.

"Because if I replay all of this and Dax is sitting across from me, he'll notice me daydreaming and give me all kinds of shit."

Her smile grew, and Grant felt the band around his chest loosen slightly. "You don't seem like the daydreaming type."

"I'm not."

"But you might daydream about me in a limo someday?" she asked.

God, she was so fucking cute. And sweet. And he would absolutely daydream about her. Dammit.

"I think the odds are actually quite good," he admitted.

She grinned. "I'll take that." Then she slid off his lap, and they both worked to get cleaned and straightened up, at least enough to walk through the hotel lobby to the elevators.

Grant was glad that she was placated by the idea of him just remembering their limo ride together fondly. But he should have left it at that. He should have probably even withdrawn a little now that he saw her getting attached. He should definitely have banged her against the bathroom counter or something, reminding them both that they were fuck buddies with health insurance benefits.

Instead, he cuddled her. All night long. His arm over her, her butt tucked against his groin, her hair spilling all over the pillow, his nose buried in her neck. And after she'd fallen asleep, he realized she'd worn her wedding ring to bed.

And so had he.

———

G rant's seminar wasn't boring.

Josie was actually surprised by that. It was a seminar, with a PowerPoint presentation given in a hotel conference room, and it was about managing finances and budgets and investments.

It should have been boring.

But she was fascinated.

It didn't hurt that he looked hot. He was in a dress shirt and pants with a jacket, but no tie. And while the suits always did something to her, it wasn't that or that he was freshly shaven—after scraping her inner thighs with his morning stubble as he "kissed" her awake that morning—or how he'd styled his hair or any of that. It was his confidence, his smile, and honestly, how damned excited he was to be talking about this stuff.

He'd said she looked beautiful when she was serving the bakery customers and especially when they chose her cakes out of the display case. Now she understood. Watching Grant in his element, happy and excited and doing something he was clearly passionate about, and very good at, was a turn-on. Plain and simple. He looked hot talking about money.

Not because she cared about money—she so didn't—but

because he did. And more, he cared about these people. She'd had no idea what these seminars were about. She never would have believed that someone could make money personal like this and that they might *care* about the people sitting in the straight-backed hotel conference room chairs. But clearly, Grant did. He was part educator, part life coach, part cheerleader up there. He was teaching them about their finances, but he was also preaching that they not only *should* take control of their money but that they *could*. They had that power. They didn't need anyone taking care of them. If they were in control of their money, they were in control of their *life*. And he was going to help them get there.

She had to know more about him now. Why was he so passionate about this? There was a story there, and she couldn't wait to hear it. He was fascinating.

He was gruff and serious and protective and bossy, but he was also sweet and, dammit, romantic and passionate and so, so sexy.

Josie sighed and sat back in her chair, watching him up on the raised platform at the front of the room with the headset microphone, pacing in front of the screen that displayed his PowerPoint slides.

He was a grumpy, suit-wearing, money guy from the big city. Who, it turned out, *did* like her cupcakes, but could show amazing restraint around them.

And yes, she was never going to get over him.

They took an hour-long lunch break where everyone was on their own for finding food in the various restaurants in the area. Grant bought Josie a salad in the hotel dining room and they chatted as they ate.

"So how did this all happen?" she asked, waving her fork in the general direction of the conference room.

"The seminars?" he asked.

"Yes. Your passion for helping women become financially independent."

"My sister and grandma," he said. He sipped his iced tea then met her gaze. "My grandma was widowed at age forty-eight. Really young. She'd never even balanced the checkbook when my grandpa died of a heart attack in the backyard while mowing the lawn."

Josie felt her eyebrows rise. "Wow."

He nodded. "She didn't know where their life insurance policies were, where the key to the safe deposit box was—nothing. She was completely scared. So she quickly started another relationship. She was afraid of being alone and thought she needed someone to take care of her. Ten years later, he stole a bunch of her money and left her for a much younger woman. Very cliché."

Josie frowned. "Oh my God."

He nodded. "I watched her struggle after that, not just financially but also with her self-esteem. She felt stupid and used. She dated on and off but had a hard time trusting anyone, obviously. Finally, when I was old enough, I decided to teach her everything she needed to know about managing her money and her finances. I wanted her to be totally secure in that and how to take care of herself. I taught her everything from interest rates to taxes to investments. We've played the stock market together for about ten years now." He smiled. "Once she felt confident and secure financially, she was able to find a guy she really liked who she could get close to—because she didn't have to worry about him scamming her. Because she knew everything about her accounts and her money and could make all of those decisions completely on her own." He shrugged. "So they signed a prenup and got married about three years ago."

Josie smiled at that. "Wow. That's pretty amazing."

He smiled.

"What about your sister?"

Josie watched his eyes harden with that question. "My sister was in a flat-out abusive relationship," he said. "Corey wasn't physically abusive, but he was emotionally and financially abusive. She never had money of her own. He didn't want her to work, insisting that it was his place to take care of her. But he also didn't give her money to spend. She had to tell him exactly what she was getting at the grocery store, how much gas she was putting in the car, when she needed new clothes. And then *he* got to decide what she bought."

Grant's voice had gone cold, and he was staring at the tablecloth instead of looking at Josie. "He didn't 'let' her have things like makeup or perfume. He said that it would just lead to other men finding her attractive. He didn't let her buy ice cream or cookies because he didn't want her to get fat."

Grant's hand was fisted on top of the table now, and Josie could feel the waves of rage coming off him.

"And he didn't 'let' her buy birth control. He said she should want to get pregnant with his babies and that birth control was too expensive anyway." Grant's jaw tightened. "When she did end up pregnant was when she finally realized she had to leave him. She needed prenatal vitamins and he said no. Said they were too expensive, and she just needed to take better care of herself and the baby. She realized that he would deny their child all kinds of things—toys and treats—but she was also scared he'd skimp on things like car seats and other safety items. So she showed up at my house one night and told me everything and asked if she could stay with me."

"And, of course, you let her," Josie said. This man was the most protective she'd ever met. Now she had a very clear window into why.

His eyes met hers. "I did. And I'll admit, I was really fucking happy when her piece-of-shit husband came over to demand she come home with him. I'm not a violent guy but breaking his nose felt really damned good."

Josie nodded. "I'm glad you did that. *I* want to break his nose, even now."

Grant took a deep breath.

"Please tell me she's fine. Totally independent and in charge of her life. And that she and their child don't have to see him?" Josie said.

Grant blew out his breath. "She miscarried at four months," he said. "So the child isn't an issue."

"Oh, I'm so sorry."

He shrugged. "It's for the best, really. But yes, she's totally independent now. Fully in charge of her own life. And no, she doesn't ever see him. I'm very fortunate to know one of the best, take-no-shit lawyers Chicago has to offer."

She smiled. "Cam?"

"Cam," Grant said with a nod.

"Awesome."

Grant still looked incredibly tense. She hated that she'd brought this all up. But she really liked knowing these intimate details about his background.

She reached out and covered his hand with hers on the tabletop. She didn't know if he wanted comforting, or if he'd find her comforting, but she couldn't not touch him.

To her relief, and pleasure, he turned his hand over and linked his fingers with hers.

"Thanks for telling me."

He gave her a single nod.

"So you do all of this in their honor," she said, resting her chin on her other hand. "That's pretty great. Do they know?"

"They do. My grandmother has come to a couple of my seminars."

"That's so great. She must be really proud of you."

"I think so. I'm proud of *her*. She changed her whole life. Her whole outlook on life."

"And now you're helping other women do that." She really liked him. She loved being naked with him. She loved his romantic, surprisingly sweet moments, she liked the idea that she was a bit of a surprise to him as well. She loved his protective side. But she also just liked him. He was a good guy.

"I'm trying to teach other women a few things so they can do that," he said. "They still have to do the work."

"I bet you get emails and letters all the time," she said. "I bet you have a huge fan club."

He gave her a grin that made her lower stomach clench. "I do, actually. It's why bringing a wife along as an assistant is a good idea."

She felt her stomach swoop as it always did when he used the W-word. "Seriously," she said, smiling. "I *completely* understand why they want to be all over you."

He gave her a slow, wicked grin. "Oh yeah?"

"Even if I didn't know how good you are with your tongue and fingers," she said. "You're a unicorn."

He chuckled. "A what?"

"A unicorn. You're this incredibly hot guy who's young, rich, successful, could have any woman, the world is your oyster. But you're a huge champion for women. You truly believe that women can and should be independent and not rely on men. You spend your weekends telling roomfuls of women how smart and savvy they are and to trust and have faith in themselves and helping them take charge. And you're motivated by love for your grandmother and sister, for heaven's sake." She sighed. "Yeah, I would be shocked if women *weren't* throwing themselves at you."

His fingers tightened on hers and he leaned in. "Well, I'm not above reminding *my wife* that there are a couple of things she *does* need me for."

Jocelyn loved when he got dirty and playful. "Oh?"

"Like reaching that one particular spot inside her pussy that makes her eyes cross and her toes curl."

His voice was low and husky, for her only, and that spot tingled at the reminder. It was true that no one, including herself, had ever gotten to that spot before Grant. She swallowed. "I'll give you that."

"And you can't suck on your own nipples, can you, Jocelyn?" he said, his eyes dark.

She cleared her throat. "No, no I can't."

He looked smug. "Good. I just don't want you leaving my seminar thinking you don't need me at all."

She grinned at him. "Well, I probably shouldn't tell you this, but I haven't really been listening to the specifics."

He cocked an eyebrow. "No?"

"I've been too distracted."

"By?"

"Your ass. Your hands. Your mouth. Your package."

Now he was the one who had to clear his throat. "Is that right?"

She shrugged. "I'm wanton now."

He snorted softly. "Really. And that's my fault?" But he looked cocky. As if he knew that it was absolutely his fault and he was very proud of it.

"Completely." She really loved flirting with him. A few weeks ago, she never would have believed that Grant Lorre was the flirting type, but he not only brought it out in her, he seemed to genuinely enjoy it too. "Before you came along I was a sweet, small-town baker who thought cake batter and frosting were these innocent, fun things that I enjoyed baking into innocent, fun shapes like ladybugs and rainbows. Now I look at a cupcake, and my panties get wet and my nipples get hard, and all I can think about is how much I want to smear frosting all over your body and then lick it off, slowly."

He leaned in. "I'm going to be doing the afternoon session with a hard-on now. Mrs. Lorre."

Her stomach swooped. "You better not. I know I'm not the only one in that room checking you out. They'll totally notice."

"Then *my assistant* better get the hotel staff to bring a podium in there."

She giggled. "I'm on it."

And Grant did, indeed, do most of the afternoon's presentation from behind that podium.

Jocelyn knew that he could see her very smug expression even from the back row.

15

I *quit.*

Grant grinned at the text from Piper and simply responded with, *Again?*

She'd sent back a middle finger emoji.

He chuckled and texted back, *What did Ollie do?* He knew it had to do with Ollie. Piper told Grant she was quitting at least once a week. He never believed her, of course, but that was the signal that Ollie had pushed his luck with her.

She answered, *He talked Whitney into buying a circus tent for the snack cake baking contest.*

Grant snorted out loud at that. Ollie was turning the thing into an *actual* circus? Of course he was. *And you said?*

I asked if he wanted pony rides and a petting zoo too. Do you want to guess what his answer was?

Grant didn't need to guess. *No way would Whitney go for that.* But Grant felt a little niggle of dread. *Would she?*

Lord, was Ollie turning Whitney into an ally? That would never do. Dax and Ollie were enough. It had been a bit of a relief when Dax had stepped down from Hot Cakes to go do his own thing. Not that he didn't get Ollie going on crazy ideas, but at least he wasn't there all day, every day. And thanks to Jane, he wouldn't be hopping on planes at the last minute to take wild trips or getting thrown into jail in Italy. Or had that been in France? Grant couldn't even remember.

She would, Piper told him. *She's almost as bad as he is. It's like she had all this pent-up creativity inside her, and Ollie pried the top off, and it's now spilling out all over the place.*

Grant couldn't help but grin at that. Whitney needed a chance to be innovative and have some fun with her work. The company had been in her family all her life. She knew it inside and out, and it clearly meant enough to her that she'd stayed on after her family sold it. She needed a chance to be a part of its growth, and if she had some things she'd always wanted to try, they needed to tap into that. For her sake, and for theirs. The woman knew the market and the product and the factory better than any of the rest of them ever would. They absolutely needed to let her take the lead on any number of things.

Except pony rides at a snack cake baking contest maybe.

I blame you, Grant told Piper. *I sent her to you when she was worried about Ollie overdoing. Why didn't you stop it?* He grinned, waiting for her reaction.

I'm very, very, very good, Piper texted back. *But I think we both know that, at best, I can distract him or slow him down. I've never been able to really stop him.*

Grant frowned. That sounded a little less confident and good-natured than he was used to from Piper.

And now he's got her all caught up in his magical fantasyland. I think she's a lost cause, Piper added.

That didn't sound good. He definitely didn't need two Oliver types on his hands. But more, Piper could *not* get sick of Ollie. Fluke Inc., and by extension, Hot Cakes, needed her. Ollie needed her, actually. Someone had to keep his feet on the ground.

Keep them apart until I get back, Grant decided. *If they can't brainstorm together, maybe we can keep this from snowballing until I can be there.*

I'll do my best, Piper said. *But you should know that I'm "forgetting" to look into pony rides, the tent order "accidentally" got canceled, and I'm hiding his company credit card.*

That's my girl, Grant said.

I'm also considering putting a sedative in his orange juice.

Okay, maybe we don't need to go quite that far, Grant said. He would not put that past Piper at all.

Fine. But I expect gifts. You know my size.

About 750 ml? Grant asked.

You've got it.

He'd definitely get her a bottle of the Disaronno Riserva amaretto liqueur she loved. Even though it was almost four hundred dollars a bottle.

And you're not quitting. Ever, he added.

I'm not quitting, she agreed. Then a moment later sent a second text: *Today.*

Though they joked about it all the time, that last word seemed ominous suddenly. Dammit.

He would deal with *all* of that when he got back to Appleby. He couldn't believe he was adding Whitney to the list of issues though.

He quickly filled a plate at the buffet table and grabbed two glasses of champagne before heading for the table where Josie sat with four of the women from his seminar.

"Well, one of us reads out loud and the other does the foot rub," he heard Josie say as he approached.

Grant set the little glass plate next to Jocelyn's elbow as the women at the table all oohed together.

"You are so sweet," one of them said to him as he took his seat.

"Oh?" He glanced at Jocelyn. "Why do you say that?"

"They were asking about what it's like to be married to you," she said, smiling at the plate.

It was covered in petit fours. Piper had, of course, handled the catering menu for the reception after the seminar. But she always did finger foods—hors d'oeuvres and little cakes and tarts—and a selection of drinks.

He also handed Josie a glass of champagne.

"I was telling them how romantic you are. How we're really homebodies and like to just be together, doing simple things." She accepted the glass and took a sip.

Okay, so they were going to make up stories about their marriage. It didn't really matter what these women thought of him, or his and Jocelyn's relationship, and this could be fun.

"Well, I hope you told them about how I showed up at your work and whisked you off for a weekend getaway to Paris," he said, helping himself to a little cake.

Vanilla with raspberry filling. Yum.

"Paris? Wow. I thought you said you hardly travel other than back and forth to Chicago," one of the women, Cristy, said to Jocelyn.

Jocelyn smiled at her as her hand settled on Grant's thigh and she squeezed. "Oh well, there have been a couple of trips. But we mostly just go back and forth between here and Appleby," she said. "Grant loves his work so, of course, the seminars are really important, but Appleby is truly home."

Okay, so he'd definitely missed the intro to the conversation. But this was interesting. Maybe this would give some insight into how Jocelyn thought a perfect marriage would look.

"Appleby is a sweet little town," he agreed. "But obviously there's not as many business opportunities there."

Jocelyn squeezed his thigh. "Oh, but honey, I told them all about Hot Cakes."

"Yes, that sounds like so much fun! Making *cake* for a

living!" This came from Margaret. "Of course, Jocelyn does that too. It's so interesting that you're both involved with baking but in such different ways."

Grant put his hand over Jocelyn's on his leg, peeling her fingers—and fingernails—away and lacing their fingers together. "I'm very proud of what Hot Cakes means to the town," he said sincerely. "But Jocelyn understands how important these seminars are to me too." She did. She'd just told him so at lunch.

"Which is why I love traveling back and forth to Chicago with him," Jocelyn said.

"Well, not to mention the bright city lights, the high thread-count sheets, and that very special cake frosting you love so much from our favorite restaurant."

She nearly broke his finger as she smiled sweetly at the other women at the table. "We do have fun traveling too," she said. "But nothing beats cuddling up on the couch together with an old movie and the chocolate cinnamon popcorn that Grant invented just for me."

"Chocolate cinnamon popcorn?" Ashley, another seminar attendee repeated.

"Sweet and spicy, just like him," Jocelyn said.

"Wow, I just don't picture a millionaire who teaches money seminars doing such... domestic, sweet things like inventing popcorn flavors for movie night." Ashley looked at Grant with a soft smile. "That's... awesome."

Grant squeezed Jocelyn's hand now. What was she doing? She wasn't supposed to be promoting romance here. This was about female empowerment and independence.

"So, do you let Grant give you business advice?" Cristy asked. "I mean, it's pretty great to have such a guru at your beck and call, right?"

Jocelyn laughed. "Oh no, but I don't really need business advice."

"That's right, honey," Margaret said. "We've got this."

"Oh, I just mean, the bakery where I work is my best friend's," Jocelyn said, popping a petit four into her mouth.

"You're not partners?" Margaret asked.

Jocelyn shook her head, and Grant had to swallow a sigh. He could see where this was going.

"No, I work for her," Jocelyn said. She laughed. "I know nothing about books and accounting and stuff."

Margaret, Cristy, and Ashley all looked at Grant.

"Oh," Margaret said. "I guess I just assumed that Grant Lorre's wife would be... a business owner. Or something." She gave Jocelyn a smile. "I shouldn't have assumed that though."

"She has her own business," Grant inputted. "The bakery is her friend's, and Jocelyn loves her work there, so she continues to work with Zoe, but she has her own business as well."

"Of course," Margaret said. "That makes sense."

But Jocelyn was frowning at him. "Well, I'd hardly call it a *business*. I do some baking on the side."

"Well, sweetheart," Grant said, squeezing her hand. "Your customers pay you, obviously."

"Sure, but it's cash," she said. "I don't have a logo or business cards or anything, and I don't even keep that close a track of things."

Grant gritted his teeth. Not just because she was kind of making him look bad—which he recognized was not entirely fair since they weren't *really* married and since it shouldn't be a wife's responsibility to make her husband look good anyway—but also because what did she mean she didn't keep close track of things? Had she claimed her side income on her taxes last year? How did she account for her expenses?

"Wow," Cristy seemed a little confused. "That's... weird."

"What is?" Jocelyn asked.

"I mean, he talks about how important it is to have full control over your finances, to be independent, and to always know that you could fully support yourself if you needed to. But then he's married to someone who... doesn't care about all of that."

Jocelyn sat up straighter in her chair. "What? I'm independent. I could fully support myself if I needed to."

She had been, in fact, right up until yesterday when they'd gotten married, Grant thought wryly.

Well, except for the health insurance thing. The entire reason for their wedding in the first place.

"So you have your own accounts and everything?" Cristy pressed.

"I do," Jocelyn said.

"And he doesn't help with your books?"

"He does not," she answered.

She was squeezing his hand again, but Grant thought it was more just general tension than sending any kind of annoyed message to him.

"So you could walk away tomorrow and be totally on your own?" Cristy said.

"Of course."

But he saw how Jocelyn chewed her bottom lip.

She couldn't totally be on her own. That was *entirely* the reason they were married right now. She needed his health insurance. She couldn't have handled that by herself.

Yeah, the reality of the whole thing had just hit him too.

He'd just taught a seminar about how women should always be financially independent, even when they were married, and that money shouldn't be a reason that anyone stayed in a relationship.

But he had a wife now because she needed money.

He'd gotten married to take care of Jocelyn.

Fuck.

It wasn't like this was a brand-new revelation. They'd both gone into this with eyes wide open. But how had he let this happen? In his mind, marrying her to help her through her health crisis had been somehow different from marrying because she needed money.

But it wasn't.

She was dependent on him right now. It wasn't long term. He wasn't going to use it to manipulate her.

Still... it was the opposite of what he taught women sixteen times a year.

Dammit.

"Um, Grant?" Jocelyn asked, leaning closer.

"Yeah?" He realized that things were tense at the table. The other women were concentrating on their food at the moment.

"I think... we need to go."

It was uncomfortable. He might have just lost three fans, but he didn't really know how to smooth this over. Leaving it alone might be the best plan. He nodded. "Okay."

She was gripping his hand again. Yeah, well, he was a little annoyed too, but they could talk about everything later.

Actually, what they needed to talk about was how he was going to make her financially independent before their marriage ended. She didn't like to worry about numbers and budgets and spreadsheets? Too bad. She was going to learn.

"I think maybe..."

He looked at her and noticed she was suddenly very pale.

"Jocelyn?" he asked, alarmed. "Are you okay?"

She sucked in a breath and shook her head. "I don't think so."

"What is—" But then he saw how she was pressing her hand against her side. Her gall bladder. Shit. He stood swiftly. "Come on." He pulled her chair out and helped her to her feet, but she was having a hard time standing up straight.

"I shouldn't have eaten those cakes," she said. Her voice was tight.

"We're going to the hospital," he told her, bending and lifting her into his arms.

The fact that she didn't protest told him everything he needed to know about how bad she was feeling.

————

A t least she'd gotten hot sex, petit fours, and champagne before she'd had to have an internal organ cut out of her body.

Josie knew she was being dramatic and maudlin. But she felt yucky. Yucky being the perfect word to describe how she was woozy and a little sore and generally crabby.

Grant helped her through the lobby of his building. He was taking her to his apartment this time rather than back to the hotel. He'd decided that they should stay in Chicago for the first three days after her surgery so she could get past the worst of the recovery before returning to Appleby.

She was actually grateful about that. And that her gall bladder had decided that it needed to come out *now* while she was in Chicago. It wasn't like she had a surgeon on stand-by back in Dubuque. The only time she'd even ever had anesthesia before this had been to get her wisdom teeth out. So she didn't really care who operated on her. Chicago was, of course, full of fantastic doctors, and she'd had wonderful care at the hospital.

Now it was possible that she'd never have to tell her family or friends that she'd even had her gall bladder out. She might be a little sore for a few days after getting home—and she was going to have to avoid fatty foods for a while, including all the bakery stuff she loved so much—but she could cover all of that up.

According to Grant, as far as their friends knew, they were just having a fabulous time in Chicago, and he wanted to keep her here with him for a few more days. He'd left it to Cam to tell everyone.

Cam was the only one who knew the truth. Grant had asked him to call the insurance company and *ensure* that there would be no snags with getting the bills paid just because he and Josie had been married for only about twenty-four hours by the time she'd been admitted.

Cam had promised to handle it. Apparently one of Cam's favorite groups to fight with were insurance companies.

Josie knew how the conversation with Cam as the messenger with their friends would go.

Cam would say, "Grant and Josie are staying in Chicago for a few more days."

Zoe would ask something like, "Oh my gosh, they are? What are they doing?"

Cam would give her a give-me-a-break look and would say, "Probably fucking like rabbits, but I didn't ask specifically. Would you like me to call him back and get the details?"

Then Zoe and Jane would exchange looks, and Zoe would say, "Do you think they're falling in love?"

And Cam would groan and roll his eyes.

And Jane would frown and say, "Grant doesn't seem like the in-love type. She's so sweet. He'd better be nice. I will make him sorry if he hurts her."

Josie frowned as she watched the numbers on the elevator lighting up on their way to Grant's apartment. Grant didn't seem like the in-love type. She'd known that from the start. And then last night during the reception after the seminar, he'd resisted playing along with her romantic tales of their marriage. What was that about?

Her thoughts wandered back to their friends discussing the prolonged stay in Chicago.

Surely Dax would say, "Grant's a great guy. Nothing to worry about."

But Jane would say, "Great guy and worthy of Josie are two different things."

Which was so nice. Her friends were really great. They loved her, and they would want her to be happy.

She wanted to be happy.

She also wanted to be married for real. For good. Forever.

Suddenly she was sad. She knew she was melancholy partly because she was still feeling the effects of the anesthesia from her surgery and the pain pills. But it was real too. She really liked Grant. No, honestly, she was falling in love with Grant.

And now that her gall bladder was out, her time with him was on a countdown.

She sniffed and Grant looked over. "Are you okay?" he asked immediately.

He was sweet. He didn't mean to be. Maybe he didn't want to be, but he was.

"Yeah," she said.

"Are you in pain?"

Yes, in my heart, her dramatic little inner voice said. "A little. Maybe. I'm okay though."

He frowned, not looking convinced, but he dropped it as the elevator arrived on his floor. The top floor of the building. Of course.

He ushered her off and down the hall. He'd already moved all of their stuff from the hotel over here so all she had was a little plastic bag of items from the hospital. She was in a pair of yoga pants and a tee that he'd brought back to her. Her hair was in a ponytail and she wore no makeup. She was as un-put together as he'd ever seen her. The morning at her house after they'd slept together with no sex, he'd seen her bedhead and with no makeup too. But this was post surgery. She was walking slowly, her head was fuzzy, and she just wanted to lie down and sleep.

"I'm so sorry about this," she said as he let them into his apartment.

"Sorry?" he asked. "What the hell are you sorry about?"

"That this all flared up like this. This wasn't how we'd planned it. Now you're stuck with me until Wednesday."

"Jocelyn."

She was in front of him in the little hallway just inside his apartment door. She turned to face him.

"I'm not stuck with you," he said. His expression and tone were both serious. "I'm actually... relieved. I'm glad the surgery is over and that you won't have the painful attacks anymore. I'm glad you're here, in my apartment and city, where I can take care of you. I know where everything is here, and here I don't have to..."

That was all really nice, and Josie found herself very curious about the rest of that sentence. "Here you don't have to what?"

He looked like he was going to try to avoid a direct answer for a moment, but Grant Lorre was nothing if not direct. "I don't have to put up with your friends and family being here and doting on you."

She felt the corner of her mouth curl. "You wouldn't want the help?"

"I don't want them in my way," he said. He lifted a big shoulder. "I want to do this my way. Having you here works out really well."

Of course he would want to do this his way. He wanted to do everything his way. She shook her head but was smiling. "Well, I still feel like a burden."

"You're not a burden, Josie."

Her eyes met his. He'd called her Josie two other times. Both when they were having sex. He called her Jocelyn almost always, but twice, when they were as close as two people could get, and he was coming undone, it had been Josie.

She didn't comment on it, but she definitely made a note of it. She wet her lips. "Okay, good. I'm hoping for a quick recovery here."

Not really. The faster she recovered, the sooner she wouldn't need him. Already he'd fulfilled his part of their deal. He'd turned over his insurance card.

But she was definitely grateful that he wanted to take care of her in these next couple of days. And she didn't mind not having her mom, sisters, grandma, or friends here with her.

Not as long as she had Grant.

That should have been a red flag. Grant could replace the people who were closest to her? Who comforted her and made her feel the most loved?

That was weird. And probably a great way to get her heart broken.

But hell, she was this far in. She was pretty sure she was going to have her heart broken anyway. And she wasn't even going to be able to drown her sorrows in cupcakes or ice cream.

No one had ever recovered from a broken heart by eating salads and oatmeal. Those were two of the main things on her list of approved foods. Anything that was high in fiber and low in fat.

Ugh. This broken heart was going to especially suck.

"Let's get you settled. You look tired," Grant said.

"Okay." She was, of course.

He escorted her into the apartment with a hand on her lower back.

The apartment was gorgeous. Way too big for a single guy to be living in. The living room had floor-to-ceiling windows looking out over downtown and the lake. Much as the hotel had. Everything was sleek gray and granite. The floor was a dark gray wood. The only light color was the white stone fireplace and the light gray area rug under the enormous dining room table.

Honestly, the table was big enough to seat one of Maggie McCaffery's dinner parties with seats left over. What was Grant doing with a table that size?

There were touches of home though. A stack of books on the table next to the couch. Earbuds on the coffee table. Tennis shoes next to the breakfast bar.

"Bedroom or couch?" he asked.

She wondered how many bedrooms he had and if he meant *his* bedroom or a guest room. They'd slept together without sex the night he'd been worried about her, but she was fixed now.

"Um... what are you going to do?" she asked, looking up at him.

"I have some work I thought I'd look over. But only after you're settled and napping or whatever," he said. "I can make you something to eat. I can run out and get whatever you need."

"Would you..." She shouldn't ask. She shouldn't get more attached. She shouldn't make more memories that would make her sad later. But then again, why not? Why not have memories at least? Why not be able to look back fondly on the few days when she was married to a man she was in love with?

That thought made it seem even more like she *should* make these memories.

He shifted closer, his hand on her back bringing her against his side. "Anything."

"Would you sit on the couch with me?" she asked. "Could you look over your work there?"

It was dumb. He could sit wherever he wanted to in *his* apartment to do *his* work. Of course.

"Absolutely."

It was also dumb how hard her heart flipped when he agreed.

"In fact, if you want to watch a movie or something, the work can wait."

She stared at him. He was offering to watch a movie on the couch with her. That was sweet. Huh, after the whole thing at the table last night.

She nodded. "That would be really nice."

He smiled. Almost looking relieved. "I'm going to change clothes quick, then. You pick a movie. I've got Netflix, Hulu, all of them."

"Okay."

He started down the hall to the right.

"Hey, Grant?"

He turned back. "Yeah?"

"Which bedroom am I using?" She could use a brush and maybe some ibuprofen.

He lifted a brow. "My bedroom."

"You sure?"

"Am I sure that my wife will be sleeping in my bedroom with me?" he asked. "Yes, Jocelyn, I'm sure."

That sucked all of the oxygen out of her lungs and all she could do was nod.

"Come on." He tipped his head in the direction of the bedrooms.

She followed him into the huge master suite at the end of the hall.

"There are two other bedrooms," he said. "Only one is set up as a guest room since my family and friends all live close and don't really need to stay over. The other I use as an office."

She nodded, her wide-eyed stare taking in everything about his room. This room was warmer than the living room, dining room, and kitchen areas. He still, apparently, preferred cooler colors but in here they were darker gray and blues.

His bed was enormous. That was the main thing she focused on. They would not have to cuddle in that bed the way they'd been practically forced to in hers.

That was too bad.

Grant sat down on the end of the bed and started removing his shoes. "Bathroom is through there," he said, gesturing toward the wide doorway leading off the bedroom. "Or there's another down the hall. This one has the best shower though."

He tossed his shoes toward the closet, almost making them land inside the partially open door.

Josie grinned at that. He wasn't totally put together and organized every single second. That was nice.

She thought of her house and the multitude of colors and décor styles. There was no one "color palette" or "theme." It was a house. A *home*. It was full of stuff that mattered to her and that made her smile. It was a bit like the house at the end of Main Street that functioned as a mini-museum for the town, but her house was a collection of the history of her family. She loved every creaking floorboard, every mismatched throw pillow, every cluttered curio cabinet—and she had three. And the pile of shoes by her back door was a little ridiculous.

Grant stood and shucked out of his pants. In boxers only, he crossed to the dresser and pulled out a pair of gray sweatpants.

Josie liked that he was comfortable enough to undress in front of her. It wasn't as if she hadn't seen it all before. And she just stood, appreciating the scene.

He pulled the sweatpants up and then took out a long-sleeved black t-shirt. He unbuttoned the dress shirt he'd worn to the hospital and shrugged out of it. It was as he was tossing it toward the hamper in the corner that he noticed her watching him.

He lifted a brow. "You okay?"

"Very much so." She let her gaze wander over his naked shoulders, chest, and abs.

He pulled the shirt over his head, tugging it down over all those glorious muscles and inches of skin. "Be good," he told her, running a hand through his hair.

"Good?" she asked. "You're the one stripping in front of me."

"I was just changing clothes."

"Stripping," she said.

"I didn't know you'd be ogling me."

"Of course I'm going to ogle you, Grant," she said with a light laugh. "One of the perks of married life."

For a second they both stopped and just stared at each other.

He'd called her his wife earlier. It was, as always, hot when he'd said it. Hell, just an hour ago, she'd had to sign her discharge papers at the hospital, and he'd quietly reminded her to sign *Lorre* instead of *Asher* just in time.

So why did *this* moment feel different?

Was it the term *married life*? Because it wasn't going to be a *life* and they were both realizing it?

He coughed after the moment had dragged a little too long. "Good point," he said. "I don't suppose you need to change clothes?" He added a roughish grin that worked to lighten the mood.

She shook her head with a smile. "No and even if I did, not so sure the big bandage on my stomach is that sexy."

He crossed to where she was standing and looked down at her. He didn't touch her, but she felt his affection when he said, "There's nothing that could make you *not* sexy to me."

She was sure *that* wasn't true but she appreciated the sentiment. On impulse, she stretched up on tiptoe and kissed his chin. That was as high as she could get without him leaning over. But it did the trick.

Almost instinctively, Grant's hand settled on her ass and he pulled her in for a little hug. He kissed the top of her head and Josie felt her heart melt.

"Movie time?" he asked.

She nodded against his chest. "Movie time. After I brush my hair and take some ibuprofen."

He shifted back. "Do you need something stronger?" The concern was back in his eyes.

"No. I'm just a little achy. And the pain pills make me tired."

"Are you su—"

She put her hand over his mouth. "I will take pain pills when I need them. I promise. Ibuprofen is enough for now."

"Fine." He squeezed her butt and let her go. "You get the brush and I'll get the pills."

They met back in the middle of the room a minute later and headed for the living room together.

And when he tucked her up against him rather than on opposite ends of the couch, she smiled. And when he watched not only *Roman Holiday* but also *Only You* without pulling out any work, she felt her heart melt a little. And when he got up and came back with popcorn with chocolate and cinnamon on it—and admitted he'd looked up a recipe for it—she fell a little more in love.

"So, me telling stories about us at the reception yesterday made you tense," she commented as she helped herself to the popcorn in the bowl balanced on his lap.

He stiffened for a second, then sighed. He looked over at her. "Yeah. A little."

"Why?" She put a piece in her mouth and munched.

"Because these women are there to learn about being happy and content without a man," Grant said. "And then you were there, not just telling romantic stories, but about *me*—someone that had just spent the day coaching them to be their own person—but also made-up stories."

She thought about that and took another piece of popcorn. She gestured to the bowl. "Not made up now."

He rolled his eyes. "You know what I mean."

"So you didn't want them thinking romantic thoughts right after you spent the day telling them that they were fine alone," she said.

"Right."

"But that's not what you were telling them." She shifted on the couch cushion, propping her elbow on the back of the couch. "You were telling them how to be confident and independent with their money, but you never said that they shouldn't have relationships."

He frowned and didn't respond.

"That's what you want them to take from your seminars?" she asked. "Really? You want all of these women to walk out totally content to be single?"

"Yes." He didn't even hesitate.

Josie felt her eyes widen. "But... it's natural for people to want to be in couples. It's what we're designed for."

"It's what women are taught from birth to think they're designed for," he said.

"You think that falling in love happens because girls are socialized to think that's what they're supposed to do?" Josie asked, a little appalled.

They'd just watched two of her favorite romantic movies. And now her *husband* was telling her that romantic relationships were figments of girls' imaginations?

"Not just girls," Grant said. "But yes, society puts a definite emphasis on marriage and coupling up. Women who don't have a partner are seen as lacking somehow. Even nowadays when we should be so much more evolved."

Josie took a breath and blew it out. "So underneath all the money stuff and all the *you can do it* stuff you teach about loans and taxes and investments and entrepreneurship and everything, your message is *you don't need men and you should be happy single*?"

"Yes." Again, no hesitation or even further explanation.

"Wow."

"I'm not saying that people shouldn't have partners and get married," he finally said. "I'm just saying that women—*people*—

shouldn't feel that *that* is the ultimate way to be secure. They should *choose* to share their life with someone else rather than doing it because they have to or because all other choices are somehow worse."

Josie sat back on her cushion. She felt the impact of his words directly in her chest.

She was married to him right at this very moment because she had to be. She'd needed something from him that wasn't love or companionship or friendship. It had been money. They hadn't chosen to spend their lives with each other. They'd made an agreement to spend a few weeks together so that she wouldn't be burdened with medical bills.

Wow.

They were the perfect example of what *not* to do, according to Grant Lorre's seminars.

"Like us," she said softly. "People shouldn't do things the way we did."

He met her eyes. He didn't jump to deny what she'd said. "I don't think that most people get married the way we did," he said. "But I do think that there are marriages—or at least relationships—of convenience out there. The people involved are may not be aware of it at the time. They think they're in love or have feelings for one another at least. But the idea of moving in together to cut expenses in half or getting married for a tax benefit or someone supporting someone else while they go to school... those are all very real scenarios."

"And you don't think two people meeting and falling in love and wanting to be together forever is a real scenario?" she asked softly.

"I think it happens," he said. "But I think it's better when it happens if each person is independent and strong on their own, and they come together because they *want* to live together rather than because it's cheaper than having two places."

She nodded. She didn't know what else to say.

"Where did the story about reading to each other during foot rubs and the chocolate-cinnamon popcorn and the whole homebodies who love the simple things come from?" he asked after a moment.

"My grandparents and parents," she said. "I could have gone on and on with stories. Sweet, romantic, in-love stories from both of them. None of them ever had a lot of money, but they've always been madly in love."

Grant nodded. "Ah."

"You're thinking all my romantic ideas make sense now, right?"

He nodded.

"Just like all of your ideas about relationships make sense," she added. "I do admire that you're such an advocate because of your sister and grandma."

"My mom has been a happy single parent for most of my life too," Grant said with a wry smile.

Josie nodded. "We come from pretty different places."

"In almost every way."

"Yeah."

Yeah. She was still a romantic, but she was starting to think that the opposites-attract thing was kind of a bunch of bullshit.

16

"If you ever put zucchini, or any other vegetable, into one of my baked goods without my permission, I will never speak to you again."

Josie stepped into the kitchen at Buttered Up completely unnoticed.

Her sister, Paige, and Zoe were squared off across the center island, a plethora of baking pans and utensils between them. One bowl was definitely full of some kind of batter. Some kind of green batter. A green that was not created by food coloring.

"You put carrots in your carrot cake," Paige pointed out.

"And whole lot of sugar and butter and cream cheese," Zoe said. "It is not gluten free, nor is it low carb or paleo or anything else."

Paige nodded. "I know. Which is exactly why you need sugar-free, gluten-free zucchini muffins on the menu."

"No."

"They sold out yesterday."

"There were only twelve, and you took six to the yoga studio," Zoe pointed out.

"Still, the other six sold," Paige said.

"And Renee Wagner called me later and asked what the hell was wrong with them."

"It's not my fault Renee Wagner doesn't understand that almond flour tastes different from white flour."

Zoe took a deep breath. "Just make the lemon poppy seed, Paige. There, lemon. That should make you happy. It's fruit."

"They use lemon juice. That hardly counts as a fruit."

Zoe rubbed a finger up the middle of her forehead. "If you do it and you're good, I'll let you do the apple cinnamon too. Those do use actual apples."

"Fine," Paige said. "But you should let me do some low-carb lemon too. We'll do a taste test and see what people think."

"They'll think the low-carb lemon muffins taste weird," Zoe said.

"Different," Paige said. "They'll think they taste *different*. But we can educate them on all the health benefits. You can have a whole new line of healthy muffins and bars."

"The bakery is called *Buttered* Up," Zoe said to Paige. "That doesn't exactly scream healthy and low carb."

"Oh, but butter is low carb!" Paige said, almost excitedly. "You can have butter and cream cheese, even *bacon* on a low carb diet. Did you know—"

"Hi, girls," Josie said, deciding this was a good time to cut in.

They both swung to face her.

"Josie!" Zoe exclaimed. "You're back early!"

"Yep."

She'd felt so good—at least in regard to her surgery—they'd come back that morning instead of waiting until tomorrow as planned. She'd seen the surgeon that morning, and he'd declared she was doing wonderfully and could slowly return to her normal activities as she felt able. She had to watch how much she lifted, but that wasn't really a problem in her normal day-to-day activities, so she was optimistic about keeping it all from Zoe. And her family and other friends for that matter.

She'd had to tuck her gorgeous wedding ring into her jewelry box at home and leave it there, of course. Which made her sad. She loved it and had already gotten used to wearing it. But it was silly to wear a wedding ring when the marriage wasn't really real. And yeah, when they were trying to keep the whole thing a secret.

Paige came around the island and pulled her into a hug. "Thank goodness!" She let Josie go and immediately untied her apron, lifting it over her long blond hair and handing it to Josie.

"You're leaving?" Josie asked.

Paige turned, grabbed a zucchini, and tucked it against her chest, and nodded. "I'm taking my unappreciated vegetables and going home."

Josie fought a smile. "Thanks for filling in. I love you."

"I love you too."

"I love you too, Paige," Zoe said with a grin.

Paige looked over and gave Zoe an eye roll. "Yeah, yeah, I love you too. But your cupcakes make my stomach hurt."

"But they have butter and cream cheese and all kinds of great stuff in them," Zoe teased.

"And gluten. Evil, horrible, gut-wrenching gluten," Paige said dramatically.

"It pairs nicely with the white sugar," Zoe said, unapologetically.

Paige sighed. "Well, when you decide to have healthy food that doesn't twist my insides up into painful knots, you let me know and I'll stop by."

Zoe laughed. "And when you stop teaching classes that don't twist my *outsides* up into painful knots, you let me know and I'll stop by."

Paige grinned. "I have a new beginner's class. You kind of just lie on the mats and stretch and play with kittens."

"I'm in," Zoe said.

"Tuesday night. And I *will* have gluten-free, sugar-free pumpkin spice muffins for you to try."

Zoe mimed gagging, but nodded. "Can't wait."

Paige laughed, gave them both a wave, and swept out the door.

Josie watched her graceful, gorgeous sister leave then turned back to Zoe. "So how'd it go?"

Zoe laughed. "Fine."

"Other than the zucchini muffins."

Zoe waved that away. "Renee complained, but Janice Conner didn't even notice that the banana nut ones Paige made were sugar-free and made with almond flour."

Josie hung her purse up on the hook inside the door and donned the apron her sister had handed off. "I guess almond flour would kind of go with the nutty flavor."

Zoe nodded. "And I had to pay Paige ten bucks on Saturday. She bet me that Wilson Thomas wouldn't know that she'd snuck spinach in the double chocolate muffins."

"She did not!" Josie said, pausing in tying the apron.

"She totally did. *And* she used dark chocolate chips because they're healthier. I caught her at it just as she was slipping them into the oven."

"And you let her?" Josie couldn't believe Zoe would let that go.

"I told her that Wilson Thomas has been buying our double chocolate muffins for ten years and that if he said one word about them tasting funny she owed me ten bucks and had to remake the batch out of her own pocket."

"And he didn't say anything?"

"Nope. Said they were delicious. Of course, your sister is also part fairy or something. She probably put a spell on him."

Josie snorted as she rounded the island and took a quick inventory of the ingredients laid out. Looked like Paige had been about to start on the lemon poppy seed after all. "I don't know about that."

"She gets people to do the weirdest stuff," Zoe said.

"Like what?"

"I went to hot yoga last night."

"You did not!" Josie stared at Zoe.

"I did. Jane did too."

"What?"

"Yep. We almost died. Our bodies are *not* supposed to do some of that. And when she says hot she means *hot*."

"How did she talk you into that?"

"A spell. I'm telling you. Maybe she's a witch." Zoe nodded. "Probably a witch. Or drugs. She brought us smoothies. They were delicious. Totally full of vitamins and stuff. But she could have snuck something else in there. We had so much energy all day. And that's when she pounced. When we were all revved up and feeling great and she said, 'Come by the studio tonight! It will be so fun!' and we said, 'Oh sure, great!'" Zoe gave Josie a look. "It was *not* great. Aiden had to literally help me get out of bed this morning."

Josie laughed. "She's not a witch and it's not drugs. It's the cats."

Zoe nodded. "You're probably right. While you're there and twisted into these unnatural positions, you barely notice it because you're watching kittens play, and you've got a big old tabby lying next to you purring."

Josie grinned and started measuring ingredients. By heart. She'd made these muffins so many times she could do it in her sleep. She did notice that her sister had some golden flax seed off to the side, no doubt that she'd planned to slip into the muffins. Josie shook her head. Paige was braver than Josie in dealing with Zoe. Then again, Zoe couldn't really fire Paige. She was a fill-in who was friends with Zoe but only because of Josie really. Paige was a lot younger and had her own friends.

Whereas Josie couldn't lose Zoe. She wouldn't survive without Zoe in her life, and she certainly wasn't willing to have a falling out over muffins.

But as she zested the lemons, she wondered what she was actually afraid of. Zoe wouldn't let their friendship fall apart over muffins either. And Zoe needed Josie. She couldn't decorate like Josie. Not even close. She could probably hire someone else, but she'd never find someone with the skill *and* the relationships in town that Josie had. She knew their customers as well as Zoe did. People came to the bakery as much because of knowing and liking Zoe and Josie as they did for the baked goods they created. It was the whole package, and she was definitely a part of that.

Why had she not really thought about her value before? About the fact that, while she loved and needed and wanted this job, this job needed her too?

"Okay, I'm here, spill." Jane came bursting through the back door of the bakery, making Josie jump.

"Finally!" Zoe said, from where she'd just pulled blueberry muffins from the oven. "I've been *dying* waiting for you."

"You've been waiting for Jane?" Josie asked.

"To find out all about your weekend with Grant?" Zoe asked. "Um, yes."

"I would have killed her if she'd found anything out before me," Jane said. She set a bottle of wine on the island beside Josie's mixing bowl, then grabbed an apron from the hooks by the door and put it on. "I'm here to help with muffins, but I was thrilled to hear that you were back early!" She gave Josie a big grin. "So we're going to combine wine night and morning muffin making."

Josie glanced at the clock. She'd come in just after closing, knowing that it would be the best time to catch Zoe without any interruption from customers. Their busy time was definitely morning, but they had people stopping in throughout the day, and there was always a little rush just before they closed from people who needed dessert for the evening or wanted something for the morning without needing to get up early to come to the bakery.

"How did you know I was back?" Josie asked.

"Zoe texted me," Jane said.

"You did?"

"Of course," Zoe said. "And we've told Aiden and Dax that they have to take Grant out for a beer or something so we get his side of it too."

"Like this is high school?" Josie asked. She *really* wanted to know what Grant said to two of his best friends about her though. Just like high school.

"God, no," Zoe said. "You'd better have had *way* more—and better—sex than you did in high school."

"I didn't have sex in high school," Josie said. "Well, graduation night isn't really high school, right?"

Jane laughed. "Yeah, well, Grant Lorre is the type of guy to give you better sex just with a hot look than you had on graduation night."

Josie couldn't argue with that. Grant made her feel things just walking into a damned room than she'd felt for the first three guys she'd had sex with. Which either meant she'd been way too easy for those guys... or Grant was special.

She was pretty sure she knew the answer.

Jane moved in next to her and peered at the recipe for apple cinnamon muffins, reading over the ingredient list and directions.

Josie stirred the poppy seeds into the batter in front of her and pushed the bowl to Jane. "Here. Put this in the muffin pans."

Jane blew out a breath. "Thank you."

But instead of reaching for the muffin tins, Jane grabbed the wine bottle and twisted off the top.

Zoe laughed. "We have a corkscrew."

"In a bakery?" Jane asked. "I couldn't risk it."

"We do." Zoe frowned. "Though I'm not sure why."

It was on the tip of Josie's tongue to tell Zoe that she had come down one Sunday evening and experimented with some wine-infused cupcakes for a bridal shower. The maid of honor had found the recipes online but wondered if Josie would do them for her. They'd turned out amazing. Josie had felt guilty the entire time she'd been in the bakery, but she'd had to make such a big number of cupcakes at once, and her oven at home hadn't been big enough.

They should add those cupcakes to their off-menu menu. With the pussy cupcakes.

In the end, she just pressed her lips together and started on the apple cinnamon muffins.

Jane poured wine into coffee cups from the front of the bakery and handed them out.

The girls sipped and made muffins for about two minutes. Then Jane said, "Oh my God, Josie! What happened with Grant in Chicago?"

"Oh!" She'd been lost in thought. About margarita cupcakes with actual tequila in them and how they could add healthy muffins with zucchini in them to the menu. She looked at her two best friends. "Um, it was great."

"I'm going to need an adjective other than great," Jane said, leaning to refill her cup from the bottle.

Zoe nodded. "This is really uncool. You always wanted details about Aiden and Dax."

The thing was, she would almost rather talk to Zoe about her ideas for the bakery. She had lots of those suddenly. Or maybe it wasn't sudden. But they'd started to gel recently. Whereas, she had no idea what to say about Grant. He gave her butterflies and made her sad at the same time.

They'd decided not to tell anyone they'd gotten married, so she couldn't tell the girls about that.

What was the point of saying anything? The surgery was over, so no one needed to know about that. Her recovery was coming along great. In fact, she'd felt so good, that they'd come back to Appleby on Tuesday rather than Wednesday. They were just waiting to make sure all the bills went through and the insurance company covered everything and to see what the final outstanding balance was.

Then they could get divorced.

At least, that's what she was waiting for. She assumed that's what Grant was waiting for as well. Considering *he* was less interested in the whole marriage thing overall than she was.

But they had to have some kind of story about their romantic trip and extended stay in Chicago. Josie tapped into her feelings about those first few days. The flight on the private plane, the fancy hotel, the amazing dinner, the rock-her-world-ruin-her-for-all-other-men sex.

She had to focus on those things. Those were the things that made her stomach swoop and her body heat and her heart pound. But in an exciting, sexy, I have a big, hot, protective boyfriend way.

It was easier and more fun to think about those things instead of the last couple of days at Grant's apartment. The days since her surgery had been bittersweet.

Grant had been amazing. He'd taken great care of her. He'd cooked—*cooked*, not ordered in. He'd run her baths. He'd brought her medication when she needed it. He'd checked on her almost too often. He'd also sat with her on the couch, took her for walks through downtown, rubbed her shoulders and feet, and cuddled her at night.

He'd been the ultimate caretaker. Sweet and attentive and a little worried, but also just comforting and nice. Nice seemed like such a blah, weak word, but he really had been.

They hadn't talked any further about their outlooks on marriage and relationships and if girls were or were not brainwashed into thinking that marriage and family should be their destiny or if that was just a natural inclination for many. They didn't talk about their very different families. They didn't talk about their own marriage for that matter.

They also didn't have sex.

The whole post-op thing had something to do with that. She knew that Grant wouldn't touch her until he was positive she wasn't going to break and he wasn't going to be positive about that until the doctor cleared her.

But it was a great excuse for her to practice a little distancing—physical and emotional—too. Things were weird between them. They'd gotten married for practical reasons but it hadn't *felt* practical. It had felt like there were real feelings there. Until they actually talked about how they both viewed marriage.

She didn't think Grant *regretted* getting married. It wasn't that. But she did think he was a little worried about her turning this into more. She had to show him that she was a grown-up and could handle this being exactly what it was and nothing more.

But to do that, she had to pull back a little. It was far, far too easy to want to be close to Grant, in every way, and if she didn't watch it, she was going to not just get her heart broken, but she was going to end up embarrassing herself.

Not having sex with him was very helpful in not becoming even more attached to him. The sex was awesome, and not that it was a huge surprise, but it made it hard for her to separate her heart from her head.

"Wow."

Josie tuned back into her friends, realizing she'd been quiet and lost in thought for too long. She'd stirred the hell out of the apple cinnamon muffin batter.

"You don't even have words for it?" Zoe asked. She was leaning on the island watching Josie carefully.

"I think that's a fair assessment," Josie agreed.

"You're so quiet," Jane said. "You're *never* this quiet about romance and relationships."

That was true. But the romance and relationships were almost never *hers*. She'd had a thing going with Dallas Ryan, a local farmer, for a little while. Dallas was hot. And sweet. And sexy. And she'd thought maybe something could come of that. She'd been feeling butterflies in the stomach about Dallas and had gushed a little to Jane and Zoe about him.

But it had fizzled after a while. They'd only had sex once and it had been great. But it hadn't been Grant great. Now she and Dallas were good friends. He'd flirt with her when he came into the bakery, but he never asked her out and she never expected him to.

He just wasn't her one.

Grant isn't your one either, she told herself firmly.

She just really wished that he felt less like he could maybe, possibly, be her one. If he felt completely differently about things like marriage and family and relationships in general.

"I think I'm just tired," Josie hedged. She had, after all, just had surgery. Not that Zoe and Jane knew that—or would know that. *Ever* if Josie could help it.

"So is he staying with you right now?" Jane asked.

"How did you know that?" Josie asked. They had *just* gotten back into town a couple of hours ago.

"Dax mentioned it when I said they should go out for beers," Jane said. "He said it was a lot more fun when everyone was crashing in Appleby and didn't have to worry about driving home."

"Yeah, but Cam is crashing at *our* place," Zoe said.

"Oh, poor baby, you have to be quiet having sex instead of doing it on the kitchen table and yelling about it," Jane teased.

"Look who's talking," Zoe said. "I know about the Ping-Pong table in the Hot Cakes break room."

Jane froze and looked up at her. "What? Who told you about that?"

Zoe laughed. "No one. But I assumed you had done it on that table at some point and you just confirmed it."

Jane narrowed her eyes but nodded. "Well done."

Josie swallowed. She shouldn't be jealous of her friends. For one thing, she was so, so happy for them. She was thrilled they both had men they loved who loved them fiercely.

But she wanted that with Grant. She wanted to know he'd be there at the end of the day, whatever time that finally ended up being, because he wanted to be there, rather than because they were, essentially, pulling off a con. Conning their friends into thinking they were having a hot affair. Conning an insurance company into thinking they were married. Except they *were* married. And they were having a hot affair.

She supposed they were only conning themselves. Conning themselves into thinking that this wasn't a big deal. When it was feeling like a really big, messy, complicated, she-never-wanted-it-to-end deal.

"So Grant's staying with you," Jane said. "And you had a great time in Chicago."

"Yeah." Josie shrugged.

Jane and Zoe exchanged a look, and then Jane shook her head and set her wineglass down to cross her arms. "Nope. What's going on?"

"What do you mean?" But Josie could feel that she was on the verge of telling them everything. She wasn't a secretive person. She loved having friends and family that were involved in her life. She was already keeping the side-baking away from Zoe and that made her feel bad enough. She'd also recently realized that she was keeping her feelings about the bakery and wanting to be more involved from her friend. She did not want to have another secret.

And she *was* a romantic. If she was crazy about Grant, and they were having a fling that resulted in him staying at her place most nights, then she would be spilling to Zoe and Jane.

"Something is going on with you," Jane said. "You love romance. Now you have a big, hot, rich guy whisking you away for the weekend and living with you... and you're not saying anything? Come on. Did something bad happen in Chicago?"

Oh crap. Now they were worried. Jane looked sincerely concerned while Zoe was starting to look mad. "Seriously, Josie," Zoe said. "Do I need to call Aiden? Do I need to go over there and yell at Grant myself?"

Josie took a deep breath. "I think I'm in love with him," she confessed.

That took her best friends a couple of seconds to digest. Then Zoe blew out a long breath. "Thank God. Okay, that's more like it."

Jane agreed. "We figured you had to be by now."

Josie couldn't argue with that. She wasn't the weekend-away type. Not only because she didn't date guys who went away for the weekend—unless it involved camping and fishing. "We had an amazing time in Chicago. Very romantic. Fun." She paused. And sighed. "Hot. Very, very hot."

Jane and Zoe grinned. Then frowned. Clearly confused by what had to be a morose look on Josie's face.

"Why don't you seem happier about it though?"

"He... we're very different," Josie said. She was going to give them as much truth as she possibly could. She could use some advice, and she really did want them to know what she was going through. She could tell them everything without mentioning that she and Grant had already said *I do*. Probably. Though actually if it came down to it and she ended up spilling that too, she wouldn't completely mind.

"You are," Jane said. "But Dax and I are totally opposite and it's great."

"You're not though," Josie said. "Not in the *really* important ways. You both take care of people. Making the people in your lives happy and lightening their burdens is always what drives both of you. You do it in very different ways, but that's the bottom line for both of you."

"She's right," Zoe said to Jane. "Like Aiden and I—we're very different in that I love tradition and routine and the comfort of the familiar, while he's more of a big-picture thinker and a risk-taker, but deep down, we're the same in the important ways. We both care about the people around us, our families and our community and serving others."

Josie frowned as she thought about her two friends and their loves. "And the things that are different about you, make you each better," she said. She looked at Jane. "Dax's playfulness and adventurous nature makes you take things a little less seriously. While your serious side makes him buckle down when he needs to." She glanced at Zoe. "Aiden has made you take some chances you wouldn't have otherwise because *he* is the comfortable familiar that you need, and you've given him the roots and home that he needed to settle down."

They both just nodded.

"Grant and I are just different." She shrugged. "It's not bad. It's just... not going to last."

"You seem different in that he's serious and gruffer and more intense while you're sweet and sunny and fun," Jane said. "Is that true?"

"Yep."

"But that should mean that you can make him take things a little less seriously—like what Dax does for me," Jane said.

Josie sighed. "Okay, the thing is, he's very into people being independent, self-sufficient, not at all dependent on anyone else. He thinks everyone, especially women, need to be able to completely make a life on their own. He's not really into part-nering up. And I'm, obviously, very into wanting a partner, someone I can lean on and share things with."

"So he's cool with dinner and sex and a weekend together in a hotel and stuff, but not full time?" Jane asked.

"Yeah. I think he'd be really happy if I had my own place, my own accounts, my own everything, and we just got together once in a while for... fun. Sex. Trips. Dates. I mean, he likes spending time with me. He's sweet and takes care of me and likes to do things that make me smile. But he hates that I don't like spreadsheets and don't balance my checkbook every month"—actually, she hadn't told him that part—"and that I'm kind of paycheck to paycheck." She winced and looked at Zoe. "I don't mean anything by that."

Zoe shook her head. "I know. But I can see why that would bug Grant. It bugs Aiden too."

"I don't need anything more," Josie said. "I don't owe on the house. I paid my car off. I don't have any debt really. I'm fine."

Zoe shook her head. "But if something would happen—"

"I have a little savings, and I have friends and family I can rely on," Josie said quickly. But, of course, the voice niggled in the back of her mind that when she'd needed her gall bladder out, she'd had to go to extreme measures. Measures that wouldn't be available the next time. Unless Grant was up for getting married again if she needed her appendix or tonsils out. There were a surprising number of internal organs that a person didn't *actually* need.

"I'm just saying it's sweet that he just wants to be sure you're okay," Zoe said.

Josie shrugged. "Yeah. He just wants me to be okay in a different way than I want to be okay."

And *that* was her bottom line. It wasn't that Grant wasn't a great guy or didn't want her to be happy. It was just that his idea of how she should be happy was different than her idea of that.

She didn't need his money, but she did want to rely on him emotionally. She wanted hugs when she'd had a hard day and foot rubs when she was tired and someone to tell silly stories to and someone to play in the kitchen with. And she wanted it full time. Hell, they could have separate checking accounts if that would make him happy. But she didn't want him bugging her about budgeting, and she didn't want him feeling like she *needed* him for health insurance when really she *needed* him for... him.

"What do you mean that he wants you to be okay in a different way?" Jane asked.

"He actually teaches women to be self-sufficient and to not need men," she said. She laughed softly. "I—the most romantic person you know—am falling in love with a guy who would very much like it if every woman decided that she didn't want to have anything more to do with men than sex and fun week-ends and *maybe* a movie marathon on the couch once in a while."

"He *teaches* women this?" Jane asked.

Josie told them about Grant's seminars and about his sister and grandma. "I mean, he comes to it from a really true place," she said. "I can't fault him for any of it. But I want the marriage." She felt a jab near her heart. She had the marriage. She just didn't have the *marriage* that she wanted. "I want the Mr. and Mrs. I want melding everything together. If I'm going to do a weekly budget, I want to do it together, to figure out where the movie date will come from and if we can afford the popcorn and Junior Mints or if I should make some cereal mix at home and sneak it in."

Zoe smiled at her. "You've romanticized being broke," she said. "That's going to be hard to pull off with Grant, even if you can talk him into a real relationship. Seeing how he's a million-aire and all."

Josie frowned slightly. "That's true."

"You've seen the romance with your parents because they *had* to come up with little ways to show each other how they felt," Zoe went on. "They couldn't buy stuff, so they made up for it in gestures."

"That made it more obvious," Josie agreed. "I mean, coming up with unique, fun, sweet date nights takes more thought and emotion than making reservations at a fancy restaurant and booking a room at a hotel." But she had a little niggle at the back of her mind when she said it, causing her to frown.

Grant had booked the restaurant because it had the best view. For her. He'd booked the hotel instead of taking her to his apartment because he'd wanted to give her that experience. It might have been easy for him to make the phone call and to afford the final bill, but it had still been done for a sweet reason.

"I don't know," Jane said. "Dax has a ton of money too, but he still does little sweet stuff that means a lot more than buying me things."

"He bought your dad's nursing home," Zoe said with a laugh.

Jane grinned. "Yes, he did. And that was over the top. But he did it because he cared about me and my dad. I guess what I'm saying is that it's also about the intention behind what they're doing."

That was so much like what Josie had just been thinking about, she sucked in a quick breath.

Zoe was nodding. "It's true. And now that I think about it, I think Grant's rubbed off on the guys. In a really good way."

Josie perked up at that. "What do you mean?"

"Well, Aiden's got millions too. But he's never offered to buy the bakery or buy me an insurance policy or give me money to do anything with it. He's given me advice and gone over the books with me, when I've asked, but he'd always been really respectful of it being my business and not just throwing money at my problems for me."

"That's true," Jane said. "Dax has never said a word about me not working at the factory or him supporting me or anything. He didn't buy the nursing home just to impress me. He really wanted to work there and because it was a challenge for *him*. I'm sure if I wanted to quit and live on his money, he'd be okay with it, but I'd be willing to bet that's never even occurred to him."

"And you think that's because of Grant?" Josie asked.

"I think Grant's taught the guys, either actually or by example, to respect other people being independent and working and doing their thing their way. I think he's instilled a definite sense of respect for women," Zoe said. "They treat Piper really well."

"They do. They tease her like a friend, but they listen to her and include her almost like she's a partner," Jane said.

"And they've brought Whitney in on a lot of stuff," Zoe said. "Even though she worked for Hot Cakes before they bought it and was part of the family that basically ruined it, they've given her a chance to stay on and help rebuild it. I think that's pretty great."

Josie did too now that they pointed all that out. Grant's respect for women and his support of autonomy was *not* a bad thing.

"So you guys are making it work," she said. "The being your own woman but still in a relationship."

"We are," Jane said.

"Of course," Zoe said. "The guys would never expect us to suddenly change."

"Well, Grant *does* want me to change," Josie said.

"How?" Jane asked.

"He wants me to be more responsible and more aware of

my budget and more careful with my money." Okay, when she said it out loud it didn't sound so bad.

Zoe agreed. "And that makes him a jerk?"

"No. It makes us incompatible long term though," Josie said. Then she winced. "That makes me sound like I really want to be irresponsible and poor, doesn't it?"

Jane laughed. "A little bit. I know that's not what you mean though."

"But would it be terrible to let him teach you about spreadsheets or whatever?" Jane asked. "I mean, Dax has taught me more about Frank Sinatra than any person on the planet should know besides Frank himself." She shrugged. "Making him happy is worth a little painful boredom sometimes."

"And maybe he could teach you about filling out spreadsheets while cuddling on the couch," Zoe said. "You both get a little of what you want."

Josie sat up a little straighter. Curled up against Grant would make learning about budgeting better for sure.

"Or you move the spreadsheet session to the *bedroom*," Jane said. "Tell him you'll listen about formulas and columns and rows, but he has to be naked while he teaches."

Josie laughed. "I won't be concentrating very hard. I won't retain a thing he tells me." But she liked this general idea. She could meet him partway. That was very real relationship-ish.

"I'm just saying, learning spreadsheets is a lot more fun that way, and it will limit the amount of time he makes you practice," Jane said with a grin.

"Well, that sounds good when you put it that way," Josie agreed.

"And hey, anything that has the words *spread* and *sheets* in it, at least has the potential to be dirty and fun, right?" Zoe asked.

"You've become downright naughty since Aiden came back and took care of your V-card situation," Jane said with a grin, lifting her glass.

"Yes, yes, I have," Zoe said, leaning back with a very satisfied look on her face.

Josie smiled. She was feeling more satisfied than she had for a few days. Maybe there was a way to make this work with Grant. Give and take. Compromise. Teaching each other something new.

And if all else failed with the spreadsheet cuddling, she could always mix up some chocolate cake batter.

17

"We need to rethink everything."

Grant couldn't agree more. Though he didn't think Whitney was talking about the same thing he was. Namely his marriage to Jocelyn.

Whitney took the seat behind her desk and opened the folder she'd brought in with her.

Grant was seated in front of her desk. He'd been waiting for about five minutes, but Piper had told him Whitney was on her way. He'd arrived early, needing to get out of the house. That sounded terrible. But he'd wanted to leave Jocelyn's house because he wanted nothing more than to *stay* in Jocelyn's house. With her. Forever.

He was going a little crazy.

Especially since finding the plate of whoopie pies in the kitchen that morning.

Jocelyn had, apparently, gotten up either in the middle of the night or very early that morning to make them.

He'd made the mistake of tasting one.

The whoopie pie was the fifth best thing he'd ever had in his mouth.

Right after Jocelyn's pussy and her nipples and her tongue and well, any other part of her body. In that order.

It had been killing him to not touch her, not kiss her. He'd been keeping his hands to himself as she recovered from the surgery, letting it be her choice when they were intimate again.

She hadn't initiated anything yet.

That was also driving him crazy. Not only because he was dying to be with her again, but because he was afraid that she was pulling away. Not just physically, but emotionally as well. And he'd never been afraid about that with any other woman. Ever.

Needless to say, he'd been thrilled to get Whitney's text last night that they needed to meet ASAP about the new snack cake they wanted to add to their product line.

He needed something to take his mind off the fact that he wanted to stay married to his wife. He was sure that would sound as stupid out loud as it did in his head. Which was why he hadn't said it to anyone. Including his friends. Including his wife herself.

"Okay," he said, trying to focus on Whitney and his job. "What specifically do we need to rethink?"

"This contest is completely nuts," she said bluntly.

Grant grinned in spite of his tumultuous thoughts about his wife. His *wife*. Damn, he liked calling Josie that. "My understanding is that it's nuts, at least in part, because of *you*."

Whitney groaned and slumped back in her chair. "Oh my God, it is. I don't know what happened. I go in to have a short conversation with Ollie about something, and two hours later we're talking about food trucks and if you can hire acrobats for community events."

"Acrobats?" Grant repeated. "Piper didn't mention acrobats."

Whitney nodded. "Ollie said we shouldn't tell her."

Oh damn. Ollie knew enough not to tell Piper every plan?

What else was he keeping from her? From them? How much had he kept from them all over the *nine years* they'd been working together? Grant started to feel his head start to ache and knew he'd be heading for his top left desk drawer after this. That's where he kept the bottle of antacids with DAX written on the side in Piper's handwriting. OLLIE was written on the side of his bottle of ibuprofen.

"And *can* you hire acrobats for community events?" Grant asked.

"You can. But they can't do tightrope or trapeze stuff, of course. They can just do tumbling and juggling and things like that."

"So how many acrobats do we have coming?"

"None. If they can't ride a unicycle across a tightrope then what's the point?" Whitney asked. "That's a direct quote from Ollie, by the way."

Grant sighed. Partially in relief, for sure. "How did this circus theme happen anyway?"

"I made the mistake—in hindsight I realize it was a mistake anyway—of saying something about the whole thing turning into a circus," Whitney said. "He just took off from there. But"—she hesitated and sighed—"I got caught up in it. It was fun. Just letting the ideas run wild, not having any restraints. I didn't realize that he's actually serious about everything he says."

Grant chuckled. "He's not. He depends on the rest of us to tell him no or that it's getting crazy. I'm sure that when he saw you were on board, he figured he was on track and coming up with brilliant plans."

Her eyes widened. "He was waiting for me to pull him back?"

"Yep."

She chewed on her bottom lip. Finally, she sat forward in her chair and shook her head. "I don't want to. I don't want to be the person who says no or that we have to slow down or that he's thinking too big. I—" She swallowed and then met Grant's eyes. "That's pretty much all I've heard from my family about any idea I've ever had here. I don't want to do that to someone else."

Grant nodded. He'd figured there was something like that going on. "That's fine. We're a team. The rest of us have your back. You keep right on brainstorming like crazy with him, and we'll take care of making sure we don't have elephants and people being shot out of cannons at our snack cake baking contest."

Her expression was hard to read. After a moment she asked, "Will you all help keep my ideas in line too?"

"Do you mean will we let you throw out anything and everything and dream big and then make as much of it happen as we can and as makes sense, but will we also be honest with you about what won't work and why?"

She nodded, her bottom lip between her teeth.

He smiled. "Yes. Absolutely."

She let out a breath.

"Listen, without Ollie and Dax being big thinkers, none of us would be where we are today. I try to give them a long leash whenever I can. I like to think of myself as the guy who finds ways to let Ollie and Dax do their thing while keeping the company solvent and responsible." He paused. "If you want to be one of the big thinkers, that's awesome. The rest of us are here for... everything else. We'll all make it happen together."

She looked touched by that, and she gave him a huge smile.

That smile and the way she lit up made Grant think of Cam. His friend was still in love with this woman. He might not admit it, or hell, he might—he was Cam and was forever contrary and doing the opposite of what people expected—but it was true and Grant could see why in that moment.

Whitney was gorgeous, but there was more than her long

dark hair and her eyes and lips and curves. There was an intelligence behind her beauty. She wasn't as bold as Zoe or as down to earth as Jane or as sweet as Jocelyn. Whitney had a classy, sophisticated polish to her, but there seemed to be a lot of passion just underneath.

It was interesting that this was the woman who'd stolen Cam's heart. Cam was a fighter. He liked to push buttons. He was downright crass when he wanted to be. He could read a room—not that it always meant he pulled punches—but polished and classy were not adjectives anyone would use for Camden McCaffery.

Maybe that was the draw. The opposites-attract thing, Grant mused. That seemed the case with him and Jocelyn to a degree. They had very different backgrounds and upbringings.

But he couldn't shake the way she'd talked about his seminars. Even what he did for a living with the guys. He made it possible for them to shine. He helped other people recognize their potential and helped encourage them to see themselves as capable of more.

Jocelyn did that too. She made Buttered Up better than it would have been without her. She encouraged Zoe to try new things. He knew the recent addition of cake pops to the menu had been Jocelyn's idea. That seemed small, but he knew that with Zoe it took a while to get new ideas through. Jocelyn had done that. The cobblers and cookies she did for the busy women of Appleby seemed like a small thing, but it was an important piece to a much bigger picture.

And Jocelyn was fine being behind the scenes and helping other people have those moments of happiness. The graduation cake for Mr. Milford had been important, even those pussy cupcakes. Those had all been her using her baking to make moments for other people.

Grant was starting to see that small, simple, sweet things could add up to big, important things. Literally and figuratively.

Damn, he was in love with her.

He was married to her.

He wanted to stay married to her.

"Sorry I'm late."

Grant looked over his shoulder to find Cam striding into the room. Grant glanced back at Whitney.

She sat up straighter and gave Cam a little frown. "How can you be late to a meeting you weren't invited to?"

"Interesting point. Guess I'm right on time, then," he said, handing two white envelopes to Grant.

"For a meeting you *still* weren't invited to?" Whitney asked.

Cam dropped into the chair next to Grant and propped one ankle on his opposite knee. "Yep. What's up?"

"Maybe something you don't need to know about," she said.

"I'm the company attorney, darlin'," he said with a slow smile. "I need to know about everything."

Whitney sighed. She couldn't really argue with that.

"What's this?" Grant asked, taking Cam's focus off his ex for a moment.

"One is the insurance papers. All the bills have come through and are paid in full. The other is the divorce papers."

Grant lifted a brow.

Cam glanced at Whitney. "Oh yeah. Don't say anything to anyone about that."

Whitney looked back and forth between them. "Divorce papers?"

"Thanks, Cam," Grant said with a sigh.

"It's Whitney," Cam said with a shrug. "She's a great secret keeper. Aren't you?"

Whitney opened her mouth, her cheeks suddenly pink. Then she snapped her mouth shut.

Cam looked at Grant, but his expression was less playful now. "Don't worry. Whitney has secrets about me that she *still* hasn't told anyone."

Grant did *not* want to get in the middle of this. "I don't want to know."

"No, you probably don't," Cam agreed. "It's just stupid shit like her being madly in love with me and wanting to spend the rest of her life with me and her giving that all up to be fucked by her family's company instead."

Whitney gasped and narrowed her eyes. "Cam," she said through gritted teeth.

Grant let his eyes slide closed and took a deep breath. He *really* didn't want to get in the middle of this. "Okay, enough," Grant said firmly, leveling Cam with a look. "If you're going to be an ass, you need to leave."

Cam just relaxed farther into the chair. "Nah, I'll be good."

He wouldn't. Cam didn't know how to be good. But if he'd stop poking at Whitney, then it was easier to let him stay than make a big deal out of forcing him out. The other option was to tell him the meeting was already over. But Grant did want to hash out some of these details of the new product, and it wouldn't hurt to have their lawyer here for that.

He decided to divert the conversation. And the best topic for that was, unfortunately, him.

"Jocelyn and I got married in Chicago," Grant told Whitney.

Her eyes widened. "Congratulations."

He shook his head. "It was... purely practical."

That's a lie, a voice in his head protested. It was that word *purely* that was tripping him up, he realized. Because they *had* gotten married for a very practical reason. It just hadn't been the only reason he'd been happy to be saying *I do* to her in that judge's chamber.

"She needed health insurance to cover her gall bladder surgery," Grant explained. "It was the easiest way take care of that."

Whitney nodded. "Okay."

Grant looked at her closely. She seemed to be accepting it all easily enough. "Really?"

"It's none of my business," Whitney said. "And even if it was, it makes sense."

Grant nodded. Okay. See, this was what it was like to deal with commonsense, practical people who understood black and white. Whitney wasn't *just* a big thinker and dreamer. "Thank you."

"And now you're getting divorced?" she asked, glancing at Cam.

Cam lifted a shoulder. "As soon as they sign the papers anyway. Everything's taken care of. No reason to stay married."

"The bills are already paid?" Grant asked, looking down at the envelope in his hand.

"I encouraged them to rush it," Cam said.

"How?"

"I'm very good at my job, and I have a lot of connections," Cam said as if it was the most obvious thing.

Both of those things were true, and Grant had no reason or way to argue them. "Why did you think they had to go through so fast?"

Now that the bills were paid, there wasn't really a practical reason for him and Jocelyn to stay married. He had figured that it would take at least thirty days for the hospital to file everything and for it to go through. Thirty days was a great amount of time for him to be sure the she was fully healed and back to normal.

It had now been three weekdays.

"Why not?" Cam gave him an assessing look. "I figured you'd want it taken care of. And that's what I do. I take care of stuff."

"They won't think that's suspect? When we end up divorced so quickly?" Grant asked.

Cam shrugged again. "I'm not sure it matters if they think

it's suspect. You were actually married at the time we filed the claim. She actually had a medical need for the procedure. The claims were filed properly, albeit quickly. They paid the claim. It went through a little faster than usual, but it wasn't fudged in any way. There's nothing illegal about it." He grinned. "They can try to deny it. I'd be happy to discuss it with them further."

Grant sighed. Cam had probably pushed the insurance claim through extra fast in the hope that they'd come back and want to fight about it. He was probably bored. There hadn't been as much legal work to do with Hot Cakes since the purchase had gone through.

Hell, it was very likely why Cam had come into Whitney's office. He'd probably asked Piper where Grant was and as soon as she'd said he was in with Whitney, Cam's eyes had probably lit up.

He was such an ass. But such a loyal, good-guy ass. He loved to fight, but he fought for the right things. And if he cared about you, he'd fight for you to the death.

That was the problem with a guy like Cam falling in love. Once he fell, he never got over it. It was very possible that he'd never get over Whitney and he'd die an old bachelor. A *cantankerous* old bachelor.

Okay, fine, so now the bills for Jocelyn's gall bladder surgery were taken care of. "These are the divorce papers?" Grant asked, holding up the other envelope.

"Yep." Cam gave him that thoughtful look again. "Do with them what you will."

"What does that mean?"

"Once you both sign, the divorce will go through quickly. You don't have any mutual assets and no one's contesting anything. There're no kids. I've made it very simple," Cam said. "But, of course, you're married until you both sign."

Grant looked down at the envelope. Right. They had to

actually sign the papers to end the marriage. Regardless of the hospital bills. "Is there a time limit on it?" Grant asked.

Cam shot Whitney a look. Grant looked at her too. She looked surprised, but she was pressing her lips together as if to keep from saying anything.

"Not really," Cam said. "I'll work it out whenever you sign. But the longer you play at husband and wife, the harder it might be to keep this simple."

Grant wanted to protest the use of the word *playing*. Which was the first red flag.

The fact that he thought *it's already not simple* was red flag number two.

The fact that he asked his next question was red flag number three.

"You think we might develop real feelings for each other if we keep this going?"

Cam looked at Whitney again. Then he nodded. "I think it's possible. Yeah."

The fact that Grant liked the idea that Jocelyn's feelings could grow was red flag number four.

"Grant," Cam said.

"Yeah?" He looked up at his friend.

"Are you going to sign those papers tonight?"

Grant already knew the answer to that question. "No."

"I see." Cam shifted on his chair, leaning forward to rest his forearms on his thighs, pinning Grant with a direct look. "Why not?"

"I need to be sure she'll be okay first."

"Is she not feeling well?" Whitney asked. "Having trouble with her recovery?"

"She's feeling great. Doctor said everything turned out perfectly."

"Then why are you concerned?" Whitney asked.

"She needs to be okay financially," Grant said. "That's why

we had to do this in the first place." He looked at Cam. "Can you put something in the divorce papers that she gets part of my money?"

Cam's eyebrows shot up. "Alimony?"

"Yes."

"You've been married for five days."

"So?"

"I'm not doing that, Grant," Cam said firmly.

"You should if I want you to."

"As your attorney, and even more as your friend, I am telling you that's a bad idea," Cam said. "I'm not doing it."

"She needs to be taken care of," Grant insisted.

His stomach was tightening, and his heart was pounding. He had no reason to keep Jocelyn married to him. He'd married her because she'd needed taking care of. She'd agreed to it because she'd needed taking care of. It was exactly what he taught other women *not* to do. He had to let her go, let her out of it. He couldn't keep her legally or financially tied to him.

But he also couldn't just turn her loose. She needed to be financially independent so she didn't end up in another situation where she was putting off taking care of something because she didn't have the money, jeopardizing her health or safety.

Grant felt his gut twist. No, he couldn't let her go completely until he knew she'd be okay.

"Okay, well, I understand where you're coming from," Cam said.

He was using his calm, reasonable voice—which irritated the fuck out of Grant because it sounded condescending as hell since Grant was supposed to be the calm, reasonable one.

He suddenly wasn't feeling calm or reasonable.

"Josie will never go for it," Cam said.

"She will," Grant told him. "I'll talk to her."

Cam lifted a brow. "I've known Josie most of her life. There is no way she's going to take money from you, ongoing, into perpetuity, just because you were married—a marriage of convenience, I might add—for five days."

She hadn't even wanted to take money from him for the surgery, Grant acknowledged. To himself only, of course. But she hadn't even wanted him to help her with that.

Fuck.

Grant shoved a hand through his hair. "I want her taken care of."

Cam looked at him for a long moment. Then he sat back in his chair. "You could stay married."

"No."

Cam looked at Whitney again. Whitney's eyebrows were up.

"Why not?" Cam asked. "You like her. She seems to like you."

"Because I..." Grant swallowed. "I don't want her to *need* me. I don't want her with me just because she needs money or health insurance. I want her to want to be with me. To choose me when she has every single other fucking option."

Whitney's eyes widened slightly but she nodded. "Do you have any reason to think that she *doesn't* want you?"

"No. But... we've fucked this up."

Grant was not used to being vulnerable. He just wasn't. He made fantastic decisions based on facts and data. He was the one who other people came to for advice and when *they* needed to be bailed out.

But—he looked from Cam to Whitney and back—if he *was* going to get an opinion on something from someone, these two would be two of his picks. They were both practical. They dealt with the real world, they made tough decisions, and they knew things didn't always work out just because you wanted them to. Hell, they both dealt with assholes on a daily basis. Cam in the field of law and Whitney inside her own family.

"We screwed this up by getting married first. For money.

And *then*"—he blew out a breath and tipped his head up to look at the ceiling—"and *then* falling in love."

"You're in love with her?" Whitney asked.

"Probably. Very likely. I'd be stupid not to be," Grant said.

"Is she in love with you?" This came from Cam.

Grant looked over at his friend. "I think that Jocelyn Asher, the most romantic person I've ever met, would like nothing more than to be in love with her husband."

Cam cocked a brow. "That is not what I asked you."

No. It wasn't. "I don't know," Grant admitted. "But I think maybe."

"So there's only one thing to do," Cam said.

"There is?" Whitney asked.

"We hire Josie to make the new cake," Cam said.

"Hire her?" Whitney repeated. Then her eyes widened. "You mean instead of the crazy contest?" She looked excited.

Cam nodded, and Whitney blew out what could only be described as a relieved breath.

"The winner was going to get ten thousand dollars and then five percent royalties on sales of that cake each month, right?" Cam asked. "So that's what we'll offer Josie. She'd be getting a monthly check. I mean, it wouldn't be millions, but it would be a decent chunk. Maybe enough to buy some health insurance on the side of her regular job."

"But—" Whitney started.

"Whit," Cam said, cutting her off. "Don't you think that someone who's truly in love should have the chance to really make it work? That they should have the people who love them and care about them do whatever they can to support them? That we, as their friends, should really want them to be happy?"

Grant looked at Whitney. Her cheeks were pink, her eyes narrow, her lips pressed together.

"Of course I do," she said. "I think if we can take away some

of these barriers between Grant and Josie, we should do that."
She looked at Grant. "And if I don't have to run that contest and
bachelor auction, I will be your loyal and grateful employee
forever."

He smiled at that, but he needed to focus on Josie. "What
about the contestants?" he asked. "Is it fair to just let Josie do
this?"

"You mean the contestants for the contest we haven't even
announced yet?" Whitney said. "No one even knows about this.
There's no one to be disappointed. Except maybe Ollie."

Oh, Ollie would definitely be disappointed. "You'll just hire
her because she's my... wife?" Grant hesitated over that word.
He'd never said it out loud to anyone other than Jocelyn.

"Of course," Cam said. "She's part of the family."

That made Grant's heart thump hard against his sternum.

"But she won't be your wife anyway," Cam went on, making
Grant frown.

"What?"

"I thought you were going to divorce her." Cam lifted a big
shoulder. "So we'll be hiring someone local, who Whit and I
have known all our lives, and who's very talented. She'll have
the income so she won't need you for that. Then she'll realize
she loves you for you and wants to be with you, and you'll get
back together."

Grant started to protest, but realized that all actually
sounded okay. "You haven't tried her cake or whatever she
would be inventing for Hot Cakes."

Cam laughed. "I've eaten more of Josie's cakes than you
have, my friend."

He said it with a tone that had just enough innuendo in it to
make Grant grit his teeth.

Whitney rolled her eyes and said to Grant, "I really like
Josie, so I have no problem with this. But she's known for her
decorating and designs. She mostly follows the recipes at the

bakery, right? We can't have her poaching one of Zoe's recipes for us. Though if Zoe wanted to be involved too, maybe we could include some joint promotion—"

"No," Grant said quickly. He could feel himself frowning. He glanced at Cam. Zoe's brother. "No offense, but I think we leave Zoe out of it. Jocelyn does plenty of baking with her own recipes. She'd be very capable of developing something for us, and I think it would be great for her to have some recognition for something outside of the cake decorating she does at Buttered Up."

Cam shrugged. "Okay by me."

Whitney nodded. "Fine with me."

Grant nodded too. This was really good. It would accomplish all of the objectives.

Jocelyn would be financially stable without him, on her own merit, with a product *she* created.

This was a great plan.

Now all he had to do was convince *her*.

And to sign the divorce papers.

And then to go out with him on a real date that had nothing to do with his health insurance.

————

Jocelyn's house smelled amazing. She'd baked. Again.

He figured that was a very typical thing in this house, and he couldn't deny that was not at all a bad thing to think about coming home to.

But he'd want to come home to this house, to her, no matter what. Forever.

So he really needed to get this divorce thing done.

And yes, he was aware how stupid that sounded.

The kitchen was empty other than the amazing aroma of freshly baked something—cookies, he thought, but possibly muffins or cake—so he made his way through the house and up the stairs. He heard the television from the bedroom. So she was in the room of the house where he most liked having her. The kitchen a very close second, of course.

"Hey," he said from the doorway.

She gave him a big smile that punched him in the gut. "Hi."

He braced his hands on either side of the door and just studied her.

She was propped up on the bed, her laptop on her thighs. She had her hair up in a messy bun, glasses propped on her nose, and was wearing a thin tank top and shorts. It was clear she was mostly ready for bed.

Yeah, he wanted her like this every night. This is what he wanted to come home to. Not the expensive furniture and high thread-count sheets. Not the city lights. Not the gourmet food delivery from some of the best restaurants in the country.

This. This woman. This house. This bedroom. And the smell of cookies. Or cake. Or whatever.

"How are you feeling?" he asked.

She pulled her glasses off and met his gaze. "Horny."

Grant froze. He blinked at her. "Oh?"

She nodded. "Yeah."

"So... better, then."

She smiled. "Yeah. Good, actually. A little tired and like we might have to be careful with our positions so I don't pull on the sore spot on my side, but mostly I feel good." She paused. "And I want you."

Grant curled his fingers into the wood doorframe. "You're sure it's okay?"

"They said to resume my normal activities as I feel ready."

He blew out a breath.

"Are *you* going to be okay?" she asked, a smile in her voice.

"Don't know," he said honestly. "I want you too. Always. But I have this insane protective streak where you're concerned."

She nodded. "I know."

"I might get partway into it and start to worry." He was serious about that.

"Well, I've always got my vibrator if I have to finish that way."

He huffed out a laugh even as his body heated, and *God, I really like her* went through his mind at the same time. "I'd kind of like to see that, actually."

She grinned. "Then we're good no matter what. I'll get the horniness taken care of one way or another, and you won't be *too* disappointed no matter how it turns out."

He nodded. "Sounds like a plan."

He started to toe off his shoes and undo his belt.

"And I have an idea that might make it even more fun and get you out of your head about my surgery," she said.

"What you just mentioned sounded pretty fun," he told her, tossing his belt and kicking his shoes to the side.

He started for the bed.

"What if I told you that I wanted to combine the sex and the vibrator with"—she paused dramatically, a mischievous look in her eyes—"spreadsheets."

He stopped at the side of the bed. Spreadsheets and sex? Sounded weird. And like combining two of his favorite things. "Go on."

She gave him a knowing look. "I thought that might get your attention."

He put one knee on the mattress and started unbuttoning his shirt. "You always have my attention, Jocelyn."

That made her lips curl into a sweet smile. "So... I've been thinking, and I've decided that you should teach me a few things about business. And I think we should start with spreadsheets."

He lifted a brow. "Tonight? Now?"

She nodded. "Yes. You teach me something. I try it. When I

understand it and do it right, one of us takes a piece of clothing off."

He let that sink in. Then laughed. "You have like three pieces of clothing on."

She looked down, then up at him with a smirk. "Two, actually."

He could see her tank top and shorts. No panties, then. Good to know. He nodded, feeling his blood heating. "So I can teach you two things?"

"Well—" She looked him up and down. His shirt was hanging open but still technically on. "You have a few things on too." She leaned to look down at his feet. "I guess it's your call on if we count the socks as one thing or two."

He nodded. "Okay. You have two things on. I have a shirt, pants, underwear, and two socks. So I can teach you seven things before we're both naked."

She shook her head. "The socks are two things, huh? Damn."

He laughed. "Two things. But how do you expect us to be concentrating on things in Excel by the time we even have a couple of items off?"

She shrugged. "I guess you either start with the more difficult stuff and make it get easier as we're more distracted. Or we start with your socks and leave the more... revealing clothes removal toward the end."

Grant had to admit this sounded like fun. A lot of fun. Even if she didn't learn a damned thing about Excel, this would be fun. And she was willing. That actually made him go a little soft. She didn't want to learn about spreadsheets. He knew that. But she was making a gesture here.

"Okay," he agreed. He buttoned half of his shirt buttons back up. "Let's do this."

She seemed very pleased as he crawled onto the bed beside

her. "I've already got Excel open and everything," she said, turning her computer to show him.

"Good girl."

She gave him a saucy smile.

"What?" he asked.

"I like that."

"Good girl? You like that?"

She nodded. "Kind of gives you a hot teacher vibe."

He gave a little growl. "I can definitely do the hot teacher thing with my favorite student."

"Oh, this is going to be so good," she said, turning her attention back to the screen.

Grant chuckled. Fun and torturous.

He moved in behind her, positioning himself so that she could lean back against his chest, and they could both see and reach the computer. She settled in against him easily, and he marveled at how amazing she felt in his arms. He took a big, deep, contented breath.

He moved her hair back from the side of her face and leaned in to put his chin on her shoulder. "I'm glad you're feeling better."

"Me too." She sighed. "It's nice to be home."

It was. This wasn't even his home, and it was very nice to be here.

"What's first?" she asked.

"Okay, well, what do you know?"

"How to open Excel."

"That's it?"

"Pretty much."

Okay, so this was going to take a few lessons. But that was fine. He liked the idea of having multiple nights ahead that they could spend just like this.

"First lesson," he said. "Blank workbook." He pointed at the screen.

She clicked and they got started.

It turned out that she didn't know much more than how to open Excel—an hour, and two orgasms later.

They lay with their limbs entwined, sweaty, and panting.

And Grant decided he didn't care if Jocelyn ever figured out spreadsheets. He'd do all her spreadsheets for her.

But they would keep playing strip-spreadsheet-tutoring whenever possible.

"So that's how you auto sum a column," he said, stroking the pads of his fingers up and down her back.

She giggled against his chest. "That might have been my favorite part."

"Yeah? I thought you liked removing duplicates," he said with a grin.

She nodded. "That was really good. But that auto summing... wow."

He hugged her close. Had he ever been this happy?

No. It was easy to come up with that answer. He'd never been this happy. Never known that simple stuff like this could make his heart pound and his gut tighten and even his bones feel warm.

After another couple of minutes, he finally rolled and sat up, taking her with him. They cleaned up, put the computer away, and got under the blankets.

Jocelyn cuddled up against his side.

"You sore?" he asked her huskily in the dark.

"No. You were very careful with me." She ran her hand back and forth over his chest.

He'd tried to be. But she hadn't acted like she needed him to hold back, that was for sure. Still, he'd been happy to do most of the work.

"Well, you tell me if you feel it tomorrow. I don't want to push you too hard," he said.

"Yes, sir," she said, a smile in her voice. "I promise to let you pamper me and spoil me and protect me as much as you want."

His heart thudded. He definitely wanted that. He wasn't supposed to. His head told him that. He was supposed to encourage her to take care of herself and to not need him.

But he really wanted to take care of her.

Was there a way to have both?

The whoopie pies. Those were the answer. If she had her own thing, something that she was proud of, that was all hers, that would support her and make her happy, then the rest would fall into place.

The whoopie pies, where he and Jocelyn had essentially started, were the answer to how they could make this last.

Grant drifted off to sleep thinking about how beautifully poetic that really was.

18

Learning about spreadsheets didn't make him want to stay married to her.

Josie stared at the papers lying next to the plate of whoopie pies on her kitchen island.

The kitchen island where she and Grant had first had sex.

The whoopie pies that she'd been trying to make that first night—that they'd ended up using in the hottest sex of her life.

That was... horribly ironic. Or something.

He still wanted a divorce. The papers were right here. He'd brought them over. He'd laid them on this island, next to these whoopie pies, and then he'd come upstairs, and had strip-spreadsheet-sex with her.

He'd also already signed the papers.

Along with them were the hospital and doctors' bills from her surgery—all marked paid—and a contract from Hot Cakes for her to develop their newest snack cake.

It already had her name and everything filled in. All it needed was her signature.

Just like the divorce papers.

It was 5 a.m. Grant was asleep upstairs in her bed. She'd floated down the fucking stairs. *Floated.*

Josie worked to breathe. And not cry. Okay, he'd signed the divorce papers. They'd talked about this. This should not be a shock. She'd known this was where he'd thought this was headed from day one. The marriage had been for a specific purpose. That purpose had been fulfilled.

Grant was nothing if not a very focused, purposeful person.

She breathed in, then out. She thought about her sister and what Paige had taught her about breathing and centering herself.

Then she crossed to the drawer that held a collection of things like scissors and tape and notepads and pens. She took a pen out, went back to the divorce papers, and signed her name.

Okay. She was now divorced.

Wow, that had been a lot easier than it should have been.

And it really sucked.

She eyed the coffeepot. Coffee didn't actually sound good at the moment. She looked at the fridge. Nothing sounded good to eat. She looked at the back door. She could... go for a run. If she was a runner. But she wasn't. At all.

Damn. She had no idea what to do.

Her sister had a yoga class at five thirty every morning. Maybe she'd do that. She could definitely use some more deep breathing and centering and calming.

She could also use someone to talk to. Someone who wasn't in love with one of Grant's best friends and who wouldn't freak out about Josie marrying him for health insurance and who wouldn't freak out about her having her gall bladder removed in Chicago and who wouldn't be upset with her for baking on the side and... all of the other secrets she'd been keeping.

Paige didn't freak out about things. She was the calmest person Josie knew. She was the calmest person most people knew.

Yeah, Josie wanted to talk to her sister.

And play with some kittens. She grabbed her keys and started for the door.

But just as she was pulling it open, she heard footsteps thundering down the staircase from the second level.

Grant was definitely not *floating* downstairs this morning.

She sighed and turned.

"You're still here. Thank God," he said. He looked like he'd vaulted out of bed. He was still wearing only his boxers. His hair was mussed, one side sticking straight up. He had stubble darkening his jaw, and he looked slightly dazed as if he'd just been jolted awake.

"I was just leaving."

He glanced at the center island. Right at the papers that he'd clearly left there last night.

"Don't worry. I signed."

"You did?" His eyes lit up slightly. "So you like the idea?"

Did she *like* the idea of getting divorced? No. Not even a tiny bit. But she wasn't sure she wanted to admit that to him. She wanted to have a little dignity here, didn't she? A little pride?

But she frowned and shook her head. "No, Grant. I don't like the idea. But it's what we agreed to, and if it's what you want I'm not going to fight you."

He frowned. "It's what we agreed to? What do you mean?"

"We both knew that the marriage was temporary. We agreed that it was for the insurance. Now that the bills are all paid, there's no reason to stay married."

His frown cleared, and he shoved a hand through his hair. "Oh. That."

"Yes. That. What did you think I was talking about?"

"The agreement with Hot Cakes. To make our new snack cake," he said. "I wanted to go over that with you before you went to the bakery because I know you probably wouldn't be comfortable talking about it there. And I'd love to get that ball rolling today."

She propped a hand on her hip. "What ball rolling?"

"We want you to develop our new snack cake," he said again.

"I got that part. I'm not going to do that."

"Why not?"

"Why would I? I work for Buttered Up. I know things are a lot better between the two families, but I can't develop a new cake for another company without talking to Zoe. And if someone is going to do that, shouldn't it be her?"

"No, *you* need to do this. You deserve this," Grant said, taking a step toward her.

"Deserve this?" she repeated. "What are you talking about?"

"You deserve the ten thousand dollars that comes with it. And the monthly royalty payment as long as the cake is a part of our product line. Which, considering the company has never added or removed any other product, will be for a very long time."

She frowned and turned to face him more fully.

He took another step closer. "You also deserve the recognition of having one of your cakes produced a million times over, sold to hundreds of thousands of people."

"I... don't want that." But her heart was beating hard. What was that?

She didn't want to do work for Hot Cakes. She didn't share Zoe's long-held belief that Hot Cakes and the Lancaster family were inherently evil—and, of course, Zoe's feelings about the company and the family had changed recently as she'd let go of the three-generation old grudge she'd been holding on behalf of her grandmother—but Josie did believe that what she and Zoe did at Buttered Up was different, and yes, better on some levels. It was more personal. It was more special. They created from scratch, by hand, and with the people of Appleby in mind.

They didn't mass produce cakes that would sit on grocery and convenience store shelves for strangers to grab without even giving it a true thought. They baked for their neighbors and friends, and they did it with a mind to tradition and the occasions that their treats would be a part of.

"You don't want to be financially secure?"

Ah, well, of course that's what this was about. "That is a lot of money."

"It is. And it's guaranteed. You can use your talents to make yourself financially independent."

She crossed her arms. "Strange coincidence that the guy who is obsessed with me being financially independent also co-owns the company offering me this contract."

He shrugged. "It wouldn't work if we weren't already looking for a new product and you weren't already a talented baker."

"Uh-huh."

"It was Cam's idea," he said.

"Really." She didn't believe that.

Grant nodded. "We were going to have a contest for people to enter recipes and a big town taste testing and... a whole event. But when I talked to Cam and Whitney, Cam suggested we just hire you."

Josie felt herself frown. That sounded a little easier to believe. "You're still setting this up for me."

"Every time I do a seminar, I set things up for women," he said. "I advise them on good investments, help them get those started, help them with how to expand what they're already doing if that applies. This is no different."

This is no different.

Right. That was the thing she had to remember. She was just another woman who had needed his help financially. This was Grant's passion. This was what gave him purpose and happiness. There had been sex—and a wedding—involved in this particular circumstance, where he didn't usually sleep with, or marry, the women he counseled, but truly, at the end of the day, she was just another woman who had gotten into trouble financially, and he'd stepped in to bail out.

He'd gotten in over his head, sure, but that other set of papers would get him out of that.

She pulled in a breath. "Well, I appreciate the option, but I'm not comfortable with it."

"You're not comfortable making ten thousand dollars and then a percentage of sales of your snack cake every month?" he asked.

She wanted to ask how much he thought that would be, she couldn't deny. But it didn't matter. She wasn't doing this. She wasn't a charity case. She hated that all he really saw was another woman who needed his help.

"I guess you still don't believe that I'm really very happy with how things are," she said. That was true. The health insurance thing aside, she *was* happy. "I don't need millions of dollars. Yes, I loved the private plane and the fancy restaurant and the amazing hotel suite, but I don't *need* them." She pressed her hands against her stomach willing it to stop flipping. "I loved the popcorn on the couch, sitting with you reading while you worked, learning about spreadsheets just as much." She swallowed hard. "The best part of the dinner at the restaurant was talking to you and hearing your stories. The best part of the hotel suite was sleeping in your arms. I don't need the city lights or expensive wine or high thread-count sheets. And I was hoping that you would realize that and... maybe feel the same way."

"Jocelyn, I do want you to be happy. I just want you to stop hiding your talent and taking less than you deserve." His voice was gruff, and he looked surprised and pained at the same time. "You hide your side-baking. You stay in the kitchen at the bakery. Even though everyone knows you do all the major decorating, Zoe still keeps the majority of the profits, and the recognition all goes to the bakery. She needs you more than you need her, yet you keep working there, making *her* business a success, while she can't even provide you with health insurance."

Josie felt a jab of protectiveness in the middle of her chest. "Zoe is my best friend, Grant. She gives me so much more than money. We're family. She's someone I can laugh with and cry with. Someone who will always be honest with me. Who wants me to be happy. Who..." She trailed off as that hit her.

She'd been keeping secrets—big secrets—from someone who had always loved her no matter what. Zoe was someone who would decorate her living room to look like Rome and figure out how to make—or cater in—Italian food and desserts, and find Italian music and watch Josie's favorite Rome-set films with her even if she couldn't take Josie to Rome for her birthday. Zoe could make movie night on the couch fun and comfortable. Zoe would listen to her hopes and dreams and would want them to come true.

It wasn't romantic love, but it was love. And Josie had been ignoring that. She'd been keeping secrets, not telling Zoe all of her dreams and what she wanted and how she was feeling. Even the bad feelings. The scared feelings about having her gall bladder out without health insurance. Zoe would feel terrible. As her boss—but as her friend—she would have been there comforting her and making her soup and watching a hundred back-to-back episodes of *Gilmore Girls*.

Josie had *really* liked having Grant there. *Really* liked it. Loved it, even.

But if he didn't want to be the one next time, if he wasn't going to stick around for it, then she'd still be okay. She had her friends. Her family. She didn't *need* Grant.

And that hit her right in the heart.

That was what he wanted.

He wanted her to not *need* him. He wanted her to just *want him.*

Well, she was there.

"I'm fine," she said to Grant. "I'm more than fine. I'm good. I don't need to work for Hot Cakes. And I don't need to be married. But I do need to go." She turned and twisted the doorknob. "I'm going to be late for work. At the bakery. With my best friend."

She swept through the door leaving the love of her life standing in her kitchen next to a plate of whoopie pies. And their signed divorce papers.

———

"You know that showing up for the end stretching and relaxation sequence and then cuddling cats doesn't really count as attending a yoga class. Even here," Paige said, coming to lie next to Josie on the mat.

Josie had needed to make one stop on her way to the bakery. She'd snuck into the end of Paige's early class and was now lying on her back with a white-and-gray cat named Grace curled up on her stomach.

"Does it really count as a yoga class when it's you and three other people?" Josie teased.

She'd been shocked to see two of the attendees of Paige's early class actually. Piper was on a bright yellow mat at the front. And Cam was by the window on a dark purple mat.

"It does," Paige said with a smile. "I'm here for whoever needs me."

"You basically come in to do your own practice, and if others wander in you let them stay?" Josie said.

Paige nodded. "Yeah."

"How long has Cam been coming?"

"Oh, he's been in a few times when he's been home in the

past. When he's home over Christmas for instance," Paige said, tipping her head to look over to where Cam was gathering his stuff. "But he makes it in about three days a week at least, now that he's been in town more full time."

"No kidding." That did *not* seem like Cam.

"Yeah. But I'm sure he was practicing in Chicago. He's really good. Keeps right up with me," Paige said, admiration clear in her tone.

Josie frowned slightly. "Is there something going on with you two?"

Paige laughed at that. "Oh, Lord, no. I do not go for the growly, fighter types."

Yeah, that's what Josie would have thought.

"He's a very contrary spirit," Paige said, folding her hands on her flat stomach and closing her eyes. "I'm happy to help him quiet some of that, but no, I have no interest in having that in my personal life. I want quiet, peace, mindfulness, calm."

Josie nodded. "Okay. Good."

"But I don't mind watching him bend and stretch first thing in the morning," Paige added.

Josie snorted softly. She could imagine. She was in love with Grant, and Cam was like a big brother to her, but she wasn't blind. He was a good-looking guy, with a lot of muscles and some very hot tattoos. "You're the tattoo type?" she asked Paige. She wouldn't have guessed that actually. Paige seemed the type to go for the nerdy professor or a tortured artist. But come to think of it, Paige had been asked out a lot and had gone to school dances and things like that, but she'd never had a serious, long-term boyfriend.

That was interesting. Her sister was gorgeous, intelligent, confident, and kind. But she wasn't interested in dating, it seemed. Growing up, Paige hadn't been all that social in general, actually. She'd stayed home a lot reading, knitting, cooking, drawing. She'd had friends and had always been well liked. She'd been invited to social events and out to movies and parties. She'd just said no thank you more often than she'd accepted. She'd liked doing her own thing and had been content at home in her own company. Content. That was a very good word for Paige. She was comfortable in her own skin, happy with her situation, satisfied with her world just as she'd made it.

Josie had always kind of envied that. She suspected most people would envy that. To know who you were and to be happy with where you were in life at such a young age was amazing. Their grandmother said Paige was an old soul. That seemed to fit.

"So what are *you* doing here so early?"

"I need you to cover at the bakery this morning," Josie told her.

Paige rolled her head to look at Josie. "Ugh, really?"

Josie smiled. "Please? I have some baking I need to do at home."

"You're baking at home but *I* have to cover at Buttered Up? That's weird."

"I'm making things for... well, for Zoe. But not for the bakery." She frowned. That sounded confusing. "I need to make some things, like gluten-free zucchini muffins and whoopie pies and some strawberries and cream cereal mix and some chocolate chip cookie dough popcorn and pussy cupcakes..." She looked up to realize she'd been rattling those off as she thought about what she wanted to show off. "I need to make some stuff before I have Zoe over for a talk," Josie admitted.

Paige rolled to her side to face Josie, propping her head on her hand. She looked very interested. "What are you talking about?"

"I've been doing this side business," Josie admitted. "Zoe doesn't know about it. And I need to tell her. Especially because

I want to expand." That was the first time she'd said that out loud. She took a deep breath. "I want to do more with it. It's all things that we don't do at the bakery. Like the whoopie pies and all the healthier muffins you were talking about yesterday and some naughty cupcakes and cookies for bachelorette parties... just things that I think would be fun to create and do on the side. Maybe even an online store. Things Zoe doesn't really want to get into. But I don't want to do it behind her back."

"You're going to start your own business," Paige said with a grin. "That's so great."

"Just something small. On the side. I want to keep working with Zoe."

"Of course. But this is great. You will love that."

"Do you think so?" Josie felt butterflies in her stomach, but she wasn't sure if they were nerves or excitement. Probably both.

Earlier in her kitchen when she'd been talking to Grant and he'd mentioned that she deserved to have the recognition of one of her cakes being mass produced and sold to hundreds of thousands of people, her heart had pounded.

She didn't want that. She didn't want her creations mass produced and sitting on shelves. But she'd had a flash of making *more* of what she was doing now. Having more people ordering and enjoying her treats. And having everyone talking about it and telling her, and their friends, how much they loved them. She didn't need recognition in the form of advertisements or logos or checks. But she did love the idea of not having to be a secret. That had been the reason for her heart pounding.

She wanted people to enjoy her stuff and know it was hers.

"I know that you'll enjoy it," Paige said. "You've always loved feeding people. You especially like making desserts. I think it's because you can make them pretty *and* make people happy with them."

Josie thought about that. Paige had something there.

"Let's face it, you could definitely make people happy with your lasagna or your chicken casserole. Those are amazing. But the cakes and cookies and stuff are also pretty."

"The strawberries and cream cereal mix is pink," Josie said. "And I put little sparkly sugar in too. Just to make it fun. And I'm thinking that I could do banana cream flavored cereal mix. Or a mix that tastes like a seven-layer bar. With coconut and—"

"*Okay,*" Paige cut in with a laugh. "What about those healthy ones?"

"Oh! If I do some of those, would you offer them here? I figure your clients might grab them after a class."

Paige nodded. "Yeah, I think we could work something out."

"Wonderful," Josie felt a surge of excitement. "So you'll fill in for me so I can get prepped to show this all to Zoe?"

"I will," Paige agreed. "But I get all the zucchini muffins you make in exchange."

"Deal."

"And the strawberry cereal mix," Paige added.

Josie laughed. "Okay."

Paige shrugged. "I eat gluten-free because it's healthier and I feel better with it, but I *can* eat gluten, and that stuff sounds delicious."

"I can make snickerdoodle cereal mix too," Josie said.

Paige's eyes widened.

"'Mornin'."

Josie looked up to find Cam standing over them. "Hi."

"Never seen you here before," he said.

"Yoga at this time of day is only for crazy people," Josie told him.

He chuckled. "You might be right." He looked at Paige. "Thanks for the practice today."

"My pleasure." Paige pushed herself up from the mat. "I better go get ready for the bakery."

"Love you," Josie told her.

"I can see why," Paige said with a nod. She headed for the room at the back of the building that functioned as her dressing room and office.

"You couldn't drag Grant down here?" Cam asked Josie.

Josie shrugged. "Well, I mean, once we got divorced, I kind of figured I couldn't really drag him anywhere."

Cam paused and then nodded. "How long have you been divorced?"

Josie glanced at the clock. "About an hour."

"You okay?"

"With that? No. In general, yes."

"You didn't want the divorce?" Cam asked.

"Let's see, would I rather be married to the guy I'm madly in love with or *not* married to the guy I'm madly in love with? I'd say married," she said, pushing up from the mat.

Cam nodded. "That would have been one of the fastest courtships and engagements ever."

"So?"

He chuckled. "I guess I was just pointing that out."

"Well, it doesn't matter. We both signed the papers so it's over."

"It's over?"

She shrugged. "Obviously."

"I did not get the impression that Grant wanted things to be over, Josie," Cam said with a frown.

"Well, maybe he shouldn't have divorced me, then," she shot back.

Cam held up his hands. "Fair enough. But..."

She narrowed her eyes. "But?"

"He's never done this before."

"Gotten divorced or been married?"

"Been in love."

That made the air rush out of her lungs. She swallowed. "Me neither."

"But you've seen a hell of a lot of love. And marriage. And romance. Your family. My family."

She nodded.

"So show him what it's about," Cam said.

Josie felt her stomach flip. "You make it sound like that's easy."

"Why wouldn't it be?"

"He..." But then she really thought about Cam's question. *Why wouldn't it be?*

Grant had good reasons for thinking that coupling up was less than ideal. But she had great counterarguments. She agreed that women should be independent and happy on their own and able to take care of themselves. But wanting a marriage and a family and to be with someone who made them feel all the things Grant made her feel wasn't bad or wrong. That didn't make her weak. It actually made her stronger.

She wasn't going to expand her baking business to impress Grant or to win him over or to convince him she could be independent. She was going to do it because over this time with Grant, she'd realized something important—she really loved baking. She was really good at it, and she loved how her food made other people feel. She'd always known that she liked it and was good at it. Basically. But it had always been a part of something bigger—Buttered Up. And her relationship with Zoe. Her baking had blended into the bigger picture.

Since Grant had started talking about how she should let people know more about what *she* did and had made her aware of how her baking made others happy—because he'd been noticing that—it had been at the back of her mind. Plus, Grant loved her baked goods. And that wasn't a euphemism. He'd gotten her really thinking about what she did and how she felt about it and how it affected others.

She was going to expand because she wanted more of that in her life. She wanted more of helping people make their special occasions perfect and fun, whether it was a birthday party with a huge elaborate cake, or a potluck at the office with cookie bars that made people smile in the middle of their workday, or movie night with fun popcorns and cereal mixes. She wanted to do more, and yes, she wanted to do some things that were *hers*. Not a McCaffery family recipe that she just followed, but something she created, something that, when people gushed over it, they were truly gushing over something she had done completely on her own.

She loved Zoe and the bakery. She wanted to keep working there. But yes, she wanted to branch out. Because of the things that Grant had gotten her thinking about.

Josie realized she'd been staring at Cam.

"You're giving me relationship advice?" she asked. "You're no expert."

He snorted. "Hey, I'm the Thomas Edison of relationships."

Josie frowned. "What? Thomas Edison? The guy who invented the light bulb?"

Cam nodded. "Sure. You've never heard his famous quote about failure?"

"No."

"Well, this isn't exact, but it goes something like this, *I didn't fail. I just found ten thousand ways not to make a light bulb.*"

Josie laughed. "So you're not failing at relationships, you're just finding ten thousand ways that they won't work."

"Something like that." He was quiet for a moment, then added, "Just take it from a guy who had it right and let it go. Once you've had the real thing, you'll never be able to convince yourself that anything else is good enough."

Wow. Josie stared at him for several beats. Then she nodded. "Okay."

Why wouldn't it be?

Cam had asked her an honest question. Why wouldn't showing Grant about love and marriage be easy? If Grant had gotten her rethinking everything in her life so easily, maybe she could get him rethinking some things in *his*.

Like the idea that a woman was better off without a man.

Sure, there were definitely some men that women were better off without. All women. And a woman definitely needed to be her own person.

But she knew, firsthand, that people could have healthy, strong, happy marriages while each person maintained their own identity and interests. She'd seen it right in front of her all her life.

Grant hadn't.

That's all he needed—someone to show him something he just hadn't seen before.

Just like he'd shown her how her baking could make people feel.

"Yeah, okay," she finally said. "I can show him about love and romance and marriage."

"Great." Cam grinned. "You can still contest the divorce. I know the attorney pretty well. Maybe the papers will accidentally fall into the shredder or something."

She shook her head. "No. I still want the divorce."

"Oh?" Cam looked confused.

"Yeah. I think I need to date my ex-husband for a while."

19

"Where the fuck is Cam?" Grant roared as he stomped into Cam's office and found it empty.

Piper wasn't at her desk either.

Almost no one was in their offices or at their desks. It was fucking early in the morning. But Cam wasn't at Zoe and Aiden's house, where he was staying, either, and Grant had no idea where else he would be.

"Probably at Cores and Catnip."

Grant swung around at the sound of Whitney's voice. "At what and what?"

She smiled and stepped into the office. "Cores and Catnip. It's the yoga studio downtown. Cores as in apple cores and... body cores." She made a circle with her hand over her lower stomach.

"And catnip?" Grant asked.

"It's also a cat café. And adoption center. Though you have to pass a major test, including a home visit, before Paige will let you adopt one, and not many people make it through her screening. So it's really just her way of collecting cats without people thinking she's crazy. Though a lot of people think that anyway."

"Who's Paige?" Grant asked. Yoga and cats? What was going on?

Whitney crossed her arms and tilted her head. "Your sister-in-law. Well, one of them."

Ah. Josie's sister. Damn. Why did he feel sad thinking about not being related by marriage to a woman he had never even met? "Well, as of about an hour ago, Paige is my ex-sister-in-law."

Whitney blew out a breath. "I was afraid you were going to do that."

He was still feeling pretty shitty about everything. Like Jocelyn turning down the Hot Cakes deal and the guaranteed money. If she was financially stable, he could date her. And eventually propose. Again. But if not... he'd likely end up proposing again anyway and then just wondering if he was going against everything he thought he believed in for the rest of his life. Just something little like that.

"It was the agreement," he said. "We got married for the insurance. We need to start fresh."

It sounded stupid even to his own ears.

"That's really stupid," Whitney said. She moved to sit on the edge of Cam's desk, facing Grant.

He blew out a breath. "I know. But she also turned down the agreement with Hot Cakes. She's not making our new cake. So she's not going to have that extra money coming in. I don't know if I can leave her alone, but I don't know if I can stay with her not knowing if it's just about money."

Whitney didn't seem surprised to hear Jocelyn had turned down the offer. She crossed her legs and braced her hands on the desk, leaning forward. "Look, Grant, take it from someone who majorly fucked up the best relationship in her entire life.

Go to Josie, tell her you love her, and beg her to rip those papers up."

"You and Cam?" he asked.

"And hey, I was eighteen. I have youth stupidity as an excuse. You don't. And don't try to change the subject," she said with a frown. "This is about your fuckup."

"Jocelyn deserves to be her own woman, to know that she doesn't need me."

Whitney laughed. "What makes you think she thinks she *needs* you?"

He scowled. "She needed me for the insurance."

"Was that her idea? Did she propose to you? Beg you to let her use your insurance temporarily in a mini-pseudo insurance fraud scheme?"

His scowl deepened. "No."

"So it was your idea? You proposed?"

"Yes."

"Hmm. And when you brought the divorce papers over, did she cry and beg you to rethink it? Did she protest? Did she hesitate to sign them?" Whitney asked.

Grant sighed. She hadn't. In fact, he would have liked to see *a little* more reluctance from her. "No."

"Did she ever ask you for your pin number for your bank account?"

"No."

"Have you checked your wallet? Are any of your credit cards missing?"

He rolled his eyes. "No."

"Did she give you any indication that she wants to move to Chicago and jet around the world on your private plane and have you drape her in diamonds?"

He shook his head. "No."

Whitney lifted a brow. "Then what the hell are you talking about, Grant? What, exactly, do you have that Josie needs?

She'd been living a very happy life here in Appleby surrounded by a town full of people who love her. She spends her days with her best friend, surrounded by cupcakes, for God's sake. She's got a great house that she has no intention of ever leaving." Whitney shrugged. "Seems very egotistical of you, frankly, to assume that she needs you. As if she's been sitting around, just waiting for you to show up and ride her off into the sunset when really, her favorite sunsets are right here, and she's already had them every night for twenty-five years."

Grant just stared at Whitney. He felt his breath sawing in and out. He felt his heart thudding in his chest. He felt his blood rushing.

Those were all really good points.

"She needed to have her gall bladder taken out," he finally said. "She needed to pay for that."

Whitney nodded and slid off the desk. "And if she hadn't been able to figure out payments or something, this town would have held a chili-feed fundraiser, or hell, her friends would have gone door to door and easily collected enough money from the town to cover that." Whitney smoothed her hands down the sides of her skirt and met his gaze. "I would have made an anonymous donation that would have covered the whole bill. Or Aiden would have. Or we both would have, and she would have been able to tuck a bunch of money under her mattress for a rainy day if she wanted to. But she wouldn't have wanted to do that. She probably would have donated the excess to something else here in town."

Whitney stepped closer to him, her expression sincere, and a touch sympathetic. "Jocelyn isn't afraid of the future or worried about her bank account. She doesn't need you to take care of her, Grant. She's always been taken care of when she needed it because *she* takes care of the rest of us when we need it. That's how it works around here. We're maybe not all completely independent, but I personally think that's really nice that we lean on each other."

He took a deep breath. That was nice. He'd never been a part of something like that.

"So," Whitney went on, "that means you need to give her something she doesn't already have that she *wants*." She stepped around him and started for the door. "And by the way, I don't mean spreadsheets or a budget or an investment portfolio."

"Right." He nodded. But he felt his mouth curving. "Got it."

He glanced toward the desk as a light flashed in his peripheral vision. Whitney had left her phone lying there. He stepped over to retrieve it.

And noticed the flash had been a new text message from Cam. It said simply *thanks*.

Cam and Whitney were texting? Nice and polite things?

Grant couldn't help it. He read the messages just above the *thanks*.

Cam: *Hey, can you keep Grant busy at the office today? Josie needs some space. She's got a plan hatching.*

Whitney: *Are you helping with the plan?*

Cam: *Kind of. More cheering her on.*

Whitney: *He's definitely in love with her.*

Cam: *I know. She's got this.*

Whitney: *Okay. I'll do what I can.*

Cam: *Thanks.*

Cam and Whitney were conspiring together to get him and Jocelyn back together? And Jocelyn had a plan?

He let all of that sink it.

Whitney stopped in the doorway and glanced back. "Oh, and don't even think about rushing out of here to go be romantic or anything."

"No?" he asked, laying her phone back on the desk. Maybe Grant could help nudge Whitney and Cam together too. She would have to come back in here later to find it. She might run into Cam then, and they could rehash their matchmaking.

"No," Whitney said. "I need you to stay here in the office."

Grant bit back a grin.

"We need to figure out what we're going to do about this new snack cake now that Josie turned us down," Whitney said. She suddenly froze. Then groaned. "Oh *no*."

"What?"

"I suppose this means that crazy contest is back on?"

Grant laughed lightly. "Yeah. I guess so."

"*Ugh.*" She looked at him. "Then you're definitely staying here and helping me go over this with Ollie. I clearly don't have enough willpower to say no to pony rides."

"But pony rides at a cake tasting contest and bachelor auction are strange, right?"

"They are," she said. "But think of the kids who will be there with their parents. Their impression of the new Hot Cakes will be fun and laughter and good times. A return to the simple things of childhood, like when you first tasted a Fudgie Fritter. It will take their parents and grandparents back too. We can have an old-fashioned lemonade stand set up, and maybe we can do some carnival games like a ring toss or a dunk tank." Her eyes got wide. "Oh, we should *totally* put the bachelors up in a dunk tank!"

"Okay, I will *definitely* be sitting in on the meeting with you and Ollie," Grant interrupted.

Whitney took a deep breath and nodded. "Thank you," she said sincerely. "I feel like I've got a split personality thing going on. And Ollie is the little devil sitting on my shoulder, telling me how much fun this will all be."

"Who's the angel on your other shoulder?"

"Exactly. I don't have one. That's going to be you."

This was good. This would keep him occupied while he gave Jocelyn some space. He wanted to go to her, but he was willing to let her figure out whatever her plan was. And he needed a little time to come up with a plan of his own. A plan to romance his ex-wife. The most romance-loving person he'd ever met, when he'd never really romanced anyone ever before. No pressure.

Still, he was grinning as he followed Whitney out of Cam's office.

He couldn't wait to see Jocelyn's plan. He hoped it included whoopie pies.

———

"Whoopie pies, huh?"

Josie nodded, watching her best friend's face carefully. "Whoopie pies. All flavors. I'm even going to play with the flavors of the cream filling."

Zoe had arrived about thirty minutes ago. They were in Jocelyn's kitchen, her center island covered with baked goods. None of them things that they offered at Buttered Up.

It was just after closing. Paige had been covering her shift all day, and Josie had called Maggie about two hours ago and asked if she could go help close up and do tomorrow's prep. Maggie had been happy to. When she'd asked if everything was okay, Josie had simply said, "I hope it will be soon." To which Maggie had replied simply, "Then I hope so too."

Josie was realizing that she had a lot of people who really loved her and really did want her to just be happy. She knew Zoe was one of those.

She'd debated over having Jane join them. Or even Aiden. Or yes, Grant. Or all of the above. But in the end, she'd realized this was between her and her lifelong best friend. And boss.

"I love whoopie pies," Zoe said.

It was clear from her expression and tone that she was still stunned by all of this. Jocelyn had come clean about the baking she'd been doing on the side. She'd also confessed that she wanted to keep doing it and expand. She wanted to do the naughty cupcakes, the healthy muffins, everything.

Josie handed her one of the whoopie pies. It was a traditional chocolate with a white cream filling.

Zoe took it, looked at it for a long moment as if it held all the answers, then bit into it. Josie held her breath.

Zoe chewed and swallowed. Then took a deep breath. Then nodded. "Amazing. Of course."

Josie felt the breath whoosh out of her lungs. "You think so?"

Zoe smiled and shook her head, setting the whoopie pie down on the plate. She brushed her hands together. "Of course I think so. You're amazing. You are an extremely talented baker and..." She sighed. "I know everyone knows that you're behind the awesome decorating, but yeah, they probably don't realize how awesome you are at the baking part because Buttered Up doesn't give you a lot of chance to really show that off."

She looked sad for a moment, then she took a deep breath. "I'm sorry."

Josie frowned. "For?"

"Not letting you do more. Not even realizing all of what was going on with you."

Josie was shaking her head before Zoe even finished speaking. "I was purposefully keeping all of this from you, Zoe. You couldn't have known."

Zoe nodded but didn't say anything.

"Listen," Josie said, "I love working with you. I'm not looking for something else or something instead. I just want to get a little creative and to have some fun on my own too."

Zoe took a few pieces of the cereal mix and tossed them into her mouth. She chewed, then smiled. "This is so you. Sweet and salty, colorful, and unique. Something to make a normal movie night on the couch or a game night around the table or an afternoon at the ball field a little different and fun.

Josie's breath caught in her throat. Okay, it was pink cereal mix. It was cereal pieces covered in white chocolate and strawberry powder and mixed with mini pretzels, cashews, and pink and white M&M's. It was silly to get choked up over someone complimenting that.

But it wasn't the cereal mix. It was how Zoe described how it made her feel. That it made her smile. And that it was Zoe.

Josie swallowed, her eyes watery.

Zoe noticed. She looked worried. "Are you okay?"

Josie sniffed and nodded. "Yeah. I just... I like making stuff that makes people happy."

Zoe gave her an affectionate smile and moved around the corner of the island to pull her into a hug. "I know." She squeezed and then let go. "I love you so much for that. I think because it's always been who you are, and I've known you forever. I never really thought about how you don't get to truly shine at the bakery. I know that you love seeing people light up about the stuff you decorate. It never occurred to me that you might want to do even more." She grimaced. "I'm a terrible friend."

"No." Josie shook her head. "I never said anything."

"Well, we can definitely do this at the bakery. We can do the whoopie pies and even make a case—half a case—for healthy stuff. We can have a secret menu for the naughty stuff and the stuff for potlucks and class treats and school so that people can still pass them off as their own if they want to and—"

"Zoe."

Zoe stopped and look at her. "Yeah?"

"I... appreciate that, but I want to do this on my own."

Zoe was quiet for a long moment. And then another. Taking that in and processing it.

"I'll make you a partner," Zoe said. "Watching Aiden and

the guys together, I realize how amazing they each are on their own but how much *more* they are together as a team. I need you. *We* are an amazing team too."

Josie felt her heart flip. She smiled. "That's really nice. And a month ago I would have taken you up on that. But..." She looked around her kitchen again. "I'm ready to be on my own a little." Josie took her friend's hand. "I don't want to leave the bakery, but I might want to eventually just do the big decorating jobs. You don't need me to be doing the simple chocolate chip cookies and things like that. You can hire someone else for that. But I'll come in and do the bigger, more elaborate projects that I love. And then I can do this"—she looked at everything on the center island—"on my own."

Josie met Zoe's eyes. "I won't do anything the bakery already does. I don't want this to be a situation like Letty and Didi. I would never let that happen," she said, referring to Zoe's grandmother, Letty, and her best friend, Didi, who couldn't come to an agreement about how to run the bakery and it ended their friendship... and started a family feud that lasted until Zoe and Aiden fell in love.

"Hot Cakes—well, Grant, and Cam, and Whitney—offered me a chance to develop a new cake for them."

Zoe's eyes widened.

"But I turned them down too," Josie said. "I love watching people's eyes light up when they see or taste something I've created. I would never get to experience that with a Hot Cakes cake. I do get to do it at the bakery sometimes, and I'm grateful for that. But I'd love the chance to really try new things and get people's reactions one on one. This is a little more personal, a little more my own thing, and I want a little bit of that."

Zoe smiled. "I love that. If you want to do this, you have my support, however you want to make it happen. You can do it through Buttered Up or on your own, but either way, I'm here for you. I love you, and I'm sorry that I haven't let you shine."

Josie gave a choked sob-laugh and pulled Zoe into another hug. After she let her go, she said firmly, "It wasn't you. It was me. I wasn't ready to shine. I was... content. I really was."

"Until?"

"Grant," she admitted.

Zoe gave her a knowing smile. "Falling in love has a way of changing your perspective and shaking things up you didn't even know needed shaken."

Josie nodded. "I hope it works that way for Grant too."

"It will."

She really hoped so. She really, really hoped so.

Just then her phone chimed with a text notification. It was Cam.

I hope you're almost done. This guy is like a caged animal.

She grinned. *A caged animal, huh?*

Cam replied, *Pacing around, growling at everyone about everything, generally losing his patience... and sense of humor. Don't know how much longer we can keep him here.*

Josie felt her heart swell. Grant Lorre was like a caged animal, huh? Grant was the levelheaded one, the one who talked the rest of them out of reacting purely on emotion.

Maybe Grant was getting a little shaken up too.

Good.

She took a breath, looked at Zoe, looked at the island top full of treats—*her* creations—and then typed, *I'm ready for him.*

———

Finally.

Grant stomped up the back steps to Jocelyn's house.

It had been fourteen hours since he'd seen her. It felt like a year.

The meetings with Ollie about the new snack cake and the contest and auction and circus had been predictably crazy and annoying. Grant had finally called Cam in as backup because, sure enough, Ollie had a way of getting Whitney worked up and excited about really stupid shit.

Okay, maybe not *stupid* shit. But when more than half his concentration had been on Jocelyn and what she was thinking and feeling and how to tell her he was in love with her and how to save his marriage... conversations about bouncy houses and how much it would cost to rent a Ferris wheel had tried his patience more than they usually would have. And they usually would have tried his patience *a lot*.

Now he was finally "allowed" to go to Jocelyn. If he hadn't known that Cam and Whitney were keeping him away on purpose, because Jocelyn had some plan she was trying to put together, he would have lost it. He'd have fired them both. Or locked them in the supply closet and come over here hours ago.

Then again, the supply-closet thing might have been great. It would have gotten *them* together and out of his way at the same time.

But now he was here, and he and Jocelyn were going to get back together.

He was going to beg her to forgive him, move his stuff into this amazing old house in this tiny, quirky town, convince her to marry him again with a huge ceremony and the-whole-town's-invited party after, and then they were going to live here, happily ever after, dammit.

But he paused on the top step, his hand on the handle of the back door, and took a big breath. He blew it out. Repeated the breath. Then opened the door and walked in.

The aroma was the first thing that hit him. As always. Her house smelled delicious. Like a *home*. Like a place people came to be comforted and to celebrate and to be taken care of.

Jocelyn didn't need to be taken care of. She needed to take care of people.

He was very happy to be one of those people. If she'd have him.

He kicked his shoes off inside the back door and headed into the kitchen.

He came up short at the sight that met him.

Jocelyn was at the middle kitchen island, tossing a salad, barefoot, wearing a huge smile and an apron and... nothing else.

"Hi," she said softly.

"Hi." Everything in him strained to go to her. But he had some things he needed to say first. "I—"

"I thought our first date should be a candlelight dinner here, in my house, that I made for you," she said.

He glanced to his left and into the dining room. It glowed with candlelight, the flames glittering off the chandelier over-head that had probably hung there for a hundred years. He pulled in a deep breath, feeling the tension drain out of him.

"Our first date?" he asked, turning back to her.

She nodded. "We've had a one-night stand that wasn't even a whole night. We've had a marriage. But we haven't really had a date."

He supposed she had a point. Their dinner in Chicago had been as a married couple as had the movies and cuddling on the couch. "Married couples can't have dates?"

She lifted a shoulder. "Of course they can. But since we're not married anymore, *this* isn't a married-couple date."

"We can fix that," he said, stepping forward. "We can rip those papers up."

She shook her head. "No, we can't."

"But if we don't want to be divorced—"

"You don't rip chapter one out of a book when you get to chapter two," she said, picking up the salad bowl. "You just turn those pages and keep going. Those pages are as much a part of the story as the next ones."

"But we're going to keep going?" he asked, his chest tight.

She smiled and started for the dining room, giving him a magnificent view of her bare ass in that apron. "We're definitely going to keep going."

Grant felt relief spill through him, and he followed her, crowding in close as she set the salad bowl down.

He quickly took inventory of the table. Pork chops, salad, rolls, wine, and what looked like a pan of cheesy potatoes.

As soon as her hands were empty, he turned her, his hands on her upper arms. "I'm sorry I hurt you. I'm sorry that I somehow made it seem like you needed me to fix things. Or if I made you feel like you were living your life the wrong way. You're not. You're happy and loved and... there's nothing more important than that. I'm sorry if I made you feel like I didn't want to be a part of that. Because I do. So much. I just need a little practice being..." He wasn't sure what word to insert there. He hadn't practiced this speech. This was all just from the heart.

"Impractical?" she supplied with a grin.

"In love," he finally said.

Her expression softened. "I can help you with that."

"You already are."

"For the record," she said, resting her hands on his chest and moving closer, "I need practice at that too. I know what it looks like. I know how I want it to be. But I've never done it. And I realize that it's going to look a little different for us than it does for others. I'm sorry if I made *you* feel like I was striving for some perfect idea in my head." She paused and shrugged. "I probably was, actually. I never expected to fall in love with a guy who likes adding and subtracting so much."

He grinned down at her, his heart feeling light, the happiness a nearly palpable thing. "Thank God you are romantic enough to know that love comes along in the most unexpected ways."

"It really does."

"And to celebrate us starting to date, we're having whoopie pies for dessert, right?" he asked hopefully, running his hands down her back to her ass.

"Actually, no."

He pulled back. "No?"

She pointed to the cake on the table.

It was a square cake, still in the pan, with white frosting.

"Oh. Cake," he said. "Okay."

She laughed. "It's okay if you think that looks very simple and plain. Interestingly, it's the most straightforward, simple, plain cake I think I've ever made."

He lifted a brow. "Is there some symbolism there? Like our relationship is actually quite straightforward and simple when you get right down to it? We don't need a lot of fancy embellishments? We are what make it colorful?"

She nodded. "Kind of." She took a breath. "I realized that what I love about baking is seeing people react to what I make. I love watching them get immediately happy when they see or taste something I made." She pressed her lips together, then bracketed his face with her hands. "I'm your cake, Grant."

He felt his chest tighten and had a hard time taking a deep breath.

"The look on your face when you walk in and see me is how people look at my cakes. When people come into the bakery and first see a cake I've made for them or are perusing the bakery case and see the perfect thing, they get this look that says that they've found something even better than they imagined and they're just... delighted." She nodded her head. "I delight you."

She did. She so fucking did. He would have never picked that word to describe him, but it was absolutely perfect.

She wet her lips and continued, "I got Zoe a t-shirt once that said *I want someone to look at me the way I look at chocolate cake.*

She found him. Aiden looks at her that way. Dax looks at Jane that way. And... you look at me that way. And *that* is why we should keep dating, and eventually, after my business is up and running, and you're used to living here in a little town and everything, why we should get married again."

He just stared at her. She was absolutely right. When he looked at her, when he heard her voice, when he kissed her, when he knew he was *about to* see her, he lit up. He could feel it. She made him happy and content and excited and like the day had gotten a little more special. She delighted him. She made him feel like all of her customers looked when they saw her cakes.

He felt a grin curving his lips. Then he thought about what else she'd said, "Your business?"

"I have a lot to tell you," she said.

"I can't wait."

She gave him a happy, excited grin. Then she glanced at the cake on the table again. "Okay, confession," she said.

"Okay."

"I was actually going to make the cake into a spreadsheet," she said, looking back up at him with a sheepish smile. "But I didn't have time to pull it up on my computer, and I couldn't remember what a spreadsheet looks like in enough detail to decorate a cake like one."

Grant chuckled. Then he laughed a little louder. Then even louder. He hugged her to him, relishing the feel of her in his arms, surrounded by the smell of vanilla and sugar. If love had a smell, that's what it would be for him.

"I love you, Jocelyn."

"I love you too, Grant," she said, tipping her head back to look up at him.

His phone dinged with a text. He ignored it.

"I'd be very happy to reacquaint you with spreadsheets. Just like the lessons last night," he told her, his voice gruff.

She grinned. "Deal. And since I'm not really wearing anything that I can strip off, how about every time you teach me something and I get it right, you can smear frosting from that cake on a part of my body and lick it off."

His body heated and he growled, "Deal."

The phone dinged again. He sighed.

"You can answer it," she said. "We're both business owners. I get that we're kind of on the clock all the time."

He smiled down at her. "Fine. But we agree right now that when we're both naked, the phones can wait."

She grinned. "I agree."

He pulled his phone from his back pocket and swiped the screen with his thumb. It was a text from Cam.

Grant frowned and read the text out loud, "I should probably tell you now that you're not actually divorced."

"But we both signed them," Jocelyn said.

Grant nodded and typed back *What are you talking about?*

As your attorney I feel obligated to say you should always read every single word in any document you are signing.

Grant sighed. *What are you talking about?* he asked again.

The divorce papers you both signed are actually cat adoption papers from Cores and Catnips. So congrats. You're still married, and you can now go to Paige's place and pick out any three cats.

Grant blinked at the message. He read it out loud to Jocelyn. Her eyes widened, and then she started laughing.

"Three?" she asked. "Not even just one?"

Grant shook his head. "I suppose you love cats as much as your sister does?"

"Oh, no one loves cats as much as my sister does," Jocelyn said. "But yeah... I wouldn't mind having a cat. Or three."

Grant looked down at the love of his life realizing that there was nothing he wouldn't do or put up with for her. "A small town, a woman who doesn't like spreadsheets, another business partner who thinks *way* outside the box, and now three cats. How did my life get so crazy all of a sudden?"

Jocelyn grinned. "You fell in love."

Everything in him softened. He smiled. "Yeah, I did."

"And oh my God! We're not divorced?" Jocelyn suddenly exclaimed.

"I guess not." He had to admit, that was pretty fucking great. They'd figured out how they truly felt, and if they had been divorced, they would have ended up together—for all the right reasons—anyway. But now... she was still his. In every single way.

"So..." She was clearly thinking it all through. "Can we still date? I mean, I feel like we still need to *date* each other for a while."

"We can absolutely still date," he said. "For the rest of our lives."

Her expression softened, and she gave him a sweet smile. "Okay. Then we'll still date. For..." She was clearly thinking something through. "Maybe six or seven months?"

"What happens in six or seven months?" he asked.

"We'll have our wedding."

He blinked at her. "A wedding? We did that."

"No. We got legally married by a judge," Jocelyn corrected him. "Now we'll have a *wedding*. Here in Appleby. With all our friends and family."

"All of your friends?" he repeated. "So the entire town?"

She grinned, practically glowing. "Yes."

Grant felt himself nodding. "Okay. Let's do it. Let's have a huge blowout dream wedding. After we date for a few months."

Jocelyn threw her arms around him. "Thank you!"

Maybe she didn't realize that he'd do *anything* for her yet, but he was sure she was going to figure it out quickly.

"And now, about this frosting and those spreadsheets..." He started to reach for the cake.

But she stopped him. "Oh, first, cheesy potatoes."

He cocked an eyebrow. "Before frosting?"

"Well, they're symbolic too."

"Symbolic cheesy potatoes?"

She nodded, grinning. "Turns out, people *can* fall in love over cheesy potatoes after all."

———

Thank you so much for reading Making Whoopie! I hope you loved Josie and Grant's story!

Next up is Cam and Whitney's story in Semi-Sweet On You!

She broke his heart ten years ago.
Now he's back -- and her new boss.
And she might still be semi in love with him.

———

The Hot Cakes Series
Sugarcoated
Forking Around
Making Whoopie
Oh, Fudge (Christmas)
Semi-Sweet On You
Gimme S'more

———

If you love sexy, funny, small town romance and, well, hot kitchens and baked goods ;) you should also check out my **Billionaires in Blue Jeans** series!

Triplet billionaire sisters find themselves in small town Kansas for a year running a pie shop...and falling in love!

Diamonds and Dirt Roads
High Heels and Haystacks
Cashmere and Camo

Find all my books at
www.ErinNicholas.com

———

And join in on all the FAN FUN!

Join my email list!
http://bit.ly/ErinNicholasEmails

And be the first to hear about my news, sales, freebies, behind-the-scenes, and more!

Or for even more fun, join my **Super Fan page** on Facebook and chat with me and other super fans every day! Just search for Erin Nicholas Super Fans!

ABOUT ERIN

Erin Nicholas is the New York Times and USA Today bestselling author of over thirty sexy contemporary romances. Her stories have been described as toe-curling, enchanting, steamy and fun. She loves to write about reluctant heroes, imperfect heroines and happily ever afters. She lives in the Midwest with her husband who only wants to read the sex scenes in her books, her kids who will never read the sex scenes in her books, and family and friends who say they're shocked by the sex scenes in her books (yeah, right!).

Find her and all her books at
www.ErinNicholas.com

And find her on Facebook, BookBub, and Instagram!

CPSIA information can be obtained
at www.ICGtesting.com
Printed in the USA
FSHW020300210620
71346FS

9 781952 280054